The Maid of Buttermere

Also by Melvyn Bragg:

FOR WANT OF A NAIL
THE SECOND INHERITANCE
THE CUMBRIAN TRILOGY: The Hired Man
A Place in England
Kingdom Come
JOSH LAWTON
THE NERVE
WITHOUT A CITY WALL
THE SILKEN NET
AUTUMN MANOEUVRES
LOVE AND GLORY

Non-Fiction:
SPEAK FOR ENGLAND
LAND OF THE LAKES
LAURENCE OLIVIER
CUMBRIA IN VERSE (Edited)

MELVYN BRAGG

The Maid of Buttermere

Hodder & Stoughton
LONDON SYDNEY AUCKLAND TORONTO

To Cate

British Library Cataloguing in Publication Data

Bragg, Melvyn
The maid of Buttermere.
I. Title
823'.914[F] PR6052.R263

ISBN 0-340-40173-7

 Printed in Great Britain for Hodder and Stoughton Limited, Mill Road, Dunton Green, Sevenoaks, Kent by St Edmundsbury Press Limited, Bury St Edmunds, Suffolk. Photoset by Rowland Phototypesetting Limited, Bury St Edmunds, Suffolk. Hodder and Stoughton Editorial Office: 47 Bedford Square, London WC1B 3DP.

Contents

Part One

"Now I am free, enfranchised and at large,
May fix my habitation where I will."

William Wordsworth,
The Prelude

1

Rehearsal on the Sands

Again he struck out due west. She watched his predatory, slightly uneven gait and once more puzzled over whether he was foolish or bold. The Sands were known to be perilous but the man went without a guide and in a direction certain to tempt danger. This time she would follow him, if only to warn him; and he had intrigued her long enough. The woman slung the shrimping net over her shoulder and stepped out from her hut onto the ripple-ribbed sands. Though they glistened still from the recent sea, they were here as hard as stucco. She walked swiftly, lightly, scanning her route all the time; in this place, as had been confirmed to her most sadly, safety lay in ceaseless mistrust.

Over by the farm she noted the same girl, Sally, stood guard on his horse, rooted, entranced by the receding figure of the powerfully built gentleman now well out onto the wet flatlands of the bay. The girl gazed out rapturously after him as if he were her Redeemer. He never looked back.

A white ghost sun showed through the thinning scuds of dull cloud, lending the watery vastness a pewter slate reflection: forbidding. The ebb tide was sucking the sea out from the greedy mouth of the bay for a few hours – when travellers could be piloted over the expanse, when urgent fishermen could race onto the Sands with their horses and carts to trawl the seabeds, when the poor, like the woman and the girl, could pick along the shifting margins; but the prodigious stridings of ocean floor would soon be violently reclaimed. And every day, the channels, the bracks, the mosses, the mudflats, the quicksands were altered by the awesome and unpredictable force of the sea.

He walked for about a couple of miles and then stopped. From the pocket of his high-collared dun brown jacket he took out some papers and looked on them intently. But before he began what he had come to do, he looked around to make sure of his isolation.

Although by now he had been out on Lancaster Sands in the Bay of Morecambe several times, he was still unused to the perspectives. He saw a hill across a hop and a jump of sand and thought it a mile or so away when in truth the distance was nearer fifteen. He could just make out groups of women, bent double as if grazing, searching, as he had learned, for cockle-beds – two, four, six miles off? A couple of carriages and several chaises and gigs were beginning their caravan from near his own point of departure – the distance gave them glamour and for a moment he imagined the deserts of the East which he loved to talk about, the ancient harmonies of timeless travel, the old silk route through Samarkand to Cathay. Down the Bay, as if they were driving into the sea on some imperative from the Old Testament, he thought he could spot the fishermen straddled across their amphibious carts. Nearer – but not too close – and anyway absorbed in the back-bowed raking and culling of the sands for the day's harvest – there were a few solitaries, but as comfortably spaced out from each other as he from them. He felt alone on what had a few hours before been the ocean floor; and safe.

Thirteen years previously he had been – as he would say when drunk or assuming his florid mood – "honoured, there is no other word for it: honoured" to see Kemble playing Coriolanus at the Drury Lane Theatre. He had taken a lot from that. It was Kemble he thought of and imitated now when he moved as the great actor had done on his first entrance and deliberately circumambulated a small space – like a dog bedding down on the grass – giving himself, as he imagined Kemble had done, a sense of his own free territory, belonging to no-one but him, to be defended against all comers.

As he made that full circle, his gaze slowly swept over what could be described as a great natural amphitheatre, a vast audience of nature crowding to the edges of the Bay, ready and overwhelmingly responsive to any informed look or voice. But the man knew very little about what he looked on. Although he was set to pass as a Lake Tourist, the Lakeland fells to the north whose peaks announced what the new visitors considered to be the pinnacles of an earthly paradise, neither moved nor excited him. It was just country. The chatter in his inn in Lancaster had been of little else but this newly discovered heaven on earth. Painters and poets, well-heeled visitors and the fashionable young were ravished by this wonderful lake-landscape. He would be prepared to mouth wonder with the best of them, when he had to. But what the man saw before him at this moment were endless and worryingly empty spaces, unpeopled, at best a temporary lodging. He loved a city. To him this prospect was dead.

He would have been able to name none of the plants on the curious terraced and sculpted limestone rocks he saw to the north of the Bay: bladder-campion, scabious, herb-Paris – all scrub to him. And as he looked up, pulling back his strong shoulders and gazing heavenwards – as Kemble had done before that final magnificent swoop back to the audience – he saw birds: there were oyster-catchers, curlews, lapwings, blackheaded gulls – but he spotted no distinction beyond large and small. To him they were merely birds, a pleasing enough decoration on a sky rapidly freeing itself of clouds, clearing to ultramarine. He turned to face the sun, now unobscured.

And this did check his breath. For in front of him, the sun hit the water-filmed sands flat and hard so that they were silver – acres, reaches, miles of silver as if a gigantic mythological shield had been thrown down before him on the ocean floor. He felt uplifted, even heroic, paused and looked down at his notes. He began.

The woman had worked her way to him, downwind, and very carefully. She pushed her hand net through the running water and put the shrimps into a hamper she carried on her back. Although it was high summer, the water was cool and her hands were soon numbed. When she stood upright – she was knee-deep in the channel, almost hidden – she listened hard and caught his murmurings on the light wind, sighs across the sands, like the singing of the cockles which could lead you to a good haul. She moved closer . . .

*

Habit, even the small hoard of a few days, had eroded embarrassment. He spoke to the empty Bay (so he had written in his Journal), "as cheerfully as a lunatic".

"I am," he began again for the benefit of the sky, the sands, the waters, "Alexander Augustus Hope, Colonel, Member of Parliament for Linlithgowshire and brother to the Earl of Hopetoun. A comfortable name, Hope, and one which my dear father thought fit to encourage with the highest aspirations by harnessing it – that's good, I must remember harnessing! – by harnessing it to the names of two of the greatest warriors of ancient times, one of Greece and one of Rome – that's very good! – one of Greece and one of Rome – that can sound like a quotation – Alexander and Augustus. Your servant, sir; your servant, ma'am: draw out the 'a-a-a-m', remember to stretch the vowels – your servant, m-a-a-a-m. Then the bow, not too deep, you are the second brother to a great Earl, and an Honourable. The Army, sir, my life – educated at home, of course – all Hopes are learned at home – ha! – it's where we put the breeding in them, my father says – should I say that? Is it vulgar? Is it funny, I mean, amusing? I'll say it with a laugh – it's where – ha! – as my dear old father – oh no! – dear old father won't do – no more. My names directed me to the Army and, happily, my inclination was willing to follow. That's not too bad. Or – my names ordered me – ordered me is better! A military man, you see – ordered me to join the Army and my inclination was happy to yield. I like 'yield'. Spread out the middle – yie-e-eld! Saw service in Flanders, 1794, brigade major of the Guards under Major General Gerard Lake – then the retreat – prefer not to talk of that – proud to have commanded the 14th Foot in the attack from Buren on Gueldermasen – Guu-eeld-er-masen – in January '95. Took the place but badly wounded: very badly: leg, chest, lamed, pension, light duties, now Lieutenant Governor of Tynemouth and Cliff Fort since '97, and turned to politics in the party of my great friend, Mr. Pitt."

The trick, so the man who said he had acted with Kemble had told him, was to "keep going", "say anything", "do it until it's second nature". The main thing, the man had said during their many hours together in that long confinement, hours, days, weeks and years in which he had fought to reconstitute himself so that he could return to life with his former appetites unimpaired – was to get used to the sound of the voice. Once the new voice ceased to surprise you, then you could forget about it: the lines would come easily. It seemed to be working.

He turned to the war with France and expressed his military man's reservations about the new Peace Treaty just made at Amiens – "the French will use it for arming up, believe me, the Frenchman wants war and Napoleon Bonaparte has a particular detestation of the free-born Englishman. Boney will never rest until he has landed on English soil. Take my word for it, this is not a Peace Treaty, this is a break in the hostilities" – he had heard that phrase on the hustings in London and instantly adopted it as his own. He rehearsed the time he had been an ensign, he spoke about his Grand European Tour with his tutor Dr. John Gillies – "this was when Europe was as easy as a man's own grounds": once again he repeated a phrase which pleased or flattered him – this one delighted him greatly and he imagined the copses, the temples, the river, the parks, the woods all laid before him as he repeated "as easy as a man's own grounds". He would pause after that and let the acres of Hopetoun work potently on his audience to conjure up the full splendour of the comparison. He referred to Italy – for the paintings – and to Egypt – for the pyramids and embalming – he had a well-fabricated passage, more or less accurately detailed, on the embalming which, he thought – having tried it out once or twice – could stun most companies, and especially one dominated by females, into a silent, shivering respect for his scholarship and experience.

He had two versions of the time he said he had spent in America and unlimited stories of London, once again, pious or profane depending on the occasion and the company. He spoke of his wounds and his injuries lightly but speak of them he did and with a melancholy fall – the Irish tincture to his speech was most emphasised here – which could not, he was certain, fail to move the delicate to trust and sympathy. He paced forward and back, waved his free hand in the wind, glanced at his notes less and less as the doing of the thing itself consumed the ulterior motive until he was not a man learning and re-learning his character but a being who had found its truest form and habitat, utterly abandoned in his flow to that moment, those words, the vision, the air and flesh and thing he was: free, unthinking, self-ravished, scarcely visible from the shoreline, finally released on that empty ocean floor.

The woman was mesmerised by him. Despite her caution she had moved nearer along the gullies until she could hear whole sentences, observe the energy and vigour of his movements and sense, as keenly as the freshening breeze itself, his desperation and his gaiety, both. At first, seeing the papers in his hand, she had thought he might be a vicar, practising a sermon – and she held onto that as a possibility despite what she heard. Although she was no churchgoer, she would have as readily accepted what he said as the content of a sermon as anything else. But he seemed too manly and too fiery for a vicar, while his clothes marked him off from the new Zealots and Ranters – they would never wear, even if they could afford, such rich and beautiful Hessian tasselled boots and so carelessly employ them in the corrosive sea paddle of the sands. But if he was not a churchman, then she was baffled. His words, the rush of water, the bird cries hollow across the wastes, lulled her and she was drawn up, out of the channel, onto the broad expanse of sands.

"Who do you think I am?" he asked, wheeling as unexpectedly as the lapwings. For an instant, she was stunned dumb.

She shook her head, put her hand to the small of her back and levered herself upright using this acceptable action to steady herself and to disguise her fear at being seen through so immediately.

"Then who are you?" he said – and she noted that this voice was not the grand, aristocratic sound of his speech, but a more common, a quieter voice, put on, she assumed, gratefully, out of benevolence.

"I work the shoreline," she answered, eventually, as someone had to stop the silence and she could not endure his direct stare however kindly his smile might colour it. Her voice sounded hoarse and too low. "I work the shoreline," she repeated, "for the small fish."

"This is far out."

"Sometimes I do come out, when there's nothing near."

"You have been following me, haven't you?"

"Yes," she said promptly, simply: he could see into her and there was no point in evasion.

"Did somebody send you?"

She looked at him and wanted to soothe the sudden inflammation of his fear.

"Nobody sent me."

"What is your name?"

"Anne Tyson."

"So why did you follow me, Anne Tyson?"

"I was," she paused, knowing care was needed to reassure him truly, seeking for the word, "concerned for you." She did not call him 'Sir': and afterwards and always when she remembered their meeting, she thought of that with pleasure and coddled the thought, rubbed it like a favoured gift.

"The Sands are dangerous," she went on, "and you kept coming out with no guide. What we call the Keer Channel is not so bad here but over there – just beyond you – that's the Kent Channel – a man and a horse can be swept off like empty shells."

"Why were you concerned for me, Anne?"

Again she paused, partly to organise her words so that she would speak plainly and clearly without the impediment of dialect, partly because she saw he needed a final twist of reassurance. Then she told her story, a story she very rarely repeated to anyone: and, cannily, she sensed it would disarm him.

"I had a daughter; my only child. She was my darling and all I had. She got drowned out here. We found her fast in the sands the next day. A fog had come up – that's the worst – and she strayed off over the cockle-beds. I stayed out looking till the tide took me away, but I was meant to be lucky and it threw me on a sandbank. She was nine. Since then I've lived on the shore, watching out. I have a shack nearby the farm where you leave your horse. I like to think I'm still near her in that way."

He nodded, took a few steps towards her and reached out his right hand, putting it on her shoulder.

"How do you live?"

"The sea does me. They call me old luck itself; I always get some sort of a catch." His hand warmed her: the light weight of it made her long to be dependent.

"You can't be older than I am. You play at being the old crone, don't you?"

"Yes; it's safer."

"If they bathed you in oils, Anne Tyson, and put you in silk gowns, you'd be as fine a lady as them all."

His face was bright, the complexion high, whipped by the weather, strong nose, fine teeth, brown glowing eyes and broad black eyebrows; he wore no wig – his hair was long, thick, grey now overtaking the brown – and there was a scar on his left cheek which dimpled as he smiled. He pressed his right hand firmly on her shoulder, disturbing her, and she arched her back and looked at him as fully. Sceptically, but trained in obedience to her social superiors, she let the old crone disguise fall away and became something of the woman he said he had spied. His left hand came up to take her arm and she noticed that the two middle fingers were bent up to the palm, clawed. Her reaction broke the moment.

"An old wound," he said and raised both hands before dropping them to his sides. "I've had many wounds, Anne, in the body and in the mind. That is why I bring myself out here. You have to mend the mind as well as the body and my misfortunes have made it hard."

"You talk to yourself."

"I talk to reclaim the man I wish to be. Does that make sense to you?"

"No," she said and his sudden snap of a grin shut out the moment when he had surely wanted her.

"So I'd better return now if the tides and the sands aren't to gobble me up?"

"There's some time yet."

"I'll go all the same. Here," he held out a small piece of silver. "In thanks for your concern."

She did not want to take it but he could not be refused. She took the silver and felt diminished.

"You are a good-looking woman, Anne Tyson – I'll not forget my guardian angel on the Bay of Morecambe."

He put his hand to his heart and bowed.

She smiled, but he was merely brisk now; that silent untouchable web spun between them had vanished from his manner and most likely, already from his memory. He bowed again, jauntily, and set off for the shore. She returned to her shrimping, huddled over in the remorseless run of water, schooling the sensations he had aroused in her . . .

*

Having resisted one temptation, he felt free to give in to another. Newton had warned him against it but Newton was too anxious. Thank God they would part in the morning. Newton had resented the expense of the delay. He failed to understand the need for these days alone on the Sands; how could he when part of the purpose was to be somewhere free of Newton's jealous eye? And so he talked of the need to prepare himself. The preparation had to be thorough: once launched, there would be no way back. There could be no mistake this time: he had been exposed and damaged too badly, he had failed often enough and he was no longer young: this was the last charge and it was into the cannon's mouth. Newton – who had never been in the front line – had no conception, the man thought, of the nerve needed, of the will and imagination he had to summon up to see himself through the next few weeks. Those mad monologues to the sea had inexplicably secured him. And – damn Newton! – now he deserved a treat! Even though he would keep it secret, it would spite the man.

"He's been varra quiet," she said, stroking the muscled velvet of the stallion's neck with light, open fingers.

"That's because he trusts you, Sally."

"Aye – he knows me now."

"Walk him down the lane a little way, would you?"

She turned the horse from the sea and they made for the narrow lane – bushy with hawthorn, dense with sycamore – stippled here and there with the silver grey of a slim birch. After the Sands, it was as warm as a burrow. They walked in silence, the horse between them. This was only their fourth meeting and yet she felt he knew her better than anyone had ever done. He gave her sixpence a time and she was forced to pay this over to the farmer whose servant girl she was – she had given him that information with no whinge – as if the sixpence were all the old fool deserved while she got such riches as these few minutes, such benefits as being next to Him . . .

"You know Anne Tyson?" he said and she nodded. "She must have been like you a few years ago. That hair, reddish brown as a new chestnut, tufted up like a helmet – a number of women in this district have that colour hair – and the blue eyes – very unsettling, Sally, to an old man like me."

"You're not a bit old! You're like naebody else. You're the handsomest man I've ever seen! And you've been so kind!" she concluded her brief eulogy and looked away, confused: that such a rich, beautifully dressed gentleman should show gentle affection for a 'nobody' was as if she had been visited by someone from an unimaginable world.

He was deeply pleased to catch such a compliment even though it had been so clumsily baited.

"No, no, Sally. *You* are the beauty. You are the beauty."

He glanced at her and, boldly, she held his look – but very soon it proved too much for her and she blushed and turned away. The broad high cheekbones too, he thought, imagining his fingers tracing them across her face, and that mouth gashed wide. The horse's hooves clopped softly on the muddy track. He felt the unmistakable imminence of great sexual pleasure and sighed with happiness. Above their heads, the sycamores threatened to intertwine and lace the lane into a tunnel.

"I must clean my boots, Sal," he said, having selected a spot. "Would you help me?"

She nodded, alert as a hare, silent.

"We'll tie him up against this gate. We'll be able to keep an eye on him there – won't we, boy?"

He smoothed the neck, as she had done, and his fingers left marks on the sweating pelt.

"Let me help you," he said, and although she was lither than he was, she allowed him to lift her down from the gate and they went together into the field.

He loved anticipation: he let it draw out until it was the finest, tightest thread.

"Here," he said. They were towards the middle of the field, warm grass reaching up to their thighs, the sun, golden now, inviting them to lie down and be lapped by the warmth. Sally knelt down, tore out a handful of grass and began to polish the boots.

The man looked down on her and hesitated, but not for long: this would be his last time with her: the red hair, the white neck, the body restless in that old gown long ago discarded by some charitable and overweight lady. His throat dried and – for he was a connoisseur – he knew he was going to enjoy a taste of what he most longed for.

"Let me help you," he said, clumsily, and lowered himself down to her so that they faced each other now, fortressed by the stockade of dense high grass, and he paused one more time. "You are the beauty, Sal," he repeated, softly. Her eyes closed, the mouth opened slightly, the want on her face was like pain. He kissed her gently, and again, very very gently, and she, used only to rough taking, to dark struggles and brutal brief unsatisfied coupling, moaned aloud at this tantalising gentleness.

He saw and knew that: there was always some part of him detached, a mind outside his mind watching, appreciating, able to conduct it all. Gorged on conceit, he thought of this as his gift. He alone, he would conclude from what he had heard and seen, loved to love and took time, took care, for he wanted, most of all, the satisfaction of the woman. He alone, of all men.

His jacket and her dress served as the bed. She was naked, white, smooth-muscled, lithe, surging towards him as he let his fingers trail over her, abstractedly, kindly, teasing her desire and spinning out his own. Suddenly he was inside her: hard but not violent and he moved and slowly, even languorously, made love to her.

This was his home; this was his landscape – the paradise of a body, not of earth and woods; the contours of flesh, the colours and sensations not of lakes and streams but of the mouth, the nipples, the vagina, the texture of hair, teeth, nails, the satin and tension of young skin, the tides of lovemaking, slow ecstatic clouds of unknowing behind closed eyes, a finger following the rippling path of the spine down from the neck, a sudden bonding of heads – like the trees in the lane – as a mouth reached to kiss a vulnerable throat, the swelling and falling susurration of breath itself binding them as the animal bodies moved and turned and locked. This was his dream of nature. Sometimes he could make the reality match the dream, but then the memory would provoke him to long for more, giving him no rest.

Afterwards they slept for a few minutes, side by side facing each other, spent but still together. He felt as if he had been absolved. The grass smelt very sweet: her hair clung damply to her brow: her body, slack now, huddled. He woke first and stroked her shoulder, enjoying the light rub of skin on skin.

"We ought to get married, you know."

The words startled her awake: he himself, too, was taken by surprise and could have believed, for a moment, that someone else had spoken them. She looked at him wonderingly, almost reproachfully.

But the words, now uttered, gathered substance. He could see himself master of a little farm along the Sands, here, living a simple life, some fishing – one of his passions – at ease and lordly in the small community, served and adored by Sally, her marvellous body, that eagerness to obey him, that deeply soothing indiscriminate serving affection. He would make his home comfortable, bring in a few books, stroll along the shore on an evening such as this and know that sexual pleasure, even satiety, was always and uncomplicatedly available.

"Would you like that?"

She was stretched back from him now as if preparing to dart forward with greater force and strike him: except that, as he knew, the appearance and appellation of aristocracy acted on her simplicity like oppression. What could she do against the power he had? Balked, she whimpered and turned away.

"The others hurt you, didn't they, Sal?" He reached for her hand and kissed the back of it. "All of them always hurt you."

"When will you be back?"

"Tomorrow."

They dressed in silence and sauntered back to the gate. He got onto the horse rather heavily – he was threatening to be stout about the upper body. She forced herself to speak.

"What did you say that for?"

"I meant it, Sal." Sincerity, he thought, was his greatest characteristic: often meant.

She stood aside as the man she knew as Hope trotted away. Then she turned back towards the sea, to the west where the sun was nesting across the bay on the Furness Fells, a celestial kingdom which she had never visited, the gold now veined with rushes of crimson as it set so massively before her, still warm, glowing on her transfigured face.

The man did not hesitate, nor look back once, uncaring and unaware of the immense grandeur of the sun now transforming the sands with a blood-red tide so that the great, greedy gob of bay became as rich as the inside of a mouth. He rode, contentedly, the two miles to Lancaster, earthed to himself, through the woman he would not see again, now confident of success.

*

Newton stood in the centre of the darkening room, his white face the only contrast in the dusky oak-stained gloom of the Royal Oak's finest quarters. As always, Hope feared that Newton knew everything he had done and condemned it. And as always he rejected that fear as foolish and fought to keep independent of it. At his best, he knew, he could have power over Newton: only when he was weak or uncertain would Newton's influence dominate and shape him. Even now he had to be on guard.

"It was my last rehearsal," he said, banging the door behind him. "I took my time."

"You did."

"Can we not have some light in this room?" Hope pulled the bell-rope and heard it jangle, faintly, down the unreliable staircases of the ancient inn.

Newton watched his partner bustle about uselessly.

"You aren't lying to me, John, are you?"

"What about?"

"You know what we agreed about leaving no scent. No marks."

"Are you accusing me?" His tone was suddenly belligerent; his handsome face curdled to unattractive anger.

"No." Newton closed the topic, having got his answer.

The maid came and soon there were candles. They ate dinner in the private sitting room. Two well-stuffed and roasted freshwater trout followed by a pair of plump young ducks, a bowl of gooseberries, cream, some of the landlady's goat's cheese and the landlord's indifferent beer. Throughout all this, little was said but they were men who knew each other's company and the silences were not awkward. The meal – like any satisfaction of an appetite – cheered up Hope immediately. He lit a pipe and smiled at the puny assault Newton had made on his food.

"If you are done . . ."

Newton nodded as Hope removed the pipe for a moment, lunged forward and took the untouched duck, chewing through it noisily as if crowing over the superiority of his enjoyment.

When he was in this mood, Newton could not catch him. Nor did he want to. It was this hugely satiated ease in himself which he envied about the man, this claiming on every offering of life which he wondered at.

"I would be happier to come with you." Newton was still reluctant to accept the parting.

"You have to see to the letters. And you need to settle the estate in Kent."

"We'll have no luck there."

"Our luck's in, come on! Isn't it?" He reached out and gripped his friend's arm playfully. "Come on. We're on our way. Look at the coach."

Newton could never resist this wave of warmth and affection.

"That's what I fear. It used up all our luck."

"It's just the beginning!"

Hope beamed at the intense recollection of the night his run of luck had ended in the fairy-tale winning of a coach and horses.

"Lucky for you, too," he said, to include Newton. "Gave you somewhere to stow your booty."

"Neither of us is free from sin, John."

Hope spurred himself to defend his innocence but at the very last instant a cold sliver of a glance checked him.

"I think it would be safer if I kept the case here," Newton said.

Both men looked at the splendid dressing-case which held two small silver pistols, all manner of silver flasks and bottles, pens, studs, trinkets, the costly embellishments of the Honourable Member for Linlithgowshire. It was Newton's prize.

"I need it," Hope said, without force. "Without the case and the letters both – I can't do it."

Newton did not reply, absorbed, it seemed, by the gleaming dressing-case.

"I have to make our fortune," the man went on, as gently as the steady candle flame. "Remember that."

"How much money will you need?" Newton asked, eventually.

"Five guineas will serve."

Newton went over to the case and carefully, almost reverently, sprung open one of the several secret drawers. The purse he took out was considerably lighter than it had been in London. He fondled the golden coins as he passed them over.

"I left no scent," he said. "No marks."

Hope shivered – then held up his beer.

"To America. A new life in a new world."

"Here's to the old one for the time being," Newton returned. "Here's hoping it gets us there."

"Hope again!" the younger man said. "What did I tell you? You can't better it."

The next day, at Hest Bank, where the conveyances assembled to be conducted the seven miles across the Sands at low tide by Mr. Carter, the pilot, a magnificently appointed carriage and four drove up just before the caravan was posted to move off. Anne Tyson, who often came to the departure point – where a small job could bring a few easy pence – stood back, stood straight and looked up into the face of the man smiling like a conqueror, high on the driver's box, alone, handling the horses himself.

"Anne Tyson!" he shouted. "Good day to you – and good luck to you!"

He whipped up the horses and soon passed to the front of the caravan, vying with the pilot, taunting and daring him all the way. Anne Tyson marvelled again at his recklessness.

As she worked in the hayfield a few hundred yards from Hest Bank and waited for him to arrive as he had promised, Sally looked out, every now and then, and daydreamed as she often did, of riding a fine carriage and horses across the great bed of the bay, a carriage like that she saw now leading the caravan.

Poor simple Sally, Anne thought, as she moved back down the shoreline; I am the one who will have to tell you that villains can give kind looks and smile while they rob you raw.

2

The Beauty

She came to the pool unobserved. It was no easy thing to do. She had known from early in her childhood that she was watched; rarely, in company, was she allowed freedom from looks which marked her out and unsettled her. Despite her increasingly refined attempts to deflect and diminish the general interest in her beauty, she had never known the freewheeling relief of consistent unselfconscious being. She had always been on show, cursed – it often seemed to her – by unsought celebrity.

Alice, her best friend, had transformed it into habits of speech – "Of course, you're the Beauty" or "If only I looked like you". She seemed to think that the wear of old habit and the comfort of long friendship blunted the arrows of envy: but, Mary felt, they were ready at any time to be sharpened and loosed. So she was wary even with her best and oldest friend. As for her work – serving in the inn – it could be a torment but to complain or resist would have puzzled and offended her parents, which she could never do: and so filial respect overcame the draining embarrassment of being goggled at, remarked on, never left alone from eyes and mouths and hands that clasped on her and would not let her be. She forced herself to subdue her anger, not wanting to give her tormentors the pleasure of seeing they could sting.

Indeed, only on the loneliest heights in the most inhospitable weather or in 'her' pool secretly, could she be free of her humiliating, disabling life.

She had come across it by chance soon after she had begun shepherding. It had taken her months to make sure that she was alone in knowing about it. There were other shepherds, woodmen, vagrants, gypsies now and then, children scrambling: but it was too high, too unexpected. Mary herself had found it only because she had been forced to slide down a rock to rescue a kid caught on a ledge. Once there, the bleating, kicking animal held tightly under one arm, she found that what had been easy enough to slide down was glassily sheer and impossible to ascend. She dropped down the rock face onto another ledge, which led around the crag onto safe ground. But below that last ledge, hidden under what had become an overhang of rock, was the pool.

It was fed by a spring which came out of the cave mouth which half-covered the collected water. She had looked up at it from the valley and not been able to spot it; the trickle which spilled over the rock spout was meagre, running down, even in wet weather, more like a smear of water than any resemblance to a force or fall. Large, almost bushy ferns grew about the place as if planted to disguise it further: it was, she discovered, blessedly safe.

For Mary it became a sanctuary and she took extraordinary precautions to keep it for herself alone. No friend was told, let alone shown it; she made her way as cunningly as a poacher, tracking and backtracking with her flocks, laying false trails, calling the dogs too loudly to flush out any nearby presence, scanning and quartering the fells rigorously. If there were ever any threat of being seen, she would move towards the person, draw away from the pool, protecting it as boldly as a skylark her nest.

*

It was mid-July and thankfully much of the hay was already in. Three and two years previously, the worst summers in memory had ruined haytime and harvest and the previous year had been patchy. Three hungry winters had frightened and weakened most of the poorer people in the valleys and even the rather better off, like Mary's father, had seen their resources threatened. Mary had noticed how some of the old superstitions had begun to creep back and not only those connected with the weather and crops. The previous evening, for instance, when some of the haymakers had come in for a drink after the last of the sleds of hay had been gathered, there had been an argument over who had the longest burning fire in the valley.

Winter and summer, day and night, the peat fires smouldered in damp cottages all over Western Europe, enlivened only by roots or by wood too knotted to work: the cheap peat smoked and smelled and the hallan drops sweated like drizzle. Hankinson of Lorton had won, claiming that his grandmother had brought it from Ireland, which made it well over a century. In his family, he said, it was still believed that if you let out the fire, the soul of the people went out of the house. Then they had talked of corpse ways and the custom of touching the body of the dead man or woman, which would bleed if prodded by the finger of a murderer. Into the long light northern night such talk had spun out, but with the hot hay banked on the sleds outside and the sky a cobalt crystal, the talk had more of the nature of relief than gloom. For this spring and summer had turned out to be wonderfully ripe – wet when needed, hot and dry when needed, the hay safely in and ahead of time, a heavy crop, and the harvest promising to be just as fine.

She instructed her dogs to guard the flanks of the natural pen she had chosen, and left her inescapable bundle of knitting most obtrusively on a rock so positioned, she thought, that it would point to her having just gone off in the opposite direction. A final look about – little movement below on the sun-sucked midday fields, a few reassuring axe-blows from the woods, faintest murmurs only from the parched streams. She sauntered across to her rock, bent down as if to pick a flower and suddenly slid down the hard hot surfaces onto the ledge and round to her pool where she drew off her long heavy dress and her shift in one violent movement, threw them into the dry ferns and stepped into the biting cool fresh lucid water.

Her white skin hardened at the touch, defining even more clearly the muscular shapeliness of a body used to working on the farm and roving the high fell land, a body well fed on plain fare and by nature extraordinarily voluptuous – a voluptuousness known to and seen by herself alone and then for a moment only as she glanced down at the glass pool before breaking its mirror image. She loved to feel the shock of cold crisping the skin, making her aware of her body in a way that seemed almost magical as she swam a few strokes, letting the coldness bathe her, exhilarating as it lapped her. She turned to lie and look up at the sky. She loosed the unusually long and heavy plait which had been coiled about her head and the thick hair spread out about her, covering the water like slowly undulating grasses, making so large a semicircle about her head that her face appeared small, vulnerable and somehow religious, the strands like rays of a blessed sun. Her white skin marbled under the faintly grey-blue water. She moved her legs and hands minimally to keep buoyant as she lay and looked up at the bare blue sky.

It was a time to think of nothing at all. She let herself seem to dissolve into the water.

She had read of saints and hermits – some of whom had lived in the district – and in her present mood could understand them very well, she thought, especially the most locally revered of all, St. Cuthbert, who had finally chosen to live alone on a tiny island, with only birds and seals for company, and for his bed a coffin out of which, she had always remembered the phrase, 'nothing could he see but the sky'. From her cave pool she did not have quite such a pure, unhindered view although she would occasionally succeed in imitating the saint by paddling her hands and achieving a particular axis: but she could never hold it for long: nor did she try very hard: saints, hermits, all those romantic figures of childhood were too hard to live by. Yet she could imagine herself as a hermit and brood into a stupor of ecstasy. As the cool water hardened its grip on her skin, she had an intimation of that state. She shook it off, turned for a moment to lie face-down on the water, let the cold tense her face and then once more lay to look at the sky.

She must guard against becoming thought of as odd.

It was odd at her age to be unmarried: odder still, in the rough and tupping of the valley, to be a virgin: oddest of all when she looked on her body which common sense told her was good for work, for children and perhaps the secret pleasures the girls often hinted at and occasionally boasted about so coarse-boldly that you laughed and only part believed. It was difficult to understand. Although she had been told she was different from all the others from about her twelfth birthday, she had joined in with the others no less wholeheartedly than before; indeed, as before, she had been a leader in the more daring games, including those which, late on warm nights, had ended in the haylofts where they burrowed for each other, the boys with hands like ferrets, the girls aching to be caught yet wanting to be seen to be bent on escape. She had loved it, loved the reek of hot hay, the safe tumbling down the stacks, the covert pressings and embraces, the sudden switching of allegiances, the instant cobweb complex of understandings, the sheer pulse-thrilling richness of it. And yet, for some reason or by some instinct, she had never let it go further than that romp of common sensuality . . . even with the one she thought she might have loved she had been elusive, ready with excuses, away . . . relieved, frustrated, almost giddy at times and always aware of that ember of shame which glowed hotter and could kindle as the days passed, as meetings and glances confirmed the denial, the rejection, and a vague but potent suffusion of unworthiness rose up like ground mist and could depress her thoughts for days on end . . .

The water: the rock: the bare blue sky: herself lesser than a pin-point to the eye of heaven: forgetting herself as the cold most deliciously penetrated to her bone and chilled her thoroughly. The sun on her face seemed far away from her body: the silence shored up the solitude: naked and almost perfectly still, she closed her eyes and watched the swirl of blood. She was as poised as a bird – a hawk, a gull, an eagle – which finds the peak of an air current and hovers seemingly motionless, seemingly painted on the sky.

Small waves lapped whisperingly against the rock: a slight breeze came around the fell and cuffed the ferns so that their symmetrical leaves arched back as if stretching themselves . . . in the woods more axes were picked up and the steel thudded into the bark with that dull ringing sound which was heard and echoed all over the valley . . . The sounds chimed and blended as she drifted . . .

She had brought a small rough towel which served well enough: she liked to keep the damp coolness on her skin as long as possible. By the time she had climbed back up to the top of the ledge, the sun had warmed her almost uncomfortably. She left her hair loose, to dry more quickly, even though its waist length was usually tucked away for efficiency and out of shyness. No one was about. She whistled up the dogs and turned the flocks down towards the valley, walking behind them – she preferred it to going in front which the older shepherds still did – knitting as she went, unthinkable that she should fall behind in her weekly quota.

In other valleys, they were beginning to wall in the fellsides and the common land, making it easier for the shepherds since the flocks could be left overnight, but much harder for the small farmers and the village people who were being told that land common to all of them for centuries was now private property. Mary would have welcomed leaving the sheep out overnight up here: heavy rain in early spring still fed parts of the high pastures through active springs and the grass was good. Moreover the long daily walk to and from the valley bottom was no help to the fattening of the flock. And even the goats could have stayed out: it would be easy enough to milk them on the hillside and carry the buckets back down.

It was early to be heading back but her father needed her that evening and there could be no arguing with him. But Mary dawdled, not urging the dogs to chase up malingerers, happy that the beasts should nibble what they could from the verge tufts and hedge banks along the way. She liked her gentle animals, knew them all well, enjoyed watching their delicate testing steps, the haughty peck at the air, the tocsin of the neck bells.

The young labourer sat on a rock just outside the village, head bent, his left hand pressing a clutch of docking leaves against his jaw. The sheep and goats took none of his attention.

Mary would have walked past with no more than a nod but – noticing the hem and skirt of a dress – he groaned, very loudly, and she stopped.

"Can I help?"

He looked up mournfully, half his face hidden by the elephant ears of docking leaves, and, gaunt from a fortnight's agony, he scarcely saw the face to which his own lugubriously tick-tocked 'no'.

"Is it a boil?" Again the young man's pendulous negative. "Toothache?"

The docking leaves moved slowly up and down like branches bowed by rain.

"Have you tried peppers and vinegar?"

"I want nae mair cures." The voice was startlingly youthful after the aged semaphore of the doleful head.

"Can I see?"

He had no hesitation in letting her do this. Over the past few days the extent of his pain and the failure of several suggested cures including the torture of a dismal though well-attended attempt to dig the two rotten teeth out of the inflamed gum with a knife had left him with something of the feeling that he was public property.

"You need some laudanum for that."

"I'll tek nae Black Drop." This was the local powerful opium mix.

"The pain must be terrible."

Mary had seen two large molars on the right-hand bottom jaw, yellow-black and broken, surrounded by what seemed like a septic gum. "You really ought to have laudanum. It can do you no harm," she said.

"I'll tek nae Black Drop," the young man repeated and stared at the young woman as if seeing her for the first time.

That he should be in such a state at such a moment! His self-pity slid off him.

He got to his feet so abruptly that he bumped into her: she laughed and stepped back and he made an attempt to return the laugh but it twisted his face so lopsidedly that Mary had to restrain any further laughter immediately for fear he would take offence.

"I'm goin' here," he said, and held out a handbill as if offering a proof of identity.

It read:

John Summers, Dentist,

Takes the liberty of acquainting his friends and the public that he is just arrived from Newcastle and will commence pursuing his profession here with the utmost Attention and Care, and may be found at the house of Mr. John Burnett, innkeeper, in Keswick, or, upon application, will wait on any Lady or Gentleman in their own house.

He begs leave to observe that he is the only Person in the kingdom who can extract a Tooth even in the most decayed state, without pain to the patient: he also professes CLEANING, SCALING and PLANTING TEETH.

From one to a Complete set N.B. He makes POWDERS and TINCTURES for hardening the gums, cleaning the teeth and sweetening the breath.
Box 1s. 6d. Bottle 2s. 6d. Duty included.

*** His stay in this place will be for a few days only.
July 15th, 1802 G. Ashburner Printer.

"I want to git to him and git back to-neet."

"Are you up in the mines?"

"Yes." But felt compelled to add, "I've just taken it on for summer work, to strike out a bit on me own. But I divvn't much like it. I'll go back to t' farm for harvest."

He was uncommonly tall, she noticed, and possibly younger than her twenty-four years: the work in the slate mines must be very hard for him.

"You should get that mouth cleaned out," she said. "Come back and I'll give you some salty water and a clove or two if you won't take laudanum."

"Nae Black Drop," he repeated again. "There's men up in them mines go mad from it, you see," he said, to explain his reluctance to take the most common and effective pain-killer. "And my father said that once the Black Drop gets hold of you – you're done."

"You'll be done if you don't get those teeth out."

"I have some salt," he said, rather proudly, producing a small hemp pouch from his breast pocket. "I rinse me mouth out every time before I have a drink."

Mary hesitated: she took an interest in medicines – her mother had passed on a number of remedies and she had collected and catalogued many more for herself: but the teeth she had seen were so very bad that a salt rinse on the way to speedy extraction was by far the safest cure. Although he was trying to cheer up, the young man's face was lined and almost grey from the pain.

"Don't let me hold you back then," she said, "but if that – Mr. Summers doesn't do the job, go to Mr. Marrs – he's a veterinary surgeon but he'll help you."

"Thank you." Feebly, the young man tried to summon up the words which would keep her in his company a little longer. But she was on her way: even though the flock was drifting slowly, it had opened up a reprehensible gap.

"I'm Richard Harrison," he said, raising his voice as she moved away.

"Get him to give you one of his powders for your gums," she said, "and keep rinsing with the salt – until it's all healed."

She went, swiftly, down the hard mud track.

He watched her greedily, lamenting his luck to see and meet her at last but in such a pathetic condition. His face, he knew, he had been told often enough, looked like a skeleton at a funeral.

"I'll see you then," he shouted, defiantly: but she did not turn round. He saw her in a pool of light, her hair lifting gently as she moved away.

But he had met her! He turned off for Keswick with that consolation at least. She was everything they said she was!

*

Her birth had been registered a few miles from Buttermere in the Parish Register of Lorton. "Mary, daughter of Joseph Robinson of Buttermere, baptised on June 19th, 1778." She was barely fourteen when Captain Budworth, on a walking tour of the fashionable Lakes, met her and planted her firmly in his best-selling book *A Fortnight's*

Ramble in the Lakes. "Her hair was thick and long, of a dark brown . . . her face was a fine oval with full eyes and lips as red as vermilion . . . she looked an angel . . . Ye travellers of the Lakes, if you visit this obscure spot, such you will find the fair Sally of Buttermere." He got her name wrong – deliberately, perhaps, to protect her – but his urging was effective. From then on, Mary Robinson, daughter of the local landlord of the Fish Inn, became a landmark for Lake Tourists, as much a part of the fashionable round trip as the 'stations' recommended by Father West, the picturesque views suggested by William Gilpin, the grand natural horrors described by Gray or Pocklington's extravagances around Derwent Water.

She became known as 'Mary of Buttermere', 'The Maid of the Lakes', 'The Beauty of Buttermere': the walls of her father's inn were scribbled over with compliments in Latin, Greek, French and English, the latter being rubbed out by Mary, now and then: and she was the pride not only of the immediate neighbourhood but of valleys beyond. Wordsworth wrote of her "delicate reserve . . . unspoiled by commendation and the excess of public notice." Coleridge, another of many admirers, looking behind her immediate circumstances for a root explanation of her grace and intelligence, repeated the inevitable rumour that Joseph was merely her "nominal father". There were those who claimed she was the most beautiful woman in the Kingdom.

Captain Budworth returned six years after his first visit – this time, to warn her. A little late perhaps. Again he is utterly charmed: "really a heavenly countenance". He notes her "well-dressed young man, full six feet high, rosy as the morning", and her best girl friend whom he persuades to help Mary let down that fascinating hair: "her friend immediately unpinned her cap and let it float; and, at my request, that natural ornament was left to flow." Then he got down to business.

"Taking her by the hand, I began . . . your age and situation require the utmost care. Strangers will come and have come purposely to see you; and some of them with bad intentions. We hope you will never suffer from them; but never cease to be on your guard . . ."

Mary's reply was polite but sharp. "I hope, sir, I ever have and trust I always shall take care of myself."

It was now four years on from Budworth's second visit.

3

"Keswick Is Ready"

"Bring me the landlord!"

The boy fled across the yard, leaving Hope alone in his coach in the small courtyard of the Queen's Head in Keswick. It had been a testing thirty miles through the Lakes from Kendal. He had made a stopover there, and, in the evening, gone down to the kitchen for a conversation which had tickled his imagination with stories of spirits and dobbins but soaked his brain in too many glasses of port. Some of it was sweated out by the journey but he feared that he would not escape the full consequences. The only sure defence was to drink again. Newton had warned him against that as well.

George Wood came out unhurriedly – demonstrating that he was at no man's beck and call – but with a welcoming, even ingratiating, air – showing that he knew where his duty and profit lay. He was almost bald – the exposed skin brown as sandpaper – built like a wrestler, which indeed he had been, with a figure which recommended the hospitality on offer and a face cast in what the man was beginning to recognise as a typically north country character, marred only by a wall eye. The boy – he was about eleven – dodged about behind him, over-excited by the steaming splendour of the four dark horses and the glittering carriage. The landlord's unhurried pace sharpened when he saw the style of his newest customer.

"Get Dan," he ordered – and once more the slightly built boy catapulted himself across the yard in a frenzy of obedience.

"George Wood," he announced. "I'm the landlord here. At your service, sir."

The man looked down on him and held his eyes for a moment, before smiling, openly, warmly. Wood returned the smile and relaxed a little.

"The horses need a good rub and then I'd like you to put them out for a day, or maybe two."

The man still stayed in the driving seat, forcing Wood to look up, intimating that he had not quite decided to stay at the Queen's Head.

"There's a lush field round the back will do the trick, sir: all the stables let out onto it." Wood spoke slowly: he valued important guests and was afraid a careless rough word or expression – such as he used to his servants – might escape and deter them.

"Do you have a good room free?"

"There's a fine big bedroom with a private parlour off it that many ladies and gentlemen have been good enough to tell me they found very comfortable, sir. And Mrs. Wood keeps the best table in the whole of Keswick."

"So I've heard," the man answered, teasing with a pause but flattering with a smile. "Very well. I'll stay."

As if he had been persuaded, though reluctantly, to come to a finely judged decision, the man seemed to wrench himself from the high box. He jumped down beside the landlord, where they found they were about the same height. The man had to force himself not to flinch at the close sight of that wall eye: squeamishness could be misinterpreted and he might need the landlord's friendship. He looked around at the buildings appreciatively.

"And your servant?" the landlord enquired.

The new arrival was word perfect.

"Terrified," he replied promptly. "I managed to coax him across the Lancaster Sands but since we came into this glorious country – which is all that tempts me to stay over for a few days, to break my journey north – such wonders! Such grandeur! – but old Peters – I inherited him from my father – for old Peters it was too horrifying – the rocks threatening to crash down on our heads, those great falls of water – simply looking about him made him dizzy – poor old man, it was a pathetic sight – he is half-blind, crippled in one leg and suffers from loose bowels – I put him on the coach back to London – that wasteful and entirely corrupt Babylon, Landlord, an abscess on the pure complexion of our noble island – and drove the last few miles myself. Not at all an unpleasant experience – such air! Such hills! – fells you call them? – such nature! You see, I'm a Lake Tourist already! Such views! My card."

George Wood took the card but would far rather have taken more of the words of the man before him. The delivery entranced him: and there was that lilt, a touch of the Irish. If there was one thing George Wood enjoyed more than another – as he would repeat – it was the sound of a good voice in full flow. And the man had the looks for it, as Wood was to relate, over the next few weeks, increasingly beguiled by his honourable guest – the powerful shoulders, the heavy black eyebrows, the scar, even the long, thick, unwigged hair – all of which showed a man ready for adventure or ready with a word, equally.

"I'll trouble you not to publish the news of my arrival," the man said, reaching out with his blemished hand to give the landlord a confidential squeeze of the arm. "I have reasons for travelling incognito for the moment. You understand."

"You can rely on me, sir." Wood's good eye glared loyalty.

The men offered each other a small conspiratorial bob of a bow.

Dan, preceded by the terrier boy, lumbered into the yard pulling on his shirt, hay covering his hair like a thatch. "Aa've been doon't 'ay field," Dan announced, angrily. "Can't deu ivvery thing at yence, thou knows."

"Take this gentleman's carriage to the stables. Then put the horses in the home field." Wood could have been Louis XIV addressing a practised courtier. Dan took the hint.

The boy rocked between the three men like a tremulous whippet confounded by too many scents. Wood glanced at the man and then nodded. "Up you go," he said and, released, the boy flew up to land beside Dan on the seat, eyes straight ahead, in his glory.

"You remind me of the monkeys in the jungles of the Orient," the visitor said. But the boy was too full of himself to react.

The mighty four-hander was wheeled about the courtyard, hooves, wheels, commands, harness dinning and jangling, the noise itself announcing to half the town that George Wood had snared some very plump game.

"I'm transporting a few possessions down to Hopetoun," the man said, as Dan manoeuvred his way round the corner, "some plate, linen, a few cases of wine – will you see it is all brought to my rooms?"

"Certainly, sir. And now – a little rum and water?"

The man nodded in an offhand, careless sort of way, his eyes still on the carriage, his mind back with Newton in Lancaster: how would he react when he discovered that he had smuggled all their loot away? "But I need it," he muttered to himself and then shrugged: and what could Newton do now? The game was on . . .

*

After a dinner served in his parlour – baked trout, burgundy and a bruisedly empurpled summer pudding – he prepared for his first saunter into the town. It was about five p.m., the afternoon heat was evaporating and those who wished to promenade would be out about this time.

The Monkey-boy – as he had nicknamed him – had taken away the luxuriant Hessian tasselled boots and glossed them to black glass. A silver threepence had more than rewarded his zeal and doubled his fidelity to this man whose carriage and horses were of such magnificence: no one else in Keswick could touch him and, once round the corner, Dan had let him hold the reins.

Hope dressed without show but like a man of considerable means. His white trousers, freshly cleaned, had front pockets with fob seals in both; his white cravat was of excellent linen and served the secondary purpose of covering up a troublesome boil which was just about to erupt on his neck – he was ashamed of this blemish, priding himself, vain, over his physical appearance; he put on his green frock coat, his black felt hat and took the leaded oak stick.

Although he was aware of a few admiring and complimentary glances on the streets of Keswick, he was greatly reassured to find that the quality of his clothes was not singular. Several others shared it – a group of young women chaperoned by one whose likeness to all of them betrayed her to be their mother; a couple of quite dandified young sportsmen not too far behind; an aged old gentleman quite of another period but faithful in every detail to its fashions. As he sauntered about the cooling streets he was happily aware of style, family, money. 'Colonel Hope,' he would say to himself every now and then – 'your servant, ma'am' – rightly imagining his eventual introduction to most of these strangers whom he hoped to greet as fellow Lake Tourists, brought up from as far away as London itself to pass a whole summer for health and recreation among the newly famous lakes and hills. Those staying at a fashionable resort such as Keswick – where there would be entertainments, regattas, picnics, dances, good company and comfort – would of course be the richer, often the very rich. And they came not only for health and recreation. What better place, for instance, to hide away a desirable young daughter for a few months until her adolescence was safely passed by and her marketability, in her absence, more freely calculated?

Keswick pleased him a lot. In his early days he had visited many northern market towns and this was as neat as any he had seen. There were some handsome buildings, no church in the immediate vicinity where he might get an inspiring sermon, but shops, hotels, offices – and there was a museum, so he had been told by Wood, and several other curiosities: above all, though, what most pleased Colonel Hope was the evidence of industry. The packhorses ambling up the broad main street, the gigs and carts, the chaises and carriages constantly flowing in and out of the winding side thoroughfares, and everywhere the heartening signs of solid prosperity – saddlers, tanners, mill-wrights, masons, weavers, tailors, woollen manufacturers, print makers, drapers, blacksmiths, whitesmiths, brewers, hatters, bakers and grocers and shoemakers, the whole inter-related mesh of trade and commerce, stinking horse manure, street cries, children, machine noises cohering, almost humming in the busy yards and alleys off the thoroughfare of the main street. The man had never tried to explain it to himself but this labyrinth of small town commerce gave him an ease and buoyancy he found in no other human concentration – neither in the most flirtatious village nor in the most classical city. London, to him, was the hum of Keswick orchestrated into an overpowering symphony.

Thoroughly relaxed, the effects of the rum and the wine still in their benevolent ascendance, he turned away from the business of the town and made for Derwent Water, called Keswick Lake by Wood, who had naturally assumed he would scarcely be restrained from racing down to its shore. He followed the ostentatiously leisured promenade of Keswick society, nodding imperceptibly, pecking his way into that idle circle. His leg was beginning to ache a little but it was a short stroll to the south of the town and he was determined that here, on this famed site, his education as a man of feeling before nature would begin. For another unforgettable statement of the friend of Kemble's had been "if *you* can believe in it, so will everyone else." He might need to believe in this 'nature': perhaps a lot would depend on it.

Hope stood on the point of Friar's Crag, looking down into the Jaws of Borrowdale and waited for the revelation; of scenes like these, great poets had written, great painters painted. Thomas Gray, on an ecstatic journey, had called this the Vale of Elysium and after the publication of his popular journal letters, numerous writers had arrived to enquire into and celebrate the fascination and beauties of this divinely compacted complex of hills, valleys, streams, lakes and what Coleridge called "their thrilling interspaces". One of the first great oils exhibited at the Royal Academy by Turner, ten years earlier, had been of *Morning Among The Coniston Fells*, painted just a few miles from where 'Colonel Hope' stood gazing. In that amazing work – he was twenty-three when it was exhibited – Turner saw Paradise in this setting: the lower half of the painting is concerned with the descent into darkness, while the top half is a world of light both ethereal and suggestive of infinity. In the central triangle, among a flock of sheep, are a man and a woman, Adam and Eve themselves, in a Cumbrian Eden. As the Colonel stood looking out from that prow of rock which is Friar's Crag, Wordsworth had begun to re-write *The Prelude*, immortalising the transforming effect of the Lakes, and Coleridge – in residence in Keswick and only a few hundred yards from the Queen's Head at Greta Hall – was probing into the religious joy to be found both in the superficial attractions and experiences of the place and in the intimations it gave of the deepest workings of the mind.

In the philosophies, the art and thought of men as profound and influential as Gray, Turner, Coleridge and Wordsworth, this small, cut-off, backward place had become at once a laboratory and an exemplar, the testing ground and the ideal itself, the Arcadia where balked political revolution and failed religion turned to nature for a new radical impulse. Until very recently it had been thought of as an empty savage wilderness. Still was, by many.

Including Hope. He had stood there looking at the prospect for a full three minutes. He had given it every chance, he thought: and the evening was a fine one. There were boats on the lake, correspondingly picturesque clouds in the sky, a breeze, fashionable strollers, signs of elegant activity over on Pocklington's Island, everything a Lake Tourist could wish for. But Hope was fascinated by the people and only by the people. He would act out the phrases but all that had really impressed him was that fine stretch of water: he ought to be able to find some good fishing.

*

"Burkett's your man for fishing," George Wood replied with the slow emphasis of the well-behaved drunk. They were alone together, late, in the snug, with port. "Burkett can charm them onto the hook." The Colonel could have sworn that the wall eye twinkled. He forced himself to look at it without flinching.

"I'll hire him."

"I'll whistle him up in the morning. He looks after High Hill toll gate. Martin can do that. Martin is his son. Allow me, sir."

He poured an immoderate measure into his guest's over-large glass.

"Who do we have here, then, roundabout Keswick? What society?"

"Not much, sir, not at what you'd call your level. There's Captain Spence at Pigmy Hall and Mr. Slack at Derwent Hall, Mr. Pocklington at Barrow Cascade Hall, Colonel Peachey on Vicker's Island, Mr. Coleridge, the poet, who writes for the *Morning Post*, and Mr. Crosthwaite with his famous museum: was it that sort of person, sir?"

"Not quite. Not exactly, Mr. Wood. Not altogether. Compliments to Mrs. Wood." Avoid the man from the *Morning Post*.

"She'll be very honoured, sir. Well, have a think, George Wood, now. There's Lady Gordon down at Derwent Bay, Lady William Gordon, and Sir Frederick Treese Morshead at Derwent Lodge –"

"No, no, I don't think so." Too married, by the sound of it and not fat *enough*.

"Oh – up a bit, you mean. I understand. It would be up and up as far as you – ssshhh – not a word. Up and up and still roundabout. Of course, with the Derwentwaters gone . . ." Wood paused to remember the romantic Catholic family who had taken their title from the Lake. "Executed, father and son, after the '15 and '45. Stayed here, at the Queen's Head, the second Earl – by all accounts a fine gentleman." Homage paid, Wood recovered pace. "Well. There's the Earl of Carlisle down at Naworth, the Grahams at Netherby, the Penningtons at Muncaster Hall, always have been, and the Earl of Thanet at Appleby, the Earl of Derby down in Witherslack, the Flemings at Rydal and Coniston, the Stricklands at Sizergh and the Lonsdales, of course at Lowther, been there for ever before King William the Conqueror, they're the great power in the country. Mr. Pitt has his seat down at Appleby all thanks to the Lonsdales."

"I'm well aware of that, sir. And of some of those you have mentioned. But, Mr. Wood – incognito's the word." He paused. "Mr. Pitt is a good friend of mine. I am proud to count myself of his party. And he needs his men. For this business at Amiens is not a Treaty – merely a break in the hostilities. To Mr. Pitt – a great Englishman." This excited Mr. Wood so much that he heaved himself to his feet.

"To Mr. Pitt indeed, sir, and when you next see him – tell him there's men in Keswick back him up and tell him, if he wants to have another go against the Frenchman – tell him – Keswick is ready." Back in his wrestling mood, Mr. Wood stood, feet apart, prepared to grapple with every Frenchman ever born.

"'Keswick is ready.' It shall be done, Mr. Wood. And he will appreciate it. 'Keswick is ready.' I will mention you by name." They drank to the Prime Minister, who perhaps of all the Prime Ministers who ever lived would most have appreciated that particular salute. "But you are still not on target, Mr. Wood, if you will excuse me, not 'warm', as we say, you haven't found the range of the enemy's lines."

"Enemy, sir? Where? Where?"

"A manner of talking, Mr. Wood, a game with words, a game, by God, I'd love to have played in the pulpit, sir, and I repeat that blasphemy, or in the pursuit of the Muse – words, Mr. Wood –"

"Don't you get a chance to talk in Parliament, sir?"

"In Parliament, Mr Wood, I only talk when I have something to say. That is why I am a friend of Mr Pitt's. Do you understand me? Only when I have something – and by something, Mr. Wood, I mean a fine thing, a noble thing, a thing that must be said by me and can only be said by me and no better said by any other than myself, I mean a thing that would touch the very tiller of the ship of state, Mr. Wood, touch it to the tiller so that my words would make it change its path through the mighty ocean of history and swing quite away from the course it was following before the words – like zephyrs, Mr. Wood, like the south-westerlies, like those fecund motions which blow our great clippers across the China Seas – those words, those *words* of mine should be those guiding winds and until I can be a guiding wind, and not before, Mr. Wood, Parliament for me is a place to sit tight and look to my good friend Pitt. In silence: value untold. You understand."

"To a 'T', sir. And I more than understand. I follow you, sir; I raise my glass to you. No – I toast you – next to Mr. Pitt – a great Englishman." They sucked down another liverish measure.

"It was the visitors, Mr. Wood. I was trying to winkle out who might be my fellow Lake Tourists. I have neither the inclination nor – I may say – the time to make the acquaintanceship of the local gentry: as for the local noblemen – too many of them, as I said, will be known to my elder brother or myself or my father, or one or other of our family – I have no wish for family connections when travelling incognito. Families can pull one down, don't you find, Mr. Wood? They can reach up from the deep as we try to paddle our own small craft and entangle us in their thrashing arms like the terrible octopus, having its serpent way with us – friendly it may want to be – but how can we judge that, Mr. Wood? – when we are thrashed about by those serpenty arms of the octopus and dragged down onto the ocean bed as I have seen, with my own eyes, once . . ."

The voice had assumed a trajectory of its own. Perhaps because of those years virtually alone, allied to the intensive preparations and the desperation of his present position, he found that an all but incontinent garrulity was taking him over. Newton would have charged him with excessive carelessness. But it had been a heavy day – the long drive, the arrival, the bracing himself to meet Keswick, the drink – and his flattering conviviality had now made him a most faithful ally: Newton would never understand that there were times when you had to be excessive, even to take what appeared the path of self-indulgence for surprisingly it could often be self-rewarding. But now he was sodden and tired, in that pleasant quagmire of alcohol and fatigue, slowly sucked into half-lights of bottomless, luxurious ease. But Wood had still not taken the point about the monied Tourists. It was too late to press further. He would find out soon enough. Wood was now his man.

With the experienced intuition of what would be waiting for him when he woke up in the morning, he held onto the landlord's company. There is a time in drinking when the only answer to excess is over-excess. Dan and the Monkey-boy were asleep in the loft above the stables where, with the other six male servants, they shared a space the size of three horseboxes: the maids were only marginally more amply bedded in two attics: the other guests – none of them suitable, the Colonel had deduced, though one or two wealthy enough to cultivate for the sake of exercise if nothing else – had long ago retired as had the landlady herself, graciously released by Mr. Wood after bringing up the second bottle of port. They were seated on an oak settle in the small snug: a peat fire had been started up to take the edge off the cool night: even the horses were asleep. The Colonel 'saw' it all – this faculty for detaching himself and looking back on himself could sometimes terrify but most often fascinate him. He 'saw' two drinking men, in the silent snug of the Queen's Head, in the small night huddle of the town raised only slightly between two dark-skinned lakes in the lap of ancient mountains themselves no more than finger tracings under the awesome landscape of the sky: and beyond that –

"Are you a religious man, Mr. Wood?' he heard himself ask.

"There's not much time for that in my trade, I'm sorry to say, but if challenged, sir, I would say – yes, I am a religious man."

"I see no life without religion," his distinguished guest went on, sober in his speech, quite without that gallop of verbosity which had so far characterised most of his contributions. "The Holy Trinity have consoled me in all my times of darkness. They are what we must all aspire to."

"Yes indeed." A little uncertain, George Wood held up his glass and there it hovered. "Amen," he muttered, finally, but did not take a drink. "There was an example of a miracle of creation not far from here just died a few years ago," he said, cheering up what he was afraid might become a difficult and philosophical conversation. "You won't have heard of a man by the name of Black Jack?" The Colonel, now packing a pipe, shook his head and Wood re-told one of his favourite stories. Here it served to illustrate 'the miracle of creation': he could use it, though, for any one of a dozen purposes – 'the equality of man', 'the influence of the hills', and even, on occasions, 'the working of the devil'. "Black Jack was a Negro servant down at Low Graythwaite, belonging to Mr. Rawlinson. He was a marvel with horses although where he came from horses had never been seen. That was why they got him cheap. Anyway, he paddled along for a year or two and then he took to learning. Nobody found out why. But soon he's reading, he's writing, he gets hold of Mr. Rawlinson's books and he's learning mathematics, and then he teaches himself music on the fiddle. Not only to play it – he makes it up for himself and there's plenty can still sing and play what Black Jack first made up.

"Now you might suppose that a lot of this would be down to Mr. Rawlinson, but not one bit of it. I've heard that Mr. Rawlinson wasn't best pleased: I'm told in fact that he put obstacles in the way of Black Jack and only loaned him the books and kept him on because of the horses: there were so many others in the country would've taken Jack on for his way with the horses and Rawlinson was an envious man. No, Jack did it all on his own – a corn chest was his writing desk, the bit of the granary he lived in was his library and study and all. Nobody understood what he was about in studying. All they knew – apart from the horses – was that he was an amazing strong man. He could swim across the lake and back without a rest; he could wrestle with the best of them – I've talked to some fine Cumberland and Westmorland style wrestlers who've taken him on and been bested. But learning was his pride and joy. And nobody could understand him on that: Mr. Rawlinson and the gentlemen would have him in after a dinner to demonstrate what he could do but I've heard they would just laugh at him and maybe give him a sixpence: there was none of them could match him, you see – our gentry up here has never been too interested in much outside land and sport.

"So he pottered on for many a year and would have died a famous man but, when he was quite an age, he took a very powerful liking to a young local lassie. He worshipped her. He was mad for her. But, poor lass, although she liked him well enough, he terrified her and she would have nothing to do with him. When she upped and married her sweetheart, Jack faded away. Went off to the woods, never seen for weeks on end, pined himself to death. They still remember him in the district but his books and his writings were taken away and most likely burned. Just think, though, sir, a man, a black foreign man in a strange cold country, doing all that by himself. To my mind – Black Jack is a miracle. Big white teeth. Always smiling."

"He must have been intolerably lonely," replied the Colonel, quietly. "Poor Black Jack."

"But a miracle." The landlord held onto the original religious theme, wanting credit for developing it.

"Oh yes, Mr. Wood, and a sign to us all. But did we see it? And did we act?"

"I would have liked a chance to wrestle him," said the landlord, rather morosely. Then, as if it followed, he added, "He was well liked by the village people."

"That's something. Well, now, Mr. Wood. Give me a candle. I suppose you've no maid to light me to bed."

"I'll soon rattle one up for you, sir." The landlord stood up with a conspicuous effort.

"No," the man said. "Tonight I'll go alone."

"It would be no bother."

"Thank you, Mr. Wood."

"I am very honoured to have enjoyed your company."

"Thank you, Mr. Wood."

"Please regard me as someone who is ready to do you every service, Colonel Hope."

"Good night, Mr. Wood."

*

Hope tried to avoid waking up but sleep was slammed shut. Sometimes there was a reprieve. Sometimes a heavy night's drinking was digested in dreams, released in sweat and he would wake with no more than a not entirely disagreeable grogginess. But two successive nights, separated not by restraint but by a reckless midday surrender, always led straight to the fiercest melancholy.

It was not just the physical symptoms – the brain stiff and parched, pains shooting behind the eyes until he could have rubbed out his eyeballs to remove the stabbing, the kidneys and liver feeling infected, livid, all his wounds throbbing as if bleedingly re-opened – the leg in particular threatening to lock into cramp, the clawed fingers tingling unbearably, mouth like an open sewer, his whole effort directed at being still, hiding from it, hoping this hurricane of retribution now meting out its punishment for the abuses of the nights would somehow pass: in some part of him – even though now he had to set his teeth against whimpering – he knew that would eventually pass. It was the depth of the unhappiness he could not bear. He thought, constantly, of the two pistols in his dressing-case: of how he could hold one to each temple: and then? What would dead be like?

There seemed no good reason, no reason at all, why he should exist. Inside the pain of his body he felt as insignificant as a single pebble on a shingle shore. He 'saw' himself, contorted on the distraught bed, a thing of complete inconsequence. The mood which gripped him was one of exhausted puzzlement: how, why, should he exist at all? Inert, he could conceive of no impulse which would make him move. He was paralysed by the futility of all being. Both the weight of the world's immense business and the certainty of its lack of need or use for him seemed to grind him to powder like two great millstones which were forever in motion.

What was this life and the point of it? Such an inconceivably brief and petty thing. Poor Black Jack – now here, now gone. And little Monkey-boy, with all the zest in the world, soon to be aged, blighted, gone. He tried to summon up the memory of Sally, disappointed, as always, that past sexual pleasures could not be relied on for present aid. All he remembered now was a bare exchange of sex, a forgotten coupling, a whim of the flesh. He could feel the slim cool barrel ends of the pistols pressing, welcomed, against the pulse in his temples. Strange comfort.

There was no reason to go on. There never was. He shut his eyes on that certainty and that blasphemy struck into the swamp of his flickering consciousness. Nothing mattered. He had lost what heart and centre of himself there might once have been. "Oh God," he prayed, "let me be of use to Thee and I will serve Thee all the days of my life. Show me a path I should follow and I will do Thy eternal will, through Jesus Christ our Lord, amen. Show me why I am here, O Lord, amen."

Such spontaneous prayers he repeated, softly, so as not to be heard in the bustling morning inn. Anyone who had overheard would have been impressed and even moved by the man's sorrow, his appeal for help, his search for a sign . . . After an hour or so, the incantations worked like lullabies and he fell into a light doze . . .

*

"Some tea, two lightly boiled eggs – make sure they are very lightly boiled – warm bread, butter and goat's cheese."

The maid bobbed at the sickly looking man in the best room in the inn. She had been ready all morning to wait on the famous new arrival but now she saw him she felt let down. She had taken great care to wet her ringlets, rub up her complexion, worn her best dress.

"You look very pretty . . ." And she did. He felt a reassuring – though muted, even distant through the murk of alcohol – but nevertheless an echo of reviving lust as he sought for her name.

"Christine, thank you."

"A name from the Christian, but also" – he sat up, his lumpen, grey face more animated, and now she saw his long thick grey-shot hair – women like Christine, like Sally, always did, always had aroused him and brought out his sincerest manner – "a name like crystal – pure, sparkling in the sunlight as you do beside that sunny window. We shall be friends, I hope, Christine."

'Oh no we won't,' she vowed to herself as she smiled and bobbed and left. She did not understand why, as she was to rush and tell her best friend, but she had 'taken against him'.

Better for that little flirtation, he got up and went across to the window. The courtyard was sun-flooded, busy, tempting. But first he must eat: and before that there were his exercises – to be done at the start of every day no matter what, for, as he had learnt in the lean years, everything depended on how strong you were. Keswick would need all his powers.

By the time he had groaned and sweated through the exercises – he concentrated particularly on his arms and chest – it was past midday, and he had been in Keswick about twenty-four hours. It was, by then, widely known in the town that the exceptionally engaging the Honourable Colonel Alexander Augustus Hope, younger brother of the Earl of Hopetoun, M.P. for Linlithgowshire and friend of the Prime Minister, Mr. Pitt, was lodged in the Queen's Head for a few days and did not want his presence in the town to be widely known.

*

"Now then, Colonel," he muttered, as he pulled on the tight white breeches. "What sort of mood are you in today? Have you eaten well? Slept well? Taking the air to clear the head? Excellent, Colonel." He sucked in his stomach and snapped the breeches on. "You have a very easy life, Colonel. You lead the life of princes and the world goes to hell without you noticing a thing. But I am beginning to like you, Colonel Hope: I am starting to hear my name inside my head." He smiled warmly at his image, seeing almost visibly, though faintly, one self settling over the other, like a halo, a crown of thorns, an aura of tension, a noose, a shiver of possession as the other self entered in.

*

He had noticed the two druggists in the town – Mary Fisher and Jonah Hogarth – on his previous afternoon's ramble. He had decided it would be impolitic to go there for his laudanum. Mr. Wood had recommended the local surgeon, a Dr. Edmonson. Monkey-boy took his card to seek an appointment: this was granted immediately and the boy guided him through the back streets to the surgeon's house. The Colonel was ushered in by a jovial humpbacked manservant who winked and beamed unremittingly, and said not a word. Perhaps he was there for contrast, for Dr. Edmonson was a fine-looking man, well aware of it, wigged after the old style but dressed in reasonably modern fashion, severe in countenance but loquacious, almost garrulous, something of a scholar and a most tremendous gossip.

He welcomed Colonel Hope into his 'little parlour' in an offhand way designed to impress his lack of interest in such a noble client but all too clearly revealing it. Hope was greatly relieved. He had feared Edmonson might be a tough obstacle. Snobs were half-blind, he had found, and if you could work out which the blind half was, you were safe. Skilfully, as he thought, Dr. Edmonson drew out from Hope his connection with Hopetoun, and his brother's titles, while being flatteringly sworn to discretion. By now they were enjoying a fine sherry.

Hope mentioned the "trifling wounds" he had suffered in what he described as various "trifling engagements" and before he could bring himself to articulate the purpose of his visit, Dr. Edmonson was on to it.

"And of course you will need your supply of laudanum!"

Hope nodded, carelessly, glancing, as he did, at the beautifully made mahogany medicine chests, compacted with dozens of small brass-handled drawers, the alluring paraphernalia of experiment – tubes, jars, lengths of pipe – the substantial library, the classical busts, all of which gave the room the rotund smack of Enlightenment certainties.

"I see you are a man of learning, Dr. Edmonson."

"In a small way, Colonel, in a modest way. We are quite a little band up here in Keswick. You will not have had time to hear about Peter Crosthwaite, our original mapmaker and remarkable museum founder, or Mr. Otley, our eminent geologist, or Mr. Pocklington, whose unique constructions embellish the islands and the banks of Derwent Water – there are several of us interested in the discovery of new knowledge – perhaps if you are staying here for some length of time I may be allowed to introduce you to our little circle?"

The Colonel intimated that he was a bird of passage – two, three days, life would move him on, although the enchantment of this spot was already working its way into his blood . . .

"The pity of it is," replied the doctor, "that I am off to visit France tomorrow. I plan to be away for three months at the least."

"London is emptying itself of those who wish to rush over to Paris and kiss the hand of Napoleon."

"I confess that I cannot but admire the man," said Edmonson. "Some of my friends hereabouts hold that he is the Devil himself. But we must admire his Method, sir, and his Logic. Now that we have this Peace perhaps we can learn from him. This country, sir, is sorely in need of Method and has never enjoyed the fruits of Logic. Do you not agree?"

His visitor nodded and got up as if drawn irresistibly to the bookshelves. He wanted to conclude general conversation and get back to the object which had brought him there. If Edmonson was off to France, he ought to lay up as considerable a stock as he could. He saw his chance. "I see you have John Brown's *The Elements of Medicine.*"

"Indeed I do, sir." Edmonson was on his feet. "Inscribed by the author." He took down the book and opened it to reveal the signature of the man whose influence on medicine was greater than anyone else's at that time – and whose strong support of opium had brought him into controversy.

"I studied under him at Edinburgh and was a Brownian against the Cullenites, just as I have been a Brownian against the Broussaisists and their damned leeches. I hope to seek out Broussais in Paris and challenge him on the matter face to face."

Hope found the page on which Brown set out the many ailments and disabilities which opium would cure.

"That's my bible, sir," Edmonson said – he read a few lines from the Beddoes translation. "You were well advised to come to me, sir. The laudanum I shall give you will be of the purest variety. What you buy in these parts is generally called the Lancaster Black Drop – very inferior and in some cases – when the user is in an already over-stimulated condition – it can even be harmful. But, to speak the truth, Colonel, I do not know how the poor workfolk in the Lancashire mills – and in some of our own hereabouts – would work or survive without it. Coarse as it is, the Black Drop is the opium of the people. What I shall give you will make you neither lethargic nor painfully alert. What number of drops do you take?"

"No more than fifty at a time," Hope lied, "sometimes, an onset of rheumatism . . ."

"I understand . . . I shall make up a good supply. If you are travelling you will be safer with proven goods."

While the surgeon set about making up the laudanum, Hope, greatly cheered at the prospect and confident that his character was holding good, went into a generous description of his experiences among the opium users of Constantinople. As he described the hour at which the opium users gathered, their quaint costumes, the ritual of the daily allowance, he conjured up exactly the sort of foreign eccentricity and strangeness for which Dr. Edmonson craved. The war with France meant that he had never travelled abroad and he delayed his work, poured more sherry, sent for his manservant to bring in some cold duck and oatmeal cakes, determined to hold onto the man telling him of the worlds he had lusted for in the wet and cold north-western corner of the warring island.

"You should meet my friend Mr. Coleridge," he said. "I'll write a note for you to give to him – call on him in Greta Hall – your landlord will direct you there – don't be afraid to interrupt him – he tells me he welcomes interruptions."

In return for his visitor's conversation – and not to be outdone in any talking competition – Dr. Edmonson let loose on his acquaintance and patient "the poet and metaphysician Mr. Coleridge, who also writes for the *Morning Post*". Once again the mention of that newspaper sent out a warning chime and although Hope nodded and smiled and murmured assenting admiration as the list of qualities belonging to Mr. Coleridge grew quite gigantically – "the cleverest man in the Kingdom, a scientist to rank with scientists, a logician to grapple with Aristotle, a poet to take on all the cliques of London" – his private and unshakable decision was never to meet this man.

Dr. Edmonson went a little too far, which he was to regret in the morning but soon forgot on his journey south. In order to impress on his eminent visitor not only the greatness of this Coleridge but the closeness of his own intimacy with him, he mentioned outstanding debts, disordered accounts, fits of melancholy which led him to want to kill his wife and wish his children had never been born, indiscriminate passions for women both inside and out of his own circle – all of which, in Edmonson's opinion, was justified by his genius which of course was enabled by the opium essential for his rheumatism and other pains.

"We doctors know our friends in the soul," he said, "especially if they are also our patients. But, in case you fear I have been a little indiscreet, I not only trust completely in your discretion – forgive me for even mentioning it – Mr. Coleridge is a man who will tell you all of this himself – if he trusts you, as I am sure he will – within hours of meeting you!"

How much of this was an excuse for his garrulity and how much was the truth about Mr. Coleridge, Hope was determined never to find out.

He left the surgery, waved off enthusiastically by the manservant, and breathed the keen air of Keswick with pleasure. Everything was now in place.

4

Marriage in Buttermere

When Mr. Fenton arrived, Mary knew that she would be able to get through it. On several occasions during the weeks when the banns were being called for Tom and Alice, her feelings had all but choked her: somehow, Mr. Fenton would settle her: she could be direct with him and talk to him as to no-one else in her life: or she could be silent and learn from a glance and be reassured. It was he who had given her the appreciation of another world, a place outside the local and confined preoccupations of this remote, thinly populated valley: he had taught her beyond his duty as village schoolmaster and that 'fine Italian hand' was only one of his gifts to this country girl, whose grace and innocence had moved the scholarly and kind-hearted bachelor to attentions which he sometimes feared had led her away from her roots and even safety. The confusion of feelings which she brought on had led to his moving away to another school in the northern fells. But he could not resist revisiting Buttermere, which he preferred to any other spot in the district. He had fallen in love with it when he had visited it as a boy on his only holiday. Nor – for he was honest with himself – could he stay away too long from Mary.

Mr. Fenton was the youngest son of a poor clergyman. He had begun teaching as a student-teacher and been reasonably contented with the prospect of a life of meagrely rewarded industry – but in early middle age he had unexpectedly received what was for him a quite substantial sum of money from the mother of a pleasant but stupid boy he had coached successfully for Cambridge entrance. He had bought an annuity. The money had come too late for him to change the bachelor state he had adopted as the only sure way to any financial peace of mind. As a teacher, his payments had had to be waited for, sometimes virtually begged for, sometimes they were offered in kind and even then grudgingly, and sometimes they were simply out of reach of the families whose children he taught. He used the legacy to set himself up in rather better style – the horse, the silver fob, and Mary noticed the almost fashionable brown jacket, the decent riding boots, the new brown felt hat – and to further the charitable work he had always undertaken: now he could give away money as well as his time.

Mary took his horse and led it round the back to the stables.

He strolled down ahead of her from the Fish Inn towards the lake. The days were long and light and the summer had been rare: dry, balmy, more a Mediterranean than a northern climate. Mr. Fenton looked up the length of the lake to the fortress of fells which lent Buttermere its utterly secured character: only one or two distant forms indicated a human presence and they shaded into the evening haze. There was a deepening purple of the crags, the water mirrored that and yet parts of the surface still glittered from the peach reflections which came off some of the clouds. It was peace itself. Mr. Fenton regretted, as he always did when he came back, that he had ever left the place. There was something about the scale, the balance of lake, fell and sky, the colours, the secluded space, the deep peace which not only appealed to what was best in him but seemed, in some way he could not explain but he knew that he could feel, to fulfil him, make him whole, in some profound way to represent him.

"Listen." He had heard Mary approaching, her long skirt drawing steadily through the long grass. "Over there, I think, don't you?"

He pointed to Burtness Wood under High Stile. The cuckoo faded after about a dozen clear calls, but they waited: it would start up again.

She glanced across to the opposite side – Pike Rigg and High Bank: the echo was so pure it was very difficult to judge the source of the sound. Both stood silently, near to an old oak, listening to the many sounds of water – the lake gently slapping the shoreline; more distantly, the tumbling splash of waterfalls; even further off from the low rush of fast streams – these and the occasional craw of a goat or sheep now the only noises in the whole valley. The cuckoo started up again like a bugle: Mary nodded and pointed to Burtness. He turned fully to her and they smiled shyly.

Mr. Fenton was a reserved, even a diffident man, but it was only with Mary that he experienced this catch of shyness. Despite their long lessons together – often as not out here under that oak – sometimes in his schoolroom, sometimes in the parlour of the Fish – he had never overcome that disturbing shyness activated, perhaps, by a powerful sexual vulnerability which could be neither expressed nor released.

She, too, as he rightly imagined, felt as aware as he did of what was between them, an invisible barrier of sensibility so intense that they feared to touch each other, so unpassable that they pretended it did not exist.

"And how are you, Mary?" The avuncular schoolmaster took over. "How's the world treating you?"

"Very well." She always said that and always added "thank you."

He straightened his back to ensure that he was as tall as she was. He wished he had retained more hair, that his face was not so axe-blade lean and that he could laugh as well as smile without the self-conscious embarrassment of the neglected and unattractive teeth. He thought – in his active superficial mind, the part which directed all his actions towards her – that such a Beauty must find him very plain, possibly repellent: his armour was his status as teacher. He saw that open, lovely young face, the glory of the hair and the gestures, the poise which he did not realise was copied from his own delicate, even fastidious manner: he sensed the voluptuous body modestly concealed in a gown which puckered under the breasts and flowed down to the ankles but concealed nothing of her sensuality. She saw a hero: the man who had picked her out, taught her, talked to her as an equal, provoked her to thoughts outside the gossip of the inn, the work in the fields, the records of the valley. He could think he had spoiled her: she knew that he had brought her alive.

To help her go her own way and reinstate herself in a life he feared his tuition was taking her away from, he had left: she saw his departure as part of what she had always forced herself to believe, that his interest in her was quite strictly and correctly that of a teacher in a willing pupil, a poor schoolmaster who could see a way to free meals and helpful gifts of victuals by continuing her education long after it was necessary.

They talked about the valley – he was compiling a small work on it – one of several, for Mr. Fenton's weakness was to start more small works than he could ever complete, but he buzzed quite cheerfully from one to the other, as happy as a bee in a bed of roses. Soon he was back in the old role and he was telling her about the origins of the dialect – "I assure you, Mary, that if your father and mother were to go to Iceland or Norway they would not have to learn a new language. The Norse tongue has been locked up in these remote hills for almost a thousand years and neither Latin nor French nor English has made the slightest impression on it. It has not been eroded nor, as far as I can discover, in the least corrupted by any outside influence. What it means, I think, is that these mountain villages have not only been isolated but also tightly bound to each other as communities – and the language gave them all they needed – including a defence against Off-comers: because you know how few understand any of it. You yourself had to learn another language when you started to help at the inn."

They began to stroll along the bank of the lake. She had worked since dawn – the wedding was a test of her father's resources – and she felt no guilt. Mr. Fenton had quickly become a favourite with her father and mother: indeed, being considerably older than most of her friends' parents – she had been born long after her mother had given up hope – they preferred his considerate company to the alternatively tongue-struck or bullocking visitations of Mary's young valley gallants.

They kept a pace or two apart, as if they were being spied on, or as if they were satisfying some ancient precept honouring chastity.

Beneath his antiquarian chatter and his careful drawing of her into conversation, Mr. Fenton watched very carefully and saw that she was troubled. This perception threatened to eclipse his own well drilled good mood but he held on: long practice had given him the support of habit. She would never confess, or even admit to being troubled and, as they walked towards the sun-cold western face of the fell, he thought, once or twice, that he could have been mistaken: she was forthright, she knew how to make him laugh, she herself laughed easily . . . but he knew that, alert to his comfort, this was no more than her bluff.

They passed Sourmilk Force over the stepping-stones and into the woods, obliged, sometimes, by the narrowness of the path, to walk in single file when a painstaking politeness would overcome them both: who should go first? Neither liked to thrust themselves into the position of being watched and followed by the other and yet neither wanted to impose.

It was this honeycomb of innocence which so profoundly attracted Mr. Fenton to the district, to this valley and to Mary. He was not a foolish man; he knew that there was no Eden outside imagination, but despite having been a schoolteacher and seeing Lakeland society often at its meanest, he still felt that here, as nowhere else he had been or, in conversation and reading, heard of, there was a life rooted in simplicity shielded by innocence. Innocence was Fenton's joy and passion: his own life, that of his parents, his choices, his vocation, all were attached to ideals and disciplines of innocence, and Mary in this valley was at the heart of it.

Fenton knew that much innocence was, in reality, ignorance: he was equally aware that there is the innocence which comes from lack of opportunity or from lack of energy, from lack of means or lack of confidence. None of these applied in the case of Mary. His teaching had in part been a testing – not only of her capacity to learn but of her moral strength: to learn without losing delight and wonder. Similarly he had seen her tested when she served in her father's inn and often in quite a barbed way by certain condescending taunts: but she had not lost her courtesy and even though she could return a wounding comment with a cutting reply, there was no erosion of her amiability.

The interflow between them was complex. I came, he told her, because I saw the wedding announced. Bidden-weddings were still held in the more distant valleys. The bridegroom and his friends rode around the villages inviting everyone who wanted to come to the day: in this case it had also, not unusually, been advertised in the county newspaper: there would be horse races, foot races, leaping, wrestling – all for prizes – and for laying on such a day's sport, the crowd would contribute something to the newly married couple. A well-organised bidden-wedding could bring in a handy dowry for a rural pair. Mr. Fenton had read it in the newspaper and immediately known he would go.

"I should have sent word that I was coming but I could not be quite sure." This was pedantically correct: both knew, however, that he had not written to her because the commitment would have triggered expectations in both of them which they would have found it uncomfortable to live with, even over a few days.

"I suppose we'll find a place to put you up." She looked at him slyly. "You might have to sleep with my father." You are always welcome, she was saying, and all of us would find unassailable reasons for being absent from home all night rather than see you be inconvenienced.

"I enjoy the old country weddings," he said, boldly as he thought, plunging into the whirlpool. And that too had accredited superficial truth: he would make his notes, ask questions of the older guests, prepare to write his sketch of local manners and customs.

But the introduction of the main theme in so general a way was saying – would you like to talk about the wedding? Are you ready? Do you need to? Mary read all this into that carefully emotionless statement and, as often before, felt grateful for his tact and equally for the unique chance it gave her to articulate her feelings. With her mother she was too proud to speak on the subject: her father's own reticence which alternated with a clumsy humour allowed her no opportunity for the relief of her emotions.

"There aren't many weddings in this valley," she said: and Mr. Fenton stopped, by the lakeside, pretending to be struck by a coil of smoke up by the slate quarries of Honister. I am being passed by, she was saying, and will I be left alone? He swallowed his reply: Mary talked to his averted head.

"Tom and Alice are the last two my age." Tom was the young man spotted by Budworth, and Alice the best friend noted on that same visit. Everyone had thought that Tom would marry Mary: everyone including Mary herself, who feared to face up to why it had not happened.

"They are very . . ." Mr. Fenton's voice trailed over the lake as if trying to divine the right, the soothing, the healing word on the face of the scarcely moving waters.

"They are very loving and I love both of them," Mary said, sturdily. "They will be as happy as can be. Tom's father's let him have the old cottage in the top field and they've built it up with stone from one of the folds and slate from over at Honister. Everybody helped out with furniture. They'll be snug as snuff."

And you will still wait on at the inn, grow older and more fearful of this public attention which has persisted too long and now threatens public isolation: and . . . Mr. Fenton could not ask the question needed to lance her hurt.

"It's funny," Mary went on, prepared to take the whole burden of it now: it would have to be enough that Mr. Fenton was beside her, even though he was looking away, even though she was standing a humble pace behind him and the place was emptily theirs, an evening sun dimming. Mr. Fenton did not turn to give her that conclusive fix of help. Dare he not? Mary caught the scent of the older man's apprehension and, so as not to presume, she tempered her words, keeping them light, undemanding. "It's funny because everybody expected Tom would marry me." There it was: she paused and gazed down at the admission like a cat surprised by the sudden slide to birth of a kitten. Mr. Fenton nodded but did not turn: yes, his stately nod agreed, they did indeed think that.

"But I was never so sure." Mary hesitated one last time: it was so hard to say this out loud, but there was an impulse which had not to be denied and although in some ways she felt herself fighting for air, she went on. "Of course I liked Tom. I liked him a lot. We've all known each other since we could run about. And he's always liked me."

They were the most beautiful children I had ever seen, Fenton remembered. The beauty of health, glossy-skinned, eyes sprayed with enjoyment, waterfalling sheer pleasure in being who they were where they were: and both had grown to outpace even that full quiver of childhood promise. To watch them grow had been the sweetest part of the schoolmaster's life.

"I don't know what it was, though," she said, "when we got older, we were still friends but there was this – it seemed like a gap between us. Nothing serious – we've never had a harsh word – and nothing that time wouldn't cure we all thought, especially when Tom went away for that year down to his uncle's beyond Ulverston and we had time to think."

And I gave you extra lessons, said Fenton to himself: I taught you to read Shakespeare and discussed my poor store of philosophy with you – which you considered, as I knew you would, to be as vast as the grain stores of Joseph in Egypt. I would dazzle you with a doggy Latin tag and bring you to a semblance of adoration by explaining things only half understood by myself. And I did these things: and – God forgive me – I knew what I was doing.

"But when he came back we seemed to have grown apart. Yet we wouldn't admit it. It had become accepted – though we never spoke out – that we would wed one day. But we never courted – not in the way it's done round here." She blushed, but only for Mr. Fenton's delicacy: she was not at all prudish or uninterested in the dark and secret alliances which happened when parents went to a conveniently early bed or a gap was found in an evening such as this for a saunter such as this to a spot such as this. "And I began to notice that both of us wanted Alice to come with us when we walked out. So we would go, the three of us – nutting, gathering the herbs for the Eastermaspudding – and Tom would always give me the lead but it was Alice, I could see, who fancied him in the way he wanted."

And did her compunctions and insights into her friend Alice's desires also play their part in her standing aside? Fenton knew how tenderly responsible Mary could be: he had nursed that sensitivity.

"I could see that Tom was a bit baffled by it all." She smiled, a genuinely affectionate smile of memory as if, before her now, was stood the puzzled suitor whose allegiance had ebbed from one shore and flowed to another without his knowledge or, apparently, involvement. "So I started being the chaperon. I felt very old-fashioned. I used to make up little plots to leave them alone with one another. And the more I did that, the more I could see I was right because Alice opened like a bud in spring and anybody could see they were going to marry." It was better now: it was said. Fenton's immobility impressed on her that she might be overstraining his indulgence and so she concluded briefly: "Mind you, I almost had to propose for them: but once it was done – everybody knew it was the right thing." Still he did not turn, but she had been given the chance to speak and she sensed, from her tiredness, that a pain had been eased. "But I'm glad you're here, Mr. Fenton, and I'll be pleased to have you there tomorrow."

To 'have him there'? Her words came to him like a chill from the lake because they assumed what she had every right to assume. That he would rescue her from the prison in which – there could be little argument, he thought – he had imprisoned her. If she were the Sleeping Beauty in the hidden valley – and he had often thought of her as that – unlikely as it was from the humbleness of her birth and the workaday common survival sense of the valley – then he was the prince – even more unlikely though that was! Surely he owed it to her now.

And had he not come this evening before the wedding to tell her that?

Still he did not turn and Mary knew that he had ceased to be her confessor and had moved on to consider what she herself banned from surface thought. But now she let it rise up – there was no shame in it, there was even some justice to be had; of course there was the possibility of affection – undoubtedly – both of them had memories of untouched, unspoken, intense intimacies in the long candlelit evenings when he had drawn her into his lair of books . . . And a score of other things: how convenient for him and how pleased everyone would be: how pleasant a solution for her and how proud her parents would be: at this moment they could dovetail blessed by all . . . And Mr. Fenton wanted to show her that he loved her: but how? And how could he dare?

Oh, she thought for an exasperated moment – see what you can have! Turn and look. Stop being such a cautious old ditherer and let yourself go for once. Once will do. I'll take care of the rest. And – at this moment she dared admit it to herself – you have given me cause to hope. I drifted away from Tom because of you – we both know that. And why did you lead me here to this courting place this evening? Come on! Do it. But he stood like a pillar of salt: time passed: and she knew he would not turn. She shivered and then, feeling weary, braced herself.

"There's a lot to do," she said. "I'll have to be getting back home. There's still a lot to do before tomorrow."

Fenton nodded gravely and turned but not to, not daring to, look into her face. Instead his eyes and the index finger of his right hand pointed heavenwards, and he stood like a preacher in a trance.

"There it is," he said. "I thought it had started up again."

The cuckoo called across the valley.

5

The First Cast

What could he say to Newton's note? The man always disturbed him. "I sit in Lancaster," Newton wrote in that heavy copperplate hand which seemed to plant sarcasm and doubt on the page by the very nature of its forceful, butting lettering, "like a hen on eggs gone cold. Nothing happens on the property in Kent – from which I conclude that our plans have either misfired or we have been seen through (now there's a possibility to douse even your ever-optimistic spirit) and from you I hear nothing at all. You could have vanished into a Scotch mist and taken a boat to one of the Western Isles – with all the plate and linen, etc., etc. – for all I am aware. This is my second letter and it serves notice that should it provoke no reply it will be followed to Keswick by its author, bent on meeting his old and gallant friend Colonel Hope, who he had heard was passing through those parts for *a short while* to expedite *some* business before moving on to *another country*." This was followed by a lurch back to civility and a fast-knotted signature, hard to unravel.

If he were to tell the truth it would provoke Newton into the next carriage across the Sands. Over the past few days he had fished a little with Burkett, been to Crosthwaite Church, laid a light siege to the maid Christine, cast out a few nightlines about the town and done a calculated amount of promenading. Nor would Newton any better understand that on a deeper level he had tried to force Hope into himself or force himself in Hope and, despite initial success, discovered a fierce resistance. There was a stubbornness in him which would not let this Honourable Colonel in; and he failed to understand it. He sensed that this not being able to assume the new character was allied to surprising and governing bouts of ease in his own old self. It was as if he were playing ducks and drakes with himself. The stone flew in the air across the surface of the water, skimming as free as a bird but only because it bounced on that surface every now and then and refused to sink at the first contact.

He wanted to be free – of all constraints, all material imperatives, of all the forces hunting him and the opportunities drawing him on.

For reasons which he could not reason – (perhaps the place had seized his spirit) – an undeniable cheeky lilt of carelessness, the rapture – long thought lost – of being the man he truly was, threatened to break through the ranks of plot, to disrupt the strategy for survival. Try as he might, the man could not cast out this devil of himself. He discovered that he liked the unwanted insurgent . . .

*

But it was a sort of madness. He also knew that. The madness of enjoying the fruits before they were grown; the madness of believing the dream to be the fact; the madness of not seizing the best chance he had ever had which would also be his last chance in England.

"My dear Newton," he wrote, "you are right to chide me. I have been remiss, but not about our prospects." Always flatter the terror, or crawl a little, or be pompous. Anything to keep him away. "I have fished Keswick like the most ancient angler, but I am about to take my leave of it. There's not a young trout in the place, no perch for our palate, no beautiful freshwater salmon which we agreed was best of all – except for char, of course, the speciality of the neighbourhood, but, as we knew, unlikely to be so lucky. (Yet I will have char if I can.) No pike either, which is a blessing. Plenty of minnows, but I throw them back in. Send me letters here still and I shall ask my new friend Mr. (wall-eyed) Wood (prop.) to sit on them or speed them to another valley by pigeon post. I have heard there's good sport to be had in Buttermere and Grasmere and I intend to make my way to one or the other for a few days. Never fear, my friend, I am in this as anxiously and earnestly as you. But we must land the right catch. I will be lucky and soon: I smell it. Meanwhile I keep myself sober, chaste and fully fit: I am a credit to the service, Newton, a credit to the sweet harsh disciplines of our beloved country. Write soon. Your letters are my guarantors." After his signature, he added: "P.S. Do not think I stole the plate, linen, etc. from you. They earned their keep here. Mr. Wood reported to me that his servants had never seen such splendour and, as they carried it up to my rooms – where it sits safely! – they felt like pirates from the Spanish main, he said, hauling off the booty!"

He read it through, a touch uneasy that its jocularity might displease Newton but knowing that it told Newton what he wanted to know. Besides, he could not be bothered to re-write it. He opened his window and hollered down into the courtyard for the scraggy Monkey-boy who had become his slave.

He enjoyed it as the boy watched him sign his initials on the letter and then sprinkle sand on it. He did the same with two of Mr. Wood's letters, in this way doing the landlord a considerable favour. Postage was very expensive – a shilling a sheet – but Hope, being an M.P., could sign or frank his envelopes and have them delivered free of charge. It was an envied privilege but a hanging offence to forge or frank falsely.

*

He did a double stint of exercise until he was clammy with globules of sweat and then sluiced himself over from the two cold jugs of water Christine had brought him up after breakfast. He dressed, carefully as usual. When he looked for his money, he found that he was down to his last few shillings. This had been anticipated.

"If it is no trouble, Mr. Wood, to set it against my account . . . I shall be drawing a considerable sum in a few days but you must know how it is, travelling the country as we old soldiers do . . . thank you . . . ten pounds will be quite sufficient . . . and you must let me spend some more of it in your excellent company . . . that evening's entertainment we enjoyed together, Mr. Wood," his voice rose in the small hallway and the other guests and servants indoors and out strained noticeably to catch what would surely be the eloquent testimonial of a compliment, "was one of the, shall we say, most boisterous *and* wise, a rare combination, Mr. Landlord, I have spent, whether in London, in Europe or in and out of ships and foreign postings in a long lifetime. I thank you, sir . . . and good day to you, Mr. Wood. And your letters, Mr. Wood, franked . . . no thanks . . . none . . . my pleasure, sir."

He made for the Druid's Well, a mile or so to the east of the town. He had saved up the site for the right feeling.

It was a profitable hunch.

The party he had sought up and down the streets of Keswick, around the lake and in the gardens, was here in the mysterious circle of fifty upright stones at Castlerigg. A young lady stood near the very centre of the circle, still on the arm of a much older gentleman whose attentive pose betokened a parental or protective association with his eager, fashionable young companion, who behaved as if she were very conscious of being watched and admired. As indeed she was. Hope flicked to alert and took in the scene: five other parties, all yielding the centre to the couple who occupied it with proprietorial ease; several guides being consulted, some read from aloud, everywhere the men pointing, the ladies dipping their heads to listen or lifting them to question, with seeming humility, the words of the scholars and their translators. Hope categorised the social substance on view as exactly as a geologist would have named the crystals in a wound of rock. Not for a moment did his eyes sweep around the mountain heights which everywhere peered down on this upturned basin of ancient civilisation. He had read his Hutchinson and felt well enough armed for any country conversation. He opened it at the relevant page.

Most meditatively – remember Drury Lane, he murmured, and, his favourite whip and spur, 'Attack, boy, attack!' – so meditatively that no one could fail to be impressed by the inner preoccupation of the handsome gentleman in Hessian boots who ruminated across the turf, he paced a slow, measured entrance to the very central point of the circle without once raising his gaze from the earth or his head from the cusp of a hand which supported its pensive load.

He all but bumped into the couple, but, just in time, he arrested his progress, drew back, seemed, for an instant, to seek for oxygen as if he had emerged from some physical deep of ocean, looked about him at the mundane world he had re-entered and then, with rapid dignity, collected himself. "I do beg your pardon, sir, ma'am." And the 'a' lingered caressingly on the practised tongue.

The tone, the address, the costume, the slight bow, the gold fob, the silver tassels: the older man read the passport signs immediately.

"Not at all, sir, not at all. It is a place that promotes deep thought."

Hope looked keenly at the man, held his gaze a moment – a glance which could have ruled a line straight from eye to eye – and then snapped to attention.

"Colonel Hope, sir."

The older man smiled widely, showing off his few but sound teeth.

"Colonel Moore, sir. And my ward, Miss D'Arcy."

Hope bowed more elegantly, muttered the line about being her servant but concentrated all his will on the first look direct. As he swivelled up he planted his most unabashed and flattering look on her, smiled slightly to animate the dimple in the scar, let his right hand trail towards his heart and, with a minute motion of his head (his hat, of course, having been flourished off) shook his long thick hair rather, he imagined, like a mane, breathing perceptibly heavily at the time so that with any sensitivity in her at all she would be in no doubt that her beauty had scored a palpable hit. She flinched to a smile, half-turned away, sparkled.

And she was, he saw, quite pretty in the too-dainty taste of the day.

Worried that the Colonel might leap into army talk for which he had neither the preparation nor the inclination, Hope let flow a hand and beckoned in all about them.

"Mystery, sir," he said, "in the lap of beauty." And, cheekily – he was much bucked by the success of his simple stratagem – he managed to throw the gear of his comment towards Miss D'Arcy on the word 'beauty'. This time she blushed. He relaxed into it.

"Mr. Hutchinson," said Colonel Moore, holding up his flat leatherbound volume, "gives us a sufficient account of both, I think."

"Mr. Hutchinson is indeed an authority, sir." So Hutchinson was in: he would trump him. "But even he may not tell the whole story." He hesitated. "Of course I am no scholar – though," a risk, "we soldiers must at times have a scholar's curiosity." Colonel Moore nodded happily – compliments here, Hope could see, would be manna. "And indeed we might say that the very greatest soldiers – Joshua, David, Alexander – who lent me one of my Christian names – Caesar, of course, our own great Alfred – the only king we call Great – Edward – and we could extend the list into the present – all have been scholars *in some manner*. I myself would claim no more than the natural store of a questioning mind." Must remember that phrase: he could see it had struck and it struck him too: he paused to give it the silent applause of a mute punctuation. "But when I see those stones here, and ponder – as I was doing when I so nearly precipitated myself upon you –" he laughed, gently, at his own folly and again rapiered a look to Miss D'Arcy who, in control now, returned to him the dreamy interest of the truly hooked – "it was Egypt I thought on. Egypt!"

He paused – thought of doing the dramatic half-circle - thought better of it. Colonel Moore was benevolent but no pushover: and melodrama too early introduced, though it could be a short cut, was always a risk.

"All of us who fear God and seek salvation through His Son must be drawn to previous explanations of the genesis of life and the meaning of death." The switch worked: on the faces of both of them came down that twilight of solemnity, a most vulnerable condition, he had found, if rightly played upon. "And these stones – so unexpected in this magnificent country – because I confess it is not for the pleasures of civilisation that I came to this district but for the informing breadth and spectacles of Nature – reminded me of somewhere I knew not where and that was my over-selfish study which all but ended in a brute collision with yourselves!" He sensed their relief: the twinkling 'brute' promised that it would not be unremittingly solemn; the man could still see a light side. "And then it dawned – Egypt! I confess it might seem a little far off – not as a country but as a comparison – and yet that was what I thought. Egypt! When I was there – force majeure, Colonel – but still time to contemplate – the Great Pyramids, the Sphinx, the tombs, the monuments of strange beasts standing in the desert – a pomp and detail, I know, quite missing from these bare monoliths but nevertheless, in some dark undercurrent of history, connected." He paused, approached a half-step closer and added quietly, with an apologetic reference to Miss D'Arcy, "if by nothing other than the stone, the mystery and," confidentially, "the human sacrifice."

"A bestial religion," agreed the Colonel.

"The slaughter of an innocent . . . virgin," the word was half-swallowed, "to satisfy a vengeful society . . . hereditary caste of priests . . ."

"A god." Colonel Moore climbed into the conversation through the chance of a correction. "They had gods for everything, as I understand it. A god for the rain, a god for the wind, a god for the moon . . ." He turned to Miss D'Arcy. "See how much simpler we have made it: as well as being the true faith we are the simplest."

"Perhaps there you have it!" Hope exclaimed. "What wisdom! We are true, as you say, *because* we are simple."

The older Colonel beamed about him and Hope tried to execute yet another manoeuvre with Miss D'Arcy – to get her to conspire (silently of course and with the finest subtlety) with him against her guardian so that the two of them could be saying "what a dear old gentleman he is" and use this to draw closer together. He thought he had succeeded but he could not be sure: her loyalty to Colonel Moore was bedrocked: so he had not scored a direct hit but then neither had she resented his attempt. He had learnt a little more about her.

"But I intrude," he said, abruptly. "Please: forgive me."

He began to back away, wafting away any attempt there might be – there was none; Moore knew his manners – to detain him.

"Are you staying in the district?" That was both civil and friendly.

"In Keswick itself," Hope returned, still, though very slowly, on his royal retreat. "At the Queen's Head."

"I will leave my card," said Moore, pleased enough that the propriety of a first encounter had run its sufficient course.

"Honoured – sir, ma'am . . ." Ah: that superlative 'a-a-a'.

Hope walked across to one of the biggest stones and examined its blank surface close up with the most scrupulous attention until the Colonel and his ward had quit the field.

Now he needed patience.

He dined at three and fished with Burkett and his daughter until the evening light finally wilted, not to darkness, it was too northerly for that, but to that active dusk in which motes of light seemed pleased to elude the half-hearted grapplings of black night. In his rooms by ten, he summoned a cold platter and a pint of beer and wrote an optimistic, almost boastful letter to Newton. "Not less than ten thousand pounds a year I'd guess . . . canny old fool in command . . . would not surprise me if . . . but convinced can succeed . . . patience and patience is all . . . please keep up your letters to Colonel the Honourable A. A. Hope, M.P." He franked it immediately and sent it off with the monkey.

But when all was done he was still in a rash of perturbation.

He burst his boil. It was a day or two premature. He had nursed it assiduously, vain of his good health, thinking that, mishandled, one boil could seed others, like a sycamore rampant. It had shifted from its deep root and was loosened so that all the 'bad' – as his mother had called it – was now gathered into the volcanic pimple. But as he tapped it, expertly, for he had suffered an onslaught of boils over a suppurating, pus-stinking twelvemonth, he knew that the hardness meant it was not quite ripe. To burst it now would be to risk the messiness of it re-grouping, possibly cloning itself across the infected area and returning in a small battalion. Nevertheless, having called for boiling water and cleansed his best knife over a candle flame, he took the risk. The immediate ease was a great reward; the dabbing and doctoring preoccupied him further. It was a contented half hour.

Christine came to collect the jug and steaming bowl. He made no attempt to flirt with her nor she with him. In another mood he might have been goaded to further efforts by her extremely obvious, even insulting, indifference, but now, if anything, he was inclined to give her credit for it. He was even capable of finding some credit in it for himself: for after all, it proved that he did not have to take every apparently unprotected woman who came into his sights. There was a rough equality between them which pleased him since it ignored and slipped through the magical armour of those clothes, the possessions, the name, the title, the carriage and four, the weight of deference and the history of servility.

He was amused to observe that she forced herself to be a blank when she picked up the bowl of pus and blood.

"Will you be wanting anything else, sir?" How disgusting he looked, she thought, sprawled in his open shirt like an ostler in drink . . .

"No, thank you, Christine. I need my sleep after all your mountain air."

"Good night, then . . . sir." The pause before the polite title was most satisfying to both of them.

But he was still untired. Another evening with Wood was not to be contemplated. That first act of over-familiarity had secured him all the credit he would ever need and besides he felt wild, restless, a mood in which he knew himself all too prone to indiscretion.

It was still hot from the dry July day: no-one could recall such a warm summer. There were fires in the heather.

He forced open his windows and looked out over the courtyard, over the town to where what he now knew as Skiddaw stood in dusky largeness, a prehistoric beast couchant. The air was full of sounds – the jangle of reins or goat bells, noises – could they travel so far? – of parties making for, perhaps already on, the lake ready to take advantage of the promised full moon, dog barkings, cow lowings, sheep, horses: the town and its fjords of fields was as restless as he with the hidden cries of the night. But the man sensed – he wanted to sense – even deeper, a disorder in the night; he longed for it.

He opened his door and called for the maid, but this time it was not Christine. A new girl answered the call for more water. She made three trips, each time carrying a pair of heavy jugs which she emptied into a small copper hip bath: and each time increasingly aware of and responding to the gauntlet of Hope's lust.

"Will you come back with a little rum in about ten minutes . . . ?"

"Joanna."

"A name to roll around the tongue," he let his tongue roll around his lips in a mock-disgusting way which made her laugh " . . . when I've had my evening bath . . ."

"Mr. Wood says he's never known nobody like you for bein' clean."

"It is a godly failing, Joanna . . . You're not local, are you?"

"Not likely. London. Extra help for summer."

"And why do you find yourself in Keswick?"

She shook her head. It brought to his notice the heap of auburn hair and, taking his time, he let his eyes stroll down a pinched but puckish face, breasts which looked firm though on the small side and the rest, as he would guess, in regular working order.

"And how old are you, Joanna?"

"Seventeen."

"Rum then. In ten minutes."

He scrubbed himself as clean as a Viking before a battle and pulled his large white linen robe around his undried nakedness, relishing the lap of texture on wet skin. The candles were all lit. The room would be like Aladdin's cave to such a girl as Joanna – fine clothes, the glint of plate, the stack of linen, the magnificent dressing-case, the several pairs of boots, the hats, the books, fobs, silks, glow of guineas on the writing table; he went to the window and did not turn around when she entered.

"Put it on the writing table, Joanna." Beside the guineas – oh, unfair temptation to the poor! Beside the heap of guineas so recently the property of your new employer, Mr. Wood. "And take out the tub if you please." Her lean strength swivelled the hip bath out onto the small landing.

She re-entered and shut the door behind her. He turned, having closed the window.

"Take a guinea from the table, Joanna. And bring me the rum. The guinea is for you."

She checked herself so as not to rush and then advanced over-slowly, first took up the bottle of rum, poured a glass, then picked up a guinea, seemed, he thought (and smiled) to test it, pocketed it, brought him the rum.

"Do you like rum, Joanna?"

She nodded and sipped: he leaned his head forward and she brought the glass to his mouth: he finished it and she let it fall on a bush of discarded clothing as he swooped down with his hand, lifted her dress clear over her waist and then, as she struggled to help him, tugged it over her head. He stood her back and looked: she stripped off his gown and, as he was there standing, he hoisted her up and held her easily as she straddled herself around him.

Still holding her he moved to the bed. Her thin lips clasped tight together, fearing any sound might betray her, she hooked her legs about him and pulled him further and further into her. He wanted to say her name but he could not remember it; he wanted to engage in the physical endearments and gentleness he so much prided himself on bestowing and was received so gratefully for so doing, but this lean, hard-bodied girl would have none of it. She writhed and twisted under him in spasms of an unfulfilled need which swallowed his own spent desire in her caverns of longing. Even knowing he was finished she would not stop but pulled herself against him, levered and bucked with a grunting intensity which made him look down on her with pity. He sought her out with his hands but she pushed him away as if he would hurt her and no reassurance satisfied her. She expected and gave no kindness, no tenderness at all. She flung herself away from him for a moment, and then returned to attack his sex but he held her off, had to use some force to hold her blind-eyed, gaunt-faced, now grasping body away from his.

This was not what he had wanted at all.

Yet, he counselled himself, he would not behave badly to her. She had whored him as he had whored so many. But there could be some, just a little, sentiment in it. He lay with her for a little while as if all had been for the best and when, with a sudden, slithering movement, she was off the bed and into her dress, he thanked her, wished her good night. She did not say a word.

She left him desolate.

In the candlelit solitude of the Queen's Head in Keswick, he lay on a rack. He knew it was of his own making but that was not useful knowledge because he could not unmake it. Nor, as he fully intended to sin more, could he with any penitential fidelity see the consolation of confession or even of prayer. His soul – if indeed that scarred and insulted figment still existed – was lost to his sight, abandoned long ago and now most likely marked for delivery to the Devil. He had reason to be in that camp . . .

At times he would claim that his father had been lashed in front of the town and put in the stocks for poaching a salmon, and told to pray for the soul of Lord I—— whose goodness had saved him from the hanging he deserved. His mother, he would say, had left home after such a humiliation, taking the three children on what had proved a pilgrimage of terror; he thanked God he had been nine years old and able to run off and fend for himself.

He got up and opened the window even wider for more air. There was less noise now in the town. He would have welcomed noise, company, a digression.

For a moment he thought of going out and joining the moon-walkers. The sky was now brighter than it had been earlier in the evening. The moon squatted above the mountains hugely, as if it had descended in majestic importance to pay a visit to this district, these mountains, this town only. The houses were shaded clear against the ground: on the hills he could see the white lines of the new walls they were building like netting all over the high ground; from the direction of the lake he heard an occasional voice, as sharp as the crack of a pistol.

It was this 'Hope' that disturbed him. He found a mirror, stuck candles at either side of it and sat, naked, before it, the sweat drying on him as the warm undulation of night air moved into the room. Alexander Augustus! What father would anoint his child with such a leaden armour of expectations? The Honourable! To whom, by whom, for whom? And yet that Honourable was such a herald. With that Honourable he could approach a ready Miss D'Arcy who would not look at a tradesman, a craftsman, let alone a common man whatever his industry or honesty. With 'Colonel' and 'M.P.' topping and tailing his rig he was unstoppable. All titles, all baubles to be inherited, purchased or corruptly obtained, none needing the effort of virtue or the talent of merit, all the gift of a grateful country to a ruling body which ground its larger numbers into the dust. And he wanted to be part of that ruling, governing, corrupting, self-enriching, self-perpetuating, invincible body which had even managed to escape revolution – he wanted to be high on its highest heap. No doubt of that . . .

And yet, on this fevered night . . . he stared at the heavy, handsome head, looked at it until it became a strange thing to him, a feeling of stone, a sight he saw from another part of the room, this unbodied head reflected more truly in the mirror than in the live skull itself . . .

Why was there no consolation in slaking his memory with the bodies of women? Or saucing his ambition with fantasies of wealth, success, escape?

It was this Hope that interfered with it all. He could not abide the spoilt and pampered younger son of the Earl of Hopetoun. He despised the ease with which he could now engage in a life beyond the mightiest exertions of the man he had been born to be.

Yet he was stuck with Hope and he must stick by him. To lose him would be worse than losing himself: it would be losing the only chance left to him for the life he had always and violently lusted after.

"But to myself I'll call myself John," he whispered to the mirror. "To myself, by myself, I'll be John, just John, plain John, the John I was christened. Good, English, John . . ."

*

Colonel Moore had left his card and the next morning, at a careful eleven o'clock, Colonel Hope called at the rented villa on the lakeside. He was informed that Colonel and Mrs. Moore had left with Miss D'Arcy on some unexpected business and would not be returning for at least a fortnight: and even that was by no means certain.

The stump of the boil throbbed: he had not cleared it. He decided on a brutal vinegar poultice.

6

The Fish

Buttermere was nine miles from Keswick by the horse road, fourteen by the carriage road – both steep and difficult passes.

The Fish Inn, now fully recovered from the wedding of Tom and Alice, sat between Crummock Water and the adjacent lake, also called Buttermere. The inn was a small cluster of a place, stables, byres, outhouses. Sometimes it was known as the Char because of its sign – a crude but unmistakable painting of that fish found only in the deepest lakes – Buttermere being one – and already considered a fashionable delicacy in London. It was the site where such a building had to be, if buildings there were at all. If you rolled a god-like pebble across the valley floor, it would come to rest on the site of the Fish, for the location commanded every aspect and enjoyed every advantage – surrounded by lush flood meadows, watered by nearby falls and tumultuously clear fell becks, sweet in its grasslands and serene in its views. Joseph Robinson had blessed his luck to marry a woman who had a certain expectation of such a fine spot and his vigorous commerce had turned a pothouse into a stopover for some of the best in the county, in the land even. He had not been so happy with the farmland which went with the Fish; his town talents (he was from Cockermouth, about ten miles away) had given him neither the patience nor the experience for such niggling country work and – as he was a man who took advice badly – his neighbours had soon left him alone to rot alone. Without the thriving Fish he would have been in debt. And it was Mary, they all said, who made the business sing. Without her . . .

On Friday morning she always went to take some food to Kitty Dawson. She was glad of the chance to get away. These days she sought out excuses to be on her own. Her father disapproved.

"It is not that he minds," her mother said, wearily, as always, explaining and defending her husband to their daughter.

"I know."

"It's just that he worries if you aren't here. He always has."

"I know." And he had. For better and for worse reasons as she had divined as a girl. But she knew also that his better self would struggle to serve her best interests and in its better moments was quite selflessly caring; and so she had long ago ignored the pettiness, the commerce and the insult of the worse self.

"Don't worry, Mary," her mother said, as she said so often these days, her own face a portrait of Anxiety, "everything will turn out for the best." The 'girl', twenty-four – unwed and such a 'catch'. "It hasn't been any good for you," her mother looked about to be certain Joseph was not within earshot even though he had just gone off to fish in the lake, "all this . . ." she added, unnecessarily, casting an accusing look in the direction of the inn parlour. "All that . . ."

"I won't be long."

"A girl like you . . ."

"You married late, mother: much older than I am."

"But I wasn't thought of as a Beauty." This was only partly true: but for her pock-marked skin she would have been much sought after: as it was she had been pursued more through calculation than desire. "And besides, my father was a Tyrant. He wanted one daughter for a servant."

She seemed oblivious of the echo this might find in her own daughter's life.

"I always go to see Kitty on Fridays."

"But it was only yesterday you were out and . . . oh dear." She held her left side: there was a pain which kept recurring whatever she did to relieve it. Dr. Lazenby at Lorton had said that she should take more rest: as if that were possible with a farm, an inn, a husband and a daughter to work and worry about.

Mary helped her to a chair: brought her the smelling salts, then a glass of ginger wine and called in Annie who helped to fuss over her until Mrs. Robinson felt first petted, then relieved and finally embarrassed.

"Away with you. It's nothing but a pain. It's gone now. Isn't it, Damson? Yes – Damson – yes?"

Damson, the cat, had been taught to 'talk' certain words and, at the command, managed a very passable 'Yeees'. Mary gave her a saucer of milk.

She felt guilty at how much she enjoyed being out of the house, even out of the village. She had rarely felt like this before but too much was now oppressing her.

It was a day of swift clouds but they were light grey, thinly spread, unthreatening, and when the sun speared through, it dazzled the lake and the foamy fell streams.

Mary paused, some distance from the little settlement of Buttermere, and steadied herself inside this deeply protected, world's end valley, the home as might be of the hidden enchantments of fairy tales as Mr. Fenton had said. But that was no help. The memory of his last visit would not leave her; there was a jagged edge to it – for had she not tried to force him against his will and had he not been aware of that and too kind to give her the direct reaction she deserved for her over-boldness? That was how she saw it and it added to her perturbation just as the sight of Tom leading hay over under the far wood gave her a quite unnecessary pang for she had never really loved him. Yet a devil was loose somewhere, a restless imp had slipped into her and would not be harried or prayed out. She who had so many reasons to be content was now besieged by envies, regrets, shameful, all of them, and she burned, on that hot July day, to admit to such inflammatory meanness. She could not understand it. Marriage would come or it would not and if it did not come sooner it would come later or she would be unmarried and what stigma was there in that? When had she ever cared and why did she care so sharply now?

The pause had steadied her for a while but then it enabled the gnawing to chew on her once more. She hurried on into the high woods to see Kitty, her basket filled with even more goodies than usual, a stock, indeed, which her father would (rightly) have called wasteful, far beyond alms.

Woods were soothing: the noises diverted her. Not only the birds, the streams, the flicker of a hare, a fox, but the vaulting noises of the woodsmen, the steady dunk of an axe, the feeling of invisible beings inhabiting the same spread city of trees. She tacked up the fell like a sailboat before the wind.

As she moved, she took note of the world close to her – the green woodpecker, its flash of holly red, mustard yellow, the great soar of a spruce, the wind whispering differently through different consistencies of leaf, hare track, badger hole, unripened blackberry, fir cones big enough for kindling, and the incessant weave of thrush, linnet, chaffinch. Had Mary been told that her knowledge of the countryside was indeed 'knowledge', she would have dismissed the tribute as, at best, a taunting flattery. Yet all around her, in their revolutionary impulse, men and women not of the greatness of Coleridge but certainly of a similar ambition were beginning to log and classify, to catalogue and proudly identify what, until quite recently, had been the terrain of a very few – the variety of nature as known by Mary. Otley at Keswick with his geology was tracing the origins of life in rock rather than parchment, in crystals, graptolites and trilobites from the millions-of-years-old fells in the Lake District rather than in scrolls kept dry in the deserts of the Middle East for a mere couple of thousands of years. The genius of English painting was turning to the grandeur and the detail of Nature – Turner, Constable, Wright of Derby, Gainsborough – all coming here, sometimes no more than a few yards from the wood in which Mary was now making her way, also driven by the strange, indefinable current of change, as powerful and mysterious as the turn of a tide, which now decreed that the study of man should be through Nature.

It had its Arcadian examples – like all revolutions it dug into antiquity for help and respectability and dynamic metaphors – and Mary could be seen, that morning, in woods as sun-speckled as a thrush's throat, as a shepherdess from the Hellenic world, a Grace from their pagan earth-suckled legends, but above all a spirit of the place. Her beauty, too, was natural – fed on plain bread, milk, eggs, fish – often char from Buttermere, but trout, pike, salmon too – and game – woodcock, wood-pigeon, cockerel and the novel intrusion of fruit. This was her father's invention and he was very proud of it.

Her father, a Cockermouth townee, had known several nautical men and took an obsessive interest in Our Fleet, Our Navy, Our Sailors: naval patriotism was his sport, the talk of his tap room. Nelson, by now, was his nonpareil. But Joseph had always been very devoted to any local news and for a long time the talk of the town had been the Cockermouth man – Fletcher Christian's – Mutiny. Joseph had followed the case with a fascination he could not explain. He became an expert on breadfruit. He attempted to envisage and explain the incredible feat of navigation undertaken by Captain Bligh after the Mutiny. He reached into any dip of information for enlightenment on the customs and manners of the people of Oceania. For hours he would brood over the significance of the case brought against Captain Bligh.

He became an encyclopaedia, a bore, a touchstone and a perennially reliable spring on the subject – most of all he brooded over what Fletcher Christian might have done – had he headed for Australia?

America? Back to England? There had been sightings, his family was powerful enough to keep him hidden and safe from the inevitable hanging "should he show his face on the shores of Albion again" – a favourite phrase of Joseph's, picked up from a knife-grinder whose preoccupation with Bligh, the *Bounty* and the Mutiny had almost equalled Joseph's as witnessed in a fierce contest of informational prowess contested in the snug of the Bull in Lorton where the knife-grinder had eventually conceded defeat and been given several unexpected commissions (including one from the vicar of Cockermouth who disliked Joseph intensely and produced a cluster of blunt knives and dullest scissors to prove it) as compensation. And in all this, Joseph had learnt that Bligh's proven and later much copied method of keeping off sickness, especially the scurvy, was to force fruit on his crew: fruit and exercise, for which purpose he carried a fiddler to make them dance every day. Exercise, on a farm, was not hard to find and Mary's daily round included flitting up and down slopes sheer enough to grip an unaccustomed calf with solid pain for a week. Fruit, though, had been the filler for pigs, the mash for cattle nursed past Christmas, at best the occasional absent-minded addition to a bare table. Joseph made it obligatory and made his wife and daughter crunch their way through apples and pears as devoutly as he would grind through grace.

Mary's loveliness, then, as she lifted her heavy skirts to seem to skim up the steep wood by the cunning zig-zag of lightly indented sheep paths, was supported on a diet, a regime of exercise and a purity of mountain air ionised by the nearness to the sea; it was also – according to Wordsworth – nourished on the place itself and the people and life lived simply there – a life he placed at the heart of the Romantic Movement.

"You always look so *well*," said Kitty, as she so often said. Mary took no notice: she was largely – though not wholly – inured against compliments. "Your cheeks are wild roses, Mary: the pink ones that blow away at once."

The walk up through the harmony of the sunny woodlands, the lightness of sensation which a testing walk always gave her, coupled with her natural health, did bring out every pleasing feature she had. And she could at least smile at Kitty's compliments because no-one was in earshot and anyway Kitty was mad.

The hut she now lived in had been well built by a woodman more than three years ago. Since that time the trees which had once enthicketed the hut had been lopped down and now the pyramidal vernal tent stood isolated among a company of stumps, like stepping-stones from the forest to Kitty's lair. Mary sat on one of the stumps, Kitty on another. Mary handed over her parcel of food and treats which Kitty took with a happy nod, grateful for the saving kindness. She foraged in it immediately to see if her young supporter had been able to smuggle through a twist of tobacco.

"Oh good Mary, blessed Mary, Mary Virgin Mary, good you girl." Mary winced at the incontinent ignition of thanks activated by the discovery of a modest twist of Joseph's tobacco. Kitty got out her clay pipe and packed it frugally and very skilfully. "We'll put up a statue to you, Mary."

"Please, Kitty. Smoke your pipe and enjoy it. Then we'll talk."

Kitty took about a dozen tender puffs and then pressed the pad of her index finger most gently on the glowing weed.

"Save it," she announced. "When it's cold. Good girl, Mary. Good girl."

Kitty moved from hut to hut every few years. The woodmen never broke up those temporary dwellings which they built to see them through the weekdays of the felling season. This reluctance expressed an unusual lack of thrift on the part of men to whom it was a necessity, but the bond with the past was strong and there was some ill-defined superstition clinging about the woods which forbade the useful dismantling of these huts built, often, to accommodate up to half a dozen men through all the taxations of a northern spring, summer and early autumn. They became the refuge of the vagabond and beggars sought them out as natural almshouses.

Kitty had lived in huts such as these and around these woods for more than fifty years. Mary had been brought up with her story which, for many in the valley – except her own generation, increasingly unable to visit her on the heights she chose for her seclusion – had gone cold long ago. But Mary had been touched by it as a girl and, as her goat herds had taken her high in the woods, she had often come across Kitty in the course of things. Eventually, she overcame her fear – with other schoolchildren she had sometimes ganged up to cry 'witch' at Kitty, delighted when she ran after them, gleefully scudding away like infant demons scattered by Beelzebub. Then Mary had seen the old woman for what she was – a pauper, trapped in her sadness, her madness, now frightened, now lost; and her story – not only for the tale itself but because it concerned someone she knew, before her, now covering the pipe's small bowl with protecting beech leaves – wrung her heart.

Kitty's father had been a woodman, born more than ninety years ago, in the reign of Queen Anne, just out of the valley in Lamplugh, a village named after one of the Conqueror's more savage barons and ever since his brutal arrival sunk in the spellbound gloom of ossified superstition. There were still – at the end of the enlightened eighteenth century, that Age of Reason which matched itself against Athens – old women in Lamplugh who were convinced that you could be led to your death by a will-o'-the-wisp or terrified out of life by the fairies. Kitty's mother had been such a black-clothed incantator, full of rhyming recipes for ills and puddings, for scalds and weather and animal magic. Her father had been glad to get out to the woods where he led a gang, made a living and found, in his daughter Kitty, all he wanted for softer pleasures. She became the elfin presence, the luck charm, the sweet pet of the forest: and when she was sixteen, she met William, four years her senior, a carpenter just out of his apprenticeship in Lorton – the next village on from Buttermere – who came every week to make the first selection of wood from her father's stock. They fell in love, all four parents were happy at the match. They were asked to wait until Kitty was eighteen and they agreed.

He was killed in a most extraordinary way. After a long morning's work in midsummer, he had eaten and then leaned back to take a short sleep. His head had been propped against a rock which had attracted the lightning of a sudden thunderstorm: the bolt had hit the rock straight on and *rolled down* the rock – so they all swore – to stab him fatally in the neck.

From that day, Kitty would not leave the woods.

At first her father had tried persuasion, but she was intransigent: brute force, but she ran back to the woods the moment she could: custodial restraint, but he could not bear the sight and sound of her pining. Finally they let her go – the mother convinced that a boggle had possessed her daughter and only too glad to see the last of her, the father, heartbroken, soon to submit to an illness which his former self would have beaten off quite easily. Kitty had stayed in the woods above Buttermere and Lorton ever since – rarely more than a quarter-mile from the rock on which her suitor had been killed.

Mary had begun to visit her regularly on Friday mornings – with Mr. Fenton's express approval and the Christian support of her mother – when she was about fourteen – at about the time her father had begun to use her in the Fish and Budworth had turned up to sketch his mischief. About ten years; over five hundred visits: and such was the silver-plated delicacy of her politeness, she had not once asked the questions she longed to ask. What had he been like? How *much* had they loved each other? What had she *felt* when she saw him dead? Did she not think that such grieving as she had showed was somehow too much for any memory to bear?

The old woman was gypsy brown, the tan so shiny on the mild skin that it was like a fresh varnish. She sat in front of her turfed teepee like a re-located squaw – the mass of brown hair loosely braided and heaped on her head like a parcel carelessly tied with twine, her forget-me-not blue eyes looking at Mary only when she thought she was unobserved, at all other times intent on the middle distance, her small, slight, quick body quivering as she enjoyed the rare comfort of proper sat-down company and felt the physical, close interest of another human being. Now and then she smiled directly at Mary, revealing a poor few blackened teeth which did not, however, impair the sweetness of her girlish shyness. It was a smile which Mary never could resist. Indeed, here with Kitty at the edge of the woods, she felt such a relief into unselfconsciousness that she bathed in it as she bathed in her pool.

They talked about the woods. Kitty knew them as well as any animal, as intimately as the dogs who worked the sheep and hunted the foxes and badgers and otters. Kitty spoke of a new lair, a vixen biting the ear of a cub, an owl on a rat, the sound of a wolf although everyone knew the last wolf in England had been killed some years before about forty miles to the south, near the Bay. From Mary she required nothing but her presence and she was not at all interested in any talk of village gavottes. Mary had once mentioned Tom to her but his marriage to Alice would, she knew, be of no significance in the intensely inward life of the old woman whom unsympathetic observers would have categorised as a mad old crone. Mary knew better. Listening to Kitty was like listening to a stream, to the wind, to the sounds across the valley floor at night: except that Kitty was a woman, had once been young as she was, had been loved, lost tragically, but lived to be a testament to single-minded passion. The ragged old woman brought out some vibrant corresponding note in her loyal young friend.

"You took her some tobacco, didn't you?" was her father's return, surly greeting. Mary confessed instantly. Joseph, who paid her no wages and feared increasingly (Alice had been a most unexpected reprieve) that his goldmine was sure to be removed from his use, could ape his former threats but do nothing. "She's been nothing but a nuisance all her life." Mary declined to reply. Her silences infuriated and mortified him.

"There's a fine young gentleman and his lady come in a chaise in the parlour now taking some tea." He paused, sore enough to want to jab. "You can go and see if they'll be wanting anything more. I've a fair idea," and here he smiled a benign leer which long ago Mary had learned to repulse but still – unawares – could cause her to coil up in herself in shame, "they've come here express to see the Beauty."

She went through as her father bid her: hating, every day more and more hating the show she was, the part she had to take up, the curio she had become, beached on the suffocating shore of the Fish.

7

Journey's End

His melancholy was a fierce and active thing. There were those at that time who cultivated melancholy to give themselves the appearance of profundity. John–Augustus tried to josh himself into accepting that his own bout was no more than that. But this was a real vertigo of despair. He had mixed laudanum with his wine, but even that had not helped.

He tried to trace the cause of this present onset – which, like all the attacks, seemed much the worst and quite irredeemable. It could happen that nailing and uncovering the cause would begin the progress of the cure. This time he traced it back to the servant in the bedroom – he blocked out or refused to remember her name – a cold witch, he decided, a witch who would find no satiation in this world, maybe even a spirit brought back to test and ruin those who had intercourse with her. He could not forget her thrashing coldness, her silent chasm of demand, his own inadequate coin of futile charity. There are few rejections as telling as a sexual rejection. She had touched on the deadness in himself and this spasm of melancholy had come to torment the impacted sin of a lifetime.

He had just enough energy to plan an escape. Burkett's daughter would saddle up a horse and ride down the east shore of Derwent Water to the Lodore landing stage. He would let her father row him down the lake and dangle out a few lines to see if a tickle of fish would tickle his mood.

John–Augustus knew what he was shutting out. In his drugged dreams he saw the silent faces crying; he saw the loving mouth distorted with grief; he knew about the humiliation and the want – all his fault, his fault, his responsibility, his wickedness, his weakness, his sin, his sacrificial past, the victim to what end – who was murdered at that powerful stone circle near Keswick? When human life was so short and had been so cheap, what was there but the living, the greed of the moment? But down came melancholy like a guillotine and he had to wake up before the steel cut the quivering cold sweaty flesh.

Burkett's daughter sat on the stallion like a lady in a tapestry and he felt his body move out to join hers; he ought to marry someone like her – handsome, workaday, submissive, as sensual as a sunny woodland; perhaps he would ask her. He could fish with Mr. Burkett – they had caught a fine pike and two trout on the lazy trawl up-lake – he could let go all those minaretted plans, those fantastical ambitions, and be what he was born to be, a jovial, lazy, loved and loving man, getting by. He helped the girl down very deliberately – well aware of Burkett's calculating and approving regard – and as his fingers pressed on that tensile waist, as her free breasts brushed his over-layered chest, as her thighs carelessly kissed his own, he saw a break in the tight-capped cloud of his misery: but he could not reach out to it. His course was set otherwise. He took the horse from her and went on alone.

He rode into the valley of Borrowdale which opened up about two miles south of Keswick. Though he had been in the district for no more than a week, he felt he knew it well. But Borrowdale astounded him. He had decided to take this, the most spectacular, way round to Buttermere principally because of what he had heard of the rich wadd mines in Borrowdale valley – opened up only once in seven years, so he had heard, in order to control the market in this unique mineral which was useful over a remarkable range, from gunpowder to dyes. George Wood had hinted, and not too darkly, about the 'lads' who knew how to get past the guards and into the mines at night: he had intimated that there was a prosperous smugglers' route through the highest mountain passes to the coast where the ore would be taken over to Ireland or down to Liverpool and Swansea. John had been alerted to the possibility of profit and so he sentenced the Honourable Alexander Augustus to a stiff course of Lake Tourism into the Jaws of Borrowdale. He trotted past the celebrated twisting and churning of the Lodore Falls without the slightest inclination to stop and wonder: there was no-one around to impress and the sudden skin of grey which had drawn tightly over the summer sky like a blind hurried him on.

He wanted to be through this valley.

From his window at the Queen's Head, and as he had sauntered around Keswick, he had become affectionately disposed to the amiably brackened rumps of the Skiddaw range: here in Borrowdale were the volcanic rocks. In fact, unknown to the traveller, who was no more a geologist than a naturalist, he was about to step over the geological phenomenon of two prehistoric ages crunching into each other as noticeably as jagged waves hitting a large smooth stone. The flames from hundreds of eruptions had once furnace-fashioned this valley and left it with rocks precariously dangling on steep hills, scattered warningly across the path, uncertainly wedged, it seemed, against the few huts which passed for homes over an ill-repaired double span of bridge which crossed the stream feeding the lake. As Alexander Augustus he was tempted to go into the village for some refreshment: it looked charmingly picturesque, even under the dull skin of grey; smoke from chimneys curling, thatch, goats, geese, the homely clutter of rustic glamour: but as John he knew only too well the new picturesque was the comfortable conscience for the old poverty. To John such a charming scene signalled want, bitter winters, spare victuals, goitres, rheumatism, at best the forgivable disgrace of pauperism. He clicked his teeth and trotted past.

Past the Bowder Stone too. Everyone had said he must stop and examine this Dreadful rock poised on a fingerpad of ground high above the valley like a Damoclean judgement. But sights or sites equally engaged him only when there was a purpose. He would pretend – for he always had his excuses well marshalled in preparation for any surprise attack of questioning – that he had been disinclined to stop because of the stone's unnaturalness resulting from Mr. Pocklington's enthusiastic enterprise in housing an old woman there whose hand – for a fee – you could shake under the stone. The Honourable Alexander Augustus had already made a favourable impression by raising an eyebrow at the antics and constructions of Mr. Pocklington on the islands of Derwent Water. Snobbery was always an acceptable proof of quality: accent could defeat learning. Augustus and John both knew that. The reflection only increased the grip of his misery.

This blackness had always affected him. Even as a boy. Like the being able to slip out of his own head and stand in a corner, hang on the ceiling, terrifyingly, silent-screamingly BE SOMEWHERE ELSE, looking back at the body left behind. So too this gnawing of himself like a fox caught in a trap forced to bite off its leg and for pain, every few moments raising its face to howl at the sky.

If he shouted aloud then – as in the high alpine passes – the rocks would crash down on him.

He opened his mouth as wide as he could and yelled and yelled again. So hard that his head felt struck. And again he yelled aloud. The sound echoed longer than a cuckoo's call. If challenged he would say that he was testing the echo – a favourite pastime for Lake Tourists whether inside the fells or on the Lakes themselves. Indeed, Mr. Pocklington and his ilk would take small cannon onto a suitable lake and fire them off for the edification of the plumper partridges who came to nest in the district. But no stone budged from John's mad yelling: nor did it make him feel much better.

The plan was not working out at all well. He feared Newton and Newton would have every justification for reproach. John–Augustus was excessively vulnerable to reproach. He could deal with anger and steel himself against pity: but justified reproach slid through his armour like a poisoned dart.

Into the Jaws of Borrowdale he rode on this fine horse, handsomely saddled by the benevolent Mr. Wood, his new friend. Though his yelling had not moved the stones it had set off the dogs and one against the other they barked and bayed, an unusual salute as he entered the bounds of the sheer-sided, heavy-wooded, spectacular wilderness.

At Rosthwaite he spotted what he knew in this district could pass for an inn.

It was mid-afternoon and the ham and beer of breakfast had lost its sustaining energy. He went from the light grey day into the gloom of a kitchen and immediately found his feet colliding with what appeared to be an armada of saucepans placed on every foot of the flagged floor. The noise alerted a woman who came in from a side door and challenged him quite sharply.

"I merely wondered, ma'am," said all of Augustus with a touch on his heart and a bob of his unwigged head, "if a traveller could find a little food and drink."

"We hev nae drink but oor own beer," the woman said, discouragingly.

She was in no mood for visitors. Apart from everything else she had spent the morning standing in a stone-cold pool hoping to gather leeches which would suck into her bare legs. But four hours had yielded only two small leeches.

"Your own beer will be very welcome."

"There are them that divvn't like it," she said, dogged, as he was to discover, by honesty. "But we can afford nowt else, sorry. Maest travellers don't get up here forby they're beggars." This was by way of explanation. She shifted her weight, he noticed, restlessly, from one foot to the other.

"And food?"

"You've come at a gay bad time. Aa was scouring out these pans for stewing some fruit, sithee."

"Ah! All these are your pans."

"Aa lend a few frae roundabout. My own wouldn't be enough. Can't waste fruit. Mind you," she admitted, "it's far frae ripe just yit."

"I'm particularly fond of fruit."

"Aa oors is to be bottled. If we don't need it, the pigs thrive on it after t' back end."

"I see. So there's beer . . . which," he held up his hand, "I'll risk and . . . ?" She let his pause hang like an insult.

"You could have a bite o' breed."

"Bread. Excellent."

"Aa made it nobbut two days sen. You'll have to soften it in milk. And we could just hev a lock o' goat's cheese."

"The food of the gods."

"Nut heer. Oor goats hev hed that green sickness lately but whativver they all say oor cheese isn't that much affected."

He discovered that this talk and barter over food had brought on an almighty appetite. Where he had felt a little pang – outside, horse-held, self-wrapt – now, delighted by the truculence of her conversation, he was ravenous.

"Beer, bread and goat's cheese – with pleasure." He put a little command in that request.

She hesitated for a moment, a dim figure in the dark kitchen, distinguished by a brown balloon of a mob-cap and a coarse sacking apron which fell from her neck to her feet like a monstrous bib: it was hard for her to accept defeat.

"You'll have to sit among t' pans. I've them aa set out, sorry."

"I will eat outside," he said, faintly but firmly. "The air –" he paused, "it is after all the nectar of the district, the essence of the mountains – to eat simple food in such air with such wonders of nature to look on – who could ask for more?"

"I'll send me husband, then," she said, huffily, and went out vanquished, pausing only to give a good hard scratch to her left calf.

The spat had cheered him up. Provided he could use the motion, he might be able to rock away at the melancholy and eventually shift it off its fierce sticking point.

Surprisingly soon the landlord came with the order and stayed, being offered a beer for himself. The beer was passable, the soaked bread excellent and the goat's cheese most tasty if rather powerful. John had spent months on a diet which would have counted this country meal as a feast fit for any Honourable Member of Parliament in the land.

The landlord, in the brightening daylight – the grey was peeling to white and the white here and there pervious to a faint yellow flash of sunlight – sat on the mounting-steps below, purposefully. He saw that the man was one who would expect privilege. His resolution to punish his wife for letting a stranger in at such a time would have to wait.

"Women are outside creation when they're busy on a thing," he said, staring across the small, scruffy farmyard – like the Fish, the inn doubled up – at a broken stable door. "There's no dealing with them."

His rich guest merely made a sound, unable clearly to articulate a word with his mouth as wadded as a feather pillow.

The landlord, who felt that the explanation – indeed, to all intents and purposes, the apology – he had made for his wife was more than enough to compensate for any gentlemanly inconvenience, was about to get back to his work in the fields when his visitor's too casually direct questions about the mines charged him to stay. He parried the stories of wealth and of smuggling: all town talk, he said, and besides, people in Borrowdale just would not be up to the scheming and deception involved, not the people he knew in Borrowdale and he had been born there – as had his wife – born there – as had their parents –

"Do you know about the Borrowdale cuckoo?" he asked, turning an amused expression on the man who might – from these questions – be from the government – they had had government people before and he would not be surprised at them sending a senior man. After all, the illegal trade, as he knew to his immediate, though expertly hidden, advantage, was very profitable indeed.

No, the man said, sighing as he downed the last spread of goat's cheese, he had not heard of the Borrowdale cuckoo. He was new to the area.

"Well, it'll just show you what simple folk we are roundabout here," the landlord said. "Not long ago, a cuckoo made the most almighty noise ever heard in Borrowdale. It must have had the throat of a raven because it cuckooed its way up and down the valley for weeks on end. Nobody could sleep at night. The dogs were set off by it and the dogs set off the sheep and the goats and the cows. Borrowdale was in an uproar from Lodore to Seatoller and back again. Of course they all went out chasing it: but it was a clever bird; it would let us get near but never near enough. Until one day it went away. They saw it go out of the valley down towards Keswick. So they had a meeting and decided they would put a big net over the entrance to the valley so that it would never be able to get in again. Day and night they worked on it, never letting up until they'd got it finished and slung up down at Castle Crags – you must have passed it coming up – fit to be a fortress on its own, and the net went across the crags and across again to the other side. Well . . ."

The landlord stopped. Clearly it was time for a vital intervention. John obliged.

"And . . . ?"

"It worked." He paused. "It kept it out," the landlord said, solemnly. "Never heard a sound from that cuckoo from that day to this. They took the net down after a few weeks but kept it handy, you know. Hasn't been needed since." He stood up and bent his knees slightly to take out the stiffness. Not a smile had threatened his expression. "That's Borrowdale folk," he said. "We know nothing of what happens outside our valley. And those mines," he gazed across at the fells but, true to his wits, in the wrong direction, "they open them up every six or seven years, they take what they want and then they close them down. We know nothing else."

John knew when he was being lied to but knew also when he was wasting his time. He registered that George Wood's information had been correct, paid his bill and – to the relief of the landlord – went on his way over the pass and not back to Keswick, which would have been more likely for a government man.

He had to lead his horse over Honister Pass but its barrenness pleased him greatly. There was, as far as he could see, nothing that need be identified or admired or paused over: just bare grey rock sheering down to a narrow track which was used for the most part by packhorses and even then not often. He felt mercifully isolated and stopped for a while to lean back on the lower bank of fell. His horse, the reins loosely looped over an upright arm of rock, noisily nuzzled into the cropped turf.

The man felt his melancholy enlarge as if – oddly – to take on the shape and texture of what was before him. In some fantastic way, he could see his mind *like* these barren screes – a frozen cascade of broken rock face lying on the more solid rock waiting only for an impulse to charge it into dangerous motion.

Mistakenly, he thought that the figures he saw high up on the furthest rocks were working the rich secrets of the plumbago or wadd mine. They were, in fact, hacking slate in the Honister quarries. Each man, John was to learn, would cut out up to half a ton of slate and load it onto a sledge which he would drag out of the open shaft and along a perilous track slotted narrowly into the fellside. He would then turn down the fell and begin to race, faster as it grew steeper, more furiously as the half-ton of slate threatened to catch him up and (as happened regularly) crush against him, until, blown with exhaustion, he reached the unloading bays at the foot of the fell. After which, his empty sledge on his back, he would walk and clamber slowly back up the steepness to enter once more into the dripping slate shaft and repeat the exhausting process.

All about Keswick he had noticed gangs of men building the giant reaches of drystone walls enclosing even the highest fell-land, the better to take advantage of grain prices in the war; gangs of men working the woods, as charcoal-burners, swill-makers, coppice-workers, plain woodmen; and, as here, men in the high mines – men spread all over the landscape, bondmen of industry, all living out near their workplace, turf huts and teepees scattered abroad, excluded from society throughout the week of their work and let into its comforts and pleasure only for a brief Saturday night escape.

It was this working landscape which he recognised far more immediately than the picturesque cataracts, the prescribed 'stations' for the Claude glass, the thrills of nature. Just as, below him, on the valley bottom, there would be vagrants, beggars, a sixth of the total population, the abandoned and the despairing, moving in strict complementary counterpoint to those over-bound on the tops. He saw himself as the only point of free will in the landscape before him, and if he could move his body with a purpose, then his mind would shake off the slough of misery and clear for action.

He mounted the horse he had led for the last hour or so and walked it cautiously down into Buttermere which he entered with the utter conviction that he had been there before. Its pleasing shape – like an almond-stone sliced open – the cliffs of wall to the south, the serenity of the lake, the promise of richness in the meadows beyond the lake, moved him with a mysterious sense of homecoming based on an unmistakable sensation of security. I am safe here, he thought: and the thought was so rare, so violent in its unexpectedness, that he looked around like a villain in a melodrama to see if anyone had overheard this God-tempting thought. I am safe here, he repeated to himself. And again he looked around, this time for the devil who was tempting him with the prospect he most profoundly desired. Only the men on the tops, only the sheep and goats on the fells, only the bare rocks. "I am safe here," he said, for the third time, and this time aloud.

Although he would have denied it, the landscape had gripped him: as an image and now as an emphatic fact of the real world, presenting him finally with a place to rest in. To the Fish.

The sky had now stripped back to blue as he entered slowly and with a surge of pleasure into the cut of Buttermere. At this time, for a short while, he was purged, he was himself as his best self should be, he was all that his great promise had held out – untainted, unbrutalised – like the Floating Island on Derwent Water, submerged for years on end, only to rise up intact now and then.

He saw Mary, standing by the doorway, looking at him directly as he rode towards her, unflinching in her look at this stranger whose jingling tackle whinnied against the soft crush of the accustomed evening sounds of the valley, the sun behind him and he, as he drew near, as intent on her. He saw her and felt – as only once before he had felt – the dizzy vertigo of a fathomless falling-away. She, too.

He stopped, dismounted, put his hand to his heart and said "Alexander Augustus Hope" – he paused – "your servant." Two wholly unnecessary words which skimmed her cheeks to a blush.

"Good evening." She neither bowed nor smiled and the words were grave but her eyes, he thought, seemed to gather all that was left of the best of the sun.

8

Hause Point

The rain began just before dawn, striking the roof so hard that he woke, startled, from a fast sleep which had been hard won. The drumming disoriented him, the darkness frightened him; he shouted out. Mary heard the calls and knew it was him but she waited. Again he called, almost a sob: she got out of bed, put on her dress and went down from her attic. He was their only guest and of course her father had given him the 'big room' – used by the landlord himself in the winter. Mary's bare feet made no sound he could have picked up and she came right to his door. She heard murmuring and, surprised, deciphered that he was praying. The muffled words were given a seductive rhythm by the drumming of the rain. She stood there until he went quiet, stayed a few minutes longer to be certain and only then returned to her cupboard bedroom next to the servants' loft.

It had the advantage of a window which was open. She leaned out of it, welcoming the cool rain on her face and neck and shoulders: she twisted up her hair to prevent the inconvenience of its getting soaked, but soon it fell loose and she let the rain stroke it. She looked out over the northern part of the lake to Burtness Wood, where the rain on the leaves made a sound she loved. Even the farmers would be glad of this downpour – provided it was short and sharp. To Mary it was a peculiar relief. The evening had been so tremulous, the physical attraction so compelling yet forced to be ignored and hidden. What had begun as a bolt of recognition and longing had been diverted into strain. The rain both expressed and unknotted her feelings. The coldness pleased her, like the chill of the water in her pool.

Awakened in alarm, Hope eventually turned to richly recollected pleasure. The rain became a murmur, comforting, like the plainsong chant of the choir at the far end of a cathedral in the city in which he had spent some of his childhood. Mary had provoked sensations of his childhood; one of them was this womb-echoing self-conscious snugness indoors, safe from outside turbulence. He had played so extraordinarily fair with her the night before, he reflected, contentedly, that it was as if he had not played at all. No calculated glances, no abrupt addresses, no stratagems, just the easy politeness, he thought, of the worldly gentleman and not even a sly request for a hot stone or a late candle to his room. Instead, he had appeared happy to let her come and go unpestered, although, like Mary, but not yet so acutely, he had been aware of a deeper affinity.

He had spent the latter part of the evening in the rather pleasant sitting room with her father, whose wish to please his handsomely connected and honourable guest had taken the form of a little boasting. The guest had been interested. With no more than the occasional nudge on the tiller, Hope had steered Joseph Robinson to an inventory of his property, his cattle, his inn-sales, his fields, his sheep, goats, fowl and fishing rights. It was odd, Hope thought, as he lay deeply sunk in the great feather mattress, how perfect and desirable such a dowry would so recently have been to John – for Mary was the only child and it was apparent that the landlord would give her everything. A good life! An inn, mine host, stories in the winter evenings, fishing in the summer, introducing some of the scientific ideas of farming which he himself had heard of but was sure had not penetrated the ancient little world of this valley . . . He lay on the goose feathers, looking at the beams, feeling the soft pelting rain massage away the binding layers of ambition, lust, wickedness, pain, revenge . . . This was where he could belong . . . And Mary as he had first seen her appeared before him again like an apparition as he slid slowly into a long sleep.

It was Mrs. Robinson who served him his late breakfast and it took no more than the tapping of an eggshell to discover from that guileless woman that her husband had gone down to Lorton with goats' cheese and potted char for the market men who called there on a Thursday. Mary was up on the fells with her flock of sheep and goats, she said, perhaps over Buttermere way or maybe towards Robinson.

"Robinson?" Hope caught the name and saw the chance to turn an early compliment. To be fair on the woman, he thought, had her daughter not been in the house then the mother . . . despite her rather theatrical tendency to clasp at her side . . . "You have a mountain in your name?"

"Oh, it was here long before us, sir, although there's plenty asks if it's called after our Mary."

"Indeed? Is Mary so famous?"

"Oh yes!" Although Mrs. Robinson was genuine in her sympathy for the anonymity her daughter strove for, she was Mary's proudest admirer. With scarcely another tug of encouragement from the Honourable Member of Parliament, she listed Mary's battle honours in print and in public praise. He was brought a copy of Budworth's (first) book; he was shown flattering notices in the newspapers; he was led to the bar and shown the compliments in Latin, Greek, French and one or two new ones in English, written – all very neatly – on the walls. Just as her husband had felt obliged to match up to the might of his guest by throwing his wealth into the balance, so she counteracted his fame with the successes of her only daughter; and yet it was done so innocently, it was modestly done.

Hope expressed himself enchanted: John was gripped by a dream of certainty. Her exceptional eminence, his own; her singularity, his own . . .

"After all of that, I simply cannot believe that the fell was not named after you – if not in tribute then in anticipation." He liked that phrase and observed that it had hoisted his reputation for conversation to the top of the pole. "I had no idea that I was entering such a Hall of Fame," he went on, and was about to enjoy a ride on an air bubble of loquacity when Mrs. Robinson addressed a cat and the cat said 'No!' Distinctly. Mrs. Robinson gathered it up and buried her face in its fur.

"Remarkable cat," said Hope, squashed.

"Damson," Mrs. Robinson replied, as if introducing them.

Annie came in; her clogs clattered irritably on the stone flags.

"Isn't it time we were cleared up in here?"

Annie's determination was catalytic.

"I was just finishing." He took a final pull of his beer: by the time he had finished it, Annie was hovering above him, her large red hands already noisily piling up the dishes.

"I think I'll follow Mr. Robinson's example and make for –"

"Lorton," Annie said, curtly. "You'll meet him coming back at this time of day."

He was capable of living with Annie's moral disapproval: her physical presence, however, was too threatening and he left rather more smartly than he had intended.

It was mid-morning and the rain had long since cleared, leaving the hills freshened, the whole aspect glittering raindrops under the sun, the track drying rapidly underfoot. There seemed nothing but crags along the border of Crummock Water and Hope, who had imagined it to be a short walk, soon regretted that he had not saddled up. This fashion for walking was tiring as well as tedious and his leg troubled him. Eventually he met a boy almost distressed with diffidence who told him enough for him to conclude that Lorton was much too far away for comfort. He turned west, down to the hotel at Loweswater where, as he was to report to Newton, "I might have landed a fine salmon trout."

A most respectable party had taken the dining room but the landlord was either too flustered or too gauche to respect the privacy which, judging from their first expressions on seeing Hope, they felt they had ordered and even paid for. The new arrival's haughty politeness suppressed their irritation; his dress and studied self-sufficiency (he had taken out a devotional book to read while sipping his brandy and water) teased out their curiosity; his amiability, when accosted, won their sympathy; introductions followed at which his card commanded their instant respect and attention.

John–Augustus noted all this with a perverse pleasure. He further let it be known – in the most careless way imaginable, like a good gun bringing down a bird without breaking a conversational flow – that he was a bachelor, a man of wealth, a friend of the Prime Minister and, in an amiable manner, on the lookout for a secure investment in matrimony. Although the latter point was delivered as a subtext it was as plain as all the rest and Miss Skelton knew herself to be in the ring.

She was not as pretty nor quite as fashionable as Miss D'Arcy, but the similarities outweighed variations of plumage. As the discussion followed between the now cosseted intruder and the male members of the small walking party which had found its grail at the lakeside Hotel, Miss Skelton was deferred to by her father, complimented by her mother, patted and plumped by her friends and avoided only by the chaplain, the Reverend Nicholson, who, Hope judged, was in love with her but too poor to press, too honourable to hotly pursue any claim.

There was an aspect of John–Augustus' character which he would suppress whenever – and it was not especially frequently – it was aroused: sympathy for the victim. But here – since he had not the slightest intention of addressing anything but common courtesy towards Miss Skelton – he could allow that sympathy to exercise itself. The girl, he thought, like all her kind, was now forced into this public auction. Put another way, she had been plucked and prepared for meetings like this as carefully as a goose is dressed for the oven. Should she not please sooner or later, she would be taboo, a mocked and patronised spinster. She was, at this moment, like a slave on a podium waiting for the bid. Or to take a comparison from fishing, she was bait: soft, swirling gracefully, juicy, to be gobbled in a mouthful, sucked in and with her the impaling point of the hard property deal also known as marriage. Miss Skelton was good bait, but this fish, thought Hope, had other food in mind.

Though his contact with Mary had been brief, formal and in no public way at all suggestive, disgust at the thought of Miss Skelton and her world suddenly and urgently spilled into his mind and he excused himself rather roughly – so abruptly, in fact, that a careful inquest was held among the company to uncover what possible offence he might have taken.

He came out of the Hotel suddenly and violently, unable to endure the privilege which had so cruelly and so recently oppressed him. "Where would they be without . . ." "Pauper . . . rip off the clothes . . . starve them . . . whip the flesh . . . see on them the scars they've given . . ." "Public prostitution . . . 'take tea' . . . how many sad wretches have been murdered by toil and neglect for their tea . . . scald them with it . . ." "Paine is right . . . the French are right . . . long live the French! . . . use their heads instead of pigs' bladders . . . put her in the Marshalsea and don't feed her for a week . . . see her prettiness then . . ." And around him had arisen the sight – seen so often on his travels – of the hundreds of thousands of vagrants, beggar men, women and children, now roving over the richest island in the world like tormented souls in irredeemable exile . . .

As he turned Hause Point and caught a clear sight of Mary's Buttermere, the lonely valley, he experienced what seemed a physical soaring of his spirits, a giddy uplift of heart. He was overcome. It was a true revelation. He held his breath. It was such an unanticipated shock that he froze, to cling onto this unique moment. He could not remember when he had felt as purely happy.

He 'saw' himself, ludicrously ill-dressed for the narrow and rock-tumbled track, gaping like a foppish caricature of the Lake Tourist: but that did not unsettle him. His feelings were cleansed of the poisons of revenge, contempt, self-hatred, envy and avarice which had worked him into a hellish turbulence of vicious thoughts.

Was it Mary who allowed him access to this source of joy? Not only her – "God is here," he said, aloud, "God and Death." A true revelation: he was humbled by it. He had been chosen, like Paul, and like Paul he would now serve. He felt as if he were in a trance, speaking the words of someone else; the pressure of this rare ocean heave of happiness had re-baptised him, and the words came from out of the air. "God and Death," he repeated, "and there is nothing else to know."

He breathed the air deeply, hauling it into his broad chest as if this particular air on this exact spot could be stored up and carried around as a reserve and reminder: for minutes on end he stood there, resisting any move which would lift the spell, gazing into the hidden valley as if in there lay the treasure he wanted.

Merlin had been in these parts, Joseph Robinson had told him. Perhaps he was Merlin come again, invisible in his magic cloak, looking for the woman who would trap and hold him secure and for ever. It was wonderful, this feeling, it *was* magical! Mary? What was his feeling for her? He was so used to the extremes of lust and commerce, of immediate gratification and protracted commercial dealing that the ground between had been long forgotten. But perhaps it was still there – a quick, unselfish affection, friendship, even a continuing passion . . . He was capable of anything!

"Have you the time?"

In one way he was glad to be interrupted – superstitiously afraid that if of his own volition he decided to leave the miraculous spot then the unique mood would not follow him and he would be like a man without a shadow. But still it was an intrusion. The question was repeated, though with more servility.

"Have you the time, sir?"

Would that he had, he thought – how shamelessly it had flashed away, that spot of his time – "What will you do with it when you get it?" The jaunty answer came out like a rebuff.

Harrison drew back his jaw as if riding the blow. Damn these clothes, Hope thought; dressed as he was, an irritable retort became a threatening social punishment. Both of them knew what damage these Hessian boots and the expensive felt hat could do to those scabbed wooden clogs and the coarse neckerchief. A word in the wrong place, a petty curse pursued into an even pettier vendetta and Hessian could crush clog for a lifetime. Both of them knew that very well, but now Hope was unusually distressed by the realisation. He took out his gold hunter watch and delivered its message almost tenderly.

"Five-and-twenty minutes after two."

The young man nodded and made as if to move on but John wanted to expunge that mean unspoken and unmeant threat.

"Is it hard work in the quarries?"

"How did you know I worked there?"

"The dust on your clothes: it would be mud if you were on a farm."

"I soon will be back on a farm, thank the Lord."

"I was going to have a smoke," Hope lied. "Would you like to try some?" He held out his leather tobacco pouch: the young man looked at it as if it would bite him who touched.

"I was thinking of a smoke myself," he said, his eyes fixed on the pouch, as if staring it down, "if I had a few minutes in hand."

"And do you?"

The young man nodded and took the pouch. He dipped his clay pipe into it – after wiping the stubby object vigorously on his breeches – and took a polite – meagre – measure.

"Fill it up," said Hope. "I've more than enough for my needs. And there's nothing like a conversation when you smoke. You're doing me a favour." The benevolence was infectious: the young man dug in. "We could sit on this rock," Hope pointed to a jutting flat stone, "and look out at the lake."

"I'm not much of one for looking at things," Harrison said and Hope's heart went out to him.

"But what about the Beauty of Nature?" he cried, at once aping and mocking his Lake Tourist's role.

"I've more time for other beauties," the young man responded and squatted comfortably, his back against the turf bank.

"Is that why you're making this journey?"

"You could say."

"Women are the spring of most of our actions," Hope offered, puffing over-anxiously at his faltering pipe, envying the steady draw the young man had already achieved.

"I don't know about that," was the reply.

Hope once again went through the elaborate mechanism of lighting the pipe, looking about him for wind, but the day was utterly calm. Harrison kept intent on the gentleman but still he noted the two boats on the lake – one had caught what must be a pike from the struggle – heard the chiming axes of the woodmen, noted the flocks on the Scale Force bank of Crummock and, more particularly, a pair of swallows playing beside the water – these and a score of other impressions gave him a richness of context denied Hope who, after struggling with his pipe, battled on, oblivious of all that was about him, to confirm and exercise his new and gloriously liberated Christianity.

"So where are you bound?"

"Home."

"And where is that?"

"Over there – place called Caldbeck." He paused and then, generously, contributed another sentence. "Beyond Keswick, this side of Carlisle."

"Carlisle . . ." Hope's pipe went out again and he decided to abandon it.

"Best smoke I've had since my teeth were pulled," the young man said, more animatedly. "Couldn't smoke when they were bad for fear of breaking them up. My mouth's had a new life since that day. They were two terrors – down at the back." He yawned open his mouth. Clearly he was eager to talk about his dentistry but Hope was after more philosophical matter.

"Do you enjoy your work in the mines?"

"Quarries. Nobody can. Negroes on plantations do better." The pipe went back in: still steadily alight, Hope observed.

"Is that why you are on your way?"

"You could say."

"I agree with you about the slavery in this country of ours today. Many others would too. My friend Tom Paine – I got this wound," he held up his afflicted hand, "fighting by his side for the freedom of our American Brothers – he has written and fought for freedom in America, in France and here in his native land. And where has he yet to plant it? Here! Here in his own country. Who can be free in this country after the Treason Trials which set behind bars and left to rot . . ."

The young man watched him very warily indeed, waiting only for the chance to be off. It was all very well for a gentleman to talk about Treason and France and Tom Paine – and he was taking care to do it where nobody was around – but one nod of agreement from him and the world could crash down on his head. His wariness turned to unease – he ought to have suspected something; no richly dressed gentleman handed you a fill of tobacco on the open road – his unease began to scramble to panic: he let his pipe go dead. The man was now attacking Mr. Pitt, calling him worse than the devil, cursing Parliament for being too feeble against him, raging – though it had to be admitted as a fine rage, a rage which at least convinced the speaker – against the law, the constitution, the King —

"God Save the King!" the young man muttered as if uttering an exonerating and protective formula: and he was on his feet. "That's all I say." And he repeated, for the benefit of the sheep, the goats, the swallows, the boats, the clouds, "God Save the King," adding, "I'll be on my way now, sir: and thank you, much obliged."

"Will you be back this way again?"

"Never," Harrison said, lying, for his whole purpose was to get back to his father's farm to work out when he could return and what he could offer Mary.

John–Augustus cast a sentimental eye on his retreat, convinced in his euphoria of pristine well-being that he had encountered one of nature's radicals, someone to whom he could reveal his new true feelings. As for his own talk – that, once begun, had, as usual, spun itself out as thoughtlessly as the wind: he believed it and quite often it was true or partly true – and if others believed it – a bargain had been struck.

A few hundred yards along the road, however, and the walking pace jolted him back to a more careful reckoning of the conversation. He picked up on the young man's unease, he recalled his own unlicensed ranting, he sensed the quarryman's fear of him. He wanted to turn back to reassure him in a more plausible way. But nothing would be plausible if he had hounded after him. It would not be credible. Once again, he concluded, a reasonable course of action was blocked by the tyranny of appearances.

The truth was, however, that he cast off the conversation as lightly as he would throw back a small fish. This precious new phial of innocence, his new self after the revelation, had to be offered to Mary.

She was not at the inn, not in the meadows, and when he finally found a sufficiently oblique way to ask where she might be, his misreading of the directions sent him along the wrong path past the wrong waterfall and up the surprisingly taxing slope of the wrong fell. From his new station he could see the three lakes – Loweswater, Crummock Water and Buttermere – lined up in the valley like three barges ready to be towed down to the shore; he could see the bivouac huts of some woodmen and he spotted more than one flock coming down from the high pastures – but Mary eluded him.

She continued to do so throughout the evening, serving him – he was still the only guest – with promptness and civility, being neither short nor teasingly indifferent, preoccupied, it seemed to Hope, and puzzlingly outside his grasp. The puzzle lay in his certainty that his feeling for her found an echo in her own feelings.

But even her elusiveness did not subdue the novelty and promise of the experience he had undergone earlier that day at Hause Point. A new spaciousness had entered into his considerations. No longer would he pound around the obstacle course set out by Newton and himself: there was a life he could live which took its time, strolled through weeks as if they were single mornings, allowed the world to come to him instead of himself for ever launching himself on it as if in unarmed combat.

He even had the amplitude to take a glass of port with Mr. Joseph Robinson and talk as well as listen to him about the Battle of the Nile. Mary had long ago disappeared but he knew – and was comforted in knowing – that she was not far off: he knew he would have the time to approach her: and on this occasion, he wanted to be sure to get her. He knew it would take great care and he knew also – inadmissible, subversive thought – that what he really wanted was to live with her here, securely, for the rest of his life: that was the earthly promise of the revelation at Hause Point.

9

Burtness Wood

Over the next two days she continued to evade him. When he was in the dining room she would be in the dairy; when he wandered out to look at the home fields she would be over the lake by Burtness Wood; when he made his way to the wood she would retreat up the fell and it was pointless, he rightly guessed, as well as being too open to comment, to pursue her onto the tops.

She tried telling herself that he was just another idle aristocratic adventurer; she had been looked over by several of the type and others of lesser breeding during her ten years in the public eye at the Fish. Usually she could cope well enough. Recently, though, her resilience seemed to have given out.

On the third evening of his stay, for instance, a couple of the wilder sons of the local gentry had turned up half tipsy from their celebrations following a squirrel hunt. They had been to the Fish a few times before and Mary had little difficulty in sousing the coarse splutterings of the pair of spoilt whelps who were nonetheless, she thought, by no means bad or wicked young men. That evening, though, their ragging had distressed her and but for Colonel Hope's intervention, she would have been in tears.

He had asked the young men if they had been to Germany – knowing they had not. Then most vividly he had described his own studies there at the ancient university of Heidelberg, capturing the attention of the two lordling drunkards by directing his talk not to his studies of the classics, philosophy, German language and metaphysics, but to the duelling societies, their codes and practices, feuds and meetings at misty dawn – sword fights to the death . . . His own scar, he said . . . in a particularly violent duel . . . the last in a succession of three . . . the first two of which he had been fortunate enough to win . . . and would the young lady of the house be kind enough to bring him and his friends a bottle of her father's excellent port? . . . (Mary went out but lingered by the door) . . . remarkable creature, he proposed, after she had left . . . (lowered voice so that she could not hear) . . . perfect example of a natural lady, did they not agree?

Modest beyond understanding, was she not? And he, Alexander Augustus Hope, Colonel, at your service, gentlemen, would not stand for another coarse word in her presence, DID THEY HEAR?

They had seen the knuckles come out of the silken wrapping and the force of it scared their wits back into good manners. On her return she knew that it was he who had plucked the sting but she was afraid that too demonstrative a show of gratitude might be misinterpreted.

So, exercising some skill, she kept out of his way. He confused her. For he was not at all in the usual pattern of adventurers. He neither leered nor lunged, he did not pinch her neither did he make a sudden and late demand for hot water and a brandy to his bedroom. He did not loiter to catch her although his apparently wayward path could seem designed to cross hers every now and then. Although he was clearly a grand gentleman – and she could sense the larger houses up and down the valley waking up to his presence like hunting dogs suddenly scenting a stag on the wind – his consideration for her – in one or two trivial matters – was nearer to the sort of decent, friendly understandings she herself had grown up with in the village. And he seemed to have no purpose. He walked to Hause Point twice a day and apart from that . . . he wrote one or two letters and delighted her father by franking one of his; he waited for him to get a full free day so that they could go char fishing; he declined all invitations and although he was irreproachably welcoming when Mr. Skelton and his daughter made a surprise detour on one of their visits up the valley from Lorton to call in at the Fish, Mary thought that she could tell that he was happier to see them depart than he had been to see them arrive. And yet he had promised Skelton he would look at some land around Loweswater, and announced that he was so taken with the district he had a mind to settle in it – a statement which brought Miss Skelton to a blush-brink of applause. Indeed, the only person whose company seemed to detain the worldly, elegant Colonel was the Reverend Nicholson, with whom he had contracted a conversational friendship based, it appeared, on a mutual zeal for the discussion of the profoundest spiritual matters – the power of prayer, the meaning of the Three Days in the Tomb, the date of the origin of the world, the precise division of responsibilities between the Holy Trinity.

This, too, confused Mary, who – privately – sensed the Colonel to be quite other than this enthusiasm for theology indicated. But the enthusiasm, she had the Reverend Nicholson's word for it, was "as honest, as questing and as pious as in any man I have ever met."

There were other confusions – he was vain, she could smile at that, and yet many times he seemed unaware of the effect his strong presence could have on others. He avoided other Lake Tourists and yet, if caught, he would be as warm as an old friend. He was fluent, learned, a man of books, and yet, she had heard him with her father on small points, as sharp as a tinker . . . too many false trails, too many different scents . . . as if he, too, were puzzling over his path . . . She kept out of his way, too experienced in public disappointment to stray into what could still be a snare.

Moreover, Mary had a matter of her own to digest which at any other time would have been sufficient preoccupation. The young man with the terrible toothache – Harrison – had sought her out and, clumsily but resolutely, he had told her that he intended to leave the quarries, go back to his father's farm, assess what his prospects were there and then come back and . . . his resolution had run out at that point but the aim was clear. He knew, he said, that he was just an ordinary farmer's son and she was a famous Beauty, known the county over, never a word spoken against her even by the men who bivouacked up in the fells – but he would have no-one else and would wait just as long as she told him to.

The earnest open strategy appealed to her. He was a good-looking, honest young man. Now that his face had regained its shape she saw a seriousness in it which implied a steadiness she liked. When he had begun she had been inclined to send him off or run away herself; but his determination had kept her listening and she had watched him walk away with his plan – it was more of a plan than a proposal – well lodged in her mind and unexpectedly endearing.

She visited Kitty, wishing the old woman really had been a witch and then she could have solved the riddles which would not leave her in peace. But Kitty – who sensed her young friend's perturbation – only talked as always about the woods, the animals, the nights. She went to her pool but, for reasons she couldn't comprehend, felt powerfully disinclined to idle sensually in the water. She would wash herself, hurriedly, and then sit in the cave, looking out across the valley, hoping that time would shift itself on soon and resolve the tangles which seemed to bind her.

On the third day of his visit, Hope and Joseph Robinson went char fishing. Mary hung around outside the stables, curious to hear her father in his element as the two men sorted out the rods. There had been a thunderstorm the night before but it had swept over and the lake was calm.

She smiled as her father began: he would have been happy being a teacher; he had often told her that and at one stage – in the nature of parents' bequeathing unfulfilled ambitions to their children – he had hoped that Mr. Fenton might consider her as a pupil teacher (just for the mornings, of course, he needed her the rest of the day).

"The char is something like a salmon," Mr. Robinson said, "but you find it in fresh water only. Generally speaking – to my knowledge – only in deep water: they have them up in Coniston, we have them here, but it's down in Windermere where they make the most of them."

"That could be changed," Hope interjected. "Why should the char of Buttermere not outsell the char of Windermere?"

"I've thought of that often," said Mr. Robinson, "but one man alone, Colonel Hope? A man needs a partner for this business. I have all this to keep me going." Mary could see her father's hand spread out before him as if he were sweeping a cloak: her father was now the man of property.

"Does it always keep to the deep water?"

"It does. We think it's because that's where it finds the water fleas. It's not an easy fish to track down. You see, you can never be sure when it will spawn. This here is the type of net they use down in Windermere – same as for everything else, really, pike, perch, trout – but *this*, here, is the tackle we use in Buttermere for fishing the char." There was a pause and Mary imagined the men fingering the fishing tackle.

"How big is it?"

"I've seen them ten, twelve inches long, up to three quarters of a pound: but you don't want them too big – the bigger they are the older they are – to have them on your plate – eight inches at the most. Here we are. There's your plumb-line."

"An ash rod."

"The best. See the four rings . . . and that bell? The line's about seventy feet long and the lead plumb has to be this size – over a pound. Hold onto it. We have six side lines come off it – different lengths, you see – with these spinners on them – they're the bait – all with hooks. I made these particular spinners myself out of bits of copper."

"Very effective."

"So you travel over deep water and pull up the plumb-line when the bell rings. If you're lucky, you have a char on one of the side lines."

"I think I have it all now, Mr. Robinson."

Mary almost laughed aloud at Hope's tolerant gravity. If her father had told him that he had also to hold the rod in his hand and drop the line into the water she would not have been surprised.

"It used to be salted char that was popular – I'm told that Henry VIII ordered it in barrelfuls – and then there were char pies – some of them three or four stone in weight: now they seem to want it potted in little jars. Mary does it. It's surprising what they'll pay for it this time of year."

"Perhaps you should let your daughter do more. 'Buttermere Char'. You could get it to Keswick and send it all over England from there."

"I would need an agent."

"Agents can always be whistled up," Hope said. "Lake Tourism could not be more fashionable. Everywhere you go there are paintings of the Lakes and prints of the Lakes and stories about Visits to the Lakes, people building villas here now: there's great interest, Mr. Robinson, and that always opens up a space for trade."

"We've had more than one or two famous writers here at the Fish," Robinson confirmed. "You'll have heard of Captain Budworth – 'A Rambler'?"

Hope nodded but it was the business scheme that had caught his imagination.

"You could have special pots made – delicate pots for the nobility, hand-painted with a lake scene to give them an extra value – and on the larger pots you could paint 'The Fish' – no, '"The Char", Buttermere, the Hidden Heart of the Famous Lakelands'. I can see the coffee houses ordering enormous quantities – if what I tasted at supper yesterday is any guide –"

"And it is, take my word for it –"

"Then in a few months you could have a thriving business here, Mr. Robinson. You could have an industry. One or two of the local lads could help you fish the char, Mary could cook it and pot it – you'd have to put the pots out to commission but the district is full of men who would work for you. Or for your daughter."

"I consider," Joseph Robinson said, rather stiffly, wanting to rein in this galloping fantasy, "that my daughter is doing good enough work already."

"But for how long, Mr. Robinson?" Hope could not prevent himself blurting out. "For how long?"

Mary moved away.

From above Burtness Wood she looked down on the lake and watched the two men fishing throughout most of the morning . . .

What attracted a man such as that to such a lonely spot? Perhaps he was reclusive – his manner denied that and yet he was very reluctant to be sought out by local society, some of which, Mary judged, was quite worthy of him. Perhaps he was recovering from the loss of some great love – that at least made sense of the aimlessness that seemed to characterise him. Most important of all, she thought, as she picked over the problems of his character, as the days went on he seemed to be so much steadier, so much easier in his own skin.

Everywhere he went in the valley now, John–Augustus sensed that he was being watched by Mary and he took that into account whatever he did. Yet, in truth, he did not have to play-act. For he had stumbled across – or it had been revealed to him – that if you act as you deeply want to act and if that, sublimely, coincides with what you aim for, then nothing is simpler, nothing is more dynamic, nothing is happier. Indeed, he had to restrain himself. For a dam had been breached; the dam which had sealed off his childhood, his best self, all his early aspirations. Since the building of that dam his terrain had been harsh, brutal and bad. But now the water flowed, water as from a spring whose source he had forgotten, the lost energy of young and wasted years ran into his limbs and mind and spirit so that he looked everywhere with honesty, with a sensation of being right in the world. As he pulled on the oars – he could not bear simply to sit and wait for the bell to ring – John was again the boy who had set out to be the man he never became. He had to stop himself from shouting aloud with pleasure. And her distance, even her suspicion, that too was part of it, part of the innocence regained.

There was this final chance – he heaved strongly, slowly, on the oars – hammocked in this valley, nursed by the safety, and with Mary

. . . the world could again be as once seemed possible. He would try in his journals that night to express this extreme contentment.

*

On the day Colonel Hope announced himself in the yard of the Queen's Head in Keswick, Coleridge, a few hundred yards away, was writing a letter which included the sentence "I have always found a stretched and anxious frame of mind favourable to depths of pleasurable impression."

On the day John–Augustus went char fishing on Buttermere with Mr. Robinson and Mary went above the woods to look down on them, Coleridge passed between them. According to De Quincey, Coleridge had "the largest and most spacious intellect, the subtlest and most comprehensive that has existed among men". He was also, at this time, at the end of his twenties, exhausted from a tormented marriage, addicted to opium, an insomniac, plagued by boils, nightmares and desperate, even murderous thoughts directed against his wife and children: thoughts which his passion for Christian goodness made intolerable. But in this spell of summer, 1802, he gained an unexpected, extraordinary access of energy and happiness which coincided almost precisely with the presence of Hope. Perhaps this came about in part because his idol and friend, Wordsworth – to whom he was in some way in thrall – had left the district to go to France and make a settlement with his French mistress and daughter as a prelude to marrying his childhood sweetheart back in England. Perhaps because after an almost fatal spasm, Coleridge thought his marriage was now bearable – although on this eight-day storming and often precipitous walk around the mountains and lakes he was to write a passionate letter to the woman he desired as his mistress while perched on the highest mountain in England. Or perhaps, like Hope, he found an inexplicable access of joy: "I must be alone," he wrote, "if either my imagination or my heart are to be enriched."

For whatever reason he did not stop at the Fish – which he had visited on several occasions; nor did he seek out or meet Mary whom he knew and greatly admired. Yet it is intriguing that on that day, he cut between Mary in the redoubt of her fells, puzzling over this ominous invasion of her feelings, and John–Augustus on the lake, drawing up char from the deep and cold lake, re-experiencing the failed innocence of his life. The three of them soon to be part of one fusion, still at this time isolated from each other: three figures representing and summarising between them so much that was central to the complex notion of the Romantic Age. It was as if, in some unfathomable way, out of an inscrutable symmetry, these three called each other up, between the lake and the fells, and were determined to bring about one of the essential public scandals of Romantic times.

So Coleridge passed through, and his journal of the day brims over with wild joy.

*

As soon as they came in from the fishing, John–Augustus left Robinson and his potboy to take the tackle and the satisfactory number of dead char back to the inn while he went over to Hause Point. He was restless for another visit, another reassurance. Having gone out onto the lake as calm as the surface itself, he had caught, as it might be, some of the immovable unsettling darkness and chill which lay for ever imprisoned deep below, like his own too-recent self. Hause Point would settle and clarify all that.

Since its first revolutionary impact, he had become more used to the experience. Now he strode out not apprehensive that he might have lost contact with that gift of powerful calm which had so effectively stilled the thresh of his emotions, but confident that as soon as he reached the Point and stood as and where he had first stopped – the experience would be renewed and reinforced, the key would fit the lock. And so it was.

The fears which had crawled back over the stockade of his new self were banished: he was unassailable on the rock of Hause Point – what could harm him but Death which here would be no great enemy? And God would surely receive him in this mood which was so open to Him.

He looked around and, seeing himself alone, got on his knees: his eyes closed, his head tight with exhilaration.

"O Lord," he prayed earnestly, "I know how wicked, how unworthy, how evil and wanting I have been and am and will be for ever. But I thank You for giving me this sight of a life of Truth. Let me keep to it. Please help me to keep to it. Please, O Lord, knowing my weaknesses, help me to be faithful to this." His earnestness became pleading. "I've never known myself like this. I almost believe that I could be like this. Please, Lord, if it is Thy will, let me –"

The sound of a horse and chaise brought him to his feet. He moved away from the spot on which he had prayed and gazed over Crummock Water. The conveyance came around the corner, quite recklessly, and pulled up at the sight of him.

An old and old-fashioned gentleman – full heavy wig, long waistcoat, antique buckled shoes – was in the chaise with a girl who could have been his granddaughter. With a dexterity that did his age credit, the old man stopped the sweating horse and accosted John–Augustus, who was much relieved to discover that the stranger's own preoccupation blocked out any interest in his own.

"I need help, sir," the old man said, "and I have no alternative but to throw myself quite on your mercy." As he spoke, the alarmed young woman – only quite attractive, Hope assessed, a little too thin in the face for his taste – glanced behind and then beyond and back again as if expecting to be set on by bandits.

Hope waited. The old man's surprisingly bright grey eyes held him and Hope knew that he was facing an honest man and felt bucked that his own present character was worthy of it.

"I have not time to tell you of our adventures or of the danger we are in. You must believe that we are innocent!" The force of this demand impressed both men. There was a pause. "But we need to stop – only a few hours – and we need to – to hide this chaise. Would you . . . ?" Here the old man's energy ran out, partly because the girl's sobbing distracted him. He took her most affectionately in his arms and the tender sight of April finding comfort in December – as Hope was to phrase it later – immediately prompted him to become an accomplice.

He directed them to the Fish, took over the chaise from them before they entered the village, drove it across the meadow to the edge of Burtness Wood, calling, on his way, to the potboy to bring some oats.

When he returned he was offered tea – without which, the old gentleman said, he never travelled. The dramatic incident at Hause Point was never referred to. Mary came in to see that they were well enough served and, yielding to a hint from Hope, stayed a while to watch, with him, the strange behaviour of this incongruous pair. It was not so much his attentiveness to her – the infatuation of old men was common enough – but her petting and cooing with him which provoked what became a quietly savoured complicity between Hope and Mary. In fact, the glances they managed to exchange, glances which played on a wide keyboard of reactions, served both to spin them together and to show each other off. It was the best time John–Augustus had spent with Mary and he saw it as the reward for his charitable act.

The dominating clatter of a four-in-hand broke the web. From outside a very loud and bullying voice demanded the landlord.

The old man went white – noticeable even under the absurd splodges of rouge – and the girl cried "It is over!"

"Please," said the man, "that shawl." He pointed to a large plaid shawl which Mrs. Robinson had used to decorate and disguise the back of a chair. Mary snatched it off and handed it to him. He placed it around the shoulders of the young woman, now almost fainting. "Take her to the window, please," he urged Mary, whispering as he heard someone striding into the hall which was adjacent. "And do not let her turn around.

"And you, sir," the old man said loudly to Hope, "would you care for another cup of tea?"

The pot was poised as a bald-headed bullock of a middle-aged man – face as bright as a carrot from the exertion of the journey – long green cloak askew – fingers coarsely jewelled – came in like the blow of a fist and demanded in dungeon-vowelled Lancashire:

"Has anybody seen a chaise? With a young couple aboard it? Well?"

The old man looked up, vaguely waving his teapot, an expression of simpering apprehension on his face. Hope rose to his feet and his full height with no little menace, which was clearly recognised by the intruder.

"We were enjoying tea, sir." The final word was almost spat out, a mean and snobbish cut. "And the ladies were peacefully enjoying the view across the lake."

The bullock stared but, having absorbed the garb, the poise, the certainty of Hope, let himself be stared down.

"I beg your pardon. I have been badly deceived and robbed. Please forgive me, ladies."

Mary turned and solemnly nodded her forgiveness.

"Are you sure, though," the man continued, desperately, "a fine young woman, rather on the thin side but a lady, no doubting it, and a terrible young scoundrel, a thief of a man who looked as if he should be hanged."

"Not I," said the old gentleman and poured himself some tea.

Hope shook his head and sat down carefully as if to concentrate on his tea leaves.

"Then they have given me the slip again. But I met a man on the road to the other village – I've pursued them over the mountain from Keswick and you know the road divides two ways – and he swore they had come this way."

"Perhaps," said Hope, without looking up, "he lied. Or perhaps your young scoundrel paid him to lie."

"That's it! By the devil, that will be it! If I see him again – good day, sir, sir, ma'am, apologies, terrible crimes, days of ruin for all of us – your servant!"

When the last sound of the coach and four had died away, Mary and the young girl turned from the window and Hope took out his pipe.

"I can never thank you enough," said the old gentleman. "But at least you deserve an explanation." He looked at the girl and held out his hand, which she took and kept while he told his story.

"I came out of my apprenticeship a week ago," he began. Hope and Mary looked at each other in astonishment but, determined to humour the old gentleman, they said nothing. "My father – who was a gentleman but unable to resist gambling – left me and my mother penniless when I was thirteen. She had no family to help her; his wanted none of us. So although I had expected a life of some leisure, I found myself lucky to be apprenticed to a carpenter in Kendal. A year or so ago, I went into Cartmel to do some work on the house of that oaf you have just seen. He has several businesses in the district – a bobbin mill, a gunpowder factory, a cotton mill, and more – and what they have in common is that the people – usually women and children – who are unfortunate enough to be employed in them are driven as cruelly as possible and paid as little as possible. He has a son who is a booby and who was loafing around his father's yards waiting only for this young lady to come of age so that he could marry her. She was the oaf's ward, an orphan and an heiress. She favoured me with her love."

Here he took off the pendulous wig, wiped his face on the yellowing lace handkerchief dripping out of the over-ornate and antique jacket and revealed himself as a young man.

"George Shelborne, sir, ma'am – and Catherine Hodge."

The introductions were reciprocated by Hope who gathered Mary into his corner as proprietorially as Shelborne had spoken for Catherine.

"We decided that the only course was to run away to marry at Gretna Green, because her guardian, as soon as he knew of my interest, first tried to get my apprenticeship broken and then announced that his son would marry Catherine on the day of her twenty-first birthday – two weeks from now. I had to take what action I could. These clothes were got from a pawnshop in Kendal; the rouge came from an acquaintance of Mrs. Charlotte Deans, the actress; the chaise was loaned us by a young friend of mine whose father owns the chief coaching firm in the town. I knew I needed the disguise because I would be able to surprise him by two hours at the most. And we would never be able to outrun his coach and four. I thought the plan had failed when, looking back on the hill there, I saw him in the valley. But thanks to you, sir," he leaned out and took Hope's right hand between his palms and pressed it, "thanks to you, I believe we are safe."

The force of the story threw the four of them into a babble of communion. Hope felt almost dizzy with the innocence and sweetness of it all. Watching the old gentleman turn himself into a stripling and seeing the irrepressible signs of affection between George and Catherine, he envied them deeply. Catching Mary's eye, he thought he caught her mind too: was she thinking the same thought?

"Let me invite you to dinner in an hour," said George, "and" – this was addressed to Mrs. Robinson, who had crept in to stand in the doorway and hear the end of the story, and now stepped forward to play a part – "please, let us borrow your daughter for the evening so that we four can be a company. Her help was crucial."

The candelabra were brought out and, with her tongue jutting anxiously out from between her teeth, Annie carried the good plate into the dining room. Mary found tiger lilies and Hope, discovering Mr. Robinson's prize of six bottles of good claret, bought two of them for the evening. A small fire was lit to make the dining room even more cheerful – although it was warm enough to do without one – and when the four of them reassembled, the small room in the Fish would have been "a credit," Hope said, in his most pleasingly generous mood, "to any inn the length and breadth of the country."

George was now dressed in the decent clothes of a tradesman with one or two additions which suggested both his independence and another inheritance. Catherine, made less thin by candlelight, had put on a blue dress which made her look even younger than her age. Hope had changed his cravat and put on his best black coat, excellently cut. But it was Mary whose bold appearance drew the breath and the admiration of all of them. She wore a russet gown, the white lace beautifully worked, her hair flowed down her shoulders and her back like a cascade, glistening softly in the flickering light, and her expression was resolved in a contentment, more, a sheer happiness that affected all of them.

The meal was organised around the char which had been caught that afternoon, and Hope was touched at the extravagant praise lobbed his way for the provision of the excellent fish. There were veal cutlets, cabbage, pease and potatoes, parsley and plain butter, oatcakes, cups of preserved gooseberries with rich cream and cheeses to accompany the claret.

The talk was even between all four of them – neither man wanting the women to leave for a moment and both women, though diffident to start with, more than capable of taking a full part in the 'manly' subjects of politics and warfare and the economy of the country which George and John–Augustus batted about, rather sweepingly. Catherine, Mary noted, was especially quick to challenge George's generalisations by reference to a local situation: Mary herself kept not so much a watch as a guard over Hope's words. George was unafraid to be republican in his views and Hope sought to emulate him.

And yet, as the evening went on and the moon rose and the wine went down, new candles, another log for the fire, shadows swaying on the walls, she seemed to become to him what Catherine was to George. The man who called himself John looked at her increasingly steadily, lengthily, certainly, and she began to hold his glances and eventually to return them.

"You say we have no liberties," Hope replied to a rather over-eloquent statement of George's, "but I can think of no time when we have had a greater chance to take what freedom we want. There are men who have been in prison for ten years and more for claiming their liberty; men who have slipped away to struggle overseas; men who have escaped to Europe to carry on the fight there – they are hounded and they *are* imprisoned, but their views are heard. And when the great and radical Charles James Fox becomes Prime Minister of this country – a day which I look forward to with all my heart – they will be liberated and with them, their ideas." Just as there was a deep well of refreshment from re-encountering his older finer feelings, so this safe release of his real sentiments was also sweet. George Shelborne was not quite as sure about drinking to the Whig who, he pointed out, was even then in Paris fawning over Napoleon – but politely he mumbled a neutral assent. Hope directed the rest of his carefully unslurred speech to Mary, who looked at him half-warily, half-dreamily.

"Liberty is all for any free and true being," he said. "We must live our earthly lives in obedience to Him but also in the service of the great possibilities He gives us. Not to be bound by manmade laws of rank or fortune or education but to show His true glory in reaching out for everything we feel will reveal His variety and greatness. I tell you, after a long life of many escapes, many dramas which might have been tragedies, what I want and would value most is to be free to choose as much of my life as is given to me – to live it by my own lights, Mary, to do, insofar as God wills it, what I want to do to the very hilt and limit."

The passion infusing his remarks had the effect of subduing all four of them. George turned to Catherine, kissed her hands and seemed content to stare at her for the rest of the night if not for the rest of his life: Mary bowed her head a little and Hope looked away, sipped at his claret, could do no more.

The silence held for two or three minutes and disturbed Mrs. Robinson, who came in with fresh candles and the welcome offer of port.

"A song!" George cried, who did not want so marvellous an evening to end. "Who will give us a song?"

Hope welcomed the chance to break the spell he had cast, seeing now that his best course lay in apparent spontaneity, and he volunteered.

"'The Bachelor's Complaint'," he announced.

Mrs. Robinson summoned Annie: Joseph had gone over to Cockermouth with his larger share of the char and would be staying the night at his sister's. Had he been home, Mary's adventurous equality might not have been encouraged.

Hope had a reliable baritone and kept time well: the words came out with an Irish twang to them.

A bachelor's life is distressing
No wife to soothe his care –
When pain and woe – oppressing,
Reduce him to despair.
Alone he journeys on
The path which all have trod;
Without a friend to cheer
The solitary road.

For him the heavenly eye
Imparts no beam of bliss;
The lips themselves deny
The soul-entrancing kiss.
He lives a lonely stranger,
Unknowing and unknown,
He shuns or faces danger,
Unpitied and alone.

He never hears the praise
Of one whose heart approves him
Nor feels the fond embrace
Of one who dearly loves him;
He dies without a tear
Of sympathy shed o'er him;
And round his mournful bier
No orphan hearts deplore him.

Applause and mock commiseration followed: George then followed with:

There was a bard in former age
Compared the world to a player's stage,
And most folks think he hit it;
But I believe and I may be right,
The world's a TUNE that we sing at sight
We learn it – to forget it.

The conceit carried through several verses which varied in pitch and volume as George fought for air against the unaccustomed alcohol. Catherine and Mary together sang 'The Lover's Complaint'; Mrs.

Robinson gave them a moving ballad about a double death on Scafell; Annie began a song, burst into embarrassment and ran out with Damson mewing 'No-oo-oo, No-oo-oo', behind her. George concluded the evening – and successfully reclaimed his right to be seen as a sober enough man – by reciting 'The Bashful Wooer' from the works of one he announced as "the greatest poet of Cumberland and Westmorland, a man living among us today, our own Robbie Burns – Robert Anderson of Carlisle . . ."

More than an hour later, John–Augustus was on the shore between Burtness Wood and the lake. He had gone out for air while Mary reverted to her servant role, but an impulse had taken him much further than he anticipated and now that he was on the shoreline he knew that he had followed an instinct which was directing him to resolve this business with Mary.

There was no doubt that – if he had ever truly, unselfishly and, if he could use the word, *purely* loved anyone – then that was Mary. It was she who was the essential element in the alchemy which had absolved him and promised him such a refreshment of security and calm here. It was she, too, alone, he sensed, who could satisfy him and he who could satisfy her. For he was aware of the violent frustration of her unused sensuality, aware too of her longing to be out of that place, that role, that trap of a life. In the life he himself might well have had, she would have been an obvious and natural choice.

Why, then, did he delay? He was not bound to the life he seemed to lead. He could go where he wanted. He could escape Newton.

He stopped every now and then to listen to the patient lapping of the water, the light breeze in the leaves, scurries and sounds in the wood which he could not identify but which helped to reinforce the solitude he needed. He would never have guessed that Kitty was rarely more than a dozen yards away from him, knowing he was the one who troubled Mary, shadowing him like a conscience.

Gradually the impulse which had taken him over to the wood, the instinct which had urged him to a resolution, worked its way to the surface. When he saw it plain he did not like it. 'You must leave her alone,' he said to himself. 'You can bring her nothing but trouble and misery. You must get out of this place and do the one good thing you'll ever have done for any woman. You must be away tomorrow – not back to Newton and the old schemes – off to something else – off to America without a penny, what does it matter? Others have done it. But you must leave this woman alone.'

For at least another hour he walked on as if to test the conclusion against all the temptations and changes he could uncover. But he knew that he was right and, much more, he felt that he was good, that he had been given this chance to act well, that he must take it and to take it would get him off on a new and better path; while to succumb would be the broad and easy road to hell.

He walked back over the warm, moonlit meadows and paused before the inn, but held on to this resolution, the righteousness firing through him like brandy.

He could not know that Mary, equally, had sensed the possibility of a real liaison and rejected it. He was too far out of her reach, she thought, she would never be comfortable with him; she would always think of herself as somehow his ward, his adopted orphan, his property; there would be no real place in it for her. As she heard him come back she refrained from looking out of her window, nor did she go down to the corridor outside his room when, a little later, she heard him groaning as he always did in the grip of a nightmare.

She would be up at dawn and away before he woke. She had forced on her mother the excuse of a visit to a cousin in Whitehaven. She could not refuse; Mary so rarely took a holiday. By the time she returned he would be gone. The dinner, the talk, the songs, the enviable lovingness of George and Catherine would be a memory, happy, but cut off from her own life as clearly as the fell top was separated from the lake.

10

Into the Valley

Exuberantly believing that he alone was responsible for the separation and still moved by a powerfully purifying sense of goodness and rightness, Hope paid his modest bill the next morning, left a parting note for George, checked himself from asking to see Mary, promised – though he lied – to return and set off at a tremendous pace for Hause Point. Here he dismounted and prayed that whatever spirit had been working within him would continue to work, that this furious feeling of benevolence to all mankind – if only a beggar would pass by and he could give him a shilling! – would not abate, that he "could truly and today start a new life, O Lord, for Thy sake and in Thy name". His own name, though, as he said that word, tolled like a warning bell somewhere behind the new screen of holiness.

By the time he had climbed out of the valley and over the pass on a day which was fretting for a thunderstorm, he was boiling with the need to act. George Wood had kept his rooms. Again the Monkey-boy together with a rather fragile-looking, unusually pretty and even smaller friend, "'Artley", proudly led away the horse. Dan the groom was again absent, reported to be "brekken in a hobstinate new nag".

Wood preceded him to his rooms bearing the precious dressing-case, which had been entrusted to his care, like a royal mace before him. Compliments and civilities were exchanged briefly – though at far too great a length for the impatient Hope – but finally the landlord left him alone. With light-fingered nimbleness he checked all the contents, drawers and secret hiding places in the dressing-case, finding everything intact. There was a letter from Newton but he was not in the mood to read it. He beat about his room like a bat in a panic.

It was Christine who came when he rang.

"Ah. Christine." He looked intently at her but there was no change and besides she no longer moved him. "I would like some beer, Christine, and bread perhaps with cheese." She bobbed and turned to go, but wheeled back when he added, "Is that other maid – Joanna?

I – she – there was something she wanted to know which I can now tell her."

"Joanna, sir," Christine reported with pleasure, smiling at his feeble deceit, "was asked to leave by Mr. Wood, because certain things started to disappear. We couldn't catch her and she wouldn't admit anything but Mr. Wood knew – we all of us knew – and she's left."

Hope's disappointment was undisguised.

Christine let him stew in it for a few moments.

"And she had a guinea, this Joanna – if that was her name – which we doubt . . ." Christine paused most meaningfully . . . "she said as you had given it to her, sir. I believe Mr. Wood'll be asking you about that. She swore you had. But if it isn't true, then of course she's for a flogging and prison: or worse."

The question hung like a hawk.

Hope regained his character.

"I may indeed have given her a guinea or two in a moment of late night extravagance. After all, the sights about here can make one dizzy." He had taken quite enough from Christine. He fired. "Whatever her failings may or may not be, I found her a most agreeable and willing chambermaid – very attractive for that occupation – far more attractive than the common run of girls, didn't you find?"

Christine flushed angrily but checked her tongue: she could not risk the job. "She waits on in the Twa Dogs now," she said, "a pothouse on the road out to Ireby."

Mutely he blessed her for the information and, after quickly slaking his appetite, he was drawn – as if he had no will of his own – to the pothouse, where he picked up Joanna, went out with her into the fields, and made love with a sweating savagery which seemed to satisfy even her and delivered him of a madness which had gathered like an abscess. On his way back he made a diversion and called in at Crosthwaite Church to let the cool sanctuary complete his cure. Mary, he thought, was now banished and forgotten. To Miss D'Arcy he was Colonel Hope; to Mary he had for a moment been Augustus; to his new self, John alone; with Joanna he had no name and experienced the inscrutable animal comfort of brief blank joy.

He arrived back just in time to avoid an overdue thunderstorm. Newton's letter contained two urgent messages:

> We cannot sell the property in Kent to Mr. Cooper as we had hoped and I fear that unless I go down there myself the business will languish. I am very reluctant to go so far when we – or rather you – could be so near a better resolution. What is your opinion? I have something which may help you. A Mr. Crump stayed here last night, a Liverpool merchant. He and his wife are on their way to Grasmere. The main inn there – the Swan, I believe. I introduced your name in the conversation, said I was your Factor, told him that you were in the Lakes for pleasure but also with an eye to acquiring property, etc., etc. In short I have laid an excellent foundation. Mr. Crump is *very* wealthy and his wife is susceptible. If you go immediately to Grasmere – unless other fish are being fried, but your letters are too vague for me to judge – (what *are* you doing?) – then I think you could do well. I will not go to Kent until I hear from you. I confess I am reluctant to go. I have an increasingly urgent desire to move altogether elsewhere. I am becoming impatient.

Hope tore up the letter. Newton would never let him go. Was this the only life he could lead? Did he have to act like this . . . ? He chewed his way through a large and over-greasy midday meal, drank more beer than he ought to have done, took some laudanum with his brandy and water to give him sleep and felt his brain ripped open by a nightmare which wolfed down his mind in the open bleeding mouths of women.

He got off his bed at five and decided to ride over into Grasmere that afternoon.

"I'll take my coach, Mr. Wood," he announced, "but if I could leave the plate and linen here I shall be obliged to you. For I shall certainly come back to the Queen's Head. But I shall take my dressing-case and, of course, my clothes, if you would send . . ."

They were in the hallway which also served as a reception area for the hotel and Hope raised his voice to include as many eavesdroppers as possible in his private conversation with the landlord. The decision had cheered him up; the bustle created by his demands reaffirmed the show of his importance; and he could still feel a breeze from the pure air which had wreathed him at Hause Point. George Wood returned the compliments at full volume.

"We shall be very sorry, sir, very sorry – Christine! – up to the gentleman's room immediately! – but of course – where *is* Dan? Go to the paddock and get him away from those horses – bought at Rosley

Fair, sir and terrible wild – account? No – won't hear of it, sir – when you leave finally, which we trust will be long delayed – then we can have a discussion on the matter of the account."

Mr. Wood's magnanimity was entirely invented from the manner in which he supposed great landlords in great cities behaved to their great guests. In the same spirit he supervised the harnessing of the horses, the carrying down of the dressing-case and boots and clothes and papers, the safe depositing of the plate and linen and two locked trunks – it was the hour for promenading in Keswick and Mr. Wood's conducting of this orchestra was not to go unremarked.

Hope had sent for Burkett: when the man and his daughter arrived, he took them to a quiet corner of the yard.

"I have a proposition for you," he said to Burkett and as he said it he weighed up his man as if he had met him for the first time. Burkett was rather small, rather bow-legged, a low centre of gravity. His eyes were narrow and he was disinclined to meet a look, but his face was not unfriendly, though strangely white-skinned considering his largely outdoor existence. The skin was one of the few aspects of himself he had passed on to Sylvia, his bonny young daughter. Hope concluded that he could trust him insofar as the man was certain of payment, but saw also that such payment need not only be in cash.

"You could bring along your daughter," he added, scenting out the conspiracy of affection and design between father and daughter and sensing Burkett's reluctance to do strictly servant work. "I had a servant," he went on, "Peters, who had to be sent back to London. I will not insult you by asking you to be my servant, Burkett, but nevertheless I could use a good man to drive this coach down to Grasmere, get me some fishing over a few days, be prepared to go the odd errand – about a week in all I would guess. I'm sure we would not quarrel about payment."

Burkett took his time. He was already owed money by Hope for the times he had taken him fishing. On the other hand, it was no great sum and Hope's custom had given him publicity. And he had his regular job which his son was keeping warm for him. As for Sylvia, there was something which could be working itself out between his only daughter and this Honourable: whether it would work out well or ill or at all, he wanted to be there to see it develop. He stated his terms and agreed.

And so a couple of hours later, it was Burkett who drove the coach and four to the top of Dunmail Raise while Hope and Sylvia walked behind to spare the horses the effort, even though, as Burkett had pointed out, two passengers were light work for four horses. The thunderstorm had washed the hills and the sky itself, it seemed, and the freshness of the evening was most amiable for a slightly strenuous stroll during which the gentleman had every right to take the woman's arm and even, over a rough patch, help her by the waist. Sylvia yielded to help with a willingness which a man less vain than John–Augustus would have suspected.

They stopped beside the resting horses and looked down on the vale of Grasmere, a prospect described by great poets as an unsuspected paradise, depicted by painters as a jewel set in nature, sought out by the fashionable, protected by the sensible, evoker of sublime epithets, a small, ovaloid dream lake ringed by mountains proportioned in a measure which touched the intelligence as much as the eye; if any one place deserves the description, then Grasmere Vale could claim to be in the very eye of the Romantic storm, in its beauty, its seclusion, its inhabitants and its capacity to draw in and draw out some of the greatest artists of the era. Said Hope:

"It looks like a soup bowl with a little puddle left over in the bottom."

And down they went into the village.

Hope sat alone in the coach. Sylvia would be acknowledged to be Burkett's daughter, she would perform some small chores, but chiefly be explained away as evidence of Hope's goodness of heart in giving his 'man's' daughter the chance of a change of air.

Though the Swan was more sophisticated than the Queen's Head, it was only a matter of minutes before servants, ostlers and maids were scampering all over the large and comfortable hotel to see to the minutest needs of the 'Honourable Member of Parliament', 'brother to an Earl', who had landed on them at an unexpectedly late hour and naturally – 'a Colonel as well' – demanded the best of everything both for himself and for his (temporary – 'from Keswick') servant and his ('pale-looking') daughter.

Mr. and Mrs. Crump, who until that moment had reigned serene in their social supremacy at the Swan, moved swiftly from slight disgruntlement to genuine delight as details of the new arrival's pedigree, accoutrements, speech and manner were relayed to them by one or other of the scampering servants. Try as Mrs. Crump did

– a sidle into the hallway, an uncharacteristic visit to the stables, even a late saunter down the road towards the village and the lake – she could not engineer an early encounter with the glamorous newcomer and so had to keep her patience until the morning.

The men exchanged greetings just after ten thirty a.m. Mr. Crump had just set his watch by the Winster long case clock when "Your servant, sir," and Alexander Augustus Hope, Colonel, M.P. for Linlithgowshire and younger brother to the Earl of Hopetoun, made his attack: Crump surrendered instantly, taking up Hope's opening words by explaining how he had met Mr. Newton, or was it Wilson? – the honourable gentleman's Factor in Preston, was it, my dear? Or Lancaster? Which was it, my dear? – uncertain not so much as to the identity of the town as to the quickest way to introduce his small and attendant wife. Crump was a kindly man and his kindness to his wife had resulted in his being made to appear in thrall to her from time to time. But one twitch of his temper and she obeyed him. Now, however, the prospect of distinguished relief from what had soon become the limited social round of a small country village – however famous – made her impatient.

"Mrs. Crump, I presume," said Hope, gallantly slicing through the knot, and then he stood back as if struck by a startling thought. "Mrs. Crump," he repeated as he, reluctantly it seemed, let her hand withdraw from his gentle grasp. "Forgive me – such a ridiculously slight acquaintance – absurd – but so extraordinary a coincidence – really – quite, quite . . ." he was lost for words. Mr. Crump was alarmed; Mrs. Crump leaned forward on her toes to increase her disappointing height and to reach forward to this man whose every title and reference made him more and more desirable. "I must say it," he went on, "now that I have begun. Don't you think so?"

"Oh yes," said the Crumps in a not unusual demonstration of faithful and spontaneous unison.

"Perhaps not," said Hope. "Too soon to presume."

"No, no!" cried Mrs. Crump and "No," once only and more thoughtfully, echoed Mr. Crump.

"It is just," said Hope, looking at Mrs. Crump as if she were a particularly testing landscape – perhaps a copse whose colours were for ever changing under sun and scudding clouds – "it is just," he said, "and I am sure, certain, that someone must have told you this –"

This – what? Mrs. Crump cried to herself, leaning forward now on a Pisan scale. Hope stretched out the hesitation almost beyond endurance.

"That you bear a remarkable resemblance to my very good friend Mathilda, younger sister of the Princess of Hohenzollern."

Mrs. Crump rocked back and blushed with embarrassed joy. Mr. Crump made a note to get the Honourable Colonel to repeat the full name of the resembled figure later so that he could copy it out and memorise it. He had no head for titles but he was sure his wife's friends at home would be interested. Hope saw that he had penetrated the female's sympathy in one thrust: Newton deserved some credit for preparing the ground but the doing, the acting, was all his own. The great Kemble would have been proud of him: he was more than a little proud of himself.

"My card, sir," said Crump, and Hope read:

John Gregory Crump, Esquire
Attorney-at-Law & Merchant
Liverpool

"And how is she?" Mrs. Crump asked, as Hope glanced at the card. He looked up, puzzled.

"Mathilda, younger sister of the Princess of Hohenzollern," Mrs. Crump prompted him. "Is she – well?"

"When I left the palace," Hope replied, gravely, and using the speech to transact the casual reciprocation of his own card, "*both* princesses – for of course Mathilda too is secure in that entitlement –"

"Of course," murmured Mrs. Crump, and looked around the hall to root out anyone who dared challenge her on this matter.

" – both were exceptionally well."

"Exceptionally?" echoed Mrs. Crump, almost a touch enviously.

"With the same natural effusion of good colour," Hope continued, deciding that excess was more apt than enough in this instance, "that I find in your own complexion, ma'am." He put his hand on his heart and bowed. Mrs. Crump made the very tiniest curtsy and then switched her face to utterly solemn.

"Your hand, sir," she said, tragically. Hope looked at the two clenched fingers.

"The cut of a blade, ma'am, the severing of a tendon, the folly of war." He stroked his scar, knowingly, and Mrs. Crump uttered the very smallest cry. Indeed, all of Mrs. Crump's not inconsiderable bulk seemed determined to contract itself before the Honourable and her movements, her voice, her gestures declined in decent proportion to her increased sense of intimacy.

Mr. Crump read Hope's card several times and knew that he ought to be impressed.

"I hope, sir," he said, not noticing the pun, "that we may be of some assistance to you in your stay in the region. It is a region my wife and myself know very well."

"The people are so natural," Mrs. Crump whispered, "so simple." She looked around, but no one was eavesdropping. "Innocents," she said loudly.

"We are, in fact," continued her husband, who took no offence at her interruptions, indeed, in these foreign circumstances, counted on them as if his sentences were much improved for being broken into, "building a property here –"

"A substantial house," said Mrs. Crump, to prevent all error.

"Quite a substantial house," corrected Mr. Crump modestly, "as we intend to live hereabouts."

"Our daughter," Mrs. Crump, by way of explanation.

Hope smiled.

"Perhaps you might meet our daughter tomorrow?" Crump suggested. "Perhaps indeed," he dared, checking his ground with Mrs. Crump every syllable of the way, "we may throw the two of you together?"

Mrs. Crump laughed.

Trust Newton, Hope thought, to miss out the most vital piece of information. So there was a daughter.

"I was about to go for a turn around the village," said Hope, switching the subject, as he thought, adroitly.

"Why," said Mrs. Crump, "so were we." Clearly the coincidence struck her as near proof of divine intervention.

"Let us, then . . ." said Hope.

"With pleasure," said Crump.

"I will just have my maid" – the emphasis was delicate – "bring my shawl," said Mrs. Crump.

Hope was quite content to saunter around the pretty little village. In the course of what appeared inconsequent, even trivial, conversation, he discovered that Mr. John Gregory Crump of Liverpool was a very wealthy man indeed. And that this wealth was not locked in land or designated for heirs: it was fine fresh wealth coming into the great port of Liverpool by the month, by the week even, in the form of Ceylon tea, Indian jute, Irish coal – Mr. Crump had an encyclopaedia of imports which he rattled off in diffident haste. The haste, perhaps, and the diffidence both, were encouraged by his wife, who did not like him to talk of Trade, considering it to be vulgar, and yet she was pleased to note that this casual reference to wealth met with a satisfactory, if silent, response.

Mr. Crump was, in fact, an extremely able, shrewd, exploitative and successful businessman and lawyer whose weaknesses were an over-fondness for his wife and an utter doting on their daughter. At the sight of a title he felt that he must bend the knee for her sake, as he knew that his wife yearned to enter what she saw to be the utterly perfect circle of society, conversation, fashion and taste described by the British aristocracy. The 'Honourable' had not impressed Mr. Crump; the younger brother of an Earl had not daunted him – he was aware, though, that the man talked to him easily and, equally, made him comfortable. He was rather disapproving of Hope's being a Member of Parliament: he knew several politicians and trusted none.

For Mr. Crump, Trust, he would say and firmly believe, was the foundation of his business and his life. He trusted the captains of his ships, he trusted his trading partners in the East, in the Indian Ocean, over the Atlantic, around the African coast; his clerks, his associates in Liverpool, his bank, his builders, his carpenters, those who supplied him with his furniture and his clothes – Mr. Crump moved in a world of total trust. If he had been told that the prime sources of his immense and, mathematically, infinitely expanding wealth were invariably polluted with the deceits and bad faith of exploitation, cruelty, oppression, barbarism, murder and vicious wrongdoing, he would have been at first amazed, then outraged and finally contemptuous, disbelieving the information. He was an honest merchant whose skills, and those of others, including thank God the British Navy, had made him rich enough to slake any whim to satiety.

Mrs. Crump had fixed on the Lake District for reasons of convenience as well as sentiment. For she, too, had her practical streak though now she tried to bury it. She had urged her husband out into the large society in and about Liverpool but the forays had not been happy. Mr. Crump was too shy or too direct; Mrs. Crump was too pushy or too arch. Nor had the return invitations been much more successful: often, indeed, to Mrs. Crump's shame, the invitations simply had not been taken up and those for whom the very considerable expense had been laid out did not attend the ball. The Lake District, which she had visited a few times before her marriage and toured with friends, seemed a golden and available corner of gentility. And besides, as she discovered, it was becoming so fashionable! The books, the prints, the articles, the parodies, the paintings, the poetry – everyone wanted to go to the Lakes and of course the war with the French had made it all but impossible for most people to travel abroad. To Grasmere, then, they had come in their own kind of innocence and plunged straight into a storm. For nobody wanted them to build their house in the paradisial village.

It was extremely upsetting and the generously exposed support of the Honourable the Colonel Alexander Augustus Hope, M.P., when they went to the site of Allan Bank was very warmly appreciated. The Colonel Hope would never know, said Mr. Crump, as he reached out to take and shake his acquaintance's hand, what a boon such sensitive and untarnished support represented. The merchant's emotion was perfectly genuine and valid. He had been shocked by the resentment he had aroused – especially from a group of poets who themselves had only lately moved into the Vale: but he had dug in and dug on, he was no coward and he would not budge, he was determined to see it built, to live in it in the season and to be happy there with his wife and daughter. The support of Colonel Hope was a transfusion. Mrs. Crump expressed her gratitude with the eloquence of total silence but with a little look which, as Hope noted and saw that it was noted, signalled that she was pierced to the heart.

On this pinnacle of enthusiasm, with promises to meet later for dinner, or tea, or supper, and do not forget our daughter and our boat of course you must use it for your fishing and good day, Colonel Hope, good day – the hills are called fells by the natives . . .

Hope had to leave. Less than an hour in their company had brought them to the boil. He had not worked out tactics to deal with what was not so much a surrender as a bid to form an immediate alliance. His success impressed him and he wanted to celebrate. But though he trawled the lower slopes around the lake most carefully, he came upon no-one.

He sought out Burkett and Sylvia and went on the lake to fish. The Crumps' boat was a splendid, new affair, more fitted for a picnic than a fishing expedition, unusually comfortable and a pleasure to handle.

Burkett observed that money could even buy speed as they swung the precisely crafted oars through the beautifully modelled oarlocks.

Sylvia tied the bait. Burkett rowed. Hope steered. They caught four trout. Hope dreamed of great wealth.

What he would like would be someone like Burkett to row, someone like Sylvia to fix the bait and himself to steer. What he would like even more would be to own the fine boat, the means to support the boat; and the further means to enjoy a style of life which could so easily include a fine boat, because that would surely embrace fine horses, fine coaches, fine clothes: Wealth. If at times Hope needed women to a point of desperate madness, so, at other times, he ached for wealth so badly that he heard his inner voice crooning for it, like the ululation of a gin-addicted street beggar, the sound suddenly there but as if never absent, an ancient and ineradicable longing.

With Mr. Crump's wealth . . . his dreams of money diverted his energy from the sexual lust which had gripped him after that effervescent meeting with the Crumps.

Without the smallest impoliteness, he managed to exchange no more than a few greetings for the rest of the day, preferring the potency of elusiveness. And he wanted to prepare himself for the daughter.

His unsettling nightmares continued, and the John–Augustus struggle which he thought had been resolved in Buttermere began to re-emerge. Perhaps the re-adoption of Augustus had triggered more perturbation and he feared to sleep. He put laudanum in his brandy which helped.

Everything, he sometimes believed, could be resolved in sex: perhaps only briefly and never more than temporarily, but often the brief and temporary were key to any future possibility at all.

Sylvia, he felt, he could sense through the creaking, sleeping inn, was available, perhaps even awake. He put the thought out of his head: a last beam of virtue from Hause Point. More importantly, he was a little wary of her father and not at all sure that Burkett was not using Sylvia as bait for a cast of his own. Moreover, the Crumps' daughter would arrive in the morning. Three counts against, then, and all urged him to resist this dæmonic demand for sex. He would punish it: he would strangle and wither it: he would beat it down . . .

But later he awoke to his own cry as creatures from under large old moss-green rocks crawled up his legs, leeching on the white skin, wetly sucking the blood, and above him, ropes, rigging, nets, a gigantic sagging cobweb of strung and re-strung hemp lines, swayed down to trap him (children crying), and wherever he looked the wide mouths of women, no other feature but the mouth, tongues thick and purple as damsons, teeth white as the flecks on fall water and hands, nails curled and black, clawing at him, at his clothes, at his chest, at his face (children wailing), ripping it away, tearing the skin from the skull . . .

He went to the dressing-table and threw cold water over his face and chest which streamed with cold sweat. He put his head out of the window and tried to calm himself by attempting to identify the night sounds. Save for the owl, he knew nothing, and his ignorance dismayed him further. He wanted to be out of this place, this vale, this county, this country, these clothes, these accents, this whole binding suffocating poisonous England . . .

*

"Our daughter," said Mr. Crump, shyly. Mrs. Crump stood in the background and moved her head a little.

Hope smiled and smiled again.

"How do you do?" he said, and held out his hand.

"Very well thank you, sir," she said, and dropped a well-rehearsed curtsy.

He guessed that she was about six.

Later that day he drew a note of credit on an obliging Mr. Crump for fifty pounds, explaining that his brother, 'The Earl', and himself were re-organising their banking arrangements, he would understand about these matters, certain they did these things better in Liverpool, great embarrassment. "But the essence of my difficulty, Mr. Crump, is the very soul of yours. It is this lovely place" – he gazed blankly but intently all around him: they were strolling up towards Elterwater – "it is an addiction, Mr. Crump, worse than tobacco, worse even than alcohol – perhaps the government should do something about it, perhaps my friend Mr. Pitt should put a tax on nature as his father put a tax on gin."

Mr. Crump concentrated in order to remember that remark in order to repeat it to his wife. And perhaps elsewhere. He would acknowledge the source – he was not a plagiarist – but his polite conversation was, he knew, poor. Figures, facts, tonnage, storage, shipping, selling, commerce which connected continents, all the romance and daring of his trade, deeply besotted him and had been his lifelong pleasure. But it was considered out of the conversational court. Mr. Crump was back at school. He took note, though: and he took pains.

"I came, I saw, I was conquered, to mistranslate the mighty Caesar," Hope went on, puffing a little uphill – curious that his heavy exercises did not make country walking more comfortable – and hoping that Mr. Crump had not heard that hackneyed quip too often – "and who could resist the lake, the hills, the trees, the flowers, the birds." He thought he had got in just about everything and moved on. "It moves for me by contrasts," he said, and now he began to take an interest in, even to listen to, what he himself was saying. "When I was in Egypt I thought at first that the sun and the desert, the empty sky and the empty sand – that there was nowhere more grand. I understood why the pyramids were so enormous and splendid, of course. There was nothing there – men had to make their own markers or monuments, and eventually they had to build an entire landscape of monuments. But here, nature itself provides the landscape and the monuments and so much more than that. As the poets say – " he could not bring to mind a single line and so he stopped, and looked down on the lake as if in mourning, intuiting, correctly, that this would have the same effect as a couplet.

Mr. Crump nodded his agreement as he too gazed down. Hope held the position for a few moments more to rest his leg and get his breath back.

"It is the people hereabouts that I like," said Mr. Crump, feeling the silence as censure and well aware that he ought to play a proper part in the conversation. "In the towns now they are so busy or so tired, poor souls, or so wretched and idle that there is no time for that calm contemplation of one's existence which is the best part of our lives and which continues at all levels in a place such as this, among the peasantry as much as among those they call the Statesmen. And I am convinced – or rather, I have been convinced – that this felicity is due to the influence of the place in which they were born and in which they have lived all their lives . . ."

As Mr. Crump meandered away on a line his wife had drawn for him and in which he half-believed, John-Augustus recalled vividly a discussion he had overheard in the stable-yard earlier that morning.

It seemed that recently there had been a rather upsetting event in this heavenly vale. A local man, known throughout his youth to be a steady worker, apprenticed to a mason, had married as soon as he came out of his apprenticeship, a girl from Rydal, nearby, and they had five children. The war made severe inroads into his livelihood and at times he would be forced onto the hills to join the gangs doing the walling, but he hated being away from his family and they too suffered from the separation and besides the wages were not enough for all seven of them. Still he managed, with great economies, to live a frugal but sufficient life. Then he fell ill and for several months was unfit for any work: the cost of medicines, the increase in debts, his feebleness when, too early, he returned to work, combined to make him look, a man in the stable-yard had said, "like a living skeletal". Everybody in the vale knew him; everybody in Grasmere admired the independence which rejected the pittance and charity of parish relief; the better-off folk spoke with tenderness of the rather thin but bonny children, so quietly obedient, and the man and his wife struggling . . . The previous week the man and his wife had been found in bed, dead. It seemed that to feed the children they had denied themselves all food and eaten grass.

There was a collection under way for the orphans.

"Tell me" – Hope was made irritable by the recollection and interrupted with the acceptable rudeness of the confident social superior, "how do you administer your business?"

Crump could not believe his luck. He began hesitantly, to be certain he was not boring his acquaintance, but seeing the same expression on the Colonel's face as had been there before, he flew on like one of his mighty clippers before the wind.

Hope had set him off because he wanted to think something over.

If he were to look at his life rationally – as in his most philosophical moments he liked to think he did – then there was no questioning the profile. He was in danger from his past. In Newton he was teamed up with someone he feared and could never finally trust. He had a reprieve which was of indefinite length but better to be pessimistic than otherwise. He needed money, above all else, money and much and soon. And he was walking with a man of Levantine wealth whose demise would permit him, Hope, almost certain access to his fortune through marriage to its heir.

In short, why not murder Mr. Crump and marry Mrs. Crump? After a decent interval.

It bore thinking about. Hope looked about him. It could not be done on this day and at this spot but he had heard and seen enough of the bouldery, rocky, unstable earth treachery of the district to know that it was possible. And Crump was no athlete nor, Hope judged, had he any real strength in that soft-skinned, cossetedly clothed body.

What would be the loss? Would Mrs. Crump be less happy with him in a year or two than she was with Crump now? Would the daughter even remember her father with the perpetual presence of Hope to blot him out? Were there parents of Crump or brothers and sisters of Crump? Well – what if there were, they had had a lot of him and would find through loss, perhaps, all sorts of qualities in themselves and others they would otherwise have missed. Even Crump himself might be better meeting his Judgement now, after a life of useful business, than later when the disturbances of retirement – already foreshadowed – would most likely have made him less of a man than he was now, less happy, less useful, perhaps even diminished, by turbulent pettiness, in the very qualities which might now ensure his redemption.

There was a place – he recalled it now – Burkett had pointed it out to him when they were fishing on Derwent Water – a sheer cliff coming suddenly out of woods and fronting the valley. Just a walk in those woods, a move closer to the edge to peer down and enjoy the full Lake Tourist sensation of Beauty in Horror, a lost footing, a clutching at Mr. Crump for help, a swinging of Mr. Crump around, a letting of Mr. Crump go down, down, down into one of the most favoured of the Lake Tourists' sites.

Hope smiled to himself: the smile broadened, and to disguise his true feelings he turned the smile on Mr. Crump; who was greatly encouraged as he had been talking about the slave trade on which much of his father's great founding fortune had been based. He knew that these were sensitive matters and he was relieved, though not altogether surprised, that this scion of the aristocracy and military England should appear so benign about the matter. There was a man who lived nearby – Clarkson – a bane of his existence on the subject. He had feared that Hope might turn out to be one of those weary and self-righteous young men who thought it witty to mock the great old institutions. He took advantage of Hope's encouragement to risk an essay on the benefits which flowed – especially to the Negroes themselves – from the slave trade even though, alas, it was now becoming uneconomical.

Hope could see Crump's artistically twisted body draped over a volcanic rock, dead but unbruised, unbleeding, ready for a sort of sanctification as the Artist–Merchant who had been determined to throw over the chains of trade and discover the zephyrs of beauty, freedom, romance and nature. Hope could picture himself comforting Mrs. Crump, shoring up the memory of her husband, praising him, assessing him, recalling '*mots*', reporting favourable comments, and then in would come the daughter, dressed entirely in black, and he would say, would be forced to say no matter what the consequences were, that the child was like the man. Crump – this would provide an opportunity for a salving weep – Crump would live on for this child herself one day would bear children . . . Hope was so dug into his happy daydream that he failed to notice that Crump had stopped to gaze at something: he himself walked several yards on before the absence of his companion impinged on him.

"Your reflections," Hope cried out to the apparently enraptured merchant, "set off my own – as do all the most acute thoughts, scattering from the hand like seeds, each of which can take on a life of its own, and I confess that I became absorbed in those great matters of morality and commerce raised by your eloquent conversation."

Mr. Crump could not have wished for better and yet he was not as responsive as Hope had expected: indeed he only barely acknowledged the compliment. Hope retraced his steps and came up alongside a Mr. Crump whose mind had been cleared and relaxed by the stimulating freedom given to his prejudices: his expression was no longer that of the tentative, diffident social and artistic explorer: he was a hard man in his office dealing with a captain whose cargo did not comply with his list of instructions.

"Look at that."

Hope looked at a flower – mauve?, he thought, groping for the colour.

"That butterfly," Crump said, savagely.

The butterfly. Hope gazed intently on its red wings, black spots, a large butterfly, he thought, and a very easy life too, bumping gently along from one of those mauve flowers to another.

"There is a man who lives in this vale," Crump said bitterly, turning a hard face to Hope, whose notion about the murder underwent a radical revision: Crump would be no willing accomplice in his own end. "He writes about butterflies and flowers and birds and in praise of the common people." Crump paused, looked at Hope for a moment as a purely formal seeking of support, and then grabbed the butterfly and crushed it.

"My wife loves the man's poems," said Crump, dusting the dead creature onto the ground. "Although the man is the curse of my existence. He and his friends would have me scoffed and hounded out of the county rather than see my house completed. But I will defeat them! Poems or not."

Hope walked back into Grasmere even more thoughtfully than he had left it.

After another afternoon's fishing, he found a way to arrange a meeting with Sylvia later that night, behind the stables. He would take supper with the Crumps.

He had more than an hour to fill in before the meal: he had a maid bring him beer. He gave her the chance to enter into a light dalliance but she appeared totally unaware of his subtle overtures, wholly preoccupied in not spilling the beer over the gentleman.

For a few minutes, Hope thought of saddling up a horse and riding the eight miles up to Keswick. The exercise would tire him – that always helped: he would seek out Joanna once more and that, too, would do something to unlock this pain of want which would rise up in him from nowhere, and beat against the walls of his mind until he thought he would never be able to bear it. Perhaps he should marry Joanna, then he would be certain that whatever lust he felt would be leeched harmless by her sex.

He ordered more beer: but the maid was just as absorbed in her task and besides, though Hope always boasted to himself that no woman was unattractive to a man who knew how to look, he had to admit that this particular maid of the Swan was not immediately seductive: she was excessively tall, awkwardly balanced, lank and thin-haired and a wart took away most of the attraction from her nose.

How far had he come from Hause Point! As he sipped his beer and sat with his back to the window brooding on the bare wall and the bedhead, he contemplated how far he had fallen and how quickly.

Had Hause Point been a dream? Or was he dreaming now? His life seemed worthless – he was used to that – but there seemed to be nothing at all to contain it. Although he had merely played with the idea, he had thought about murder this morning and who was to say that given propitious circumstances and the required degree of desperation, he might not indeed . . . murder? For even as he recognised its horror he still retained the possibility that it might be available, as a way out. For he was lost, in no one mind, in nothing but urgent, insistent needs – lusts lashing him into lunacy. He dressed for dinner reluctantly.

He should go back to Buttermere, go to Mary, tell her as much of the truth as she could bear and marry her. Only then, he knew insofar as he was certain of anything, could he lead a life free from these ceaseless responses to envy, desire and pain . . . But Sylvia would be waiting for him, later, and there was Crump to be re-engaged. He went down the stairs and was stopped at the sound of voices.

"Allow me to present myself – Colonel Moore, Mrs. Moore and Miss Amaryllis D'Arcy, our ward."

"Honoured, sir," the diffident voice of Mr. Crump returned the introductions.

Hope eavesdropped through the formalities, re-grouped and entered with an air of weariness which lifted instantly at the sight of Miss D'Arcy. A second bite!

Explanations, laughter, invitations to be Mr. Crump's guests for supper, accepted, pleasure – further coincidence. Mrs. Crump, it appeared – to her intense delight – had known poor Miss D'Arcy's mother – a most delicate, sensitive lady.

"And your father – if I may speak of him too – was a man all of us admired . . ."

"All of us," said Mr. Crump, risking an interruption of his own, shaking his head a little over-vigorously for sorrow but the idea was right.

"I'm sure my husband won't mind me saying that it was not his wealth which made us all respect him – although I've heard my husband say many a time that the wealth of Mr. D'Arcy of Moss Side by Manchester was of an enormity to make the sultans and pashas of the East take note – but it was not for that, not at all, that we, all of us who knew of him . . ."

"My wife never met him," Mr. Crump interrupted, helpfully. The look his aid received from his wife guaranteed that he would hesitate – on this social occasion – to interrupt again.

"It was his reputation, his name, his . . ." Mrs. Crump was sinking, after such a thoughtlessly cruel puncture, "his reputation," she repeated, "for being such a good man, such a very good man – oh my dear!"

Miss D'Arcy was in tears. They were not, Hope observed, as Mrs. Crump and Mrs. Moore surrounded her with attention, the welled-up tears of spontaneous emotion – not if he was anything of a judge: there was something spare, almost dry, if the word could be excused, about the tears; he noted their dryness carefully while, in mime show, semaphoring to Colonel Moore and Mr. Crump 'the female of the species' and 'over-sensibility' and 'poor child' and 'let the ladies resolve it but although we are men of the world we too are not unmoved by the finer shades of feeling, especially for those fallen on life's remorseless battlefield.' The miming drew the men together just as Miss D'Arcy's tears drew the women into a quick companionship. Indeed the little incident could not have been better judged to give them, as a group, a history and a common recognition of similar social sympathy, of good manners under stress, even of kinship that they alone in the Swan, in Grasmere and perhaps for many miles around, should have shared in Miss D'Arcy's private grief and dealt with it so skilfully and properly.

Supper was a triumph of the sort Mrs. Crump very rarely experienced and she would have been hurt had anyone pointed out that Mr. Crump's fine and very expensive claret which flowed like spring water was something to do with that success. It was, as she was to say time and again, "a true congregation of hearts and minds".

On entering the dining room, Hope had manoeuvred himself next to Miss D'Arcy and given her to understand that he was overwhelmed at the self-control of her behaviour in the face of such insensitivity as that displayed by the over-enthusiastic Mrs. Crump who, nevertheless and for the sake of harmony, had to be tolerated – if not forgiven. Miss D'Arcy took the compliment, appreciated the censure and the mocking of Mrs. Crump, and smiled the smile of the dumbly adoring at Hope, who was alerted by such a perfect response but nevertheless willing at this stage to receive it at face value.

He scored a further success with Colonel Nathaniel Montgomery Moore who, on the visit which he, his wife and Miss D'Arcy had just taken to Dumfries, had encountered none other than Major General Gerard Lake, "who told me about your great gallantry at Guelder – Gueld –"

"Gueldermasen," Hope pronounced carefully.

" – with the 14th Foot," Colonel Moore continued: he acknowledged no correction. "Said you commanded it like a true Englishman, sir, and fought like a Roman. He had nothing but the highest praise for you, sir. I said I was proud to have your acquaintance – and so I am. And the wounds, sir – you bear them very well: the leg, Major General Lake told me, was very badly crushed."

"Oh sir!" said Mrs. Crump faintly and for a moment she threatened to be the second act to Miss D'Arcy's opener.

"Windows!" said Colonel Moore and he rushed past his hostess to try to open the windows, which stuck. The loud tugging and pulling that followed – the instructions from the Colonel, instructions from the landlord, banging of levers, banging of latches – eclipsed any small performance Mrs. Crump might have been inclined to give and when the company was finally re-seated she was wise enough to let it pass.

But it had given Hope an opening. He had rarely felt better. A huge gust of energy blew him back on course. Miss D'Arcy was back in the game, he could see that. She would not be easy – then so much the more fun, the greater test for his skills. Mrs. Crump's talk of the girl's father's immense wealth – which surely she had inherited – had abolished all that fruitless toying with marriage to the innkeeper's daughter in Buttermere. That had been the weakness of the self-defeated. What Hope needed was a stage, a part and an audience. He had all three and felt that at last the play was under way: this was why he had struck north; this was why he had learned his part (and God bless Major General Lake of Dumfries and God keep him there); this was his great opportunity and 'O Lord,' he prayed to himself, 'if it is true that You have love even for the worst of Your sinners and let Your Son welcome into Paradise the thief on the cross who by a single act redeemed a life of evil, then remember me at Hause Point, remember how I tried to obey Your will and how I saved that innocent young girl and help me here because I swear, if I succeed in my intention here, I will lead a life of charity and Christian duty to the end. But for that I need Wealth, O Lord, I confess it: without it I am worthless; just let me get my hands on it and I will be an ornament to Your name.'

He looked up, as Kemble had looked up, and then picked off each of the attendant five with a dimpled smile which impelled them to treasure his grand simplicity and unaffected openness.

"Pain," he began, "is one of the strangest phenomena on earth. I have been where men have suffered pains which would have murdered any of us here" – he nodded to Mr. Crump – "but those same have not only endured it but seemed to ignore it" – here he nodded to Colonel Moore, who straightened his back – one old soldier understood by another. The Colonel breathed in a sentimental sigh of agreement. "I speak not only of the Army – although as Colonel Moore knows probably better than I, the acts of heroism you see there in the face of pain – wounds, cuts, torn limbs" – he looked at Mrs. Crump; she swayed slightly – "severed arteries, gashed heads" – Mrs. Moore was unaffected – "and all the terrible lacerations and disfigurements received on the human body in modern warfare" – Miss D'Arcy nodded; she was intrigued – "but I speak of the self-inflicted torments of the Indian, the Negro and the Mussulman."

He took up his claret, drank, and moved to an anecdote which he had found scarcely ever failed and would surely, he was convinced, see him through this supper party as the man of wide travel, wide curiosity, the aristocratic rover who had finally come back home to live by the more profound, more refined things of life.

"There is a sect in India which eats broken glass," he began, abruptly. "I have seen them with my own eyes. It is part of their religion, a religion I do not scoff at as it holds many elements which match our own even though it lacks the truth of ours. At one of their great festivals they have the ritual of driving out the devils from their bodies. First the drummers come on – I may say that no women are allowed to take part in this ritual and the ladies here will perhaps agree with me that they are fortunate in that omission. These drums are quite extraordinary – from the colossal to the size of a cup, they make sounds and rhythms which are undoubtedly barbarous but are nevertheless compelling. Indeed, the more they play the more I may say drugged you become with the sound and the beating of it until you have to prevent yourself swaying around with the natives. They are chewing a drug plant and drinking their quite disgusting beer or spirit – I had only one sip and did not stay to analyse the taste but rejected it instantly – the dancers – wearing headdresses feathered like exotic birds and daubed all over with signs and scribbles –

messages to their gods, I assumed – then begin to pound the earth in a movement which matches the drumming perfectly and, like the drumming, is powerfully affecting."

He found a matching rhythm. "Faster go the drums, faster spin the dancers, rush torches show off the paint and the sweat on them – they begin to smash small bottles of some holy liquid and first stab themselves with the broken glass – with no apparent injury, they do not even bleed – and then they eat the glass itself. I swear it. The glass is put into their mouths as they whirl around in the shadows and lights of the torches and they chew and swallow it down – showing it in their mouths – putting out their tongues afterwards to prove either that the tongue is not cut or that the mouth is empty. I asked, afterwards, how many of the young men – they are mostly young men – died as a consequence and was told none. The broken glass kills the devils inside them and makes them stronger. I asked . . ."

Later, in his room, he remembered Sylvia. But it would be too risky: even more certainly he felt, bright and keen as he was now, that she was part of a trap best avoided. Or left until later. Sylvia would wait. He took out a pipe and poured a little brandy.

Outside his window the moon had risen over the fells and it was reflected exactly in the round lake. Hope nodded his appreciation as at the perfect execution of an ambitious manoeuvre: it was indeed a favoured spot.

11

The Proposal

"Harrison o' Caldbeck?"

"Reet." The younger man stood his ground.

"I knew some Harrisons at Wythop."

"Cousins."

"And there's one or two in Cockermouth."

"I've heerd Mother say we'd kin theer."

"None of them was up to much," the older man said, unkindly.

There was a pause.

"We can't pick who we have for relatives," was the eventual reply.

"So you're off farming stock?" The older man sought another opening. "There can't be much to farm around Caldbeck, can there? There isn't an acre of flat land for miles."

"We manage," was the reply. They were in a little porch at the back of the inn: Richard Harrison looked at Joseph Robinson's untidy meadows. It was a critical look and Robinson was stung.

"It's low land brings out the real farmer," he said.

"Or not," the younger man concluded, swiftly, still staring into the middle distance. The reply brought Joseph Robinson an unease he could have done without: after all, he ought to be in the commanding position. But this young stranger from the bleak Northern Fells seemed very capable.

"Is there something you've seen you don't care for?" Joseph asked, a little weakly.

"I'd need to think on that," Richard replied, still without turning his gaze to the older man.

At that time there was a growing interest in Cumberland and Westmorland wrestling, partly because of the growing interest in everything in those two fashionable and enchanted counties. Fine wrestlers such as George Wood of the Queen's Head in Keswick could now earn twenty-five guineas on one of the great lakeland wrestling days: more, of course, if they put money on themselves. Some said the sport came from the Norsemen, others muttered about the Romans who after all had been in the area for several centuries and left little else but stone, and one literary aficionado had just written a treatise tracing it back in direct line to Jacob's wrestling with the angel.

It was a peculiar sight. Two men dressed in long underwear would shake hands and then bend forward as if making a deep bow to each other. This position would be retained and they proceeded each to rest his chin on the other's shoulder – heads nuzzled close together like horses lodged in affection – and then swing their arms in order to take a grip on the flattened back of their opponent. Once the grips were taken, the wrenching and twisting, the buttocking and tripping and hyking, the turning and thrashing and throwing began until one man was floored, his grip broken. The event would conclude as it began with a handshake.

The two grappling at a conversation on the porch – one a capable wrestler in his time (famous local wrestlers like George Wood and himself often ended up as innkeepers), the other, Harrison, a contender for honours and prize money on that very day – were like the wrestlers when seeking for a grip. This is when it can look most puzzling and most comical to the ignorant. Two men crouched against each other, bums stuck out, arms swinging up from the grass to the grip in salmon-like curves. But the cognoscenti know that the grip can be everything: in itself it can decide the entire bout.

And so Harrison of Caldbeck and Robinson of Buttermere – wrestlers were always known by name and village both – were circling about each other's conversation trying for a grip. Every time Robinson seemed to get a hold, Harrison wriggled away. The older man was eager to engage him, keen to get the trial of strength over with, aware, perhaps, of limited strength. But Harrison was a long-headed young man. Whenever Robinson struck for a grip he moved quickly and broke it, never allowing the older man to settle. But he had to watch very keenly: Robinson had won notable bouts.

"D'you fancy your chances today, then?" Robinson said, deciding that talk about his farming, not unlike the farming itself, alas, would give him no advantage.

"There's some awkward fellas down here," Harrison replied. "They take a bit o' weighing up."

"Would I put money on you?"

"I nivver bet," said Harrison, "save on certainties."

Robinson nodded. He had used the same reply himself on occasion.

Harrison had arrived for the Sports on the previous evening, taken a couple of glasses of beer in the Fish – complimented the landlord on his brew – and then gone to sleep out the night in a barn. To the crowd in the tap bar he had seemed no different from any other young contender down for the Sports. But Robinson, eternally vigilant over his love and his interest, had seen and noted the direct force of the man's design on Mary.

More worryingly, he appeared to be welcomed. Mary had spent a little time in close conversation with him and even stroked his cheek at one stage. Robinson was surprised and a little alarmed at such an untypical gesture. He had taken the trouble to seek out the young man in the morning and tease him into conversation – as he thought subtly, but Harrison was immediately aware that he was being sized up. So far, Harrison had enjoyed the advantage.

"Will you be headed back home after the wrestlin'?" Robinson asked.

"I might stop on a day or two."

"Have you business roundabout?"

"Summat might crop up."

Robinson had learnt all that he wanted to know and more than he cared to hear.

"I'll be seeing you then," he said. "But we all get very busy around here this time in the season. None of us has time for much else but the work in hand."

"I won't keep you then," Harrison said, nodded cheerfully and walked away. A lot of swagger in him, Robinson thought, a lot too much. He made a click of disapproval loud enough for the young man to hear.

Once Harrison rounded a corner he took a very deep breath and leaned against a wall. He had been on his mettle throughout. He feared that Robinson had seen through him and played with him. He gave no credit to his own moves and answers because he had all but forgotten them. Robinson knew his game and would do all he could to spoil it: that was what mattered.

He had not caught a glimpse of Mary but she would be at the Sports: she had said so when they had discussed his teeth: her questions had been more curious than tender and even when she had touched his cheek it was to prove for herself that no bruising remained. There had been a steady diminution – since the operation – in his own interest in dentistry but she had tapped his experience out of him and collected it with care.

Harrison had come back to propose marriage.

He could not afford too many jaunts like this – especially as his father had been less than joyful at his return. They did not need an extra hand until harvest, he had said, or even later when they could lay off the casual help and Richard and his father would be more than sufficient labour to see the small hill farm through the winter. This expedition was sanctioned on the understanding that there was good money to be won at wrestling. Guineas were nowhere else so easily available.

The wrestling was to be the prize event of the day and several carriage loads had come across from Keswick and Cockermouth and even further to the small but picturesque meeting in the much lauded Buttermere. One or two of the local gentry would be entering the wrestling; several were in the horse races, although events such as the long leap and the high leap attracted less fashionable clients.

Harrison knew many of the wrestlers and the rest of the morning passed pleasantly enough as he moved around the quacks and the pedlars, tinkers and gypsies and show people who were an enjoyable contrast to the farmers' wives selling their freshly imprinted butter, with their buckets of eggs, the vegetables and poultry, rabbits, game pies, potted char, rum butter. A few of the men had taken a rare day off from the quarries and the recognitions were more generous than Harrison had anticipated. He suspected that they might think he had used the incident of the bad teeth and the convenience of a farming father to bolt from that tough and dirty job. That, in part, was the truth. But he wanted to assure them of a more overpowering reason: he needed to re-establish himself on his home ground as firmly and quickly as possible in order to launch himself on Mary. Of course he never mentioned that.

The Fish was crowded from mid-morning, with tables in the yard and extra help in every room. Mary loved days like this. She liked the sensation of so much enjoyment around. She liked the people – many of whom she knew well, and at least as importantly – many of whom knew her well and had known her since early childhood, before the mark of fame had set her apart. In the mass her singularity dissolved. She was reduced to the landlord's daughter who served at table: it was the sort of anonymous commingling in which she found a great relief. She liked working with her father too on such days because she could be commanded by him without being suspicious of him.

Joseph saw the wrestling day as one of his great sea battles. The inn was his vessel, the valley was the ocean, out there before him were a horde of small boats and pirates, flare ships and decoys, occasionally an enemy frigate or two hoving over the crest of a hill, sometimes a rich galleon sighted nearby which had to be pursued and boarded. Mrs. Robinson was banished below decks and confined to the kitchens from which emerged a steady issue of victuals from forenoon to midnight. Mary was his lieutenant and they worked together wonderfully well.

All his talents were called on on such a day – his powers of calculation, of decision-making, of patience, of amiability, of firmness and above all of steering his excellently stocked, freshly painted and cleaned up vessel of an inn through the increasingly unpredictable currents of the day. Hot sport, heavy drink, the aphrodisiac of leisure and the compulsion to press into the very gut of pleasure combined now and then to threaten choppy waters, even a storm.

Joseph knew his allies. Like Nelson he was thoroughly familiar with those on whom he would need most to rely. Every Buttermere neighbour and old wrestling foe would be given a free mug of beer as his first drink and throughout the day Joseph would ask a little – often useless – favour here, another there in order to keep them within his ken: so that they kept their eyes, he would say to himself, on the signals coming from the flagship. Mary would be sent out like a rowing boat among the waiting fleet – a word here, a suggestion there, showing again the presence of the command vessel. Not that he anticipated great trouble – most of the fell people were there to entertain themselves in ways which might appear rough and sound loud but came from characters largely tolerant, polite, gentle, qualities widely commented on, coming from the ease of great and graceful physical strength, the pacific, solitudinous nature of the daily lives, and a long experience of continuing community. Yet Joseph knew that he was right to have his armaments in place: you could never trust the gypsies or the tinkers – against each other, let alone anyone else: quacks, drunks and ranters would drift from their positions in the line and cause trouble just by bumping into the orderly armada of hill folk who knew how to hold steady but had never been fond of strangers.

While the vagrants and beggars shifted around like floating fireships of guilt, capable of their own frustrations.

Mary knew his commands well. Sometimes she would anticipate them. She kept a tight grip on the new hands and was particularly good at swabbing down the decks after a boisterous boarding party had come and gone. There were several times when Joseph could stand outside the front of his inn, or on the for'ard deck of his ship, and have the time to contemplate his next manoeuvre, calm amid the storm as all the great commanders always were. And for once he knew he was fully appreciated by his Buttermere neighbours and even by his wife.

The day was bright enough, a quick breeze sending a fleet of light clouds across to the east, the sun warm but not hot, dry underfoot.

On an outcrop of rock, Kitty Dawson looked down on the valley for a few minutes. From where she stood, the business of the Fish, the activity around the field, the movement of the crowd at the country meeting – dressed in a range from the metropolitan fashionable to a package of rags – made scarcely a blemish on the landscape. The lake was undisturbed, the steep fells even more silent and bare than usual, the small movement spilling out of Buttermere village no more distracting than any cloud shadow across the crags and turf. She smoked a peck of tobacco and decided, as she decided every year, not to go down. She would hear any news that mattered. The longer she gazed down, through the tendril of tobacco smoke, the more the meeting merged into the older, stronger established patterns and colours of the valley floor until, eyes half-closed, she saw it disappear into the ancient landscape . . .

Joseph Robinson was aware of what was good for business but he was also a man who prided himself on his love of sport: this meant that he had a responsibility to knowledge and experience. He had to judge the wrestling which would be the chew in the conversation of the valley for weeks. In mid-afternoon, he hove to, dropped anchor and took Mary the few hundred yards to the sports field, basking a little in their ceremonious passage – the work and self-forgetfulness of the day brought out every best quality in her and yet, paradoxically, although at the pitch of her beauty, she herself was more unaware of it than at any other time. But others saw it and the crowd shuffled free a space to let them through. Joseph went into the ring to confer with the other deep judges of the sport. Mary took the opportunity to look around the small country fair.

Richard Harrison came up to her as she was standing in front of a pedlar whose display included a cluster of ribbons: red, blue, yellow, green.

"Tell us your favourite colour," he asked.

Mary smiled but shook her head: she wanted to be under no obligation. The young man gauged her reaction and bought an emerald green ribbon which he handed to her. She could not refuse and indeed found it quite easy to accept. Cured of his bulging toothache, refreshed by some days in the open air on his father's farm and steeled by his resolution, he appeared as a handsome, personable man – about the same height as Tom but from a different local stock – blond hair flecked with auburn, skin pale, lean-shanked, eyes duck-egg blue.

Joseph saw that Mary had escorted the Caldbeck man to the wrestling ring and an instinct of apprehension unnerved him. She would not, could not leave him for this boy! When he took a green ribbon from her and tied it loosely round his waist, Joseph was even more disturbed.

As Richard took the ribbon from her he had said, "I'll borrow it for luck." She had not the heart to embarrass him by refusing a request so diffidently expressed.

The contest got under way – a series of knockout bouts inexorably leading to the final pair and, after seeing Richard – and Tom – win their opening bouts without much difficulty, she wandered away, suddenly keen to be on her own.

There was no-one by the lakeside: the wind cuffed the water lightly and took the murmurs of the crowd behind her yet further away.

Where was the man called Hope, she wondered. What would he be doing at this moment?

On her return from Whitehaven she had surprised herself by feeling compelled to go to the room where the four of them had enjoyed the dinner. *So much.* She had felt flattered, nervous, tentative, bold to be acting the companion to the even bolder Colonel: but she had also felt locked into that happiness; of right. And then she had run away from it. But he had not asked after her; unsuspected questioning of her mother had told her that. Now she had to let that night, her feelings, her certainties about his feelings, her inflamed stirrings of the senses – all be lapped away. A louder shout than usual took her back to the ring.

She was in time to see the recovery of one of the young gentlemen who had begun to torment her on that night until Colonel Hope had silenced him. Harrison of Caldbeck, she was told, had upended him savagely after the young gentleman had sought an advantage by what would, in a common man, have been punished as an inadmissible move. So Harrison had lost the first fall unfairly: in the second he had twisted his man feet up and then let him crash to the ground. There was no third fall: the gentleman had withdrawn.

The final was between Harrison and Tom with all the sympathy on the local man. Alice sought out Mary and they watched appreciatively as the two strong, tall, graceful, beautifully built young men whirled each other about, endured two dog falls – draws – and only after several lengthy spasms of athletic tussling arrived at the deciding fall. Which Tom finally won.

Harrison leapt up instantly to hold out his hand and immediately looked about for Mary and shook his head. Noting the gesture, Joseph moved smartly over to his daughter and escorted her back aboard. The rest of the afternoon and evening would be far too busy to allow them any helpful solitude.

Harrison was still there in the morning. He followed Mary as she took the flocks out of the village. From his porch, Joseph watched with a sullen and rather bleary eye: the night had been long on reminiscence and several barrels had been tapped to celebrate old victories.

After the fair, the village had regained the wholeness which, Mary perceived at times such as this, was vitally precious to her: perhaps this was her love. The place itself, the arrangement of those low, recently rebuilt stone farms and the few mud and wattle cottages, the eternal comfort of the lake's shape and colours which seemed not to mirror but to temper her mood, the rise of fells which gave her sensibility its reach. The valley was her, she moved in it as through the natural expression of her mind and feelings. The keen blustery morning summoned up exactly the braced mood she sought to capture.

She made a mild attempt to evade him but he cut across and landed in front of her, sitting, as she had first seen him, with the sheep and goats dithering and teetering before and around him. He held up the green ribbon.

"I forgot to give you this back."

"So you did." Both of them smiled at the device.

And she took the ribbon, without a promise. But paused.

"You know why I really came here," he said, and the words might well have been memorised because he stared up at her in rather an abstracted manner as if his mind were on something else.

She did not reply. It was as if a light blow, say on her cheek, had suddenly distracted her from the braced confidence of her early mood to an unwelcome uncertainty.

She wished he would stop. She liked him. Over some months . . . a year or two . . .

"You know what I'm trying to say . . ."

Now he *did* look at her and the look was almost forlorn. In that look she saw her life with him and it was a decent life: the small farm in high northern fell-land, the farm coming in part or in whole to him, several children, heavy days, quiet times, a life she often yearned for – a plain and ordinary life away from this coddled valley, a place in which she could start again.

But at this moment the thought of leaving the valley – her home, her existence – and not being here if, by some chance, *he* should return . . . yet this expectation confused her. She had not experienced it before. The man was an aristocrat, inconceivably wealthy, brother to an Earl, a Member of Parliament, a Colonel – that he had been amiable for a couple of passing days was surely something she could accept, absorb and forget. But the expectation would not be driven out . . . and yet Harrison was a fine man and there was something about his miserably presented directness which made her want to scoop him up. A wave of tiredness came upon her, this time the full tidal memory of the strains of her life at the inn, her age, her vulnerability, her need to stand alone . . .

"So . . . ?" He wanted her to agree to walk out with him: to accept his first and formal step on the path to marriage.

It was his honesty she could love, she thought. And he would be a man who would not try to trample on her. He would listen: there would be an equal life there: he smiled and tapped his healed face.

"And I'll let you pull the next bad tooth," he said and stood up, reached out for her.

12

Credentials

"I accept," she said.

He kissed her hand, delicately, a mere whisper of the lips, stood back, looked intently at her until she was forced to smile back at him, and pressing her left hand in his unclawed fingers, swept his blemished hand across the landscape beyond them: Bassenthwaite Lake, the valley, Keswick, Derwent Water, Catbells, Newlands, an Arcadia which his gesture seemed to offer her as his gift.

"Only time," he said, carefully, remembering the very intonation of these precisely rehearsed words, "will enable me to show you how much your acceptance means to me. Only time and," he paused and once more kissed her hand, "our greater love."

Miss D'Arcy smiled again: she stood above him on the rise of Latrigg Fell and was impressed more than she had anticipated by the gallant and handsome figure he struck, posed so elegantly against the mountains.

"I should like to marry soon," he said, abruptly, as if the thought had ambushed his feelings, "and here – here where we met."

"I too would like that," she replied, steadily. "I can think of no better place to be married." The steadiness was a torment: at last she would be free.

"There –" Hope pointed towards Crosthwaite Church modestly huddled below " – where saints have visited and so many have worshipped quietly for over a thousand years."

She nodded and then, as steadily as she had accepted everything he had so far said, "Colonel Moore will want to write his letters, of course. But when we have the answers . . ."

Hope asked his question silently, merely an abstract, puzzled look, leaving her to wade through the potential embarrassment. Miss D'Arcy – Amaryllis – held to the silence as resolutely as he. She was not cowed.

Any feelings Hope had for her – and though they had included a certain measure of respect and the possibility of desire, they had not been strong – now alchemised into a quite violent dislike.

"I do beg your pardon," he was forced to say.

She composed herself at some leisure before answering.

"We discussed – the Colonel, Mrs. Moore and myself – the probability of this –" she left a coy blank for the word 'proposal' to etch itself on the wind, "and of course," she giggled just a little, "we made our plans."

"Was it so transparent then?" Hope asked, gaily, and smiled and smiled . . .

"*I* was always certain," Amaryllis confessed with such resolute frankness that he totally disbelieved her. "And during those two weeks in Grasmere, Mrs. Moore became convinced that you would –" again the blank and again the word was conjured up between them like a spirit conjured from the mountain. "Colonel Moore, of course, was always a doubter."

This time Hope's quizzical look did prove a sufficient prompt.

"He thought you would be too Grand," she said, rather gleefully. "Of course, he did not say that and he would deny it if I accused him of it, but . . . my father . . . your brother the Earl." Miss D'Arcy looked very thoughtful. "Even though my father was convinced that, with our name – it is French – we must have come over, like all the best families, at the Conquest . . . and Colonel Moore had heard . . ."

Here she hesitated. Her shyness, he judged, was entirely genuine.

"Yes?"

"From his talks in Dumfries . . . that you . . . in Vienna . . . had been, were, engaged to – I believe you mentioned the name to Mrs. Crump."

Hope was instantly alerted, which enabled him to respond gently and convincingly. Privately he condemned the benign Mrs. Crump to a slow spit. He could see her uncontainable familiarity turning his whimsical early compliment into an item of confidential gossip which might well – had Miss D'Arcy been less resolute – have harmed his chances. He paused – a marked pause – turned away, took a couple of paces laterally – so as not to be too ridiculously far beneath her – and managed a reasonably sincere sigh – given the short notice.

"There was an arrangement, I freely admit it," he said, bravely breaking it to her and gazing out across the valley as to a disappearing dream. "Indeed, it was one of the many subjects . . . time, Amaryllis

. . . but you have driven so much out of my thoughts. These few days with you have been like this country before me here – a new paradise, an enchanted place so rich in itself that it needed nothing else. Any thoughts of others, any memory, any meetings or encounters have simply disappeared – as dark places are driven away by the sun. Yes, in Vienna, a lady, I will not say her name but assure you that any conversation I had with poor little Mrs. Crump was most decidedly not on this subject and not about this lady – she has clearly clutched at a reference and taken it for a confidence – in Vienna, this lady of, I may admit it, royal connection, formed an attachment for me which was not reciprocated but proved most difficult to disengage. In Vienna, of course . . . my only conclusive recourse was to leave the city, which could not be arranged as quickly as I would have liked since I had army business there which demanded my attendance. The rumour, therefore, was given time to breed and, for my own honour's sake and for hers, I could do nothing, nothing, but endure it . . ."

Miss D'Arcy came across to him and put a hand on his shoulder with proprietorial affection. He left her hand unattended and the non-gesture had the force of a faint rebuff. Secure in his dislike of her, he was in control.

" . . . Letters? . . ." He murmured, eventually, vaguely, his eyes resolutely on the landscape, her hand rather guiltily withdrawn from his shoulder.

"Please – let Colonel Moore talk to you about it."

Hope looked down the fell where Colonel and Mrs. Moore were strolling with unskilful aimlessness, taking care never to look up towards the two figures on the rump of mountain. Hope smiled to himself. Just when the game appeared to be won, the odds had lengthened. He turned to Amaryllis and delivered his most accomplished smile.

"I take it I am to be investigated? I will try to find it entertaining," he said. "To be spied on!" His smile was relentless and Miss D'Arcy who, until then, had felt none of the virulent force in the man, was pushed into embarrassment. He made her feel cheap, disloyal, childish and socially inferior.

Mrs. Moore tapped her husband's arm complacently.

"She's done it!" she said. "He's taken her arm. Don't look."

How had his wife managed to spot it when she, too, he could have sworn, had kept her eyes off them was a puzzle to the Colonel who tended to the view of Woman as Eternal Enigma.

*

He had not a quiver of anxiety over the business of the letters.

"It was in her father's will," he said, evenly. The two men were in the small back parlour which George Wood kept for discreet purposes, "and although it is . . ." Stuck for the precise word, the Colonel made a small gesture with his right hand which then efficiently used the momentum to pick up his claret. "Amaryllis talked to me earlier. She wanted me to overlook the letters. I think she is afraid that you might be embarrassed. But of course I must carry out her late father's wishes. You will understand there can be no question of that. Her fortune, you see, is very large." He nodded almost sadly, as if the weight of the wealth were altogether too much for him. "Very large," he repeated dolefully. Hope understood his reluctance to be parted from it.

The problem was to prise him away. In Miss D'Arcy he had implanted a slight sense that she might have offended the Earl's younger brother and could be denied entry into the world for which her father had cultivated her. Would that take?

"You have not enquired as to the size of the fortune," Colonel Moore said, in a tone which suggested that Hope was somehow in the wrong for this negligence.

Hope smiled and mimicked the Colonel's previous gesture including the picking up of his claret. He only sipped: tense, waiting for the right opening.

After going to the door and reassuring himself that they were entirely alone, Colonel Moore recited the wealth of his ward. Mr. D'Arcy had been very, very rich and very shrewd. Hope smiled and smiled.

"Those letters . . . ?"

"It is quite clearly laid down. You give me a note and three or four names and addresses. I write to them and include your note. Once they have replied, well then! You and Amaryllis can be married in a trice!" The heartiness of the latter part of his sentence was in response to a sudden visible stiffening on Hope's part.

"I could never agree to that," he said: he smiled no more and let a silence grow uncomfortable.

Colonel Moore was confused. Part of the confusion came from the unworthy pleasure given him by the prospect of holding onto his ward a little longer. Firmly, however, he regrouped and readdressed himself to the task. "I am afraid, sir, that it is a stipulation. One which, in your case, is, I realise, unnecessary, tiresome, perhaps worse – but I will explain all that, I will tell your referees of the peculiarity of this circumstance, the onus will be on me and trust me, Colonel Hope, I shall not let Amaryllis or yourself down. My wife and I consider this to be a most fortunate match. It is in Amaryllis's best interests and she has told us that she is certain of happiness with you . . ."

Her face flashed up in Hope's mind's eye and he abhorred its prettiness which he saw as entirely calculating, unaware of her lust to be free – through marriage.

"But we must . . ." The Colonel repeated the gesture which led his hand to the glass.

"I understand," Hope assured him. "It is the delicacy in myself which I find insuperable. This is no criticism of your position. You have your duty and as one soldier to another . . . but I have this damned reluctance." He smiled, quickly, warmly, and in that dart of charm Colonel Moore saw the pressing attraction of Amaryllis for this man. "Perhaps I can overcome it in time . . . but it is too much of . . . forgive me . . . of a market, an auction, a commercial venture . . . And of course I am not an unworldly man – the Earl, my brother, whom I'm sure you will meet, will assure you that I am, by his standards, too interested in confirming and enlarging the wealth of the estates – and indeed on my visits to Egypt and Turkey and the New World I have, I may say, made a purchase here, an investment there . . ." He narrowed his eyes and saw Hope the Merchant Prince, the aristocrat at large on the Rialtos of the world, feared, admired, dipping silkenly between caskets of treasure, tranches of land, ships, silver mines, paintings, furniture, the collector, the connoisseur, and sending all back to the lonely Scottish estate which burgeoned with those foreign infusions of antique wealth, material goods . . . "No," he concluded, pulling himself reluctantly out of his Croesian day-dream, "I am not an unworldly man. But," he went on, deliberately hitting a harder tone, "as you will entirely appreciate, sir, there is a man's own sense of his own honour. A sense which can work against his best interests – for I need not repeat how much I respect Amaryllis, how entirely delightful and suitable I find her and how wonderfully rare she is for me who has – as man to man I can tell you what you must guess – several times been urged to marry. Amaryllis is the first woman to whom I have proposed and I trust she will be the last. But I am afraid . . . letters . . ."

Colonel Moore was on the rack. The man was so plausible, so persuasive; he himself – in his better self – would surely also have felt opposition to the posthumous demand of a tradesman, however rich, however Norman his name. It was as clear an indication as he could ever have wished for that Hope was not primarily interested in the immense dowry.

"If it were my sole decision, then of course, of *course* I would never press it."

"I understand." Impulsively, Hope stood up, reached out and took Moore's right hand in both his. "Please believe me, this is my obstinacy – you are behaving honourably, honourably – I realise that I am jeopardising my chance of great happiness – but we know – both of us – there are times when the greatest danger has to be faced, the greatest risk taken because that small persistent voice will not allow us to escape our duty to ourselves. I am very much afraid, sir, that . . ." Hope stopped abruptly, before he was overcome. Colonel Moore, moved and perturbed, would have stood up to encounter the man squarely on but the pressure of Hope's grip kept him down in his seat.

"Perhaps we can talk again tomorrow," Hope concluded and left a rather fuddled and flattened Colonel Moore to his own company.

Hope had talked himself into a state of indignation. How dare this man demand his credentials as if he were some arriviste from the Colonies whose background had to be sniffed out and tracked down because his foreground was presumed to be so suspect! His rank was way above that of Moore: the Hopes of Hopetoun were far better stock than the Moores of wherever they sprouted up! Miss D'Arcy might be a young woman with a remarkable inheritance, but there were others, and money was not the sole factor at moments such as this.

He imagined, with pleasure, the unusual difficulty Colonel Moore would have in presenting his defeat to Miss D'Arcy. For surely he ought to have been able to explain to Colonel Hope, to persuade Colonel Hope, to arrive at a gentlemanly agreement – and what precisely had Colonel Hope said? And when would he be back? And what was to be done?

The man who called himself Hope went down the sleepy cow-crossed and vagrant-strewn main street of Keswick with the speed and determination of the utterly resolved. It was late afternoon. The Colonel and himself had entered negotiations after a celebratory two thirty dinner for which Mrs. Wood had polished all her arts and cutlery. He was well fed, well soused, bursting in strength and eagerness for life, King of the mountain-town making for the pot-house and Joanna.

He was careless of any consequences there. She would never be believed and he was discreet enough for all normal purposes. In the end he would simply deny it and accuse her of false witness. His dress, title, manner and reputation protected him from her range of accusations. He would never be the luckless, dirty, shrivelled-looking man in the stocks – put there likely enough for stealing no more than an egg. Hope tossed the woeful prisoner a small piece of silver.

Joanna, he was told, by a rather uppity landlord who rejoiced to see privilege spiked, was out in the fields. Doing what? The leer was the answer.

A flare of anger scorched Hope's mind. He took it for granted she would be there to service him whenever he wanted it. He knew that, essentially, he had not yet utterly satisfied her and that was unbearable. The lust he had was to slake her own unmistakable lust. It only worked if she could be brought to the surrendering pitch of exhausted or ecstatic release.

He went behind the pothouse along the path he usually took with her, knowing, in a way which twisted him savagely, that she would not bother to keep their secret places private.

They were ambling back, Joanna and her late hot lover, a tinker by the look of him, sodden with sex, Hope thought, she too carelessly satiated to fasten her dress properly, he altogether swaggering in the success of his rut.

Hope could have slit their throats.

He let them pass, acknowledged them barely, made the faint pretence that he had chosen this path by chance for a late afternoon walk, even gazed up at Skiddaw, and their gurgled laughter mixed in with his own longing for the gurgling of their necks to gape blood. He strolled and forced himself to stroll. He had the faintest intimation that Joanna despised him.

"But what have I become?" he cried out, suddenly aware of the ridiculous, ineffective, by-passed figure he was, trailing aimlessly into woods whose trees he could neither distinguish nor enjoy. He remembered Hause Point, he remembered the abyss he had so often fallen into. He sought out St. Kentigern's church nearby at Crosthwaite.

It was a place he had visited three times – once to be seen; the second time to appreciate the sermon which he had afterwards discussed outside the small West Door with the vicar who had been impressed by his distinguished visitor's passionate piety. And once, before as now, for solace and solitude.

He entered into it as if for sanctuary. The clean loud latch clicked behind him. The smell of flowers and beeswax. The peaceful dust motes by the sun-struck windows. The scabby, festering evil went out of him at the touch of this holy place. He took a seat near the back of the short nave and was disappointed to see, a few pews before him, a knelt figure, praying intensely. Before he could go out so as to wait until he could have the place to himself, the figure levered himself up, bowed to the altar, and turned and saw him.

It was Nicholson, the young clergyman he had met in the Lorton Valley, shy, the unsuccessful wooer of Miss Skelton, poorly paid, but on several occasions a most useful conversational refuge for the restless Colonel.

"I always call in here when I am in Keswick." The chaplain, keen to make amends for what he perceived was an intrusion, took the flustered course of staying on and saying more. "And I believe it is a church favoured by yourself?"

"It is."

"Do you know about our St. Kentigern?" Nicholson wanted to loiter with the man who – in his eyes – could pluck with ease a flower he could only look on at a distance. He was fascinated by the power he saw inside the rich clothes, the allure of the title, the estates, the enrapturing confidence of the Army, the experiences . . . In an attempt partly to offer a tribute and perhaps in some way to attempt a readjustment of the balance against him, he recited what he knew of the church's founding saint.

"He had a remarkable life," the chaplain began, rather wistfully, and Hope saw in return an over-thin, rather knobble-nosed, receding, flat black-haired though still youngish man hypnotised by Fame and Glory. "Don't you think all really great men are extraordinary from the very beginning? And evil men too? Look at what they say about Napoleon." Nicholson glanced around the church, warily, afraid that the invocation of the name of this secular devil might disturb the Christian bones. "Kentigern's mother was a northern princess called Thanew whose great love was for the Virgin Mother on whom she modelled herself. This was a century or more after the Romans had left – not that they influenced these parts very much – they built their walls and garrisons and roads and left the wild fell folk alone. But it was a time of several kingdoms and Princess Thanew was proposed to by a neighbouring king. As she wished to remain a virgin, she refused. Her spurned suitor laid a trap for her. He drugged her and then violated her. When her father saw the evidence of this sin he condemned her to death. She was tied to the wheel of a chariot and sent down the steep sides of one of the great hills. But she prayed to heaven and promised that, should she be spared, she would devote the first fruit of her womb to Christ's service. The chariot turned about; its lead pole stuck deeply into the earth and she was saved."

There was an innocence about Nicholson's story-telling – practised for the valley children whose company he most enjoyed – so remote from the recent thoughts and experiences of Hope that he was immediately beguiled by it. He could have applauded the saving of the Princess and his obvious appreciation gave Nicholson confidence.

"But her father was still determined to do away with her. He put her in an open boat, with no oars, at the mouth of the River Aberlessie which, the chronicle says, was called 'The Mouth of Stench' because of the thousands of rotting fish cast on the sands. Again she prays and for three days and three nights she is swept through cold northern seas until she is cast ashore on the sands of Culleross on the north side of our Solway Firth. She is weak and ill but her first prayer is not for herself but for her unborn child who is dedicated to Christ's service.

"She wanders about the shore, which is bitterly cold, but then the north wind blows a heap of ashes some fishermen had left on the strand into a flame. She adds to the fire with driftwood. And it is by that fire that Kentigern is born – about 518 – and to that fire, just as in the Gospels, that shepherds came and cared for the boy whose mother, her work done, is dead."

Hope felt a heave of sentimental sorrow threaten his eyes at the vision of this brave young girl, on the bleak shore, dead in delivering her child. Nicholson himself was always moved by this story and felt affection that a man such as Hope could be so touched.

"Nearby there was an old hermit – Servanus, who became St. Servanus – and he took in the child and over the years the child became his dearest friend, his Myn Ghu or Mungo. You'll find a lot of churches dedicated to St. Mungo – it was Kentigern's pet name. We know the boy was pious and tender and determined. He went into the monastery. Like little Samuel it was his duty to trim the lamps of the monastery and keep them burning. We know he was envied and bullied by his fellow pupils and that even at that age he had the gift of healing – restoring a robin which had been cruelly killed by his fellow students."

"The gift of healing," Hope repeated, "and the gift of miracles?"

"Yes . . . and although he himself wanted the contemplative life, he was drawn out into the world and given the episcopate of Strathclyde, at Glasgow, when he was twenty-five years old. He fought Christ's battles there for ten years – it must have been like our brave missionaries now going into the wildest and most uncivilised parts of Africa – because the pagan King Morken was his enemy and envied the fame of Kentigern. Still, he let him alone. Kentigern's own example was powerful: he went always on foot, lived temperately, went into cold water each morning even in winter, lay at night in a stone coffin with ashes for a mattress, and yet he was a man of business, his parishes grew, churches were established the country over, and always in one hand he held a plain pontifical staff, in the other a psalter."

As Nicholson went on, telling him how King Morken died and his children swore to kill Kentigern who came south to Carlisle and then – learning of the paganism of the fell people – into the heartland of the lakes where he founded many churches, established missions, stood up to his neck in Derwent Water to read the Psalms and then went down into Wales . . . Hope saw himself, the ascetic, the missionary, the preacher, the proud foe of great kings, the saint of God, the healer, the miracle worker, the chastiser of his own flesh: and in some way he felt himself shriven. 'O my Lord,' he murmured inside his mind as the young chaplain unrolled more and more miracles and spiritual honours of St. Kentigern, 'make me free of evil thoughts, evil deeds, this wicked life . . .' and the murmurings of his internal prayers gradually absorbed more of his attention so that when Nicholson eventually stopped, he found his listener remote, unaware, it seemed, that the history was over.

Then like a gunshot in the lichen-silent church, Hope asked:

"How do you become like that? How do you do it?"

Nicholson smiled, opened his hands hopelessly: the gestures were a futile response. Hope's intent look was of a man who wanted to know, who wanted a true, rapid and helpful answer. Nicholson looked away as he replied:

"It is God's grace."

"And how do you earn that?"

"That is in God's hands."

"But there must be something you can do."

"Hold the faith and believe in Him."

"You could do that and get nothing," Hope replied. "If someone wanted to be *certain*: what would he do?"

"There is nothing certain in this life except our death."

"Everything is certain," Hope said. "Everything you do is certain. He knows what you are. Why does He let you do it?"

"He sent us His only begotten Son so that we could be free."

"How are we free? How are we free unless we fight for freedom and like as not break one or more of the Commandments?"

"God works in mysterious ways," said Nicholson, daunted by the increasing vehemence of the man.

"Why? Why does He have to be so mysterious? What about those of us who are not saints or healers or holy men or men like you or in any way find it easy to do His service – why is He so mysteriously absent from us? What did we do?"

"There is original sin . . ." Nicholson began.

"Before I was born? Is that it? And if I have no chance before I am born, what chance do I have when I live my life? No. He is not mysterious. He is very clear. Those who are with Him, those who are not, and those who know neither way and have to spend their lives in the torment of doubt."

"Is not that the condition of us all?"

"No. Most doubters either think they have grace or care for nothing but the day itself. I understand that. I too, at times . . ." Hope reined himself in, pulled back from the edge of his desperation, ". . . at times have been led to think that way."

"But you have come through," Nicholson affirmed. "You have sought Him again."

Hope was trembling and afraid that he might give too much away. He found it difficult to breathe. The dislocation happened and he saw this stout, handsomely dressed man, almost gasping in front of a pale-eyed, pale-faced clergyman, the two of them in the consecrated atmosphere of a church which could trace back its foundation on that spot through about thirteen hundred years. He saw the place claiming him – this was where he ought to be, to root himself and be rid of those burrs and thorns of fortune, the corruption in his mind and flesh, the evil impulses of his behaviour. He saw himself stripped bare, lashed, hair-shirted, meek before injustice, stoic in the face of punishment, as pure as a sanctified wafer at the altar.

"I am staying at the Queen's Head," he managed to say. "Please come and see me there later in the evening: we can talk further then."

He practically ran out of the church, confirming, to Nicholson, the burning urgency of the remorse which had smitten him. I was in the presence, Nicholson thought and was to repeat, of a most religious man.

Hope walked rapidly from the outlying church towards Keswick which now seemed like a net, dropped on him when he was unaware, leaving him pinioned . . .

Miss D'Arcy was with Mrs. Moore in the parlour in which he had so recently talked with the Colonel. That now seemed long ago: and before even that the far past of his proposal – like a holiday which disappears from all feelings in a mere day or so. George Wood conducted him to the parlour with reverence: high class was meeting great riches with talk of splicing these two irresistible institutions and it was happening in George Wood's back parlour.

Mrs. Moore soon abandoned her pretence as chaperon – encouraged by the unexpected surliness of Colonel Hope who seemed, to her and her ward, in a mood unlike any other they had found him in and unlike any they could previously have invented for him.

Amaryllis had put on a dress which had arrived only that noon from London. The ironing, altering, re-tailoring had all been done against the clock and pushed through only because of the tyranny of Miss D'Arcy. She had felt a shadow in the morning after her acceptance which, she wanted to tell Augustus, had been far too long delayed. He had pursued her – politely but unmistakably and through two weeks – at Grasmere. She had been playful. He had travelled back to Keswick with her even though it had not been his previous intention to do so. She had been flirtatious. He had taken her to most of the local beauty spots; arranged for cannon to be fired over the lake for their echoes and the quaint museum to be selectively open when they visited the place. She had dawdled. Luxuriating in the public attentions of such a suitor, she had drawn it out too much, perhaps, so that the final acceptance had come after the optimum moment. The news brought back by Colonel Moore after what they had all supposed was no more than the formal punctuation had almost panicked her.

Her new dress was the very latest fashion, vastly expensive, unmistakable plumage.

It was a walking dress. There was a straw gypsy hat, tied down with a rich half-lace handkerchief. The muslin gown was ornamented with knitted work crossing the shoulder. This was echoed at the bottom of the dress. The body was drawn around her rather large breasts, shawled with a light yellow sarsenet scarf. Lilac gloves, half-boots made of kid – she looked, as she sat rather apprehensively in the country inn parlour, as if she were waiting for Mr. Gainsborough.

Once again the gust of dislike unnerved him. He was taken over by it as he had been by the piety which had moved him so completely in St. Kentigern's.

"Would you like some tea?" she asked, timidly.

He shook his head. Even her timidity seemed to him a sham. Here were goods: enter a bidder: auction begins. He had no ability to sympathise with her.

But he must be careful. He needed her to play her game.

"Please," she asked, genuinely fearful now, it seemed to Hope, who relished the fact, "will you sit down and let me talk to you?"

"Of course." His reply was as light and harmless as a butterfly. She was unnerved again.

"My father," she began and paused, and Hope hardened his feelings even more. She was using the man's death to work at his sympathy. But he nodded sympathetically and, as he was about to sit down, he pressed his clawed hand sincerely on her shoulder. "My poor father would have been so proud of me today." Her eyes sought out his to divine what the real mood was: Hope jammed her gaze with a glazed and bland smile. "He would have admired you – greatly. As I do. He would have been so happy that his daughter – his only child –" the pause-calculating arrived once more and pushed up Hope's resistance another notch " – had accepted and had been so proud to accept the proposal of a man as distinguished as you, sir." She stressed '*accept*' and yet, as she went on, her sentences drifted over his head as the phrase 'as distinguished as you, sir' looped now pleasingly, now mockingly around his mind. Who was someone like him? Was he someone like himself? Was there someone like him? " . . . and of course he had to take the greatest possible care. I'm sure that – your name – everything about you – but the will says and quite emphatically and Colonel Moore –" an element of anger there " – is a man who will see it through to the letter."

Hope was charming. He glowed with a rich and handsome flush of compassion. He sighed her sighs and, in his gentlemanly manner, raised his eyes against the mocking Fates. But he would not budge.

She dare not ask him whether his proposal was thereby withdrawn. He did not answer this anxiety, feeling no cruelty in letting it dangle.

He left her after about half an hour and went down to the lake to see Burkett. He had intended to put in an hour's fishing but there was an impatience which he could not appease by the sport and so he turned aside into the fields which took him across towards Portinscale. Burkett had looked disappointed: ever since Grasmere when the trap the fisherman had sprung – and which had seemed so foolproof – had simply not worked, he had been a little abashed. Both he and his daughter seemed diminished: they had stepped out of their class, allowed themselves to imagine things and been very properly put in their place. Hope was aware of this and not unhappy about it.

The calm appearance of a saunter through the fells concealed immense upheaval. What was he to do ? Colonel Moore was not the man to betray what he interpreted as his duty and his trust. Amaryllis would not have the strength to overthrow the Will. And yet a way had to be found.

One of the reasons for his choice of this area was its proximity to the border with Scotland. Once over the Border, in the village of Gretna Green, a marriage could be legalised within half an hour – as George and Catherine would have done by now. A licence, a payment, a swift ceremony and it was sealed. His only real hope was to get Amaryllis to cross the Border with him.

First let her fear build up: let her come to believe that this prize, this catch of the season, would leave her not only as if she had never met him but somehow spoiled. For, so her fear would run, he had not been able to accept her trading character. He would stoke that up. But whether she would finally flee across the Border with him . . . Again like a fist slammed in his mind, his antipathy for her jarred him. No-one as protected as that would ever be so abandoned as to defy her guardian. And it would be hard. Bitterly, Hope thought, as he walked along the margin of the northern shore, ignoring the spectacular, breath-catching view down Derwent Water and deep into Borrowdale, she simply had no real love in her. None of that selfless sacrificial gambling of an entire life, present and future, which the deepest and wildest love could breed. How could he be expected to love anyone like that?

But a way had to be found to marry her. In his latest letter, Newton had again threatened to arrive. This time it would be even harder to put him off. Hope had written an evasive reply which he would frank and give to George Wood to post for him but he doubted that he could deter him for much longer. He was now frightened of what Newton might do. He had had time enough: Newton was right. He had been relatively easy to control in the north while it was clear that all the going rested with Hope but in London, Newton had been much more sinister. And it was Newton who had been the murderer. Hope flicked his head to one side as if dodging a blow: there had been no need to slaughter those two old booby servants; but Newton had ignored his protests. No witnesses. Throats slashed wide open. He could pay off Newton from a fraction of Amaryllis's dowry – he must see that Newton had no idea as to the real size of it – then he could be rid of him.

And then . . . as always, Hope could lull himself sooner or later into a mood of self-satisfaction at the prospect of a future rich, secure, free, and attainable . . .

By the time he came back to the hotel it was dark. Wood met him at the door. "There's a clergyman to see you, sir." By now Wood regarded himself as something between his esteemed guest's confidant and his protector. The Colonel, the Honourable, the Member of Parliament had given him more access to what nearly approached aristocratic companionship than he had ever enjoyed. Moreover the gentleman was scrupulous beyond praise. When he had come back from Grasmere the first thing he had done – despite George Wood's vehement protests – was to pay back the loan and bring his hotel bill up to the mark. No gentleman had ever behaved like that before. It was the sort of behaviour Wood expected only from his fellow tradesmen. That a gentleman should do it showed an uncommon understanding of the difficulties involved in running businesses with too much debt outstanding. Wood liked to think there was friendship in such unusually honourable behaviour: friendship shown in his willingness to frank Wood's letters, in his refusal to lay any blame on that slut Joanna, in his clear affection for 'Monkey-boy' (whom everybody had now nicknamed thus), in his little compliments to Mrs. Wood. For all these reasons, the unexpected visit of the clergyman was passed on with ponderous confidentiality.

This back parlour, Hope thought, as he entered it for the third time that day, is like a little theatre: Act I, Colonel Moore; Act II, Amaryllis; Act III –

"Reverend . . . Nicholson." Hope remembered he had invited the chaplain to call on him.

Rather embarrassed that he had waited . . . as if he had been hanging on . . . shy, although it could not be the surroundings, he very gratefully accepted the offer of claret, knew it to be a good one and said so . . . did not know quite what to say . . . he had found a peculiar empathy grow between himself and this handsome, strong, elegant, privileged man of the world when they had been in the little hill church of St. Kentigern's. At the same time he had sensed a tremor of – he did not know what.

Offering the meagre purse of local gossip, news from Buttermere, Nicholson spoke about Mr. Skelton's plans for building a large stone manor house in the area; dwelt longingly on the prospect of Miss Skelton and said something about the wrestling which included a mention of Mary of Buttermere and a young man from the north of the county walking thirty or forty miles just to see her and make his feelings known to her.

"And what are said to be her feelings about him?"

Nicholson, already a little confused by the claret, was flummoxed. How could he know – and about a matter of such small importance to such a man? But he did his best. Hope did not pursue the matter but saw that the claret was finished rapidly and went up to his room, his brain twisting around obstacles, snaking over the barricades of his common sense, scaling the walls of his strategies.

He wrote a decisive letter to Newton and then tore it up and burnt it. He scrawled several pages in his journal – without the usual reward of redemptive ease.

He punished himself through two bouts of his heaviest exercises, until his upper arms ached, his stomach muscles felt cramped, his legs watered, head dizzy. Cold water sluiced but did not cool him. Jealousy had pierced his side like a spear.

The next morning, shortly after dawn, he had his carriage and four in glittering readiness. The Monkey-boy, hastily found acceptable clothes, was up on the box, his dressing-case – the inherited, wealthy proof of his existence – set inside the coach like an ark, an altar, a talisman, a passport – and with Wood seeing them out onto the empty streets, he moved off through the cool, misty town, into Newlands Valley, over towards Buttermere, his heart hammering him on to get back to her before it was too late.

13

Home

As he drove down to Buttermere, he saw the valley covered, the lake covered, the village itself covered with a quilted pearl mist. He went into it like one entering a magic realm. The horses slowed to a delicately hooved walk down the steep track. The Monkey-boy looked solemn and frightened as the large coach drifted through the opaque swathes of mist like a cortège through a dream. Hope, now John–Augustus once more, held onto his patience for dear life. There would be nothing to see from Hause Point. He would go directly to the inn.

It was a ghostly village and the sounds of the horses and the coach, often so jangling and cheerful, were melancholy in the shrouded vale. To Hope, who had imagined sunburst and welcomes, the return of the prodigal and Mary in all her glory, it was an uneasy arrival.

Mary was not there. She had gone over into Lamplugh with her father and would not be back until the afternoon. For a moment, Hope thought of wheeling the carriage around and driving back out of the mist to the clear possibilities of Keswick. But he quenched his impatience and soon the Monkey-boy was importantly engaged in stabling the four horses while his master sat down to one of Mrs. Robinson's giant meals, inimitably served by Annie and watched over by Damson who would contribute the occasional 'Yes', 'No,' 'Good' or 'Day'.

Even in this quiet and easily lovable domesticity, Hope could not throw off the sense of unsettlement. It sat in his stomach like a small serpent, sucking at the intestines of his doubts, puffing its desperate poison into his blood. The force of it drew all his energy from the outside world and he spent the misty day in a collapse of inertia, as if utter immobility were the only way in which he could cope with the threatening fears inside him. The short stroll to the lake's edge tired him. He took brandy and laudanum and slept grimly in the main bedroom throughout the afternoon.

He woke to an evening clear of mist, bright sky, leaves glistening from an afternoon downpour which had not disturbed him. He heard Mary's voice.

The sound pierced his heart and he knew, finally, that this was his chance. His great sacrifice in leaving her might have been noble but it overestimated his capacity. The attempt to board Miss D'Arcy had been to fight the good fight on his previous self's behalf but he had no heart for it and besides, Moore's objections could be fatal. But that was not the point! Joanna, of course, was an irrelevance, as all such would ever be – he was certain of himself there. It was Nicholson's talk of St. Kentigern, he liked to think, which had settled it; there were men who had found their purpose and held to it, who had heard the voice as he heard the voice of Mary which dissolved his despair as surely as the night was dissolved by the day.

To enjoy more exquisitely the pleasure of encounter, he forced himself, in mock parody perhaps of the self-abasement, even flagellations of the monks and hermits, to take slow care with his dressing and shaving before restrainedly descending the few stairs to the parlour where she was and where she turned to greet him with undisguisable love.

Later that night they walked on the shore of the lake but across the other side from Burtness Wood: she would not go with him on the more familiar path which she had taken with Fenton.

Mary let the silence gather around her like a secret protector.

"I could never do it," she said, eventually. "It could never happen."

Hope was careful. He had attacked immediately and abruptly with the proposal. She needed time.

"Do you want it to happen?" he asked, very quietly. He had not yet mentioned the young man spoken of by the chaplain: she neither. He presumed then that it had been little more than rumour.

They were beside the lake on open ground just a few hundred yards from the village, walking critically apart: but his quiet question widened the gap still further.

"Why did you ask me?" she said.

He saw her already shadow-edged at the small distance, her hair stroked gleaming by silver moonlight, her bearing tense as if braced against assault.

"I am in love with you, Mary," he answered, gravely, and the words fell from his mouth with the unmistakable pulse of sincerity. "I want us to marry. I want us to spend the rest of our lives together."

"Here?"

"If you wish."

"And say I do wish?"

"Then here."

"What would you do here?" Her tone was harsher now, to his surprise. "There is nothing for you here. Fishing for a day with my father: spending a morning with Mr. Nicholson – but what else is there in this valley for you except fields and society you have been shunning – a society which would laugh if you married me."

"Let them laugh."

"It would be me they would laugh at."

"And your friends. Tom, Alice, your friends . . ."

"Oh . . ." The lightest brush of scorn now? He could not be certain. "They would think you a great catch. They would clap their hands red-raw and then wonder, like me, what we would do with ourselves after the wedding day." Her anger showed up his polished sincerity.

"I like it here, Mary, and it is for ourselves we must live."

"You like it here for a day or two, for a little adventure, for a glance at our famous Lakes. But you would never be able to tolerate the dullness of it. It can drive me half-mad of a winter and I have the inn and books and I've been born and raised here. You would want your friends and your parliament – what about that? You talk of politics at any provocation though sometimes I wonder which side you are on – now you were for Mr. Pitt, now for Mr. Fox; then again it seems to me, you want to give good riddance to all of them, and have a guillotine brought over from France. Unless you go into Society here which will always, always regard me in this valley as a curiosity, doubled again in curiousness through . . . marriage to you – unless you go into that Society your talk will be with farmers and strangers who have neither the education nor the inclination for such conversation."

"Are you saying we must leave here?"

"We?" She paused. "*We* . . . could not stay."

And now he paused: but finally – with an effort of which she was unaware – said: "Very well. We could go elsewhere. But," he went on, "I would like it to be a place such as this. If it could not be in this county, then up in the Highlands or in the hills of Wales where valleys still remain remote and innocent. I am tired, Mary."

"Is marriage such a rest?" Even in the dusk he caught her smile.

"For me it will be a rest from many things," he said. "So . . . ?"

She turned impatiently. They had reached the trees and she wanted to stay on the open shoreline. Past her he saw the moon-rippled lake, the black wall of Burtness, the deep purple of the fells, the sky hazy with rays of cloud quite white from the moon.

"You may . . ." Mary hesitated: why was she such a strong advocate against her own cause? Against what she wanted so much that she had to stand apart from him not only for propriety but to prevent the touching, the stroking, holding which she felt so powerfully drawn to. "You may have found this place such a haven after all your travels that you have confused me with the place and your feelings for the place with any feeling you have for me. That sometimes happens."

With such a truthful guide as this, he thought, surely he would be safe. She would prompt only his best instincts, encourage only his finer thoughts. This place and herself – were one: but they could find another place and she would make it their own.

"Why don't we go into Scotland tomorrow?" he asked urgently, "we could marry there instantly and have done with it. What you are talking about are problems in prospect. The longer we wait, the bigger they would grow. Let's be married, Mary, and throw *that* at them!"

"I'll not be carted off to Gretna Green and married over a blacksmith's forge!" she said, conclusively.

"So."

"Why do you want to?" Her confusion was as visible as a rising of ground mist. "To marry me? You scarcely know me."

"I have told you. I am in love with you."

"But how do you know?"

"You know."

"How? I think you must have been in love other times – several times, I'd suppose. What is it that says this is . . . ?"

"I know . . . do you?"

" . . . Perhaps . . . if it is that thing . . . but what if it is something else and you have gambled everything on that thing – and it is the wrong thing?"

The innocence of her persistence enthralled him. This was Arcadia. This was how life should be lived.

"The only certainty is Death," he replied, grandly. "For the rest we must have Faith."

That she too believed.

The light thickened between them, like desire made material, and yet, their eyes now fully accustomed to the dusk, they saw each other clearly. Perhaps the layer of darkness was useful cover, both romantic and practical: for this loving meeting beside the lake between innkeeper's daughter and great gentleman of the realm was Romance itself, and yet for Mary it was also a court where his cause could be tried and the darkness gave her courage.

"What would your . . . ?" she hesitated and then stopped.

"My family? You see, I can read your mind. My brother – who is all the family I care for –" he rather liked that phrase: had he read it somewhere? "*All* the family I care for," he repeated this, he hoped, implying fissures, wounds, ancient divisions and present battle lines, "would, without doubt, think you the best woman in the world. But, to be frank, I do not care what even he thinks. You must realise, Mary, whether you take me or reject me" – he paused – and then, regretting the element of manipulation which had slid through the forces of his sincere commitment, continued: "And please don't do that: take time, as much time as you want, but for God's sake, Mary, don't reject me . . ."

His plea was suddenly hoarse: even his accent changed, she noted, and for the first time she wanted to comfort him, to reassure him that yes, he was loved, she would take care of him.

"You would not be ashamed of me, then?" she said.

"How can you ask that?"

She summoned up her courage.

"You say you want to marry me and live here – which I would find impossible: or live in some remote place in Scotland which would be like this, like Buttermere. But you don't talk of the Town, or your estates, you don't talk of taking me –"

"Into Society? But it is Society I want to be rid of."

"I may at least want to sample it, before avoiding it," Mary said.

"So you shall. In time. When we have found our own place and built a nest there."

"A place such as this?"

"This place is you. Why do you pull away from it? You live through this place."

That too she believed.

"But you – your travels, your politics . . . what is there here for you?"

The question was distressed and Hope dug into himself.

"Mary." It was the first time he had begun a sentence with her name and the intention and the effect was that of a declaration: he stopped in the lush wet grass soaking his glossy boots; and she, after a hesitation, was forced to stop also.

"Mary," he repeated, "we know each other very little in some ways, although there are other ways in which I believe tonight we know each other better than we shall ever do. The deepest ways and there are deeper still where we will not fail." His tone was sensually undisguised and she blushed, unseen, in the semi-darkness. "But what you do not know of me is of me in the world you imagine I came from: the Army, London, Vienna, Egypt, the Indies, Parliament, my brother's estates, the courts of princelings across Europe – how can you know about my life there? I will tell you if you ask. I make this vow, Mary, that on my heart and honour I will answer truthfully any question you ask even if the answer might do me harm in your eyes. That I swear."

The urgency of his sincerity heated him to a sweat even though the late summer evening was cooling. "I want to cast all that off. You must understand the force of my wish – to be free of all that. I have lived more than half of my life and at last I can see what I value: liberty, simplicity, to be with one woman I truly love and to see a world grow up around herself and me. I have done with fine clothes, great routs, assemblies, pageants of lives lived in and for the public eyes. I want to be unwatched, hidden from the demands of others: all this I saw possible in you and in this place but most of all in you."

He took her hand, held it hard. "Mary – you are right that my ideas can seem to contradict themselves – why? Because inside my head there is a storm of opposition as I fight to pull away from the old and binding trade routes of a life laid down for me and beat my own tack across this ocean of existence. Once, in the wars, I was asked to be a spy – this was in Holland – it was where I got this small scar – and then I took on the name John. It was of course for reasons of security but that name and the fact of being plain John wherever I went in those perilous few weeks of spying gave me, most curiously, a sense of peace and liberation such as I had not felt before and feel now again, with you. Will you, please, Mary, know me as John, call me by that name in private, let me be the man I want to be – not what inheritance or fortune has made me but what I want to make of myself. You see, Mary, through you, I can be the man I most long to be. Oh God, Mary, help me to be that man!"

She was shaken by his vehemence and the strangeness of his confession.

Between them now were the fierce lines of sexual attraction: the thought pounced on Hope's mind that it was altogether mad that he, in the prime of his life and she in hers, both longing to experience a pleasure so common and trivial in one sense, so mysterious and wonderful in another, should stand not even touching, able and willing for custom and manners' sake to allow an uncrossable barrier to be made of the grassy interval between them. But he had to wait for the exact moment, like a navigator poised for the passage between the rocks. Not yet? A night lost, a night less, the night perhaps when all the chemistry in the body and the alchemy of the senses of past, present and future might have fused into the new free true man he wanted to be. But Mary was iron-locked in chastity and caution and he was self-sacrificed to his purpose, for these moments as chivalric as Sir Bedivere himself.

The slap of water on the shore was a mocking sound. Like skin slapping on skin.

The low rush of wind in the woods like the low groan of incomprehensible satisfaction.

The smell of wet earth the exhausted sigh of consummation.

And for a full minute they stood apart, each as tall as the other, immobile.

Then —

"I must go," she said. "I must go!"

He watched her walk swiftly and then begin to run along the lake, up the rise which would dip over into the village, and he breathed out a breath which seemed to take all strains and tensions whatsoever from his body.

He was home.

14

An Alternative

"My dear fellow!" Colonel Moore's greeting was angrily over-effusive. "We thought you'd abandoned us all in Keswick."

It was noon of the following day and Hope had just risen after a night tormented by some of his worst nightmares – bottomless black-walled glassy-surfaced prison cells dark and above him the loops of chain and ropes rat-mangled and he a white face struck wide-mouthed in horror as the vast machine turned to crush and break and slowly rip him sinew from bone, inescapable agony. He had cried out, hoping for Mary, but she had not come.

He looked at the fresh face, the well-powdered wig of the Colonel for a moment in complete non-recognition. Taking this as a calculated affront, the Colonel failed to conceal his anger.

Mary came in with tea. Hope had not seen her that morning and the sight of her resolved all his feeling: there was no mistaking it. She would heal him. He simply beamed at her: warily but surely she returned a smile. Colonel Moore was not amused by what he saw as a commonplace pothouse flirtation.

"Miss D'Arcy," he announced, cutting to the nerve with the accuracy of the furious, "has gone for a stroll to the lake with my wife. I am sure we would be welcomed most heartily: especially yourself, sir; Miss D'Arcy is quite shocked at your unannounced departure after so many weeks of being so very attentive, indeed the very model of a suitor."

Hope watched Mary but her hands did not tremble nor her face betray her. Yet he knew that the very blankness was a reaction. How well she hid it! Together they would be unstoppable – they could change the world. He would take her to America where they would conquer the new continent. Who could stand against them? Who would question them there? Or want to sniff out where they came from, hound down their antecedents, previous employments and convictions? She was not a way out of his old world but the means to find and conquer the new.

Mary left without returning his inexplicably jubilant glance.

Moore took the silence to be a reflection on his peremptory manner

– a characteristic which was a virtue in war, so he would say, but a liability in society.

"I met a very good man called Newton," Moore said.

Hope was fully alert.

"Do you know him?"

"Newton . . . ?"

"Solicitor from Chester . . . once in the same line of country as yourself – Parliament – got out because of the scoundrels he found he had to deal with – no offence, my dear fellow –" once again this phrase of endearment came as easily from the Colonel's lips as thick-gummed adhesive. "Your name came up – can't quite remember how – and – (forgive me, all this complication about D'Arcy's will but I do feel bound by it, you know, I really do) – well, the long and the short of it was I said – so you know Colonel Hope, then? Yes, he answered, though Hope may not remember me. What sort of fellow would you describe him as? I took the liberty – forgive me – of asking – his appearance, his manner – that sort of thing. Well – though I should not be surprised – he drew you to a 'T' – not a bit out of place: you were exactly as I see you before me now."

"I'm relieved to hear it."

"No offence intended – this will, a ball and chain, you know."

Hope nodded and wished he could order a brandy but did not want to bring Mary back into the room. He took out his pipe for an uncharacteristic morning smoke and used the action to let Moore stew. It was little less than spying on him! He worked his pipe into the pouch in a clear demonstration of dissatisfaction.

Moore contained himself against saying more in this matter. He was still stinging from Hope's arrogant treatment of him in Keswick. Even this unsuspected and very convenient reference from the man Newton had not quite damped his suspicions. Two letters sent off that morning should settle the matter: they did not follow the precise request of the will but responded to its spirit. Even more importantly, they responded to the new and imperious impatience of Amaryllis who had made it quite clear that she was not going to let a great match go by for the sake of parchment and protocol.

"I think we had better join the ladies," Hope said, after the pause, and by his tone managed to make Colonel Moore feel that he, Moore, ought not to have been neglecting them. Again Moore felt faulted by this animal whose spoor puzzled him.

He kept Moore waiting further while he sought out the kitchen to find Mary there with her mother, as startled to see him as if Jove himself had dropped into her humble cavern.

"Mary," he said. Her back was to him. "Mary," he repeated with no impatience and softly.

She darted round to look at him, her eyes condemning.

"This can all be explained and it has no bearing at all on what I said last night. You will agree with me when I tell you, as I will, later. I have known this man Moore for some time – since my Army days – and he has pestered me with his ward ever since I arrived in the district. It would be impolite of me not to give the poor girl the time of day, but that is all: good morning, Mrs. Robinson."

The mother all but bobbed a curtsy, entirely flummoxed by his direct, though to her gnomic, address to her silent daughter. He nodded and went out into a grey dry morning, the lake, slate as the clouds.

"Miss D'Arcy – what a pleasure!"

"Colonel Hope."

"And Mrs. Moore! Well now: what a fine morning it is."

That Irish twang again, thought Moore: affectation!

And both women, he noted, sorely, paddled about like happy little skiffs on a pond.

Miss D'Arcy soon engineered their isolation: and again Colonel Moore saw how adeptly he was being out-manoeuvred: he took out his anger on his wife's selection of dress – "Unaccountably ill-chosen for such a primitive spot as this."

Hope decided to guide Amaryllis – now on his arm and leaning towards him confidentially although no confidences had as yet passed between them – towards the spot on which he had talked so momentously with Mary the previous night. Partly because he wanted to revisit the place – as he wanted to revisit Hause Point – to renew his spirit, possibly in some pagan awareness yet remaining in such a character as he, on the spot where something so vital had passed; partly out of a cruel perversity and as a harsh though unperceived snub to the wealthy young ward.

She made, he observed dourly, all the expected Tourist remarks on the lake itself, the woods, the 'pretty rustic charm' of the damp, insanitary, small, overcrowded cottages. Hope was now so affianced to the place that he could take it for granted: it was and would be *his*:

effusions only over-egged it. Nothing needed to be talked about in such artful ways. Here were peace, fish, company, Mary and safety. "A cuckoo!" Amaryllis remarked, pausing to hear the effect and by her pose create one. Hope felt a grimness clamp inside him.

She picked up his disapproval, burnt off her superficial nervousness, kept his arm but leaned away from him now, erect in herself: and began to play her hand.

"I understand your anger," she said, "no – I have thought about this – I have thought about little else since we parted.

"I am sorry – truly – that you were asked to submit to such a humiliation. I did not fully realise – until I reflected on it – how impossible your position was. How intolerable! I had – of course –" she looked away and blushed, "never invoked the will until now. I had no way of anticipating its effect. But I ought to have understood. I am to blame for lacking the imagination to understand your feelings. And believe me, sir, I have blamed myself a very great deal over the past few hours."

Hope was persuaded. She had never spoken as convincingly. Moreover the energy she brought to her defence was far richer than any she had shown so far. It gave her fashionable prettiness a flash of attractive beauty: her body was tense as she spoke and Hope was interested to see that the rather large breasts rose supply and temptingly as she forced through her argument. He drew her to him and pressed her arm in affectionate forgiveness. She stopped, stood back half a pace and looked straight at him. Behind her the lake, the woods, the fells: her face clear in the morning light.

"I will make you a good wife – if you will still have me."

Her directness left him no escape. Besides, sincere desperation always moved him – and he caught a true whiff of it here. He liked her better than he had ever before liked her and, as often happened to him when he was emotionally locked in, the words which came were meant to serve the moment which was all his world.

"Nothing has changed," he said.

"Despite the matter of the letters?"

"That will be forgotten in a week."

"And we will marry here." She looked around and pointed out the tiny Buttermere Church which stood like a toy on a promontory of rock.

"Keswick," said Hope thoughtfully, "has more . . ." He left the sentiment unexpressed, describing it in tone and gesture. Amaryllis nodded, and understood.

Colonel Moore was not particularly happy to see them eventually stroll back towards the Fish in such obvious accord.

They took tea in the parlour: Annie waited on them.

"Isn't this where the Maid of Buttermere lives?" Mrs. Moore was a great sightseer.

"She's gone off wi' t' sheep," Annie said, miraculously finding the table with the tray unslopped. "On t' fell tops."

"A shepherdess," said Amaryllis. "How classical!"

"I saw her earlier, didn't I, Colonel?" Moore prodded out his question.

"You did."

"Frankly, I can't see what the excitement is about."

"I'm told she's wonderfully graceful," said Mrs. Moore. "And her hair – they have written poems about her hair."

"Her hair," repeated Moore flatly. "Didn't notice the hair."

"She is very famous," said Amaryllis, sipping or rather lapping up the tea rather smugly, Hope thought: and he waited to deflect what threatened to be a criticism. "I envy her," Amaryllis continued, surprising and pleasing Hope. "I would like poets to write about my hair. Will your friend Mr. Coleridge do that?" she asked Moore, who ignored the question.

"There is no comparison," Moore announced, stiffly, "between a lady such as yourself and a village girl who happens to catch the eye of one or two adventurers and writers."

Hope smiled. "You suggest that Great Beauty has to be bred?"

"Of course."

"As great intelligence, wit, charm –?"

"Everything but brute force," said Moore, disliking the catechising tendency of this discussion. "The lower orders cannot be expected to enjoy these qualities. Their lives don't allow it. On the whole you will find that they are small, ugly, ignorant, smelly and coarse: but as the Bishop of Llandaff said in his great sermon, that is God's wisdom in creating both the Rich and the Poor. If they did not have their place, we would not know ours."

It was then that Hope decided he would after all re-enter the lists for Amaryllis. Until that moment he had been aware of a vague benign feeling, like a wispy ungathered gauze in his mind, which would bring to an easy resolution the difficulty of his now inconvenient attachment to Amaryllis. He would have found a way to let her go. That was banished. His riposte to Moore would be to take his ward to the brink.

"God's wisdom," he said, "is truly beyond our understanding."

"I never question it, sir," Moore replied in a very military manner.

"Should we seek to comprehend it?"

"Only if we are professional churchmen. The rest of us are there to go along."

"And yet," Hope stirred his tea unnecessarily and a genuine thoughtfulness replaced the mild baiting which had left Colonel Moore ruffled, "is that the God of the New Testament, the Father of Jesus Christ? Or is God the Jehovah, the Old Testament God, the Terrible God, who makes such great divides in society, who allows such vast injustices and crimes and violent upheavals – wars, earthquakes, floods, slaughters, famines, plagues – is He the God for our times? Or do we not rather want the gentle Saviour from the village of Galilee – perhaps a village a little like this, Colonel – who with His brothers and friends – common people, Colonel, men such as you would find today in the valleys around here – set out to change the world – what boldness! – to change human nature itself from the Old Jehovah's cruel laws to the Sermon on the Mount, to the teachings of the parables, to turning the other cheek and loving thy neighbour – even a common neighbour? I can think of few in the New Testament – Caiphas perhaps? – who are in our terms well-connected – but is it not through the views and hopes of these common Apostles that we should comprehend and reach out to Him?"

Hope's unselfconscious rumination confounded the company to silence. Moore knew that he was being got at again and was now without limit or quarter the enemy of this overwhelming chameleon, who could fill the parlour with his presence. Mrs. Moore was rather afraid of deep religious talk unless delivered from a pulpit by a vicar and on a Sunday. Amaryllis was quite touched by what Hope said. She had not been impressed by his teasing of her guardian on the subject of 'The Poor': she could not understand why Hope, who benefited so obviously from the system and enjoyed those benefits so plainly, would attempt such drawing-room republicanism. His religious concern, though, she sensed was much more true and she absorbed it carefully as part of her growing intelligence on the man.

"Too much talk of religion spoils it," Moore offered, finally and rather sulkily.

Mrs. Moore nodded.

Hope looked to Amaryllis.

"I see how we ought to live our lives," she began, rather timidly but obedient to Hope's unspoken prompt, "but sometimes I fail to see how we can carry out laws made for such a different people at such a different time."

"That is a very sound comment," said Hope, and he slapped his knee in applause. "Very sound."

"I would love to see, and study, different peoples," she went on, cleverly changing the prickly subject under cover of his encouragement, "the Lakes are the most beautiful place in England, but I would love to go abroad."

Hope noted the tactic and approved of it. He had jolted them enough with his religion. Such people would never understand about Faith; they had never needed it as he had, he thought, never longed for it as he had. They were damned, as the Ranters would say: and he? He was one who would be forgiven unto the seven and seventieth time because the Lord dwelt within him. This realisation – which came to him very rarely – made him glow with great good feeling and he looked on Amaryllis more kindly than ever he had done. She was, he observed, a very handsome young woman, richly dressed – he could gloat over her clothes, the frills, the laces, the hidden folds leading to hidden pleasures – and now talking most sensibly as well-bred young women should.

"Travel!" he interjected. He was suddenly and joyfully blinded by an idea which solved everything – everything! "Yes." He turned his full attention on Amaryllis and – as at Grasmere when he had pursued her through the two weeks of lingering walks, sudden picnics and excursions to Windermere to row under the moon – she felt his embracing force and praised her determination to follow him into Buttermere and seek him out. For she had almost lost him. Colonel Moore would never again be the petted and applauded elder.

"I have travelled so little," she said, her direct look inviting him to take her around the world.

"Yes," he murmured, still so gripped by his idea – almost a revelation – that for a moment he was disconnected: he 'saw' them all there – four bodies in that space – that small space – and wondered who they were, what they were doing there and knew fatalistically that they would return to darkness so soon – two women, two men – all of them would be gone and those crude walls would still be standing.

"Travel is impossible." Colonel Moore's gunshot re-entry into the conversation called him slowly back to himself. "The French are simply using the time to re-group. This treaty's no peace treaty at all: it's a cessation of hostilities, no more." He looked to Hope for approval, sensing from Amaryllis's behaviour that he had better make his own peace and his own treaty.

"I don't think so," Hope replied, "though I have heard that phrase used – and used by men of the world such as yourself. But I would guess that the Frenchman wants peace every bit as much as the Englishman. And we can't be over-run, you see, being an island. Bonaparte's an army man, Moore – you appreciate that – we're a naval nation" – he liked the sound of that, would use it again – "as our host in this inn would tell you if you afforded him the opportunity." Moore was put out by this reference to a common landlord: once again this unconventional Honourable was exercising some fashionable snobbery over him and he resented it.

"I fail to see what an innkeeper has to do with our conversation," he said, as he thought restraining himself.

"Mr. Robinson is a most unusual innkeeper."

"Nevertheless," said Moore. And that was his sentence.

"He illustrates," Hope continued, now buoyantly recovered and returned to the company – his great new idea safely tucked away to be returned to at leisure – "the deep affection the English have for their navy and for seamanship. We are an island floating off Europe and thank God for it! The sea is our passage and our defence. If we forget that, then we are lost – but, as Joseph Robinson will tell you, we do not forget that: we are a nation of sailors, watermen, fishermen, navigators; we live on the sea, we have our independence because of the sea and Bonaparte will never be able to overcome that."

"The navy's full of traitors." Moore was flustered, though again he did not quite know why. What had led to the strange paean to the sea? "Look at what they did at Spithead and the Nore. Look at that gang of thieves and murderers at Tilbury – republicans, rebels, traitors, putting a blockade on this country, on their own nation in a time of war! The navy has done well, sir, but don't tell me to admire them. They are rebels. They want to overthrow our King and

Constitution. They are scum and as soon as we're done with them we should hang the lot. Except that hanging's too good for them!"

"I was talking of travel," said Amaryllis, firmly. She gave her guardian a sweet and steely look. Her moment of return was not going to be sabotaged by such man's talk.

"And I was saying," said Hope, unfailingly cheered up by his knack of being able to tip Colonel Moore into a spin of fury, "that the Peace gives you the opportunity. For of course you are far younger than I" – his smile was almost roguish, to Moore's disgust – and Amaryllis felt a tingle of blushing pleasure in the complex flattery she was receiving, "your youth has been confined by war whereas that same war released me across Europe and even into the East. While before it, travel was my obsession. I felt – and still feel – that there could be no better life than to see as much of this glorious globe as possible."

"It's very tiring, is it not?" Mrs. Moore had been waiting for a chance to make a contribution for such a long time and it was very disappointing to see what little effect her remark had.

"I would travel," said Hope. "I would follow in the footsteps of my old routes – you would be intrigued by those – and then – more exciting still – we could find new places to go where neither of us had been . . ."

Amaryllis smiled fully with pleasure and relief. So he was talking openly of their being together, travelling together, living their life together! Her mission had been successful. She clapped her hands as if in appreciation merely of what Hope was saying.

"There are some places too romantic even to think of," she said. "The Old Silk Road to Samarkand: we would never be able to go there, would we?"

"That would not be travel," Hope said, "that would be adventure. That would call for boldness and endurance, for such strength and will as might not be your concern."

"Perhaps we –" a pause, a delicate, confidential, triumphant pause on those two binding letters, "could build up towards that?"

"Surely. And meanwhile – the Rhine, the Alps, the Dolomites, Tuscany, Athens, the Nile . . ."

"Europe will be in flames again by Christmas," said Moore.

"Then let us go as soon as possible," said Hope, gaily, "let us take the bird out of its cage and release it into the gardens of the world."

He was in full swing now and none of them could resist him. Even

Moore had his vanity stroked and was brought into a good humour so that by the time they left – Hope having explained (to Amaryllis's further comfort) that he was looking for some land in Buttermere – all was for the best with the best of all possible men. He waved them on their way and secured a place for the Monkey-boy up beside the driver. The boy was carrying a confidential note to Newton.

Hope took his favourite stroll down to the lake. He stationed himself in a position which would enable him to see Mary coming down from the meadows he was beginning to know well. He would soon unravel her, he thought.

This new amazing idea – this revelation – now slid out from under a stone and basked in the late afternoon sunlight of his mind. It would solve everything. Would it be possible to secure Miss D'Arcy abroad and Mary at home: both? Could it be managed? Why not?

He searched for Mary for the rest of the day but she was not to be found. It was as if the valley had swallowed her up. He would give her time.

15

Newton

Hope often found that his lies became reality. There were times indeed when he consciously used a lie in order to trigger off a reality. He would often boast, when young, of some athletic feat which he had not done and then find, quite soon afterwards, that he would indeed accomplish it: it was as if the boast cleared away an obstacle. Spurred on by this, he would lie about achievements and use the lie as a goad, a talisman, an objective or as all of these as he made his shadowy way through a life which had always lunged towards glimmerings of light without greatly discerning their source or strength: thus he had been scorched as often as he had been rewarded.

He had told Amaryllis that he was staying on in Buttermere to consider buying some land. When he woke up the next morning to discover Mary already gone and her parents genuinely ignorant as to which pasture she had taken the flock, he set off, on horseback, to look out Mr. Skelton or the chaplain and find out about land prices and prospects in the neighbourhood.

Mary's absence impressed but did not perturb him. He understood it and admired even more both the sensitivity and the depth of her feeling. Her value grew. For he, more than most men, knew of the alluring, tantalising, cruel chasm between their appointed stations in the hierarchy of British humankind, 1802. His kind were more likely to take a Hottentot for a wife than an English village woman. Moore had expressed the general views of the time and indeed in some respects his tongue had been gelded to politeness by the female company. Mary, in the world of Hope, was an invisible labourer, a plaything or a whore. By treating her as an equal, and as a possible wife, he had strained her credulity and he appreciated her qualms. And yet he knew, as he reached Hause Point, stayed his horse, and looked around slowly like a chieftain over his lands, that she was bound to him: in that certainty he glowed and the embering of his better self found its only and, he suspected, final, life.

*

Mary watched him ride up the valley, saw him linger at Hause Point and wondered again what the attraction of that particular spot had for him.

"Why do you think he goes there?"

"Does he?" Kitty was not looking.

"I've seen him sneak off there at all sorts of times – he thinks nobody notices —"

"What does he do there?" Kitty asked.

"Just stands: once I fancy I saw him kneeling – Tom said *he* had seen him kneeling."

"Is he a man for religion?"

"He talks about it a lot."

"Is he?"

" . . . I believe he is," Mary said, after thought. "*That* I believe he is."

As her young friend glanced away, Kitty looked at her closely. She knew that the children in the valley would pretend she was a witch as Kitty herself, when a child, had teased old women and run from their mild curses. But now she longed for the powers witches were credited with: she wanted to change herself into a swallow and dip beside the man on horseback at Hause Point, to study his face when unregarded. She wanted to change herself into goose down and be in his pillow at night so that any secrets would be known to her. She wanted to change herself into a morsel of food to be swallowed and pass by the man's heart so that she could discern whether its beat were true or false. She wanted to be a mendicant confessor who would draw him down from the great stallion and ease him of all his secret mind. Or she would wind magical silk around Mary and leave her as she was – hunched over her knees, fixed on the man now riding slowly away from her – leave her cocooned until time had revealed his true purposes.

But Mary was in love with him. Kitty knew that and it chilled her.

"Why am I so doubting, Kitty?" Mary asked, not wanting an answer, using her friend as a staunch against the insanity of talking aloud alone. "I've had not one moment's quiet since he came back." Even to Kitty, she dared not use the words 'proposed marriage' – perhaps because to say them would be to take the luck off them. "But what should he want with me? I can see that he would want to have some sport – that's what you expect – I've had plenty of that to cope with. Why isn't it that? What possible gain can he enjoy from . . ." (marrying: unsaid) " . . . me?"

"I liked that man from the north," Kitty said, crooning into the silence. "I came down from the wood to watch him last time he was here. I liked him. You like him."

"Yes."

"Marry him, Mary: marry him. Time you were married." Kitty rocked on her haunches, the empty pipe clenched at one side of her mouth, her body compensating in intensity for what she feared was a lack of force of will to influence her troubled young friend who was clearly in danger. "Marry *him.*"

"I don't love him," Mary said and failed to add that she had written a letter, that morning, asking him not to come again.

It had been an impulsive gesture but one she did not regret. Although she did not want to see Hope until things had settled in her mind after the unmistakable significance of Miss D'Arcy's arrival, still she was sure enough to know that she did not love Harrison. She would not have him wasting his time and thoughts on her. Nor would it have occurred to her to have kept him going as a fallback. He had to be told as soon as it became certain to herself that she would never marry him.

As she had addressed the letter, she had thought of Mr. Fenton, who lived quite near to Harrison, and she had written him a letter too. His wisdom was badly needed. She still had that letter with her: she had held it back and the boy had gone to Keswick without it. And as the morning drew on, she knew she would not send it. It was beyond her old teacher and, in an angry flash of self-awareness, she knew she was glad it was beyond his schoolroom precepts. He had used her for a sport of his own. And expected her humble thanks! She would tear up that letter . . .

*

Hope was delighted to fall in with the Reverend Nicholson. On an empty sunny road, on such a glorious day, he was just in the mood for amiable discourse. He got down from his horse, greeted the clergyman with flattering familiarity and walked on with him towards his church at Lorton.

"Is Mr. Skelton still in these parts?"

Nicholson was pleased to tell him that he was, and with his daughter – now, Nicholson was relieved to understand, no longer under consideration by this dashing and ornamental stranger – and after he had shown off his church, he would escort the Colonel to the small hotel where the Skeltons would surely be found at midday.

Hope did not want to go inside the church. It was unusual for him not to plunge into such a place but an instinct made him defer that pleasure until a later time. Nicholson, a little nonplussed, wandered rather aimlessly around the graves pointing out the longevity of some of the natives: a longevity, Hope remarked smilingly, matched and balanced by the brevity of the lives of other, less fortunate natives.

"It appears that in Lorton," he said, "if you reach the age of three, you have a fair chance of lasting until eighty-three. Achieving that first number, though, seems to be beyond most of your parishioners."

The good Reverend Nicholson, given his cue, spoke movingly on the poverty and ignorance in the district, the lack of medicines, of proper food in the shank of winter, of superstitious and damaging customs . . . Usually Hope would have joined in all this with great vim – it was a theme on which he could be eloquent – but again, he was disinclined: a question had been gathering in his mind throughout the walk with Nicholson and now it burst out.

"How long would it take to get a special wedding licence?" he asked. "What is the fastest you could do it?"

The questions surprised him but as he asked them he felt purged and resolute. Nicholson was amazed: he stood rigidly still and for the rest of his life retailed and retold this moment with awe. Hope smiled encouragingly at the scraggy, nervous, black-crow figure, a signpost among the gravestones; the hills were clear, sharp against the sky; across the fields, men, women and beasts moved in slow and ancient patterns; his feet felt clamped to a steady earth.

Nicholson's restrained politeness fought hard against his galloping curiosity.

"Two weeks," he answered, eventually. "That is, here – or no, a little more. But – if you went to Whitehaven – if you were to apply through Whitehaven –" he paused to allow the vision and power of one of the great ports of England to infiltrate Hope's consciousness: Nicholson was proud of Whitehaven's commercial eminence; the multitude of ships, the merchants, noise, money, crowds excited in him an inclination to proxy boastfulness which the Lakes could never do; in Whitehaven, Nicholson thought, lay the future of the world. Miss Skelton detested it.

"White – haven . . ." Hope encouraged him by repeating the town's name in two parts: as he pronounced them, a thrill of harmony went through him – what words!

"Maybe even a week," Nicholson risked.

Hope nodded and turned away to conceal the thrash of feeling which was resolving itself towards irresistible action.

He fingered the coins in his pockets. Three guineas and a little change. He owed George Wood a fair sum: there would be a bill to pay at the Fish – he would defer that; his bill at Grasmere was still outstanding – a quick return there might winkle another fifty pounds from Mr. Crump, but Crump was a card to be played carefully; he would have to take out a note against someone very soon. Moore? That would be a good game. Moore would be unable to refuse. The thought cheered him up even further. When he turned around it was with the three guineas in his open hand.

"Take these for the poor of the parish," he said to Nicholson, "to do with as you decide."

Nicholson's gratitude added even further to Hope's rising stock of benevolence and by the time he and the chaplain turned into the small hotel he was ripe as a falling plum with every Christian virtue: eager, aggressive to burst out.

To Miss Skelton's dismay, this manifested itself in a playful but relentless cataloguing of the glories and benefits of being the wife of a local clergyman. Nicholson wriggled in embarrassment but yet, Hope knew, he wanted the pleasure of the implied possibility to go on even when the pain of the young woman's rebuking and dismissive manner was most acute. When Hope finally stepped outside with Mr. Skelton to enjoy a smoke, they left an exasperated Miss Skelton – who, over the next few days, re-wrote the meeting in terms of Hope trying to make her jealous, or test her – and a critically expectant, rather forlorn young Nicholson who, over the next few days, re-wove those minutes into endless lengths of sweetest, faintest possibilities.

"Land in these valleys," said Mr. Skelton, "is not as cheap as you might think for such a remote spot. Most of it is owned by the nobility – and you yourself, sir, need no lessons in how sacred the land is to our aristocracy. Has there been a more tenacious group in the history of the world? In these parts we have families – the Lowthers are a good example – who collected the core of their property a hundred and fifty years before the Conquest and still hold it – and have built on it ever since. And so unless – as you will know from your own estates – unless you have a special entrée – land is unobtainable. But that is what we expect. What makes it more difficult here is that some of the farmers have freehold tenure. They claim antique rights and over the common land too: it's been the devil's job enclosing some of these parts, I can tell you."

A devil's job, Hope suddenly thought, with a jab of dislike, that you would be very used to. He saw Skelton, with his careful country clothes, he remembered his disdain for the servants in the hotel, and once more Hope's better feelings rose up from vaults to which they had been so long confined and took strength from the sense of goodness which surged through him. A goodness which embraced not only Christian charity but also radical politics and a personal itch to dent pomp and mock snobbery. It was a dizzy draught which, he knew again as at Hause Point, came from Mary. She sprang some vital element from his true character.

"They insist on holding onto their rights, do they?" Hope asked.

"They can be very obstinate," said Skelton.

"Don't you know how to break them?"

"You have to get up very early in the morning," said Skelton, thoughtfully, trying to imply that he did indeed get up very early in the morning and also there was more to this than could be discussed casually over a puff of tobacco: deep manoeuvres were under way – and of course under control.

"The trick, I suppose," said Hope, "is to take all the common land from them first. That should ruin their economy and go some way towards breaking their spirit."

"Exactly." Skelton nodded approvingly at this sensible insight.

"And then if you're lucky they will be forced to sell."

"That is how I came upon the lands I have further up the valley. Grand old family, the Forsters, been there for ages – simply couldn't survive. Very pious and decent people. But they just had to sell."

"Sell or starve . . ."

"I'm afraid so. The Law of Life, Colonel . . ."

"Were there many bidders?"

Skelton tapped his nose conspiratorially and emitted a deeply clubbable hiccup of laughter.

"So we must all be on the lookout for starving farmers?"

"No need, sir." Skelton was totally unaware of any hidden meaning in Hope's blandly delivered question. "I myself have rather over-bought and unlike your peers, I am not averse to selling the odd acre."

Hope put in a first bid there and then but insisted that business prevented him from staying to drink to it. After a brief exchange with Miss Skelton he left, accompanied for the first mile by Nicholson, whose company he liked increasingly.

"A week, then, for a licence," he said, as he got on his horse.

"In Whitehaven," Nicholson confirmed. "Only in Whitehaven."

Hope left him standing in the middle of the country road, gazing out after his new friend as if Hope were a vessel carrying with him all his fortune and pushing out into the wide ocean from the golden port of Whitehaven.

*

Mary had sought out Alice to confide in her but when she finally manoeuvred her into a solitary space – the two of them knitting with automatic, unregarded energy – she felt herself lost for words. The feelings simply were too difficult to express without appearing vain or coquettish or puzzled and confused in a way that would seem silly.

But Alice knew Mary like a twin. She was fully aware of the effect of the intrusion of Hope. She had not spied but she had seen. For a while she was content to work largely in silence, with the occasional marketing of village chat, around them the pleasant mull of sheep and goats, the jangle of a bell, the light bark of a dog as it trimmed a stray back into the loose group, the day now balmy, chiffon clouds, a party of Lake Tourists walking loudly down towards the lake.

"Is that Harrison coming courting you, then?"

Mary shook her head and, with relief, recognised how acute was Alice's perception of what was going on.

"Never again?"

"No."

"So what did this Colonel say to you?"

Perhaps it was Alice's pregnant ballast which gave her such solid ease: Mary envied it.

"He . . ."

"No!" Alice even stopped knitting. "Marry?"

Mary pressed her eyes shut and nodded.

Alice allowed a few moments of deeply respectful silence.

"Marry?"

"Yes."

"Oh – Mary."

She stood up, came across and threw her arms around the neck of her friend which gave Mary, at last, the chance to burst into tears. Alice was always easily infected by strong emotion and she too flowed with tears – of delight, of astonishment, of congratulation for her friend who seemed likely to be hoisted from this anonymous rural drudgery into the Great World of carriages and visiting cards, new silk gowns and your own servants.

"You deserve it, Mary," she said, and then repeated as if it could be a benediction, "you deserve it, you deserve it . . ."

Mary shook her head violently, checked her tears, looked at Alice and then, instead of speaking, set off crying again to see her friend's large potato face so funny-moved and awash with pleasure at her anticipated good fortune.

When she repossessed her feelings, she said "But *should* I . . . ?"

Alice was startled: made no reply.

"Should I?" Mary persisted, drying her cheeks, immeasurably calmer for that cataract of tears, "*should* I – do it?"

Alice was unable to offer a reply. She knew Mary well and had accepted immediately that there would be no question either of her making an error or of her trading favours for false promises. And so what on earth could be the objection to this marvellous gift of fortune?

"It's a funny thing to say, Alice, but I can't really work out what sort of man he is."

The hard-thought-on and strictly protected secret, the essence of her insecurity, was presented to Alice for examination.

"Everybody here will be very pleased," Alice said, slowly, whispering as if the sheep and goats and dogs might overhear and start the rush of gossip. A little formality entered into Alice's speech and Mary was uncomfortably conscious of a change of tone in her best friend's attentions. She shook her head as if to shake off a web.

"Please don't tell anyone. Please."

"I won't," said Alice, her fingers quickly and tightly crossed.

"I saw that! No crossed fingers. Swear."

"I can't swear."

"You have to." Mary was rarely grim and her severity daunted

Alice. "Swear on this." She passed Alice a copy of *The Rape of the Lock* – one of the several books given her by Mr. Fenton, a neat, small copy, easy to carry about. Alice drew back as if it were a bible blessed in Jerusalem itself.

"Swear!"

Mary was on her feet now and memories of rare childhood battles when, overtaxed and desperate, Mary had finally turned on tormentors with unlicensed violence suddenly pricked their images onto Alice's thoughts and she stretched out a hand –

"Both hands!"

– both hands and –

"Swear."

"I swear."

"And may God strike you deaf and dumb, Alice, if you break this vow. Now spit!"

Rather gratefully, Alice spat.

Mary's anger was removed as easily as a cape and she sat down quite cosily with her knitting. Alice said nothing for a few moments for the sake of her dignity but she could not contain herself for long –

"Where will you be married?"

"This is all sworn?"

"Yes."

"He wanted to go off to Gretna Green right away," said Mary, gaily, testing her own reaction against that of her friend.

"Oh, Mary!"

"Should I have done?"

"Oh, Mary!" The reproachful tone allowed for no qualification. "You didn't say no?"

"I did."

"Oh, Mary!" Yet another and different peal on those three syllables was rung out, this time in anguish.

"In fact I haven't yet said I would marry him."

"Mary!" Now the name sounded like an alarm.

"For all I know he may have given up and gone away. There are plenty more fish in the lake."

"But if he wants to marry you," said Alice, slowly but shrewdly, "he must have thought about it a great lot. He won't blame you for being cautious. That'll just stoke him up. He'll be back."

Mary knew, in a half-smug, half-mad, love-lost way, based on no material evidence, that he would indeed be back. And yet at times she wished him gone for good.

"Do I want him back?" she asked, quietly, stubbornly, as if to herself.

But Alice was done with mystery and awe.

"You must do! Don't be silly! Think of everything he'll give you. Think of all the things you'll do. Oh – Mary – if only I weren't carrying, then maybe you would take me with you for a little bit. I could be your maid. I should love it!"

Mary's confusion was stirred even more deeply: but to attempt to untie the knots in Alice's statement would be fruitless. She did not want to 'think of all he'd give her', or think of thinking of that and least of all be thought to be thinking that: she shrank from such possibilities of what would be slander and yet they were unavoidable. She realised with a weary depression that the burden of 'appearing' in public at the inn would be light compared with the burden of being thought of as a calculating fortune hunter. Was 'John' sufficiently sensitive to comprehend that? She smiled to herself, seeing as sharply as Alice before her the questing dimpled smile of the man and knew it would most likely be beyond him. And Alice her maid!

"I could never let you be my maid!"

"I should be good at it."

"Don't pretend to be put out, Alice. You know very well what I mean."

"It would get me out of Buttermere for a while. Think of that."

"What would Tom say?" It was a considerable satisfaction for Mary, at long last, to find the opportunity and the nerve to tease her friend about her marriage: until this moment it had lain between them a little like the sword between the virtuous knight and his sleeping lady.

"He would miss me," Alice replied eventually, "but," she paused, "I could nag him into it. I'm sure of that." She nodded owly wise to her friend and gave her summation of her experience of marriage: "Nagging has its place. Besides, he would know I'd want to be with you. I don't love him any more than I love you. He wouldn't expect anything different."

"Would you come with me, then?"

"I'd follow you round the world, girl."

"As a companion. It would have to be as a companion."

Alice smiled, shook her head but kept her peace. She could see her friend in silk – indeed when Mary put on that grand dress given her by Mrs. Spedding, who had taken such a fancy to her the previous summer, no one could have distinguished her from a lady. But herself, she would collapse with nerves into such a dress, walk like a lumpkin, sniffle in company, blush like a blood sunset at the least thing and generally be as awkward as a goose indoors. But she saw that Mary was on the verge of being upset and changed to the subject she was certain most pressed on her friend's mind.

"He's so handsome!" Alice said. "Even if he weren't all the things he is – he's such a handsome gentleman. His hair so thick and long and the grey so distinguished. That scar which makes me shiver when I think of it but when you see him smile it seems to shine from the smile in some way. And a strong-looking, fearless-looking man – with none of the airs, with none of the fancy parts . . . of men who haven't half the claims to them he has. He speaks to me, I'll swear, just as he'd speak to the finest Duchess in England, and it isn't just the time of day but he'll ask me questions and make it easy for me to talk back to him. Not like Reverend Nicholson who hops from one leg to another and goes into long explanations of things I can never make head or tail of although I know he is a good man: but he's not an easy man. Colonel Hope . . ."

Mary enjoyed the balm of such talk and because of that did not even allow her usual scrupulous sense of fairness to qualify Alice's peremptory opinion of the Reverend Nicholson: an omission which later pricked her conscience. She was concentrating, though, on the destination of her own feelings and Alice's supporting presence lapped about her like the secure water in her secret pool.

*

A few hundred yards across the valley, Joseph Robinson sprang out of the hedge like a highwayman and Hope's horse stopped short, pulled back and away to one side. Hope got him steady but rather brutally, Robinson observed.

"Well, landlord, what is it? My money or my life?"

"I'd lay claim to neither, sir," said Robinson, bowing to excuse his sudden appearance.

Hope dismounted. From Robinson's manner he was sure he detected a whiff of potential irritation.

"I am glad to see you in such a lonely spot," he said, holding out his hand and giving a very firm return to the landlord's rough grip. "I have been blaming myself for not speaking to you earlier."

Robinson said nothing.

"About your daughter," Hope added, as if it were unnecessary: but the wary puzzlement on Robinson's face made him wonder whether it had been necessary. If not, why had the man so obviously waylaid him? But the man was cunning.

"I would like to think I had your consent," said Hope, drawing back while going on, "to my paying attentions – to your daughter."

"Attentions?"

Honest puzzlement or a bait? Hope had not calculated on the burden of parents and he was unrehearsed.

"I find your daughter most charming."

"The whole county finds her charming," said the father in a tone of brisk defensive pride.

"More than that . . ." Hope was struggling – what rights did this barrel-bodied innkeeper with a head like a duck's egg who just happened to be Mary's father have to steal in the way and squeeze out these pips of confession?

"Are you saying you want to court my daughter, sir?"

For fear that he might be flying too high for safety, Robinson looked away as he asked that question, his eyes scrutinising the fell behind Hope as if determined to seek out a lost sheep.

Did the man have to be so direct?

"Yes," said Hope, gracelessly.

"Will you be in earnest, sir?" Robinson was still after that sheep, if anything, even more determinedly.

"Of course!" The retort, haughty, did not shake the landlord who stood his ground.

"Am I to take it then, sir" – perhaps the sheep was further up, towards the tops; his eyes moved higher and Hope began to be uncomfortable. Was someone approaching? Ought he to be warned? – "that if she returns your feelings the next step would be the next step as is usually taken?"

"You mean marriage?" Hope was impatient to get this over with. There was no help for it now. He ought to have been better prepared. He had been ambushed.

"The same."

"My answer is positive."

"That is – a yes?"

"Quite so."

"In that case," said Robinson, his eyes even further raised now and screwed up – he was looking into the sky as if the sheep might have shot out wings and ascended to join the heavenly flock – "you have my permission." And he stuck out his hand.

Hope took it, but this time only lightly.

Robinson's gaze came down to earth and, phlegmatically, he announced, "I came out to find you to tell you that a Mr. Newton is here to see you and requires you urgently."

Hope felt tricked.

"Forgive me if I ride ahead?" A saving common politeness brought out the request but he was halfway into the saddle as Robinson gave his assent.

The older man watched him gallop away and stood quite still for a while. He wanted time to think this over and went to the waterfall where he was building steps to make it easier for the Lake Tourists to climb up alongside it: Coleridge was to commend Mr. Robinson's steps in a burst of cascading prose later in that week when he came again into Buttermere having entertained Charles Lamb and his sister. Robinson worked slowly and thought matters through carefully. He had finally lost her, then – that was the lament whose keening was beginning to sound to his innermost ear: and to a man he knew he could not throw off . . .

Mary saw John – as she now called him to herself – and the other man walk quickly away from the inn. She saw also that they knew each other well, that their business was urgent and private and that John was troubled. It was an insight into him she had not known until then and the effect of it was to allow her to see a glimpse of a space for herself in what seemed such a foreign and well-armoured life. She could nurse his vulnerability. The men took a boat and Hope himself rowed directly down the lake.

"Your vouching for me in Keswick was unnecessary," Hope said, curtly. He looked around – there were fishermen further down: he slewed the boat round towards the woods and let the oars loll. He was determined not to let Newton dominate him.

"Maybe I should not have come," said Newton, willing to abase himself now that he was here. "But the truth is that I owe money all over Lancaster, I have no credit in the place. I dare not draw on anyone for fear of arousing suspicion, my position was becoming more desperate every day. It would do neither of us any good were I to be discovered."

"Very well. Very well." Hope was impatient, moody, suddenly depressed. Newton was a curse. "But what do you want now that you're here?"

"Miss D'Arcy seemed a pretty little object. Mountainously wealthy. And you have conquered her heart?"

"Yes. So? There is Colonel Moore – he leeches on her – he'll never let her go however much salt I rub in."

"What about your plan for carrying her over the Border?"

Hope looked away. Why was it that Newton could be so hateful to him? He had been an ally; he was making legitimate enquiries of a business he was part of; he was accommodating, anxious to be friendly – but none of it was convincing. Hope could browbeat him from time to time, especially when he was not consciously attempting to do so, when a sudden gust of temper overwhelmed him and knew no bounds: but Newton was the begetter and the cold perpetrator: with him now, Hope was aware that however far he had roamed, he had always been on the end of a rope.

"Why did we not just go with what we had?"

"What we had was not enough," said Newton. "Even the dressing-case . . ."

"I still have it. I'll show it to you later if you disbelieve me . . ."

"No, no . . . even that and the coach together would not have done much more than to get us comfortably to the New World but with all the vexation we have in the Old." Newton's lean face fell into its bitten bitter lines. "And the New World will be like the Old in this: those who have will rule and those who do not have will grovel and scramble and be trampled over and forced to beg – John – remember – to plead, to run like rats into sewers and shiver there until a danger passes. The New World is full of men like us and I dare swear it will be worse than here in its brutal way. We are a brutal match for them, aren't we? But how much better and easier and happier, John, we will be with the wealth of that pretty little object." Newton now dropped even a semblance of politeness. "We made a contract, John; if you regret it then regret it but don't make the mistake of trying to get out of it. It will stand until we succeed, John, or until we fail. You weren't thinking of breaking it, were you, John?"

Hope felt a chill, as if a breeze had suddenly licked off the lake. Involuntarily, he shivered. Newton noted it but did not react. He now looked at his man with eyes which seemed to liquefy his threat.

"You weren't, were you, John?"

"Why did you have to murder him?"

"I have justified that: and besides, they'll never pick up the trail. The dressing-case is the only evidence and that came from another source. There is no connection. You mustn't worry, John: have I ever betrayed you?"

Newton leaned across and not so much patted as caressed Hope's knee: the larger, stronger, fiercer-looking man accepted this strange comforting and indeed seemed soothed by it. "You were too long alone or with those who denied you what you most need," said Newton, softly.

Hope felt the elegant hand draw delicately across the fine cloth and then touch more firmly, rhythmically. He closed his eyes and saw the Piranesi vaultings and dungeons of his nightmares, the ropes of vine and scaffolds of gaunt, almost fleshless men he had known. The world was evil; brutish, unjust, cruel, empty, vicious and Newton knew that, Hope thought, knew it so powerfully that he could conjure up the truth of it even on the languid lake now faintly tinted with a dust which some would see as blessed. Newton talked on about that time alone, abandoned, terrified and all the time touching him, knowing, as he did, how dependent the man was on touch, on the felt and experienced pressure of flesh for the desperate reassurance of his vitality.

As Newton's murmur became an incantation, the vision from Hause Point rose up like a sun from the couch of his memory but the dark certainties of Newton inked over it and Mary too, standing, he could see as he left his body, standing guard over him, so near to him, she too was helpless before the remorseless bleak credo and history of the man who had seen in him a perfectible instrument for his own greater ends. To Newton, Hope was the latest of those whom he had warped for his purpose. His dæmonic digging out of the man's will and of any trace of sympathy, second thoughts, decency, compunction, was made crystal glorious in the proof it gave him of his power: to take this sensual, strange and curious creature and work him, work him to a purpose: the working itself at times more pleasing, more, much more seductive than the purpose, as the boat swayed on the lake and Hope held on to find some place in his mind to keep faith with Mary . . .

16

The Prisoner

One of the images of horror which rested on the floor of Hope's mind undisturbed for years but, if touched, was ready to strike with a sting which could make him cry aloud, came from his time in America. He had heard of Indians who would lash a prisoner by the legs to a pair of horses which they would then drive in opposite directions, ripping the body in two. This image – he had never seen such an act but heard it verified on several occasions – was like a needle on a nerve and he would literally toss his head about as if trying to shake it off. When he woke, that night, the two ripped and bleeding halves of a body – his body – seemed imprinted on the moonlit wall and he bit his hand to stop his cries.

He dared not go back to sleep and opened the curtains to let in the bright white night. Though it was warm, he shivered and took his bottle-green greatcoat to the window. Soon as bored by the silver shades of fell and lake as he was frightened by the blood and blackness of his nightmares, he took up some paper and began to scribble. Writing had been more than a consolation: at times in his life it had been the only existence he had.

He had learned that writing about pain could relieve that pain.

It was light enough to see the page, but he was used to writing in poor light: many a time he had written in the dark, carefully measuring out the width of the page with his thumb and forefinger.

He had learnt, too, that to write about someone you feared could chase out the fear: even Newton could be subdued on the page. He had forgotten Newton's power.

*

"Newton came to me like Our Saviour," he wrote. "He knew how much I feared silence and how poorly furnished I am for loneliness. In the months we were together in that place he comforted me and bound me to him and though he left before me he would send me tokens and gifts to keep his bond. He held on."

*

When Newton left the prison, Hope had still six and a half years of his sentence to serve. It was then that he did the most extraordinary thing, so curious and mysterious, in fact – and it is a fact – that it seems implausible. It has an indigestible flat mereness which is perhaps a distinguishing aspect of reality.

He went to his window one day and looked out across the exercise yard, across the wall, across a Scarborough side street and into another window where his gaze was met by that of a young, plain but not unhandsome, intelligent and sweet-looking woman. Some power came, related, he remembered thinking, to the power Newton exercised over him, some force came into him and across that imprisoned and inhospitable space, he looked and bent his will to cast a spell on her. For half an hour they gazed at each other as if unblinking until finally she turned away.

The next day, at the same hour, he was there: and so, after a few dying minutes, was she. "Once again I held her: I knew I needed to hold her: my life was in that gaze." And the next day. And for weeks, for months with now and then a day or two missing but that somehow prepared for. Gifts came, but only after the first year, as if a whole twelve months needed to go by to test the silent power of that daily vigil. And finally brief words in a large clear hand "to which I, eventually, replied as briefly. For it was not here the words which were the bond, but that meeting of eyes."

For more than six years. "For two thousand three hundred and forty-eight days I stayed at a window little bigger than my head, and looked on that woman who kept me from hell. I never released her. Newton will never release me."

*

He managed to see Mary the next morning without being observed by Newton.

"He is a solicitor from Chester who has come to drag me back to business. I shall have to go out of the district."

"For how long?" Mary lowered her head: the words came with a guttural sound which excited him.

"I don't know," he said, and added, truthfully and cruelly, "for ever, if Newton has his way."

"And you?"

"Perhaps there is nothing to hold me here."

"I need time."

"Then this can be the time you need."

"When will you return?"

How very proud she is, he thought, that such a simple question should come out with such forced and evident reluctance: as if to ask were to beg.

"When would you want me to return?"

"Whenever you wish."

Her answer was plainly delivered; he was to be allowed the freedom to interpret it as he liked. Those were the words, though: her looks said, just as plainly, 'come soon' and he left jubilant at her dismay.

Newton and Hope drove from the Fish. Mary did not watch them go.

They called in at the Queen's Head but only so that Hope could leave a letter for Miss D'Arcy. While Hope took a drink with George Wood, Newton evaporated into the market-day streets, appreciating the possible danger of a too close public association with the widely greeted Honourable Colonel. He remounted the coach on the edge of town.

After eating, some miles south of Ambleside, they went to the studio of William Green, who had set himself up as both painter and merchant. In the good weather he would be out doing his work: when the weather turned he would be available in his studio to discuss and sell it. For favoured customers he would interrupt this routine and take them on one of his favourite rambles, pointing out views and aspects which would often turn up again when they returned to his studio for tea. The new prosperity, particularly of the southern lakeland with its picturesque villas, enabled him to prosper – quite remarkably – in landscapes in a way similar to an urban painter making a living from portrait painting. Hope wanted to buy a small watercolour, if only to pay Green for his trouble, but Newton steered him away from it.

The further south they went, the happier Newton grew. He became a sightseer. He peered at his Hutchinson and sought out Father West's 'stations' where he could admire the very best views; he was prepared to seek out any natural eccentricity, for all the world as if he were a new convert to Lake Tourism. Hope, whose time in Buttermere had given him, in his own eyes, the status of a native, talked down Newton's enthusiasms and enjoyed that play of superiority.

Yet the later taste of it was sour. He was no more than Newton's creature. As they made south for Cartmel, and Newton promised a great future in America, talked of the fortunes they would make, crowed over their cleverness so far, patted the D'Arcy plan into even better shape and deluged his handsome rather silent companion with compliments, Hope felt a plan slip into his mind, brood there, steady itself, and then emerge fully formed when he came to the northern edge of the treacherous Bay of Morecambe and looked out over sands which had claimed so many lives and swept bodies out to sea without trace.

*

He put it all down in his Journals:

> Yesterday we walked into the Bay, across the Sands and without a guide. The weather has been wild, foul and dirty. Our only previous exercise since coming to this lonely spot was a rapid walk along the shore and then quickly, thankfully, back to the inn for all the comforts of a spiced rum punch. In the snug of this ample inn – the weather barred out and all within soused in warmth – Newton has come as near as I have ever seen him to full ease and careless contentment. He is now in full agreement with my intention to hold off Amaryllis for a while, a scheme greatly helped this morning by the arrival of a letter in which the dear girl announces that she is already ordering her wedding trousseau and tells me of the friends who are proposing presents to her. I will reply in a day or so: briefly. Newton appears to delight in these inn-bound days and I have humoured him. Yet I could not keep that terrible thought long from my mind and even when it stole across on tiptoe and deep in the distance, like an Arab boy far off flitting towards a well at dusk, even then I would catch the recognition of a smile on Newton's lips as if he had heard the thought spoken or seen what I was imagining.
>
> The murder always takes place on the Sands.
>
> And so when we went out onto the Bay, Newton was in a curious manner forewarned – which only added to the unique curiosity of the man. I was in a state approaching exaltation. Before me, across the Sands, was the spot where I had begun what could be my last adventure; beside me was the man who alone bound me to the chains of the past; in the hills behind me – as we walked – was the object of all my affections, the key to peace and freedom.
>
> I remembered about the tides and, from the words of Anne Tyson,

the fearsome bore of water which unleashed its force up the river channels. So I was aware that I had little to prevent me from carrying out my dream and completing this story which would free me to complete the next. I am much stronger than Newton when it comes to a struggle. I would take him far out, and at a late time, and stun him as the tide began to come in. And Newton would be washed away.

That was my purpose as we set out at about ten on a morning of blustery but dry clouds, grey white like loose bandages trailing across the sky, the fishermen way down the Bay. The cockle gatherers were to the north that day, and so I veered south, the Sands as firm and docile as a beaten footpath across the meadow.

Walking out into that Bay was like making for the edge of the world. Or the moon might be like this because soon we lost all sense of others – they were mere spots of movement in the far distance and we were together in an isolation which was not unlike the isolation of a prison cell. We were bound together in this space which seemed vast but was always no more than the space we carried between us, walking closely together, while the rest of the world was indifferent to us.

I had purposefully kept my plan uninformed in its particulars. I knew myself well enough to know that a particular plan would agitate me in advance and that agitation would certainly transfer itself to Newton. As it was, I knew that he must be aware, by some shadow on my mind, of what I intended.

But he gave no sign of it. Indeed I had never seen him so amiable. He took my arm. He told me how well the mountain air had worked on my complexion – "black eyebrows, bright blue eyes, brown hair, shoulders like Atlas," he said and followed with even more fulsome effusions and compliments of which I have always been most wary. I, who like to give compliments, invariably suspect those given to me. Is that because mine are not untainted by the groping for advantage? So I fear are the compliments of others.

I had calculated as follows. High tide was a few minutes after half past midday. We would walk out into the Bay for a little less than two hours. I would fell Newton and then run back to Cartmel, reckoning that the time required for the return run would be that of the outward amble. Even were Newton to collect himself after a quarter hour or so, he would be in no state to beat the tide.

Had I not been for so long used to carrying contrary feelings in my mind I would have begun to scream as we walked out into that Bay – Newton was so mercilessly cheerful and flattering and skittishly inquisitive, hanging onto my arm, my words, my stories, his eyes glittering with appreciation, skipping about the Sands like a bee flitting from one ripe flower to another but always returning to me to claim my arm and urge me on to more stories of London, of America, of women, of wars, duels, all the picaresque baggage of a life which, when told aloud, seems bursting with Life Itself, but to me, where I live, on the inside of my mind and heart and soul, appears as vital and nourishing as the catacombs of Rome. (Which I visited with a gypsy man who tried to rob me and may still be in the catacombs.) To Newton my life was a pageant, a chronicle of conquests, a quarry for him to dig, a well spring to suck at and as this went on I was holding in my mind the knowledge of what I had decided to do.

I began to worry how I would do it. To commit a violent action you need to be surprised or set on a single course. You need to be defending or attacking and in both cases you need a compelling sense of exactly who and what you are.

I was too many people. I was the entertainer, the friend and the confidant of Newton; I was all the past selves he teased out of me and that past went through my mind like a procession from the graveyards on the night of All Souls. Also I was with my beloved Mary and, if I admit the whole truth, still stained by the occasional pulse of speculation over the great wealth of Amaryllis. The stroll itself was as much soothing as bracing, more the way to dispel anger and intensity than to shepherd and use it.

I grew silent and looked at my watch. It was several minutes before twelve. As if respecting my silence and understanding it, Newton held onto my arm firmly and matched me step for step.

He is much slighter than I but wiry: yet finally much weaker.

Without him life would be simple and clear. God would forgive me in His infinite mercy and besides I would be doing no more than the public hangman should have done many times over. Newton owed a life.

I heard our breathing like the panting of tired dogs.

In the distance I fancied I could measure the tide moving in. We were between the two deep river channels which even now ran fast but when the tide swelled were gorged with such a power of water that no-one could hope to stand against them.

I stopped. Newton held onto my arm.

I looked away from him and saw, over towards Hest Bank, a woman alone and wondered if it was she who had once followed me. What had she said? 'She worked the shoreline'?

And I waited for the spirit to come to me, for the heavens to open or my own self split into the act which would release me to a life of goodness and rid the planet of an evil man. God knew all this and He would surely see the gains to His glory.

It seemed to me I heard the echo of a roar of the sea far off but coming closer like an army now proclaiming its threatening might.

And then the spirit, the I, left me and I saw us both there on the Sands, two specks no greater than the grains of sand themselves, two – what were we? What were those objects upright still, locked arm in arm – my mind, my conscious mind, rose up from the body, went out of it and hovered in the air like a kite, like a kestrel on a support of air waiting for the faint movement, disturbance, flicker which would take it to its prey. Where was my call? Where was my prey? What was this so clear and unmistakable distinction between the I, eye who saw, was, and the body linked to another body on the floor of the Bay?

Often I have been terrified of such moments.

Now I let it float. I let it hover there. My soul.

Previously I would tussle and sweat to pull it back, to haul it into the body, for without it I would be dead or if I did not re-entrap it I would be mad. Surely Bedlam was this: poor bodies separated from their souls as I was – as Christ is my witness – as I then was for a full time.

I feared it no longer.

This was true peace, passing all understanding. This was the beginning of the communion of souls. If I dared to stay apart and alone I would be taken up, like pollen, and blown by the wind to where the almighty inscrutable plan willed and there find another life.

"John." Newton's voice was tender and low. It was far off but I heard it. "John." He repeated the name several times but did not stress it or raise his voice. Nor did his tone betray urgency or fear. Tugging quietly. "John."

Oh, but I wanted to soar, to stay aloft, to be so gratefully and finally freed of that thing on the floor of the ocean. Let me be, I heard a voice say: but not aloud. Let me go free.

"John," the voice repeated, tolling me back, "John." And again "John."

Let me be.

Let me wait and be taken by the wind to where it wills. That will be my will. Such freedom and clarity in that soaring. Such lightness.

"John."

Lightness and singleness.

This is what I am, I thought, this pure light hovering spirit at the will of the wind way above the salt mud and dull bodies lumped on the floor of a mouth-open Bay. This insubstantial being is . . .

"Let me be," I murmured aloud now.

He squeezed my arm, carefully.

"Let me go," I said, but as I said it, like the bursting of a bubble, like the ending of a dreaming, like the breaking of a spell, like all these but multiplied and rending me in two even as I was joined together, as I spoke this second time I was returned to myself, enfeebled, slightly sweet-sickened, bereft. I turned to look down on the face of Newton.

"We have to hurry, John," he said, still gently and looking at his watch. "I talked to our host before we left. The tide will be full in less than an hour." He looked even kindly at me. "We don't want you to drown, do we?"

Had he not gently urged and led me off the Sands, I would have been overtaken by the tide, to be landed on some neglected shore, dead in body.

17

Fixing the Day

He was sick and feverish for more than two weeks and Newton nursed him. In the calmer times, he would walk a little, although he seemed to panic at any suggestion that they walk into the Bay or on the Sands; he would only go along the very edge, near the old cart track, and never be out when high tide brought in the rushing wall of cold booming water. At Newton's bidding and sometimes at his dictation, he wrote letters to Amaryllis, explaining his incapacity, assuring her of his devotion, promising his return, dissuading her from attempting to visit him this far south and in the wild weather that had set in. Unknown to Newton he wrote a single note to Mary, not mentioning his illness (for he knew she would immediately come to nurse him), but promising to return.

He wrote little in his Journals, but one entry speaks of his "abhorrence of Newton and yet I dared not show it especially when he was being so kind to me."

Newton seemed if anything even happier than before, fussing over his friend, commandeering the small snug, spicing the rum punch himself, organising a restorative diet, all but waiting on his friend whose figure and looks were improved by the wasting refinement of illness until into that bold bullish figure crept something more elusive, 'poetic' was how Newton described it to himself, although 'haunted' might be more accurate. For John was much of the time abstracted, seemingly beyond reach.

When they talked it tended to be abrupt and with a rather desperate undertone.

"Is Rank, then, on this Earth, everything?" he asked, late one evening, the logs low, the candle flames swaying in the draughts which breezed through the inn. "Is it all we should strive for? More than Wealth? More than Affection or a Christian life?"

"A Christian life," said Newton, "is all very well for a Christian man. But even he is helped by Rank and by Wealth. With Wealth he can be charitable – as you are to the boys and beggars of Keswick when you walk along the street scattering your pennies like seed corn.

With Rank you can bring justice into an unjust world. You can judge lives and spare them, you can correct them and make an example of them. I have never yet met a man of God or a man of the world who did not think the Lord was wise in creating both rich and poor and if He makes the division – as He has done – then clearly it is preferable to be one of the rich. And in some matters to have Rank is to be richer than to have Wealth. To have both, of course, as you have," Newton smiled and reached out to touch his friend, who shivered a little from the last traces of the fever, "and with the Plantagenet inheritance of good looks, wit, a fluent tongue and the charm of Old Nick, there is nothing to prevent a man reaching the very heights."

"Is that what you want me for?"

"I am your friend."

Newton's reproach stung the sick man and Hope continued, in expiation, "But we know that Billy Pitt has sold titles like a drunken Irish tinker at a horse fair. We know that all sorts of dishonourable slave-traders and men of vicious practices at home and abroad are now preening themselves in sashes and ermine; their wives are often as not bought in from the pastures of the older aristocrats, themselves no more than a clique of butchers ennobled for slaughter or out of craven toadying – and yet they can look forward to centuries ahead when their names and rank will roll down English history in all the begged and stolen glory of a thief's coat of many colours. Why should we bow to that?"

"We do," said Newton. "When you are liberal to the poor in Keswick, you are considered all the more liberal because you are the younger brother to the Earl of Hopetoun. When you bid good day to polite society in the town it is considered all the more lustrous a 'good day' than any I could give because the Earl of Hopetoun is your elder brother. When you are friendly to a man like Wood, you make not a friend but a slave of him because he cannot conceive friendship for a man who has access to the nobles, the Dukes and Earls, perhaps even the Court itself – a world more foreign to him than America and about as approachable as the Milky Way. We adore Rank. We crave it. Why? Because we need to abase ourselves. We know we are poor sad miserable frail creatures and we want to worship. The next world is all very well and for many it is all they have and they abase themselves for eternal life, but if this world is also available then we abase ourselves in this. We are all base. It is our natural condition. To pretend otherwise we raise up idols or petty gods or temples or failing all of that, Kings and when they fail – as ours did by his execution – we make do with Rank even though we know how rank it is, even when we see the Prime Minister use it like an alloy to fill out his debased guinea, even so we want so much to look up and to be beaten down, to curry favour and to be stamped on, we want so much to have the reminder of the dirt we crawl in and the belly we crawl on. And how better than to look up and know that those you yearn to be are themselves no more, even less than the dirt you are but you are so base that you still look up and still yearn?"

Newton's reply had gone from argument through rhetoric to a diatribe so vituperative in tone that John, wrapped as he was in his immense bottle-green greatcoat, sipping hot rum punch and fed by a fine embering fire, felt a cold rash of goose pimples rise up over his body as if in protest at such utter contempt expressed for the world and the flesh.

"Is there nothing that can be good in us?" he asked.

"One man can try to help another; from time to time," said Newton, and then he gave John an unequivocal cobra stare which flung them both back to that walk on the Sands. "But even between two such men, evil and destructive thoughts can never be wholly blocked out." He paused. "Can they?" he whispered. "Can they?"

John shook his head: but he would not be entirely put down.

"There are men who work for others. There are men – look at Tom Paine – who put their lives at risk for others, who want Man to be Free, who fight for the Rights of Man –"

"They want power!" Newton's interruption was savage. "They see a new world where Rank is not as potent as the force of the mob and they seek to gain power over the mob by promising them all the privileges of Rank without pointing out the absurdity which is that such a world where all were equally privileged would simply find new names for old and Rank would re-emerge. Those Paines and Robespierres saw that and wanted to be the first leaders of the new order."

"So no-one acts for anyone but himself?"

"No-one." Newton paused. "But at times – at times like this, John – two men can be comfortable with each other and there can be a pause."

"And love," John said, playing the first small hand he had held for some time, "is that not a giving of yourself to someone else?"

"The love of a man for a woman?" Newton's contempt was so plain it had no need to strike.

"Or a woman for a man."

"Women see men as providers or protectors. Or, as your Miss D'Arcy, elegant and splendid ornaments which they can afford and hope – ha! – will hoist them into a higher Rank from which they can peer down on rather more of their fellow women than they peered down on before! It's all empty, John. The life of this earth is the life of the meanest poorest body on it: everything else is vanity and detestable frivolity – 'love' most of all. Above earthly existence there is nothing dignified and so we invent catalogues of grace and beauty and nobility and delight: they are nothing but spoils – all of them – the spoils of the fortunate to be plundered by the brave."

"What if love can give you that 'pause' you spoke of?" John said, finding obstinacy in him now. "I know myself," he went on and here spoke ringing truth, "that what I want most on earth is a sense of peace, a place of calm in my own mind, a feeling of ease in my skin, to be without this swarm of envy and scheming and greedy reaching out and wanting to have what I have not got, be where I am not, do what I am failing to do: and what if this 'love' can give that?"

"It can seem to," Newton admitted, "I have heard that and I have seen it for myself. But it is an illusion. I have heard and seen that too. And it leaves you more bitter, more restless, more disjointed than before."

"So what is there?"

"To seize the reins and ride roughshod over the world as we will do," said Newton gaily. "To play for the highest stakes – for Rank, for Wealth, experiences which are new, however dangerous and vicious they might seem. To drive life into the ground!"

John raised his glass and Newton drank with a flourish.

At other times, Newton would be practical and once more in the character in which John had known him in Lancaster: anxious, fussing, clerical, the pernickety nagging polar opposite to the cunning and destructive fury of the Newton who could inveigle and dazzle his man.

"We must sell something," he said.

With John fully restored, they had decided to begin the journey back into the Lakes. The bill at the inn would have to be paid and, through Newton's extravagance, it had come to more than eight pounds. This left them with less than five pounds in cash.

"We'll call in on Crump at Grasmere," John said, always superior in conversations such as these, and greatly improved in his health by the prospect of going back into battle. And as Newton shrank he blossomed.

"Crump might not be there. And we will have to repay Crump soon."

"And Wood."

"Wood is a peasant. He will wait."

"Crump is a man of business. He will wait only for so long. And Moore is a Colonel."

"You have not borrowed from him."

"I intend to."

"Who else?"

"Various tradesmen in Keswick." And elsewhere. Mary's father was now owed what for him was a large sum.

"We must sell the plate and linen."

"Who would give us a good price in these parts?"

"We cannot sell the carriage. That would maroon us. Nor the dressing-case. That would be too dangerous." Newton – in John's view – was comically agitated by his inability to solve what seemed to John a puny difficulty.

"First we'll borrow from Crump," he said.

Which they did, a day later, in Grasmere, and just in time as Mr. Crump was about to embark – without any parting pain – for Liverpool to look after his business. Mrs. Crump was to stay and be the presence, beating off the opposition to Allen Bank. Colonel Alexander Augustus suspected that Crump's eagerness to supply credit – indeed to supply twice as much as was asked for, knowing, as he did, how inconvenient it could be for a gentleman stranded in such a remote part of England – might have been in part a bribe to provide company for a wife who was unashamedly in need of it. But their company at tea was all the interest he received. Immediately afterwards the two men parted. Newton had to go.

Newton had been forced to recognise the danger and expense of his accompanying his friend into Keswick.

"I have to bring it to a conclusion as fast as I can," John said. "I will even try to take her into Scotland. But when she knows she is going to be married, when Moore knows, more importantly, then I'll be under hourly scrutiny. You know I've been ill. You know I've found all this much harder than I suspected. I had not realised how much of a show there has to be all the time with this boring Lake Tourist business and besides, the Honourable Alexander Augustus is becoming tired of the affair. Moore will have all his hounds out. I've dodged pretty well so far; I've ducked invitations with plausible excuses; I've gone to church but to an unfashionable church and at an unfashionable hour; I've refused to saunter by the lake at the expected time and discouraged comment if I could, but . . . I'll need letters and I'll need to be free to move fast, and frankly, Newton, you take up too much of my time." He paused. Newton, who had drooped as Hope had flowered, now slipped back into that reptilian watchfulness which, in other contexts, transfixed his friend. But here Hope was in command and he reached out with both hands to shake the man's bony shoulders in brawny affection. "You are a spellbinder, Newton. You are so much more interesting than anybody else that I can't keep away from you. And I have a natural tendency to defer to you when you are near – not always: sometimes I make my own way regardless and you admire me for that, but at an anxious time like this, I would want to talk it all over with you and that takes time, it would be remarked on – remember Moore is implacably our enemy – and when it is done – we'll be away and then, *then* we'll be together."

Newton let himself be convinced.

He went to stay at a very modest inn near Kendal.

Hope drove into the yard of the Queen's Head with as much noise as he could generate and, to his great satisfaction, the grooms, the maids, the Monkey-boy and wall-eyed Wood himself were soon dancing out onto the cobbles of the yard, welcoming home the Honourable as if he were the son of the Great House returned to claim his inheritance.

And indeed there was something of that about him as he walked down towards the lake, scattering pennies, greeting all he met with that easy smile, suddenly back to his great self which filled the small streets with a feeding sense of life. People felt bucked up just to see such a confident, finely dressed, healthy animal man on top of the world, free with his greetings and caresses: and he in his turn was lifted as on an air bubble by their pleasure at seeing him. Perhaps, he thought, my main purpose in life is this: to stroll around in a high good humour and say hello to people.

"Ah," said Colonel Moore, attempting joviality, "our prodigal."

"Except that my wild oats," replied Hope, bowing all but imperceptibly in return for the rather exaggerated effort of Moore's, "were, alas, taken from medicine bottles."

Miss D'Arcy instantly composed herself to commiseration and yet again – and after all his resolutions! – Moore felt done down by the man whom he simply could not fathom.

He had tried to explain his unease to his wife and now, while the two women practically begged Hope to get sick again so that they could show the full extent of their concern for him, he called up his definitive summary to her.

"The fact is that in my service I met all types. And men I would serve with on the field of battle but never allow into my society at home. That is as it should be. War is for warriors: society is for those who belong. But this Colonel Hope – I'm sorry, my dear – I cannot place him. He looks like a warrior but yet there is something wild in him which service such as he has had – and remember that diplomatic stretch in Vienna – ought to have polished. He fits into no known type and say what you want but to an old soldier that is a warning sign." It had been no help to his temper to be told by his wife and later by Amaryllis to whom his statement had, disloyally, been transmitted – that the fact of Hope's fitting into 'no known type' was of course the very heart and soul of his unique attraction.

He watched him now. Surely his manners were too elaborate: even his laconic poses were elaborate. And his speech – what was it precisely about the fluency that was unsettling – was it the soft Irish brogue which crept in for no great reason other than the pursuance of seduction, for so it seemed to an increasingly aggravated and frustrated Moore.

But the ladies purred and purred.

And the man Hope took it all as his due.

Moore could stand it no longer.

"I thought of taking a journey up to your brother's estate at Hopetoun," he announced.

His wife looked amazed but knew enough to say nothing.

Scenting either another obstruction or a new insult, Amaryllis blushed.

Hope smiled and yet his blue eyes were so cold that Moore had to steady himself against flinching.

"May we enquire the purpose?"

"I thought," said Moore, ignoring with some difficulty the bolts of disapproval issuing from the unplacid eyes of his ward, "that I would introduce myself to the Earl your brother, in order to reassure him of the . . . proprieties . . . of the . . ." Struggling now, he received help from no-one, " . . . nature of the family and its circumstances into which . . ." Flailing badly he lunged for an ending, " . . . you will marry."

"But he would never have doubted it," said Hope, smoothly and instantly. "There would be not the slightest doubt in his mind that the woman who had so generously consented to be my wife would in every possible way be suitable. Indeed," with Moore already crumbling, Hope moved in closer, "I would guess that your visit might bewilder him. It would certainly confuse him. It would turn his view of the world upside down. It could even astound him." Each sentence was like a snub and smacked across the room to the unforgiving shame of the two women, heads now bowed. "But by all means if you intend to make yourself known to my brother – have you ascertained that he is at home? – if you are fully determined to go to prosecute this most original enterprise, then I shall write a letter to make sure that he receives you. Otherwise the poor fellow – he is very high on form – will not know what to make of it. He is very correct about matters such as these. I would not like – I could not bear – to see you turned away or worse kept waiting but not received or worst of all received but in total ignorance – on my brother's part, that is – of the matter and the meaning of such an unusual encounter. Have you pen and ink and paper?"

The silence was savage.

Mrs. Moore staged a sudden attack of an ancient ailment of the heart which had been useful on previous occasions such as this.

Amaryllis fled for the smelling salts.

The Colonel tapped the mantelpiece and issued orders to his wife from a distance.

Hope opened a window.

The moment passed and, with Mrs. Moore fully restored, the four of them went out to saunter down to the lake, the Colonel and his wife trailing several dozen paces behind the lovers who made for

Friar's Crag, nodding and greeting the few Lake Tourists sensible enough – Amaryllis observed – to stay for the most reliable and picturesque month for true Lakers.

"You will notice," she said happily, "that only the richer are still here. September weeds out the poorer."

Hope smiled irresistibly and she responded warmly, pressing his arm, and giving him a look of tenderness which touched him into a daydream of their marriage. There would be serious wealth. He had forgotten how keenly this prospect appealed to him and as they walked between great elms and beeches and looked down the lake into the Jaws of Borrowdale, he listened to her plans for their wedding. He responded sensibly to her questions as to where they would go on their honeymoon – "To Scotland," he said immediately, "to Hopetoun, of course!" – at which her face was illuminated; he even fenced a little with her over some details of procedure and arrangement, but the hinterland of his mind was entirely preoccupied in harvesting the wealth that would so soon be his and setting it out around the acres of his fantasy. Wealth could be power, most readily the power he had always wanted – to lead a life of liberal hedonism unlimited. Amaryllis D'Arcy was his key to that treasure.

He stayed a few days and was seen to be a perfect suitor. Wedding clothes were bought, Colonel Moore decided against his visit to Hopetoun, all that remained was for a date to be fixed.

Hope received a letter from Mary.

He went to see Amaryllis.

"A final short exile from the court of your perfect love," he said, knowing how much she enjoyed his over-ornamentation from time to time. And it kept the thing light.

To Burkett who helped the Monkey-boy harness the horses he said, "A last pass at char-fishing."

Just for the exercise, he said, he himself would drive the fourteen miles over into Buttermere.

18

Lorton Church: October 2nd, 1802

It was what he had dreamed of.

Mary met him, as she had whispered in the parlour that she would, at the edge of the village and led him north towards Hause Point. He saw and understood why she was keen to avoid the stretch of pasture beside the lake where he had first proposed to her. Although in one way he was entirely convinced that he understood Mary and appreciated her in a way which was available to no-one else, there was a continent of her life foreign to him: that steady accretion through peace and honest work and friendly security of a character deeply set and rooted in its place and time and context: all discoveries made there delighted him.

Yes, this was how he had dreamt and imagined her, leading him away from the totemic circle of her village, even of her own particular valley, out towards Lorton.

She walked half a pace in front of him and although she answered him politely she preferred to be silent. He was happy to let that be and indeed his work was cut out to keep up with her: she walked very swiftly and his leg, which the damp air had stiffened, began to drag uncomfortably. It had been a rainy day.

At Hause Point he claimed a stop for the view. Mary was thinner, he noticed, and paler, and it suited her. He too, he was quick to compare, was thinner and, from the mirror, he had seen that it benefited him also. He had begun to cultivate it, eating and drinking less, launching even more furiously into his exercises, treating his skin to a little oil to keep the ruddiness down.

Soon they walked on in complete silence; the strength of her concentration was such that any remarks he made were like children's arrows bouncing off the bark of an old oak: her fixity impressed and intrigued him.

It was still damp, a little drizzle now and then, the fells purpling with misty mizzle, the greens of trees drenched greener, their green swan song before the winds and colds of autumn drained them yellow and blew them down. The Tourists had largely departed and the roughly kept road was empty but for the occasional mule pack on its way to or from the quarries or, once, a vagrant, a woman with two children, one a baby still at her breast, who told them how she had walked over from Newcastle after her husband, a sailor, had been lost at sea leaving her with nothing more than the name of his brother who worked in the Honister Quarries. She was half-starved and almost destitute but determined to get there in the hope that the brother "might be the true brother of my dear husband in his kindness and sense of duty and at least find a way to nurture his little nephew" (the boy was about four and very thin) "and niece" (here she indicated the blessedly sleeping child she was carrying). "As for myself," she went on, "I have neither hopes nor fears. As long as the children are taken care of I will stay, go, work or, begging your pardons, lie down and die. It makes no difference."

Mary was in tears at the story and told the woman to call in at the Fish where she would be fed and could restore herself and the children. She told her to explain to Mrs. Robinson that they had met and gave her a bracelet as a token of the promise: the bracelet to be delivered up to her mother. Hope, too, was moved and gave the woman a shilling, the boy a sixpence and the baby a kiss.

"How can we think about ourselves," Mary said, as they watched the ragged woman strike out for Buttermere, "when this goes on all around us?"

Hope could think of a dozen replies but offered none. There was something holy in Mary's open-heartedness, he thought, and debate could have no place in it.

She led him to the churchyard in Lorton and went through the gate and into the church porch, out of the drizzle. Their capes glistened with a sheen of water but after they took them off and shook them out, the warm air restored them, aided by a small silver thimble full of rum and milk which Hope had providentially made up in his flask before setting out.

"I don't want to go in," said Mary, firmly, as Hope rose from the porch benches – on which they sat face to face like petitioners – "I don't want to go in yet."

He sat down and looked at her, though again, as at Hause Point, she looked away. Perhaps it is the mildness of the rain which makes the complexion of the women in these valleys so soft and clear, he thought. Or was it only to be found in Mary? No – he had seen more and better-looking country girls here than he could remember seeing anywhere, more independent too, and cleaner. But in Mary there was an apotheosis – in Mary . . . he dawdled over superficial speculations such as these, maintaining the silence, made rather nervous by the effort she was summoning up . . .

"I have heard, sir," she said, without looking at him, "that . . . that you have been paying court to Miss D'Arcy in Keswick. I have heard that you are engaged to her. May I be told if that is true?"

Was that all?

Oh, Mary, Mary! How could he measure what her honesty might do for him?

He hesitated, theatrically, but she did not recognise the gesture, being too concerned for the truth. Recognising the failure of his gesture – she swelled his sensitivity to its utmost – he gnawed his lip for shame and changed his tactic. He had planned well ahead. He knew from the sad tone of her letter (which had not directly mentioned Miss D'Arcy) that he would be challenged. "For bait," he would say, "Miss D'Arcy was the bait to tease you back to me!" He had even rehearsed it on the way up the Newlands valley. Mary would surely ask him – was it true that he was courting Miss D'Arcy? Yes, he would reply, without giving anything away. She would pause, chastened, saddened, and then, like a knight on a white charger, he would race in at the moment of her greatest vulnerability to say "Miss D'Arcy was only bait. I used her to bring you back to me. Don't you see? Your refusals and coldness drove me even to this cruel trickery. I know I have behaved unforgivably to Miss D'Arcy but it was for your sake – you drove me on to this cruelty! Now, Mary, make me the promise I want . . ."

But the rehearsals were useless. Faced with her puzzled and honest enquiry, his buckish deceits dissolved.

He thought of a way to answer which was as near the truth as his present circumstances could possibly allow.

"It is true I have been what is known as 'courting' Miss D'Arcy though I am not engaged to her – that is not true. There has been no talk of a wedding. But I have, I freely and honestly admit, been in her company, been her companion, expressed my admiration for her and all in all, in the common gossip around here, may well have been considered 'courting'."

"They do," said Mary, looking at him directly. "That is what they say."

"Why did you turn away from me, Mary?"

"I gave you my reasons."

"I answered them."

"I could not see why a man with your position in society – with all the world to choose from! – should wish to be hung about with a country girl."

"Did you not believe me?"

"It was not a question of belief."

"What was it then?"

"It did not seem possible: or right."

"But I proposed it."

"I know." She looked at him, anguished, searching, "but I could not feel that it was right. Why should you do it?"

"I told you why." He paused. "Love."

"Oh, 'love'. That can come and go. As it seems to have done with you, in Keswick."

"Were you jealous?"

"Yes."

"Then you do care for me?"

"I never denied it."

"Why did you turn away from me?"

"You say that. What do you mean? When did I turn away?"

Hope gazed out down the church path to the old gate, beyond that to empty fields, a grey sky, drizzle, and breathed in deeply: these moments were the most sweetly enjoyed of his entire existence. She was his: all he had to do was to reel in, gently, gently, and then – "I came to you with everything I had, Mary. It was not easy for me, neither. I admit it and my manner may have betrayed unease. It was not easy for me to discover that the end of a lifetime's search for a companion, for a woman I could respect and love, ended in the remote, small, secluded valley of Buttermere." He smiled, charming a corresponding smile from her. "And I admit I may have been graceless." He raised a hand to fend off her objections. "But I was taken by surprise, ambushed by this sudden revelation."

He spoke now with hypnotic sincerity and Mary's pain and the tension of her resolution which had brought him to the church to face him with the truth, was washed away like the absolution of sins. 'Stop,' she wanted to say, 'you need go on no more: I believe.' But, sensing that, he kept the line of his monologue taut so that even her apparent surrender would not let her off his hook. "And I confess I was confused. I am, after all – the man I am. It would seem on the surface not an extraordinary but certainly an unusual and noteworthy match as much for me as for you. And I had no precedent. Was I to approach your father – well, of course I ought to have done and would do it, as we all want, if our lives could be lived again, but I confess I was confused. It was you I wanted to sound out, it was you I needed to know for I have known no-one like you and so there was a confusion from the beginning. I was trying to get to know you but at the same time – and I admit it but I can see even now no better solution – I could not but seem to be compromising you. Had I been brought up in that valley with you, I would have known all I needed to know: had you been a woman of Miss D'Arcy's type, on the market, then I would have known all I needed to know. But I was without that knowledge."

He paused. "Nevertheless I was so moved by what I felt for you that I was happy to go blindly on and ask for your hand. This was rebuffed. What had I done? Had I mistaken my own feelings, had I mistaken your feelings, was I being clumsy and offensive where I thought I was being direct, was I running before my horse to market? I was miserable and decided that the only way was to leave you alone. Either you would write to me or forget me. But I could not forget you. It was I, not you, who made the return. It was I, and not you, who came to try to restore what there might be between us. Yes, I was thrown into Miss D'Arcy's company: yes, I walked and talked with her and escorted her to two, two only, engagements in the great social swirl of that mountain town and, yes, I am certain now, but only now, that I went beyond propriety. But, Mary, it was, if I may say so, not entirely my fault. I was bound to you. I tried to leave the district and went as far south as Cartmel only to fall ill in a fever . . ."

"I can see you have been ill" – this was her sole interruption.

" . . . and as soon as I was well I beat back north, pretending I was for Hopetoun but knowing every mile of the way that I would have to stop in the Lakes near you just to *be* near you. And yet I dare not come into Buttermere again uninvited. I dare not, truly." Now his eyes moistened and tears were prepared to fall and soon they did. "I was weak for this love but it needed some nourishment. What if once more I came and once more I was rebuffed? What then? You may think me foolish – I too think myself foolish; I cannot understand what happened to me, a soldier, a man who has fought in revolutions, stood his punishment, challenged life to its worst – but in some way I cannot even imagine, the very soul of my life depended on my love for you being returned and consummated. How could I come to see that love once more wounded by your absence and flight or killed by another refusal? Miss D'Arcy was no more than a poor consolation and I will not forgive myself for it – although I am certain no harm was done as no honour was infringed – but Mary, don't you see?" Hope himself was incapable of seeing, the tears were now real and his eyes luxuriated in them and it gave him a deep refreshing sense of being shriven.

Mary took his hand. He grasped hers and pressed them to his cheeks where her skin could feel the copious wetness of the tears, their genuine passage. He drew her to him and she sat beside him, still as comforter, although it was he who took her in his arms and she yielded without hesitation as he pressed her to him, his hands, seemingly blindly, even helplessly, moving over her body, which responded quickly, almost swooningly, to what became caresses. He kissed her on the mouth at first as gently as a cobweb and then gradually harder until they were locked together like stags tangled in horned combat.

She would have yielded, he recognised, in that small self-conscious part of a mind not quite altogether given over to the mingling of their senses, bodies –

The Reverend Nicholson opened the door of the church, looked on, looked away, looked back again and felt his face go brim scarlet.

"Good afternoon," said Hope. "Is there a service today?"

"Not . . . not today," Nicholson replied after a struggle. "I was redistributing the hassocks," he added, compelled to make an excuse for walking out of his church. "Miss Skelton – Mr. Skelton's cousin – a spinster of this parish – has kindly donated a new set to mark the Peace with the French and . . ."

He stopped as Mary, quite suddenly, burst out laughing. At first he was offended but the laughter was so clear, so unmocking, so brilliant and happy that his mood somersaulted and he found he was joining in. Hope, too, maintained his serious dignity only a moment or two longer before catching the infection and soon he was wiping his eyes a second time.

"Mr. Nicholson," he said, when they had subsided, "you are the very man I was looking for. How kind of you to drop in!"

This provoked a bashful chuckle soon followed by a stand of at the ready, at your service.

"Perhaps, Mary," Hope said, still holding her hand, Nicholson noticed, with fixed concentration, "if you let me have some private words with the Reverend Nicholson. Will that be in order?"

Mary looked at him directly and drank in the infinite fidelity of his gaze. "It will," she said.

"And I can speak . . . ?"

"I can speak too," she said, smiling.

Hope, in the abstract, would have calculated himself annoyed with such an intervention: in the event he felt his spirits brighten, as the burden of expected and traditional feminine dependence indicated a willingness to support its own weight.

"She is a rare woman," he said, awkwardly, even shyly, in this new discovery.

"Everyone in these parts has thought so for many years," said Nicholson, who now relaxed into the role he saw anticipated from him. "Do I assume you intend . . . ?" But the thought of it was too much for him and his attitude betrayed that sense of improbability: Mary fired a little and replied steadily.

"Colonel Hope has asked for my hand and after careful consideration and constant warnings to him of the difficulties for both of us in what he is asking, I have willingly consented."

A lump came to Hope's throat. He would treasure and bind himself to this purity, this unassuming modest strength – beyond doubt the real glory of the world!

"We would like to be married soon," he said, "as soon as possible."

"And quietly," Mary added. Hope had not dared for such instructive co-operation. He himself had been so hesitant over framing such a request that he had abandoned it. "It must be done quietly," Mary repeated. "Colonel Hope will have various arrangements to make abroad – with his family, I mean, and others, undoubtedly –" was she telling him to uncouple any hint of an obligation to Miss D'Arcy or at least giving him the chance to behave as honourably as she clearly understood he would want to? – "until the day itself, we would want it kept quiet."

"Special licence?"

"If that will be quicker," said Hope.

"In Whitehaven then?"

"I will *not* be married in Whitehaven," Mary said. "I will be married here or not at all." She turned to Hope. "When we are married you may command me – although I had rather you let me find the way myself. But the law gives you that right. Until then, though, I can have a will of my own. And I will be married in Lorton Church." There was no room for argument.

"And so you shall. And Mary, never lose your will. I'll not tyrannise over it."

It was quite a good political simile he thought, and he noted, with some pleasure, how both Mary and himself were heightening their speech out of excitement and perhaps also to impress the clergyman with their self-possession: he had, after all, discovered them wildly distrait at the door of his church.

"You and I will have to go over to Whitehaven to get a special licence," Nicholson said. "I would go by myself but if you came with me . . ." Rank would galvanise the law.

"We'll go tomorrow," said Hope. "Let me offer you breakfast at the Fish and a good horse to Whitehaven."

The Reverend Nicholson could not bring himself to spike such enthusiasm by a recitation of the list of charitable works he had planned to do on the next day and so he agreed and spent much of the rest of his afternoon rearranging his obligations. He breathed his secret to no-one, not even – though he was badly tempted for the focus of power and lustre which would accrue to him – when Miss Skelton and her groom passed him by in the new trap – splashing his legs with mud only a little – as she exercised with her piebald pony. But he brooded over it a great deal and in his evening prayers included a prayer that the prospective marriage between two such dashing and outstanding people should be turned to the good of mankind and the greater glory of God.

That evening, Hope and Mary explained it to Mary's parents – several times as it turned out, for Mrs. Robinson wanted to be absolutely and beyond any possible doubt certain and Mr. Robinson spent the first half hour mutely shaking his head and saying "Oh, Mary" or "Who would've believed it" or "If anybody deserves it she does" and, most frequently of all, "We should be running up the flag, shouldn't we? We should be running up the flag. Tots of rum."

When Mrs. Robinson finally and conclusively comprehended the news, she wept and her sobbing broke out randomly all evening unchecked even by the cat's suspicious cries of "No-oo".

"There was never any such thing heard of before in our family," was a line she found and stuck to: and from time to time she would glance almost pleadingly at her future son-in-law and say, "We're respectable people, you see, sir."

After the interrupted ecstasy of that brief unconsummated embrace, Hope was anxious to see Mary alone, naked and in bed.

Her interest and most of her attention, though, seemed to have switched away from him and be directed to her parents who appeared to have aged, or to be suffering some slow somnolent sickness needing constant prodding and re-animating. Hope's jealousy spurted up even here, although he admired and publicly applauded the efforts Mary was making to help her parents adjust to the news. But he could not abide her not being consumed with himself and left the parlour on an excuse for air.

He found that he needed it: as often, the false excuse turned true in action. He lit up his pipe and wandered across towards the wood. The rain was holding off but the air was damp, an almost palpable curtain of moisture to be brushed aside.

He would go back in a few minutes and offer the parents one hundred pounds drawn on a bank in Tiverton to settle their mortgage and sell the place up. That should be enough reassurance. He thought that underneath the public shock, Joseph Robinson was a sly old fox who had noted Hope's precipitate willingness to have 'just a country wedding' with 'no more frills than you would otherwise have had'. The hundred-pound note from Tiverton might materially convince him.

Hope refused to consider any other consequences.

He kept uppermost in his mind – with no great difficulty – the unique feeling of voluptuous comfort, of violently eager sexuality and infinite tenderness which his brief embrace with Mary had imprinted on his body's map and mind as surely as a lightning rod can scar a rock.

The problem, as he had realised, sadly, hundreds perhaps even thousands of times before, was that great sensual pleasures were very difficult to compare with one another and most unjustly elusive in the memory. He thought, now, as he reached Burtness Wood and let his feet take him almost automatically along a route he was now so comfortable with, that Mary would be the most satisfying woman he had ever made love to. He had noted the beauty of her face – which mattered – her grace – which mattered – and the unmistakable yield and reap of her body – which mattered most of all. She was a virgin. That would be difficult and it was a novel obstruction but he would do his best. She was, he now knew for certain, wanting love, wanting it badly and longing to let go the too-long-dammed-up force of it. And he the grateful river bed to receive the flood from that reservoir and conduct it through the winding meadows of his art to the shores of that limitless endless ocean of a moment, painful stabbing sweetest drawn out moment when the world itself became the things you were and there was an intimation of immortality in that wordless cry, a cry without meaning save as an echo to the vastness from which the climax of great love could, might, provoke a recognition.

He tried to measure her possibility against others and failed. He tried to conjure up the fine beddings, the hurried jubilant snatchings, the stolen, flagrant, dangerous pleasures – but whenever he reached out, they flitted away like fireflies before a slow hand. Women in full dress in salons in daytime, women in undress in their homes at night – husbands asleep a room away, women in hedgerows, in alleyways, in doorways, in public (sitting on his lap, skirts demurely spread over his knees), on horseback, in carriages, in prisons, on battlefields, in hospitals, women who had scared him, hurt or mocked him, women who had paid him, women who had made him pay (both hated: neither sought: both the result of pity), ugly women, fat, thin, tall, short, common, wealthy, toothless (several), aristocratic, black, Indian, hairy, one-legged (in Rotterdam), mad, and some entirely amiable handsome sweet understanding women – all, he thought, with no less but no more satisfaction than that of a woodman who sees a tree well felled – all, according to their several situations, as well served as he could manage at the time. Only very rarely and then only under duress had he ever loved a woman for anything less than thoroughly felt lust. He was proud of that. Those occasions under duress had been gratifying too in one respect: the reluctance of his member to follow the dictatorship of authority.

But that was all past.

And what had it left? As the smoke wreathed around his face in the darkness he found that even his strongest concentration could evoke only the fading sights of a white inner thigh, the glory of a perfect pink-nippled bosom, skirt, petticoat, stockings, hair, mouth, a kaleidoscope of objects, of fragments when what he wanted was a whole figure, with a face, a name, a place in his life that he could return to and against which, to get some measure of his present condition, he could match his feelings for Mary.

She alone was coherent. Maybe that was the surest sign.

When he returned he found that he had loitered longer than he had thought. Mrs. Robinson and Mary were in bed. Mr. Robinson had built up a fire and produced a bottle of port which he proposed they sink before retiring in honour of the great event. Hope wanted to be in bed or in Mary's bed or she in his or anywhere but in the parlour of the Fish with a rather dolefully determined landlord already sentimentalising on his daughter as if he had lost her at sea. "She was always that handy, from a little child, helped about the place, could charm the birds down off the trees and her mother's abiding comfort . . ." But he was caught. In the position he found himself in it was necessary for him to behave better than expected, to be finer than good and especially on this night, to show the graciousness of his rank and character.

It was a considerable sacrifice. He had never in his life found the slightest merit in the postponement of available pleasure. His only consolation, as they 'tacked' (Robinson's word) through the port and then – stand to, my hearties! – a second bottle! – was that his first encounter with Mary might be difficult for her and so the more sober he was the better and the more thought out his strategy was the more certain of both immediate and long-term success.

And then an even happier thought reached up through the ripe squelch of port: she would want, to be entirely at her ease (as he needed her to be were this to redeem him fully), a final and literal proof. The licence would do it.

With a head feeling swollen to a pumpkin he set off for Whitehaven in the morning together with a conspiratorially roguish Reverend Nicholson.

Mary watched them go and, unusually for her, cut across the field to see them again as they rode off to the great sea-port town. They would be away two days and she had promised that in those two days she would make her wedding gown, prepare herself for going away "to Scotland, of course", he had said in the fantastical hubris of his godlike proofs of love, "to Hopetoun itself, where they will take you in like the lady you are."

She was frightened of that. As she walked back across the long-grassed wet field, she reckoned up the price she was already – just this one day after the event – paying. She was frightened of the world of her prospective husband. She knew enough of it to know it could be generous, understanding, a discriminating patron and enviably gracious. She was also aware that intruders, outsiders, those who did not belong to that class as she clearly did not belong, could be ripped to pieces as surely as a canary flitting its safe cage would be torn apart by ravens and crows. She was frightened of that and wished she had one last time before her consent urged on Hope his responsibility in that matter – to see her through.

Already, it had disturbed her domestic tranquillity. Her father looked at her with a gaze which alternated between amazement and reproach; her mother, all morning, had avoided her, ducking out of her daughter's way, not knowing just how to cope with this monstrous new fact in their lives.

Why could she not rush to tell Alice as she would have done had Hope not been the man he was? Why did she not want to raise the whole valley for her wedding, to send for Askham, the best fiddler of all, to call up favours in cakes and flowers, in bridesmaids and young men on horseback who would crack through the day like the cavalry and make it unforgettable? She would have done that for Tom: she would have done that for Harrison. Why did she not turn towards Burtness and tell Kitty? Because Kitty, she was certain, would not be happy for her and she feared the douse of apprehension. And so feeling as lonely as she had ever felt, Mary took herself off to the pool which had been a calming and restorative place for her many a time: and sat beside it trailing her fingers in the water, looking at her ripple-broken reflection as if looking there could divine the enigma.

There was a cunning wind which curled about the corners of the fellside and disturbed the water. Even when she let it be, the surface was so uneven that there was no clear picture of herself. She decided against bathing and then felt rather lazy and guilty with herself, as if she had failed some important test . . .

But when Hope came back the next night, waving the licence like a flag, when he showed it to her and kissed it, when he ate greedily and rapidly and then went directly to his room, then she had only a new and unique happiness in following him and lying with him.

Once begun, she could see no reason why anyone would ever want to stop.

At first she lay stretched out, not tense but a little uncertain as he stroked and touched her, bent to harden her nipples, now brushed now stormed her body with hands that moved without a pause.

Her hair spread over the bed like a silk, lush coverlet, dividing and parting her white skin, concealing and then highlighting the voluptuous body which turned to his and wrapped about him, locked hard around him until they could be no closer: he could go no deeper. This first thrust had penetrated to the hilt and she held her breath, concentrated her senses, let the hard unimaginable bonding be absorbed: with rapture. Her eyes, which had been closed, giving her a slightly sacrificial, nun-like appearance, opened happily. She smiled: the first wholly equal exchange, perhaps, there had been between them. And then she began to move, to draw him, let him partly go, to pull him into her, totally at ease and resolved now and swept by this craze for his body, wanting him, as he did, to have, to hold, even to hurt and to break into this driven coupling.

Her demand and her force provoked him to the limit that first time. He fought to hold himself back so that for her it would be something she could never exceed – and for him too in the strain of that added effort was an aphrodisiac which goaded him on. But however high he lay above her, however hard and slowly he drove, she would absorb it, smile with wilder boldness and dare him on.

The sudden indrawn concern on her face warned him; he held on, plunged faster; his cry and her moan united in jarring vibrant blank release.

They rested, nuzzled, spent. Her hair was wound across her breasts. His head lay there and could have rested there for evermore. Now, she thought, she could understand: and now, she knew, she was his equal.

Throughout the night they excited and tempted each other, Mary growing even stronger and bolder as the calm darkness – an occasional splatter of rain like gravel on the window pane – fed and taught and unleashed a long-denied desire for the touching, coupling, languorous feeling, holding, being held, the slow tidal flowing of sex which overwhelmed even Hope who lay, sheathed in sweat, the dawn light glancing off the shine of it, wondering what else life could possibly give. What else so emptyingly gratifying; what else so freely blown on the current of physical serendipity; what else so peacefully, harmlessly, other-pleasingly complete? This was the consummation and as the sun rose again he woke from a feigned sleep and moved once more inside her to feel the silk and flesh quick sway of this magically alert oblivion where two bodies were one body but in some way the body did not exist: only the pleasure, only the idea of the pleasure, only the amazement at this symbol, this formula, this landscape, this dream . . .

*

A week later, on the 2nd October, 1802, Mary Robinson and Colonel the Honourable Alexander Augustus Hope were married by the Reverend Nicholson in Lorton parish church. The bride and groom were pulled back the few miles to the Fish Inn, Buttermere, by four young men from the village who had uncoupled the horses of the groom's fine carriage. The wedding feast followed the local pattern although the more boisterous outside sports and games were omitted. The bride was considered to be quite miraculously beautiful: a woman who had gained great fame from her grace and looks she was thought that morning to be far more handsome and dashing than she had ever been. Nothing was left out of the day which could have added to its zest and local rural charm. There was music and dancing until well past one and it might have gone on until dawn had not the bride and groom retired at midnight on account of the early start they were to make the next morning on their journey to the country seat of the groom's brother, the Earl of Hopetoun, in Scotland . . .

It was Mary who wanted to go to bed. The previous seven days and nights had driven her into a playful but insatiable and often violent lust for his body, for him to have her, for her to have him: she could not see him without wanting to touch him: he could not touch her without wanting to have her completely. They were radiant with what should have exhausted them but seemed to exercise them fit for ever greater pleasure. In that time, both of them looked and felt and acted and were seen as quite apart from all the rest, as if their private joy was so intense that it cast a ring about them inside which they spun as silent and indifferent to our world as a far-off planet in the universe.

There was a bright half moon. The curtains were open. She was asleep and he looked at her, naked, her hair down to her waist. Gently he criss-crossed her body with the fine strands gleaming in the moonlight on her marbled skin. Her face was as mysterious, he thought, as the Gioconda's. This was the best of his life. Please God, let him remember. She woke, smiled, opened her arms and took him into her.

19

To Scotland

They left the valley later that morning. Monkey-boy sat alone holding the reins like the chosen slave of an Emperor making his triumphal entry into Rome. Hope had sent for him a few days previously. George Wood had been happy to lease him out, business was beginning to fall away as the nights drew in and the weather turned, and Mary had made a favourite of him. At first Hope had thought of Burkett for the job and he would have been more reliable on the busier roads they would use into Carlisle and on the high road to Scotland but an unlocated suspicion had swung the decision away from Burkett. Perhaps there had been a sullenness, a too lightly masked attitude of resentment, or was it a feeling that Burkett was a hunter and he the prey? He could not specify but he had listened to the warning. On the busy roads, he himself would drive: and the horses were docile.

Mary had cut the boy a bottle-green jacket – a parody of the elegant coat worn by Hope – and found some brass buttons in her father's rummage box – old sea captain buttons – which she had scattered across the cloth, half for use and half for ornament. A decent pair of breeches had been found, to replace the near bottomless rags he was wearing and, almost best of all, the cobbler in Lorton to whom Hope took his boots for refurbishment discovered a pair of small boots unclaimed for years and sold them off for a few shillings. Add to this a fine scarlet cravat which Mary made out of an old handkerchief and Monkey-boy was set up.

He was only too happy to leave the couple in the coach where, blinds drawn on the country road, they spent the morning as they had passed the night until both of them reached an almost ethereal dimension of experience as the sexual obsession fed on itself and renewed itself seemingly without end. Now and then the boy would pull up at a signpost and either spell it out – loudly – or, in extremis, ask for urgent assistance but mostly he was content to whistle and look about him from his great height, the four horses walking or at most – the roads were very poor – trotting before him, too skinful of pride and cheerfulness to be at all aware of the passionate coupling in the blinded coach beneath him. Through the valleys he went, waving to men and women at harvest, loudly greeting men with sickles already cutting back the hedges, head pecking about him like a thrush hopping about a lawn. To vagrants he threw a haughty greeting, before the packhorses and mule-men he was silent, bent on manoeuvring his large vehicle without giving any cause for criticism, to lesser carriages he was cheerfully arrogant, full of himself, never had such a wonderful time with the four horses before him, the coach which he had polished up all the day before, as indeed he had burnished the harness, and inside his master and new wife on their way into a new country and a famous country seat. Who would have dreamt it a week ago playing chase around the Moot Hall in Keswick with other bits of boys from the town!

He worshipped Colonel Hope and saw himself saving his mistress time and again from the most dangerous traps – tigers pouncing and shot just before their claws sank into her unguarded skin – but most of all – robbers – he kept a sharp eye out for robbers especially when he knew himself to be in the environs of Cockermouth, a metropolis well known to Keswick folk for the dissolute manners of its inhabitants and the dark unpredictable nature of the events visited on it. The most terrible things were commonplace, he knew, he had heard, in dread Cockermouth: three-headed calves were born there; women fell down in fits and strangled themselves in the public road; wild gangs from the hills rode into the town and terrorised peaceful churchgoers. He was glad that Colonel Hope had two pistols – he had seen them in that fine grand dressing-case – he himself had a very thick length of hawthorn at his feet and if any robber came at *him* . . . Fortunately it was a closed day for robbers and the boy took his blind coach through the middle of Cockermouth unmolested. Indeed, had he not known better, he could have thought it seemed a pleasant enough little town, very like Keswick.

A few miles further on, Colonel Hope pulled up the blind and told him to look out for an inn. The boy scouted the land like a gun scanning the air for game.

Mary and Hope were drifting on a plane of weak, deeply satiated pleasure which broke into quiet private laughter at the least excuse. When they got out of the carriage at the inn – appropriately at a village called Mealsgate – the sight of Monkey-boy ramrod-backed high above them, his many buttons winking at all points of the compass, induced a bout of affectionate teasing which made up Monkey-boy even higher. He recognised the assumption of friendship and was flattered.

They had the best meal the inn could afford – which was rather meagre pickings, a scraggy dry chicken served as the centrepiece and the support group no juicier. The meal was redeemed by an excellent bottle of claret, a case of which Hope had brought along with him.

This had been given him by George Wood. It had been an unremarkable but rather jolting coincidence.

A couple of days before the wedding, Hope had found himself short of money. He was already in debt to Mr. Robinson and the debt would grow as the wedding preparations went on and Hope promised his share of it in the near future. There was also his own well-indulged keep, and payments along the way for fishing, stabling and the generous gestures to the Reverend Nicholson or a clutch of Lake Tourists who might provide an audience, take his fancy and accept his hospitality.

He decided to write to Colonel Moore. Once he had the idea it delighted him. He sent his highest regards to Miss D'Arcy, hoped she was well, looked forward to seeing her very soon but regretted that he would be absent for about ten days in Scotland "to put the final stamp on the matter which concerns all of us so closely." As he had not expected to stay in these parts for so long – "and you, sir, if anyone, know what it was which drew a few days out into weeks, weeks spent in the discovery that I have finally found the woman with whom I wish to spend the rest of my life" – he had made no arrangements for credit in the neighbourhood. "I enclose therefore a draft for thirty pounds to be drawn on Mr. Crump of Liverpool" – address enclosed. "Would you be so kind as to settle my account at the Queen's Head – I detest even trifling bills outstanding – and dispatch the change to the Fish Inn in Buttermere?" Compliments and observations on the weather made up the page.

On the day of the wedding itself, George Wood had turned up at the Fish – he had been intending to come to Buttermere for some fishing for some time and now that business was slack . . . He brought not only the change from Mr. Crump's note for thirty pounds but an extra ten guineas from Colonel Moore "in case you should meet with any unexpected expenses along the way into Scotland." Miss D'Arcy had added a brief but tender note – and no doubt, Hope concluded, it was she who was responsible for the extra ten guineas. This had led him to speculate on the possibility that he might have underestimated her character, and indeed, had it not been his wedding day . . . But that frivolous line of thought was stamped out.

Wood had not only brought the money, he had also hauled over a case of claret for Colonel Hope as a "mark of respect". It was more than that. Although to Hope their conversations and encounters had frequently been of not much more importance than time-killers, to Wood, whose rough background, trade and wall-eye kept him outside polite society, those moments had been quite wonderful. He had never met a man who talked as well as Hope – "he knows more than Peter Crosthwaite's museum," he would boast to his old farming and wrestling pals, "and he talks to me" – this was the vital part – "no different from what he would talk to the highest Dukes and Princes all over Europe, the Nabobs of India, the Emperor of China, I've no doubt. George Wood is just as much to Colonel Hope as they are and I tell you, that is rare, that is very rare and I respect that gentleman more than any gentleman – and I have met many in the Queen's Head." This would be followed by a silence which dared not be interrupted for it was as if a vow were being taken to buckle on a sword and go out into the world of snares and delusions with the arms of Colonel Hope as his standard.

George Wood, then, may well have been pulled over to Buttermere for this genuinely promised spell of fishing but pulled over at that particular time because he knew that Colonel Hope was in that noted valley. The payment via Moore of his account in full might well have alerted Wood to the possibility that he might never again see him. Hence the journey, hence the princely gift.

Hope's welcome was even more than Wood could ever have anticipated. Indeed, the man, who was an innocent, rigidly unassuming, if anything self-deprecating individual, who would describe himself – at his highest self-estimate – as one who 'soldiered on', was touched almost to the point of tears by the way in which Hope – admittedly a little flushed but that could well have been the excitement of the wedding – drew him into the company, and to its centre – Mr. and Mrs. Robinson – announcing him as "my good friend George Wood, who has done me many a favour and whose hospitality I would recommend to the Pasha of Baghdad himself."

The marriage and the bride riveted Hope in Wood's esteem unbreakably. "Only a true gentleman, only the truest," he announced a few days later in the Queen's Head with the few old and close friends who would creep in out of the colder weather once a week to stick the red hot poker in the punch and comb through the seven day tangle of business in the town, "would carry off a thing like that. Not that she could be faulted. You have never seen a woman look like that woman looked on that day. We all know Mary. We've all seen Mary. We're all proud of Mary and she's kept herself well and never lost her head, we all know that as well. But – I wish Mrs. Wood had been there to describe it for you – the dress it was – and that amazing hair of hers they write about in books, that was – flowers there were and – on his wedding day, Colonel Hope brought me into that wedding feast as if I had been – well, I dare not say a brother – but a sergeant, say, or more likely a corporal – somebody who had marched with him through the thick and the thin of it all. It was a wonderful day for me and I salute them both."

So Hope had cash in hand and the distinction of a fine wine to call on whenever local supplies faltered.

By late afternoon they were in Carlisle and Mary wanted to stop over. Hope had promised that he would buy her suitable dresses and all the other sartorial refinements necessary for her appearance in Hopetoun. She thought Carlisle would provide but he insisted it was too small a town: he would have her dressed "in Edinburgh. It is a truly great city. In Edinburgh you will find fashions ahead of London even and the dresses I will buy you there will be down to the last detail everything that is required by the Scots."

He would face no consequences. They would go to Edinburgh and after that to Hopetoun.

To Mary, Carlisle was a great enough city and she peered from the carriage window at the battered castle – "several centuries old," Hope answered her. "King Arthur had a castle here – so did the Romans and before them the Druids" – and gained a concession in being allowed to ask Monkey-boy to drive down past the Cathedral to the ancient cross with the mediaeval town hall, wooden pillared, barnacled with traders, hawkers, tinkers, the streets full of horses and cattle, cries of street sellers, there a group of actors advertising a play that evening to be given by the local celebrity Mrs. Charlotte Deans, there a procession on its way back from the courts, the judge so severe even in that unforced ritual amble to his lodging that Mary shivered, there a glimpse of the riddled alleyways known as the Lanes and then, with great determination, their youthful coachman attempted to slew the horses round the hairpin which would take them down the Scotch road.

But the horses had been too long in the country and perhaps the boy was a little tired by now. They would not go as he urged them to.

"I think you had better get out and help him," Mary said.

Hope, who had been in a shallow sulk because Mary had got her way over going through Carlisle, found release in action.

He looked out and instantly sized up what was not a very worrying scene: the boy, in fact, was doing quite well, keeping the horses relatively calm, avoiding their stamping indiscriminately about the place and upsetting baskets, vegetables, stalls, children, dogs, poultry, beggars . . .

Yet Hope sprang out as if to the rescue of one furiously distressed. The boy was both ashamed and annoyed – he swore he had it under control – but there was no option. Hope took the reins and as he scanned the busy world below him, found it hugely energising and called out:

"Mary! Mary! Come up here with us."

He drew the coach in towards the side and the boy jumped down to open the door and make a show of assisting the entirely capable Mary up onto the box. He then scaled it himself, fast as his nickname, not to be left out of what became, with Hope grandly walking the horses towards the Scotch gate, an event in itself. The splendour of the equipage, the dominating and expansive nature of Hope, the extraordinary beauty of Mary, even the comic counterpoint of the old-man-faced boy all but buried under brass buttons, drew the gaze of all the crowded walks and Hope waved, bowed, acknowledged the crowd; it was a progress.

Beyond the crumbling old wall, through the Scotch gate, appeared the cause of the high density jumble and traffic of the place – the great fair which spread over the Bridge and onto the area known as the Sands, beside the River Eden.

This time Hope could not refuse Mary's wish and he left the boy with the horses and some pence to buy a few apples for the animals and a trinket or two for himself when the hawkers clustered to the carriage.

Even though it was still light – the sun only just in the west, the castle only beginning to purple into shadow – flares had been lighted to vivify the gathering which teemed about them and they walked, Mary thought, as if they were climbing up the middle of a waterfall. She held onto Hope's arm and felt glad of his greater strength and experience: responding to what he thought of as the sweet pressure of dependency, Hope turned to her and, in a voice half-drowned by the crowd, said, "I have never in my life been as happy as I have been this last week, the days, the nights, not a moment has been wasted or empty, not one. They have held more life than I had ever imagined possible. Thank you."

Formally, he kissed her hand.

Mary, finding in this declaration the same quality she had yielded to in Lorton Church, wanted to throw her arms about him and would have done, even there, had he not suddenly whirled her round to show her some tumblers springing through hoops of fire.

There was a band playing near the gibbet where a magician using that macabre association had set up his show and was making great play with a noose which lay like a halter around the neck of his assistant. Hope wanted to see the trick through but Mary was feeling a little tired, the magician would not be satisfied until a much larger crowd came to the beating of his tambourine and his assistant's cries of "She escaped hanging! See the miraculous cheating of Death! See the noose defied by a woman!" Besides, Mary found it too sinister. She preferred the dancers – from India, from the New World – the dogs on their hind legs – the parrots and tame white rats – the shows of muscle – and the quieter and most numerous stalls of all, for clothes, boots, silks, knick-knacks, combs: she admired a pair of gloves, lilac, trimmed along the edges of each finger in white, with a crest on the back of the hand.

"Would you like them?"

Mary smiled only.

"You shall have them."

Two shillings and sixpence. He did not barter.

He insisted she wear them even though she was loath to spoil them and too shy to point out that this was the first present he had given her. They rediscovered Monkey-boy flustered but intact.

On through the eight or nine miles of flatland, some of it near marshland, to Longtown, which stood just on the English side of the Border but already in the speech of the inhabitants and in the pendulously low-browed and poor cottages – many still of mud and wattle – precursing Scotland. Hope drove most of the way while Mary, who would not be inside, let the boy sleep gently on her breast. But Hope insisted on waking him when they approached the town.

"He will never forgive us if we let him enter asleep as if he were a child," he said, and Mary saw the kindness in this.

So did the boy, who came defiantly awake ready to challenge anyone who would dare suggest he had momentarily closed his eyes, let alone gone to sleep. He took up the reins as if he had just a second before handed them over and clicked and clucked his tongue, flickered out the long whip which he had almost got the hang of, called out loudly to the potboys and grooms in the yard and made a most satisfactory noisy and noted entrance into the courtyard of the Graham's Arms.

It was past eight and all of them were tired. Hope took the best suite of rooms and while Mary unpacked – he said they would stay for two or three days until certain letters had arrived, arrangements been finalised – he wrote a letter to Newton.

He had delayed it for a week and even now, even after those nights with Mary, it was hard to write. But he willed himself and succeeded, finally, in composing a short note which said, quite simply, that he had married the woman he loved, that he wanted to make his life with her alone, that he hoped Newton understood and he would stay at the Graham's Arms waiting for a reply so that their affairs could be organised to their mutual satisfaction.

After he finished the letter he franked it: "A. Hope: Free", and rang for the maid – a slender, sleek, black-haired, button-eyed little flirt, in the delirious few months, a year or two at most, of her prime dazzle. Yes, she would see that it was sent off immediately in the morning, is that all, sir? Yes. He himself, he told her, and his wife, would wake late after a long day's travel. At which, as he had anticipated from his tone, she giggled in flattered complicity. He gave her sixpence.

He heard Mary moving about in the next room but the letter had jangled his nerves. He had told the truth to himself: he had what he wanted and he could will his life to hold it. He had told the truth to Newton – something of which, until even the day before – he would have thought himself incapable. Now he must tell the truth to Mary.

He went through to their candlelit bedroom. She stood by the bed, naked, her hair gathered before her thighs like the Venus of Botticelli.

*

George Wood had meant to stay over in Buttermere for two or three days but he was so full of the importance of the event he had not only witnessed but in which he had participated and so aware of the value and profit in being the messenger who brought this amazing news to Keswick that, without great regret, he saddled up early the next morning (which unfortunately was dry with light grey clouds, ideal for char), paid off rather too liberally the cottage woman who would lend him her (only) bedroom on these trips, and got back to Keswick by noon.

By the middle of the afternoon the facts – often greatly exaggerated – of this unlikely and unequal match were widely known, and Wood was receiving gossips high and low as they invented imperative reasons for calling at the Queen's Head, all pressing the landlord for more and more details. There could never be enough details. From the women on the clothes and the wedding feast and the honeymoon; from the men on how the man had looked, on why he might have done it, on whether his brother or any close relative or friend had been with him. The women sometimes flustered poor Wood who could not remember the colour of a bonnet or whether or not the famous hair was filleted this way or that; the men gave him to understand they would come back later and over deep draughts delve the intelligence to its source.

It was Colonel Moore's duty to take the news to his wife and Amaryllis. He knew that they were very unlikely to have heard anything as the dressmaker from Manchester had arrived the previous evening and the plan had been for the women to spend the entire day in a purdah of pins and samples.

Moore learnt of the marriage from Mr. George Bott, a collector and dealer in local rustic curiosities, a man whose information about the town was so well developed that if you sliced him into sheets he would have been a newspaper. Even the word of Mr. Bott, though, was not sufficient testimony in this momentous instance and Moore all but galloped up the street to the Queen's Head, where Wood was addressing a gaping cluster of locals much as one of the Ranting preachers, spellbinding a native congregation.

Local opinion was jubilant: Mary was not only a favourite but as it were a champion for the people of that region. The hills, the lakes, the woods, the waterfalls – those were God-given and always there and, many thought, peculiar objects for so many to make such a fuss about. Tourists proved that the Rich had nothing to do that was serious. But Mary was their girl: fell-bred, never above herself, and lauded in print and ballad and story by great men and poets everywhere. That she had captured such a fine and generous man – as all agreed, to Moore's intense irritation (although it proved his suspicion that there was an irredeemable vulgarity about the man) – this was a wonderful thing for Mary and, by association, for all of them. Moore beckoned Wood aside with his undisguised field command manner and pumped out of him the confirmation he needed.

Back on the street, his chest tight with the stress of what he had been told, he route-marched himself on a slight detour to the lake, made sure he was well apart from anyone else, and then inhaled deeply and with huge, ballooning, vengeful satisfaction. He had been proved right! The power of self-righteousness and self-congratulation thrilled through him. He was right! Hope had been a man to be suspected. He, Moore, had divined that with the instinct of a lifetime's service. Hope's unmanly, over-gilded manner, that unsoldierly fluency of speech, the feminine jibes and the odd subservience in those ceaseless compliments – all the criticism which he had been forced to choke down was now released in a cannonade of outrage. But, for a few moments, he nursed the outrage, he fondled it in his mind, he let the thought of imminent victories trickle healingly about the wounds which he had been forced to suffer by his wife and ward over this vile and deceitful suitor. Moore had his moment by the lake.

What broke it was the abrupt realisation that he was carrying a note from Hope for thirty pounds drawn on a Mr. Crump whom he had not met and might not exist! He began to walk even more urgently to his villa. He would remit the draft to Crump that afternoon. He would also go through with his intention of writing to the Earl of Hopetoun if not to admonish him for the failings of his brother then at least to point out the distress said brother had caused to a young woman whose parents had died when she was tragically etc. Moore thought he could make a cool hand of that and wished he had a secretary by his side to whom he could dictate those phrases which flowed out of him as he bounded with joy into the villa and leapt up the stairs into his wife's drawing room not only unapologetic but relieved that he had caught the women: Amaryllis, Mrs. Moore, the dressmaker, two maids, the dressmaker's dwarfish assistant, at sixes and sevens, pins between teeth, mirrors cluttering the furniture, cloth the floor over, lace and frills and wild sketches and Amaryllis like a statue in the centre of the room, draped over and triumphant.

"Ladies," said Colonel Moore, deeply secure in his battle plan and quite happy to take any initial skirmishing flak, "I must ask all but my wife and Miss D'Arcy to withdraw."

It took a moment to register but the protesting cries of the two named women died in the throat after a closer look at Colonel Moore's expression.

Amaryllis connected it immediately with herself, knew that whatever the news it would not be good and forced herself to put aside the shapes and lengths of cloth and helpfully usher out the four aides who were inclined to bump into each other and be unsure whether this called for a major evacuation or a minor retreat. When they were gone, she stood (Mrs. Moore was sitting), holding onto the back of the chair, and faced up to her guardian.

"Well?"

"He is married," Moore said, and though he may not have intended it, the sentence was cruelly expressed, even delivered with a sneer, and it cut Amaryllis like a fine whip across the cheek. Indeed, she flinched and swayed on her heels for a second as if she had been physically struck.

"When did you learn this?"

"George Wood told me. It is the sensation of the town."

Still his voice was harsh and he could not bring himself to give the fullest explanation in one easing statement. She had, after all, made him suffer over the weeks. More than that, she had challenged, successfully, his authority and forced him to climb down, before his wife, before Hope, before his own opinion of himself.

"Are there any details?"

Amaryllis's knuckles were white, Mrs. Moore noticed. She herself was so stunned by the news she could look neither at her husband nor at her ward. She concentrated on Amaryllis's knuckles.

"Wood appears to have all the information one could wish for and much that we – you and I, my dear – would be happy to be without."

Still the vital elements were unsaid: and Amaryllis smiled. The first impact of shock eased just sufficiently for her to see the game Colonel Moore was playing. She knew him well enough to know that now she had to beg.

"I would be most obliged and most grateful to you, sir, if you would not spare my feelings in this way and tell me all you know so that I might . . ." That was as far as she could get.

Moore hesitated.

It was not pity which moved him to speak – he considered his ward's behaviour to him over the past few weeks beyond forgiveness and therefore beyond pity – but he found that he was bursting to get it out. He wanted to tell somebody. He had to.

To draw attention to his own dignity, he let the hesitation grow into a pause which he twisted into the silence for a few intolerable moments longer, then –

"It is that innkeeper's daughter! That person in Buttermere at the pothouse. The one they all call 'The Beauty' in their native delusions. Her. It is her he has married and taken off into Scotland!"

Mrs. Moore shook her head: it would take her some time to absorb this.

Amaryllis went even paler, the fine bones of her face now gaunt – clear.

"Are you sure of this?"

"Wood was at the wedding feast. He described it all. There was a special licence got from Whitehaven."

Thus he blocked her next question – a question which might have given her a grain of relief for she could have queried the speed of the match, pointed out the necessity of banns . . .

"A special licence," Moore repeated, almost gloatingly, Amaryllis noted, and understood that he felt he could now taunt her at will.

"She is a lovely woman," she said.

"She is a common serving girl," said Moore, with venom.

"People speak widely of her beauty and her virtue."

"The people's opinion is ignorant, prejudiced and of no account."

"Colonel Hope must have shared that opinion."

"Hope has behaved very badly, very badly." Moore, catching a faint scent on the wind, perhaps, left it at that. "If he were here he would have a great deal to answer for."

"I think we made him answer for too much as it is."

"We were cautious. And, you see, with good cause."

"You offended him. And the result is – I have lost him."

Amaryllis had all but reached her limit but she was determined not to give Moore the satisfaction of seeing her in tears.

"You are well rid of him," said Moore, intemperately. "No gentleman would do this. No gentleman would run away and marry a servant girl on whatever provocation. And you gave him none. I acted according to your father's instructions and wishes and I dare say he has been proved right beyond all doubt."

"The proof has cost me the man I wanted for my husband."

"Had he wanted to be your husband, he had only to wait a little longer."

This near truth was intolerable.

Amaryllis delivered a jerky marionette of a bow and left the room almost at a marching pace, a piece of material from a proposed gown still clutched tight in her hand with the clamp force of a death grip.

Moore looked to his wife for some comment on his performance, on the news, on Amaryllis, on the scoundrel Hope, on his, Moore's, great and wise foresight!

She was sobbing and waved him away.

*

The immediate neighbourhood of Longtown is flat and marshy to the west, leading out to the treacherous Solway Firth and deeply wooded to the east, largely the land of the Graham family which emerged as one of the bloodstained victors after three centuries of Border Wars. The plains to the south back to Carlisle are dull and north into Scotland are more flatlands. For those who enjoyed slaughtering animals and game or hooking out salmon and trout it must have appeared another Eden but few sought it out for leisure of any less murderous variety. The centuries of national, local and family wars had left the place denuded of population. It was known as the Wastelands. Those battles and feuds, possibly the longest recorded family feuds on the planet, had taken life and blood elsewhere. There were few settlements of any size and none of much interest.

The inhabitants had become nomadic farmers on the tops and the great buildings were fortified churches, pele towers and castles. Only the strongest stone buildings had held their ground and they were few. The rest was still little more than a huddle of hovels here and there heaped on the blood-soaked landscape – twelve thousand killed in those three fields in a morning; eighteen thousand lost in that estuary in a day. It was a country where Irish gypsies wintered and were comfortable, a place that outlaws made for and, in long remote valleys, ancient Border families would still send out the young sons from eleven years and upwards – the Armstrongs, the Elliotts, the Robsons and Grahams and Scotts, the Douglases, the Hetheringtons, the Nixons and Johnstones and Maxwells – to take revenge for a slight real or imagined and come back with evidence of spilt blood. Dour, grim and as locked in its own incestuous quarrels as any cursed kingdom in the Bible; a place to pass through quickly and not meet a direct glance in the face; a barren land where the wind keened over the marshes and out of bare scrub riders would suddenly appear with menace.

To Mary it was for those few days a paradise.

An observant, sensitive, careful woman, she had been disarmed and transfigured by her love for Hope and his for her. This was a New World of experience and what she had known before was left behind like an old, abandoned country. There was too much in the present for the past to have more than a fingerhold and she walked around the neighbourhood of Longtown as if it were that magical kingdom where buttered larks fall from the sky into your mouth and the rivers flow with diamonds. She was in an enchanted castle and like a lady in a legendary tale she, with Monkey-boy as her squire, strolled about the gory wastelands unaware, as if they were fields of gold.

Hope had stayed a day and a night and then, with a believable show of great reluctance, announced that he had to go to Dumfries to make sure that his brother would be at the house. He must also draw some money – he had got embarrassingly short of ready cash – and re-write his will (his solicitor was at Dumfries). This final piece of news he delivered as a gift but in such a way as to emphasise the possible tragic undertone. Mary had felt even further weakened by the largesse of his devotion.

He had taken a man from the Graham's Arms to drive him, explaining to the boy that he wanted him to stay as chaperon to the new bride. The word chaperon had almost compensated Monkey-boy.

He got on with Mary very well. Although Keswick was a town of not many more than a thousand inhabitants, the tourist traffic and industrial connections made it a different species – in the boy's eyes – from the 'country' which he affected to find dull, unworthy of a civilised man's full attention and liable to give you unpleasant shocks such as putting your foot on what appeared a soft pad of mud-earth and going up to your knee in sludge which threatened to suck you in entirely. Mary had pulled him out and wiped off the worst with grass. But his townee ways entertained her and she allowed him the superiorities which he thought accrued by right to someone important enough to have been seeded in an urban centre. He acted the page, the squire: she acted the mistress-bride, but never the lady. She disappointed him a little there: he enjoyed saying 'My Lady' very loudly when people were passing or they were in the Graham's Arms and was abashed when Mary forbade him to do it. He would have liked a little more respect for his position, more bowing and 'can I help, me lady'-ing, but that was resisted. Yet she encouraged him to assume the role of her protector as they wandered around.

Every path to Mary was an adventure. To stroll at such leisure was a novelty. Or she could sit in her drawing room and be waited on by the maid who was such a sweet and chatty girl and could once have been a friend . . . It was all a marvel and a wonder and the lilac gloves were laid on his empty pillow.

*

Newton read the letter quickly, put it away and finished his breakfast. Then he went out of his decidedly inferior accommodation into the thriving town of Kendal and made his way through the over-pressing crowd until he came to the river. He walked along its bank, past the industries using the fast-flowing water for the famous Kendal products, and kept his course until he was clear in the country.

Needing to be strictly alone, he quarried his way into the landscape and went way beyond the old motte and bailey mound of the first castle until he found a safely isolated spot, a cleft between two hillocks, drumlins, where no harvesters would pass, no shepherds were in sight, no peat smoke, dog howl or children's cry betrayed habitation: then he read the letter again. And after some hours of considerable upheaval, decided on his response.

*

On his way back from Dumfries, late, a darkening, windy, damp afternoon, trees creaking, horses unsettled, shots from the woods like the remnant of a war, Hope decided he would get down and walk the final three or four miles back to Longtown. The young groom from the Graham's Arms was not totally surprised: his temporary master had shown several signs of engaging eccentricity on the journey. He had discovered, for instance, near Gretna – he had insisted on going to the famous forge where the blacksmith/priest had hammered out so many wild and unauthorised marriages – an impressive and isolated lump of rock called the Lochmaben Stone. This, he had been told by the guide who had detached himself from the bellows of the forge to escort the wealthy and liberal-looking gentleman down to the banks of the Solway where it lay, was a local Truce Stone. "What happened," said the guide, looking up at the lump, lichened and beaten by weather but untouched, surprisingly for such a long-standing and significant monument, by any sign of civilised man, any number, letter, pictogram, not even a scratch from an idle dirk had cared to or dared to infringe its natural features, "what happened was that aince a year the families would gather at the Stane heer. The English frae over theer," he hoisted a thumb over his shoulder without deigning to turn but Hope followed his direction across that tongue of firth called Solway and noticed fishermen way out on the sands with their haaf nets, "an' us frae roundaboots hereaboots and we settle accounts. Cattle would be paid back and twelve men on either side would be set up tae judge the other fella and so on until aa was cleared up and they could get on wi' their business for anither yeer, things bein' cleant up if you see what aa'm sayin'."

Hope was delighted.

"But look at the place," he said, indignantly, "no care taken of it, nothing to tell you how important it is. This –" he flung out his half-clawed hand to the rock, "is a sight worth a dozen of their lakes and waterfalls. Lake Tourists! It is as sensible to worship the weather. The weather, the lakes, the mountain fells – they are just there. This stone had to be hauled here –" he looked to the guide for confirmation: given. "There's no stone like this in this area?" he looked to the guide: another nod. "It would be drawn here, by men who wanted a place of peace in the barbarous countryside we have heard this region was for so long – peace-loving men dragged this stone here. And here it stays for centuries. A place where feuds are settled and justice is done and who comes to see it? Very few?" The guide concurred. "*Very* few?" A sad nod. Hope fumbled for a sixpence, found a shilling and decided it made no odds. "This is the most moving sight I have seen since I came into the north of the country. Thank you." He flipped the silver coin over to the bellows blower who clapped both hands over it and nodded for the last and deepest time.

So when Hope dismounted, scribbled a note to his 'dear wife' and said he would prefer the exercise of his legs to the jolting of his hindquarters, the Longtown groom filed it away as another little anecdote for future parlance and was not displeased to drive an empty carriage down the road. The girl he was courting was hired at a farm just outside Longtown and with luck he might catch sight of her in the farmyard, lure her over and, if all the winds were in the right direction, give her a ride in this majestic carriage. He might even, if the heavens were looking the other way, climb in beside her . . .

Hope let the carriage lumber and jangle into the distance before he set one foot before the other. Even then he paused for an extra minute or two to listen to the growing anger of the wind at the trees. This was when he liked Nature. He could feel pitted against it. Now, as he began to walk, he was buffeted quite violently by the wind and the rain slashed across his face: it made him feel alive. The clouds, too, were as he liked clouds to be: massive, brooding grey shot with white and even silver-backed filaments scudding across the sky as if scowlingly fleeing the wrath of God. It grew dark soon, the light heavily absorbed in the dense woodlands now making a timber canyon of the badly rutted road. Gradually the sense of immediate vivacity gave way to the much more profound feeling of desolation which he had been repressing for the past twenty-four hours. As his mood darkened and his pace slowed down, the wildness of Nature which had seemed exhilarating became the weary, abstract and endless moan of injured innocence, the trees bending and protesting as they bent, the clouds flashing across the hilltops seemed a sign of the strains and disturbances in himself. Quite suddenly, he felt lead-limbed and found a bank to rest on.

The wind rose higher, now blasting through the trees, boring through the wood, until he could feel he was out on the ocean as he had been often enough, on a night when the ship seems frail and the seas and skies so mockingly powerful there can be no science but faith to see you through.

Desolation came up like the fast rush of a high tide and soon he was axed by it, head literally hanging down on his chest as if the neck, that vital channel between brain and body, had been snapped.

What on earth was he to do?

Was he altogether an evil man? Beyond all redemption? Surely the Lord had forgiven worse than him but they had confessed – how could he confess? Or they had given up their broad and easy evil ways and turned to the strait and narrow road that led to God. How could he take that path without hurting the person dearer to him than anyone had ever been? How was he to be good without destroying the woman for whose sake he wanted to be good?

"Can You answer that?" he muttered to himself and then, stiffly, as if indeed he had been injured, "Can You?" He raised his voice to compete with the soughing boom of the wind. "Will You tell me how to do it? Please. I'll do anything You ask if You will tell me how to do this thing: to tell the truth, not to hurt Mary and to keep her love. If I lose her love then I am lost anyway. I have to keep that. She is my last chance. Perhaps she is my only chance. But if I tell her the truth I will hurt her terribly – You know that. And that will risk losing her, losing her love. You know what an innocent lamb she is. You know all about Mary. Your mother was a Mary. She was probably put in charge of the sheep, too – in the Holy Land – I've been there – sorry – I've heard stories from those who have and they've told me about the sheep, their bells, the goats, those barren hills, how all the parables can be found in a day's walk from Jerusalem to Jericho. But that's as may be. I'm just trying to get You to understand – no, I'm trying to get Your help. Perhaps You don't want me up there? But it was You Who said there would be more rejoicing in Heaven for the return of one sinner . . . You said that: and I believe it. And You said 'Come unto me all ye who are heavy laden and I will refresh you!' Well. Here I am. So heavy laden I can't stand up and *that* is true. I will sit here until I have an answer. Why does everything have to be a test? Never mind. So is this *the* test? I tell Mary the truth, hurt her, lose her, prove to You that I am true to Your faith and then . . . ? What? Mary will be harmed. I will be alone. You will have me back sinning in half a day. Should I be talking to You like this? Should I be talking to You at all? I've never found it difficult and You've answered me before now. Oh yes. In Scarborough, bless You, O Lord, for I was rotting flesh. That time going to America, a night like this but in a colossal sea, and I prayed and You plucked that small bark safely to the shore. And I have to talk to You now because there is no-one else – no-one else on this entire earth of Yours – who will listen and understand as You listen – but do You understand?"

Hope slid clumsily onto his knees. The thick, cold mud came through his breeches immediately. He closed his hands before him and lifted his head into the rain, seeing the turbulent clouds, buffeted by the wind now whining through the creaking branches and drawing louder through the trees.

"I need a sign. I need to know what to do. I will wait here in this no man's empty land where, I am told, You have looked down on hundreds of years of butchery here whose meaning only You in Your infinite wisdom can understand, I will kneel here until You show me what I must do. But if You would have me to use – and I can be of such use! If You give me the sign I will work and fight for Your ministry like a crusader in arms – if You want me in Your fold, then You must tell me how I can, as I must, as I have to, tell Mary the truth and neither hurt her nor lose her."

He stayed kneeling until his thighs locked with cramp and the rain had battered him into a saturated statue. No coaches or horses passed in the darkness. The cold came through his legs and then into his arms – the rain running down his upturned sleeves – in spasms of pain but he would not unlock himself from his suppliant pose.

Like someone trying to shift a rock way, way beyond his powers, he forced his mind to dwell firmly and solely on the goodness of God and his faith in the intercession of Christ. "Please God," he would murmur at times, or merely, plaintively, on the moaning wind, "Please." Eventually it was as if his mind were as stiffened and locked as his body. If only he could make the force of his will impose itself on some passing spirit of this bloodied place, a spirit which would be affectionate remembering perhaps a similar dilemma. He could not dare to reach the glory of God as the mere and desperate sinner he was but surely in one of God's million million ears his thought-willed prayer would be heard and responded to? Surely to one of His million million eyes the sight of such pleading would bring alleviation?

If only he could stay still enough, long enough, and his mind which had done so much that was bad could use those forces for good and press on the mercy of the Lord. "Please God," he said and the words became neither prayer nor plaint, merely two shapes of sound, whispered syllables in the wind which roared them away to the east. His whole mind and body became one muscle and the muscle cried to be heard, to be answered . . .

About an hour after midnight, Mary forced them to get out the coach and lamps to look for him – provoked at last to use her new authority as a lady over the easy reasons and excuses of the groom. She reached him just in time, tumbled sideways onto the road, in an attitude which looked very like that of a child curled up into itself, desperate for comfort.

*

His fever was short but violent. Mary had experience of his strength and she herself was a strong woman, but she was forced to call in help more than once on that first bad day as he threatened to get up and walk back to Hause Point. She could not understand why but it was Hause Point to which he kept returning. He had been sodden and stone cold: she told them he had been stunned by a falling branch – the bruise was hidden inside his thick growth of hair – nor was it a large bruise but sufficient, clearly, to lay him low and then the bitter rain had got to him.

She knew this was a lie. There was no bruise and his knees, she could see, were padded with mud which could only have come from kneeling. But there had to be an explanation and that which she gave appeared plausible.

Already the favourite, he now became the centre of attention. The Colonel's health was enquired after by someone or other every few minutes and the Graham's Arms moved in slippered sentences during the thirty-six hours of his violent assault on his sickness. For that, it appeared to Mary, was what was happening. It was as if the illness were as specific as a devil inside him and he was using every nerve and fury to exorcise it. There was no sense in which he was the passive body branded by this destructive condition. The condition seemed deeply lodged and had to be torn out with shivering fingers and trembling hands.

"Please God," he would say, "take him away. Take him out of me!"

"Please God" was repeated so plaintively, so longingly, obstinately, angrily, patiently, sorrowfully, that Mary could not bear to hear it without feeling a fire cut across all her senses. It was as if he were pleading for help which would not come and she could not give it. She felt distressed at her inadequacy.

When, finally, the sweat broke and sluiced off him and the spasms began to ebb, there was a period when he babbled. Mary sent the sharp-eyed maid away, saying that she would rather look after him herself, and besides it was over, people could know he would be up and about soon enough, it had been a fierce struggle but a short one. She was disturbed by the babble.

Talk of "my real family is greater than the Hopes, Mary. We were descended from kings, my mother told me. She never lied. We are descended from the Plantagenets, my mother said, and being kings we should always live like kings. She liked me to be a king. The Plantagenets were cheated and swindled and murdered but they will return and then the country will be a fine country once more . . ." Talk or, more, mere stubs of phrases, to do with "the children must stop . . . nothing can be done when you don't feel . . . Newton is the man . . . is that not enough for you, is *that* not enough for you . . . ?" and broken sequences which as he dozed and waked over the next dozen hours began to make some pattern in Mary's mind and shape into a message which she could not decipher.

Broth, gruel, eggs beaten in butter and milk, rum, a thin slice of venison, soft nursing such as he had never known and within a few days he was up and walking and well enough on the fourth or fifth day to take out a couple of horses and ride Mary up to the Lochmaben Stone, where he explained, insofar as he could, its historical importance and then, beating down her protests, made love to her urgently, in the open, pressed against the Truce Stone. She did not enjoy it.

It was when he got back from that outing that he received a letter.

He took it out of doors to read and came back in a mood of terrible gaiety. "We shall have to go back to Buttermere," he announced, waving the letter like a flag of surrender. "My brother has sent me credit to Keswick, and he points out," he glanced at the letter for confirmation, "that he will be closing down Hopetoun in a few days' time to make a journey abroad, to take advantage of the Peace, that's it! To settle business he has in France – to see if he still has any business in France! – and we can go south, he proposes, and stay with him in London – just imagine – in London! Mary – London – the greatest city in the world – St. Paul's, Smithfield, Covent Garden, Drury Lane, the Court, the Thames . . ."

His voice was far away as her head grew lighter and stranger but she held on. The very bones in her skull seemed to swell in fear and a cry split through them but she would not let it out. Her flesh ran with the panic of terror but she forced the muscles of the mouth to smile, the neck to nod the head at her husband's talk and plans and bright promises. It was as if her heart were being slowly ripped in two. For she knew he was lying, and more, she saw he might always have lied.

Part Two

"It is not by mere Thought, I can understand this man."

Samuel Taylor Coleridge

20

'The Romantic Marriage'

According to the Editor of the *Morning Post*, the 11th October 1802 was a slow day for news. "To fill in a space on the page" he included a short colourful piece from Samuel Taylor Coleridge, resident in Keswick. He had been trying to persuade Coleridge to write full time for the *Post* – he considered him to be the most brilliant journalist of his day just as others considered him to be the greatest thinker and talker but none, alas, gave him the accolade he sought most eagerly: of greatest poet. A week before in the *Morning Post* he had published what many consider his last fine poem, 'Dejection Ode'. In view of Coleridge's future censorious attitude towards the man called Hope, it might be interesting to note that 'Dejection Ode' was addressed to his mistress and followed a year of drugs, debts, broken promises, illness and severe domestic discord in which he had confessed to wanting to murder his wife and children. His mistress, he called her Asra, had rejected his overtures and even been embarrassed by them. The piece of 11th October was called 'The Romantic Marriage'.

The 'Dejection Ode' was published on the day that Wordsworth's marriage to Mary Hutchinson was announced. Mary was a childhood sweetheart. Her character had much in common with Wordsworth's characterisation of Mary Robinson. Wordsworth's previous great love was the French Annette Vallon, whom he had just seen this August at Calais, leaving her – after nine years' fidelity under great stress – with a small sum of money and their illegitimate daughter.

Coleridge envied Wordsworth, who was unfailingly supported by women who loved him, served him, wrote out his poetry, recited it by heart: even his own longed-for 'mistress', Mary's sister Sara Hutchinson, seemed much fonder of Wordsworth. Coleridge's genius was now, late in 1802, turning from the pursuit of poetry – Wordsworth, he thought, had blocked that route to him – to criticism and journalism. His intelligence was such that even from the small and remote mountain town of Keswick, he sent off to London, three hundred miles away, essays and comments on politics and events which showed a wonderful grasp of argument and detail. 'The Romantic Marriage' was a much lighter piece.

The publication of this article brings the story into the public domain.

*

THE MORNING POST. OCTOBER 11TH, 1802. PAGE 3.

The Romantic Marriage

> On the 2nd instant a Gentleman, calling himself Alexander Augustus Hope, Member for Linlithgowshire and brother to the Earl of Hopetoun, was married at the church of Lorton near Keswick to a young woman celebrated by the tourists under the name of The Beauty of Buttermere . . . she ought indeed to have been called The Grace of Buttermere rather than the Beauty . . . She has long attracted the notice of every visitor by her exquisite elegance and the becoming manner in which she is used to fillet her beautiful long hair: likewise by the uncommonly fine handwriting by which the little bill was drawn out. Added to this, she had ever maintained an irreproachable character, is a good daughter and a modest, sensible and observant woman.

Coleridge then goes on to describe Hope's "address to a lady of youth, beauty and good fortune" (this is Miss D'Arcy) " . . . the wedding clothes were bought," he writes, "and the day fixed for their marriage when he feigned a pretence for absence and married the Beauty of Buttermere."

Paradoxically, this expunges doubts and reservations which Coleridge (Moore inspired?) had held.

> His marriage, however, with a poor girl without money, family or expectations has weakened the suspicions entertained to his disadvantage. But the interest which the good people of Keswick take in the welfare of the Beauty of Buttermere has not yet suffered them entirely to subside, and they await with anxiety

> the moment when they shall receive decisive proofs that the bridegroom is the real person whom he describes himself to be. The circumstances of his marriage are sufficient to satisfy us he is no impostor, and therefore we may venture to congratulate the Beauty of Buttermere on her good fortune. The Hon. Alexander Hope, the member for Linlithgowshire, is a Colonel in the Army, a . . . etc.

Coleridge was six years out in Mary's age (he gave it as thirty) and also wrong about a day being 'fixed' for Hope's marriage to Miss D'Arcy. The doubts he mentions – as to Hope's real identity – might well have more to do with the embarrassed and post-hoc reparations being made by his friend Moore than by any more general opinion. Crump was to cash the bill for thirty pounds which Hope had sent to Moore a couple of days before the wedding. Wood, whose livelihood depended on a regular assessment of creditworthiness, was convinced by Hope as were a great many others – the Reverend Nicholson, Skelton and, of course, Miss D'Arcy.

It was indeed a slow day for news. Newton read and re-read the page on which the article was placed. Nothing else compared. He was told, for instance, that "the Archduke Constantine of Russia, a Prince whose character and manners have been set in an exceedingly unfavourable light by Mason in the well-known *Secret Memoirs of the Russian Court*, is said to have behaved on some late occasions with ill-bred and offensive rudeness to Prince William of Gloucester." "The Dutch Government," the same column went on, "is now sending out large supplies of ammunition on board its Indian ships to the Cape of Good Hope and the Isle of Java." Without a break in the line the column's next entry reads, "Female fecundity seems to have assumed new powers in French Flanders since the era of the Revolution. Mrs. Filibert aged fifty-eight years and resident near Valenciennes was delivered the other day of a fine female child . . . Michaelmas Frankfurt fair has been miserably dull . . ."

Almost a quarter of the page was taken up with verse of one sort or another – Original Epigrams includes some lines "On the curious circumstance that in the German language the sun is feminine and the moon masculine". There is shipping news from Deal, Portsmouth and Plymouth: "October 7th sailed the *Amelia* and *Galatea* Frigates for Portsmouth. Came into harbour the *Rusario* sloop of war to be paid off." News from Cheltenham "which could scarcely ever boast of so much company at this season of the year as at present." Some of it undesirable, judging from the final paragraph: "Last night villains picked the door of the Cheltenham Bank but got no booty, the cash being always removed at night in one of the proprietors' dwelling houses." News from Margate: "the Earl and Countess of Jersey stay six weeks longer." And following that: "a certain Colonel is evidently smitten by the charms of the Hon. Miss Fitzroy. The parties appear to understand each other and it is not improbable but they may pay a visit to the Hymeneal altar without taking a delightful trip to Gretna." A long notice from Drury Lane, an even longer notice from the Norwich Musical Festival, deaths, appointments, birthdays and a brief, bottom of the column account of Captain Sowden's "Aerial Excursion with Monsieur Garnerin. That H.E.'s countryman, Volney, furnished Captain S. with the several ideas, cannot be doubted, if we refer to his survey of the Revolutions of Empires where, speaking of himself, as having been lifted up into the uppermost region by the wing of Genius, he says 'that although he had eyes more piercing than those of an eagle, the rivers below appeared to me no more than meandering ribbons, ridges of mountains irregular furrows, and great cities a nest of boxes, varied among themselves like the squares on a chessboard'." Newton tried to imagine being high as a cloud, scouring the land below for Hope's carriage, but he failed. He cut out the article and folded it into his wallet.

Coleridge's (anonymous) account was instantly taken up by other papers and widely reprinted. It may indeed have been a slow day for news on 11th October 1802. But matters would soon speed up and the *Morning Post* would keep an eager, increasingly excited, and ultimately frenzied public well informed.

*

George Hardinge – "a Welsh judge and a very singular gentleman" according to Coleridge – was a senior justice of Brecon, Wales, a Cambridge scholar who had married an heiress, an author of biographical notes, a noted non-returner of borrowed books and the original for the character of the waggish Welsh judge in *Don Juan*.

He was on his way from Edinburgh back to Brecon – a progress not too difficult to discover – and stopped over in Carlisle when he received a letter from someone claiming to be an old acquaintance (though Hardinge could not recollect the rather illegible name) who wanted him to know that his old friend Colonel Hope was in the Lake District and badly in need of advice. It would be a great favour to your dear friend, the letter insisted, if you passed through Keswick and sought out the Colonel who was too proud to call for help but would undoubtedly appreciate it. The proprietor of the Queen's Head would be sure to know Hope's whereabouts.

Mr. Judge Hardinge had always promised himself a few days in the Lakes, primarily to enable him to hold informed conversations in which he would commend the Welsh hills at the expense of the Cumbrian with a detail which it would be impossible to counter. He was sole master of his time and on the morning of the 11th took a leisurely route into the Lakes, stopping at the Crown in Wigton for an excellent game pie and a creditable local beer – he noted "the number of male inhabitants who stand on corners and occasionally muster up all their energies in order to issue a careful spit" – and from there his carriage took him via Mealsgate, through Ireby – "there was the remains of what I was told had been a busy market around the old cross: once a wealthy village now being set in decline by the new industries" – alongside Bassenthwaite under Skiddaw – "more massy than our Snowdon but without the grandeur: here we Welsh have the edge" – and into Keswick – "more of a Welsh town than an English: Cumbrian stems from Cymru – companion – I felt instantly at home there."

George Wood welcomed him to the Queen's Head and once more the scurrying of stableboys and town boys brought a few minutes' theatre to the cobbled yard. Wood thought that Colonel Hope had gone into Scotland with his bride: but he could well be back in Buttermere by now.

"*Bride*, is it?" Hardinge was delighted. "And who is the victim?" Wood obliged. Hardinge instructed his manservant – who knew Hope well – to go into Buttermere the first thing in the morning.

21

Langdale Chapel

They had travelled back in silence, sat apart. It was not a sullen separation. Both were troubled with private thoughts so desperate they welcomed the silence. They also noted it and now and then one or the other would break it, to be friendly.

"Did you ever look in that?" Hope indicated the dressing-case which was on the seat beside him and facing Mary: they sat diagonally inside the coach leaving the boy the freedom of the reins. "While I was in Scotland I imagined you spending some of your time gazing into it."

"I never opened it," Mary said and smiled, a small sad smile but meant to be reassuring.

"Most women would not only have opened it, they would have used it."

He unlocked the case, displaying it to her as if it were an object worthy of particular awe. Mary had never seen a single thing as beautifully made, appointed and cared for. All the four bottles silver-topped; the brushes thick-backed in worked, patterned silver; the neat lady-like pistols; the little drawers for studs, buttons, pins; the mirrors; hidden spaces for jewellery; the whole as reverently handled by Hope as if the dressing-case were an altar and the objects sacramental vessels.

"I believe you – love," Mary bit on the discomfort of the word but had to pause, "that dressing-case . . ."

"It's seen great service," he said, easily, "Egypt, Rome, Vienna . . ." and again she wanted him only to stop these lies although how did she know, how dare she assume, what was her evidence and more important what was her reason for this sudden repellent conclusion?

The coach jogged along the uneven roads, only achieving a smooth trotting run on the few stretches of made up surface.

When they passed the Roman cavalry camp called Old Carlisle the boy asked if they wanted to turn down into Wigton – which he had heard of as a mighty place, famous over the globe for its game pie and beer – but neither Hope nor Mary had any appetite and they went on to Cockermouth before they stopped and then only because Mary surmised the hunger pangs of their growing coachman.

"I'm glad to be coming back into this valley," she said, impulsively reaching out to him as she caught sight of Loweswater, the first of the three lakes hung down in the Vale of Lorton like a triple pendant between the bosoms of the hills.

"So am I," he said, taking and gripping her hand tightly. "I never wanted to leave it."

"You need not, then," she said, intuiting something true and important in his melancholy sentence. His dejection appeared so heartfelt that she let her own doubts and terrors slip away. "We can stay here. I don't have to go to Scotland. Or London. I've always been happy enough here and with you I would be so much happier."

He brought his blemished hand to close a double grip over her releasing hold.

"We could buy a good house. A free-standing house, of course, with a little land, near the lake," he said.

"I would still like to keep a small flock of sheep and goats," she said, smiling rather mischievously. "Until I have better things to concern me."

"The houses are well built here," Hope said. "Good stone and slate. Weatherproof. Secure against anything."

"You would become the leading light in the valley."

"I would have none of that. A peaceful life, an open hearth, a little fishing, a few friends and you, Mary. There is nothing else on earth I want . . . Do you believe that?"

"Yes. I believe it."

"It is the truth. I swear."

"You need not swear. I believe you."

His look was unbearably anguished yet tender. She had to withdraw her hand and turn away from it. He confused her moral nature too much. She could not feel clearly or right and so her actions were now peremptory. He interpreted this as evidence of her being overcome with the prospect of such peace and security and felt at once optimistic and guilty.

But even that unexpectedly warm and affectionate show was only temporary. Hope was soon pitched back into depression as he recalled the precise wording of the letter from Newton. Mary, re-passing the fields and houses which she had passed by so recently so happily, was bracing herself against the questions. The future had become impenetrable as any of the large darkening silent fells between which the coach rocked and waddled its way.

They arrived at about seven. Mary made a great deal of the little of her honeymoon and her parents went to bed convinced she had been gloriously treated. Hope drank far too much brandy, which, on top of his only recently recovered condition, made him stiff drunk and Mary had to half-carry him to bed where he fell into unconsciousness immediately. Except during his illness, it was the first night since he had brought back the licence that they had not made love – for which she was grateful because she could not dissemble. Her moral unease was immediately translated into physical reluctance and doubt. Mary listened to his faint purring snoring and his bursts of nightmare almost distraught with apprehension.

*

Hardinge's manservant, Richard Jenkins, rode smartly up to the Fish and assumed it must be the inn which had been named, although, as he was to tell other lesser servants two days later, in the kitchen bar of the Queen's Head, "it looked no more like an inn than a cottage, look you. In Wales, we have not many inns in Wales, but when an inn we have got, look you, like an inn it appears and not like any ordinary cottage, see? I was on my guard from the moment I saw the place, take note. Outward appearance is not much, they say, but what other and better and more convenient appearance have you got to go on, see? And I knew my Colonel Hope, I knew that gallant gentleman from many a good night – which became good morning! look you – with my master in some of the best places a gentleman can get drunk in London or anywhere in the world I dare say if you went to the trouble to go about and make drunken comparison. I knew that Colonel Hope would not be seen skinning a rabbit in a low-roofed, mean-windowed, small-doored, groomless, nigh servantless, peat-fired hovel of a pothouse calling itself an inn such as this was I saw before me. Therefore I may say without exaggeration and may the Lord be my witness as indeed He is the witness *and* the judge of us all – even my master himself – I want you to know that before I dismounted I had my suspicions."

There was a boy in a multi-buttoned bottle-green jacket brushing down a horse in the damp morning air and it was to him that Jenkins applied for information on the whereabouts of Colonel Hope. The boy proudly pointed out the figure of a man – "only half-dressed, he was," Jenkins reported, "no jacket or coat whatsoever. Just the shirt with the cravat blowing in the breeze like a windmill."

Jenkins gave the boy his horse and went across the field with the letter. As he drew nearer he saw that the man had a note in his hand to which he was referring distractedly "and he was talking to himself, look you, a sure sign, gentlemen, and a most terrible thing." Jenkins hovered for a moment or so out of courtesy but finally pressed on, only to stand off again, in puzzlement.

"Well, man, what do you want? You've been stalking me for half an hour."

"I'm looking for Colonel Hope, sir," he waved his letter and he added, to stave off the malevolence in the eye of the preoccupied gentleman, "I have this letter for him from his old friend Judge Hardinge."

"Well?"

"The boy over there – with the buttons – told me that you were Colonel Hope, sir."

"And?"

"He must have been mistaken, sir, for I see you nearer now and I know you are not the Colonel."

"Let me look at the letter."

The Judge, who was no stinter of title, had lavished all of Colonel Hope's titles on the paper. Hope studied it a moment, opened and read it and then looked up and presented Jenkins with a face on which the hard malevolence had been erased. He smiled so charmingly that Jenkins was encouraged to smile back – he noticed the scar running into the dimple and somehow the observation was a comfort.

"You are . . . ?"

"Jenkins, sir."

"Jenkins. This is not for me. It is for my brother. I remember him telling me about your master. I am Charles Hope – not Alexander – Member for Dumfries, not Linlithgowshire. But I will be glad to pay a visit to the gentleman. As a matter of fact it fits in very well with my own plans. Would you tell him that, Jenkins? I am working out some thoughts and do not want to interrupt myself by going back to the –" the merest pause, a keen sense of the Jenkins view – "little pothouse over there. We Lake Tourists, you know," he stretched out an arm as if bidding the scenery to take a bow or strike up, "are happiest in the rustic dwelling house. Nature, Jenkins, is a mighty force and the more we humble ourselves before it the more we can appreciate its majesty."

"We have very big mountains in Wales also," Jenkins said.

"I'll be in Keswick tomorrow."

"Thank you, sir . . . and how is your brother, sir? The Judge will kick me downstairs and up again if I did not ask."

"The last I heard of Alexander he was in Vienna. I think he had come to prefer abroad to home. But we are not an epistolatory family: not much time for letter-writing, Jenkins, not, that is, between ourselves."

"Epistolatory was known to me," said Jenkins. "The Judge is full of Latin."

"Of course. Good day to you."

"Shall I take back the letter?"

"That won't be necessary."

"So I left him down by the lakeside with two letters," Jenkins reported in his minute account to as attentive an audience as he had enjoyed for a long time, "one in each hand, see, like equal weights on the scales of justice. And I knew, as God Himself is my Judge, that I had met a man whose soul was roasting on the spit."

*

Newton's letter left him no option. He had to go to Keswick. He had no intention of calling on Judge Hardinge and took the risk of Newton's further opposition by delaying his trip by one day to give Hardinge the chance to move on.

And it would be another day with Mary.

Yet somehow he seemed to spend all that day avoiding her; and she him. The Reverend Nicholson, hearing that they were back, walked over to a welcome from Hope and the men spent the afternoon fishing, quite successfully, for char. Nicholson also got the bonus of the offer of a ride in the coach to Keswick the next morning . . .

Mary managed to find a few things which had fallen behind in the neatness and organisation of the house and the inn and used this as a springboard to an energetic cleaning and scouring – despite Mrs. Robinson's protests that this was not what a lady should be doing – and so her day was washed and scrubbed through. Whenever she stopped for a few minutes, fear threatened to panic her . . .

There were no visitors that evening which relieved Mrs. Robinson who had feared that Mary might make the whole world topsy-turvy by insisting on serving as before. She and her husband were now a little in awe of and confused by their daunting son-in-law. They were incapable of engaging their daughter on the old terms. But the roots were deep, the ties tranquilly bound. This need be no more than a shadow flitting across the surface of the lake. They, like Mary, like Hope, were in suspense.

Mary went to bed early but Hope had no inclination to spend an evening with a bottle or his father-in-law. He pottered about the few outbuildings as the dusk gathered, loading the carriage for the next day, fidgeting so much about the granary that the boy caught the anxiety and suspected he may have done something wrong.

Hope was about to go into the inn, to their room, when he had an impulse to repeat the walk he had once made up the lake and beyond to where the high fells had given him the feeling of an impenetrable fortress.

He walked swiftly, enjoying the pull on his legs, the cool evening, the calming, droning susurration of the water on the shore. The moon was rising and as he walked through the woods it brightened steadily so that when he came clear of the trees it was like walking back into near daylight. Moonshadows draped the great fell shoulders. In the still lake the moon sat like an impassive jewel. "There can only be miracles now," Hope muttered, "only miracles. But there were miracles. You had the Red Sea open and then close again: You sent down locusts: You changed the water into wine and blinded Saul with Faith so that he became Paul and a saint. And there are still miracles – I heard of miracles all over Italy. A Virgin appeared to an entire village I once passed through and in Toledo there was a man with the stigmata clear for us all to see."

Kitty Dawson, who had stalked him through the woods, looped up the fell and kept him in view as he walked up to the walled-in, rock-fortified end of the valley.

"What am I to do? You give me no sign. You give me no help. If I am left to myself You know that I will sin. Why will You not listen to me? You were sent into the world to save sinners, those who truly repent. Look at me. I am that sinner and I truly, truly repent. Why have You abandoned me?"

But the whispered words found no echo, not even among the rocks.

He turned and looked down the valley, moonlit, a splattering of stars up, one or two dim yellow candles picked out here and there, the bark of a dog, ceaseless lapping of water.

It was over.

*

He knew she only pretended to be asleep but he respected it. He wanted to talk but what about? There was an innocent tact, he thought, even in her dishonesty.

He undressed quickly and blew out the candle. Moonlight found its way into the room and lit up the dressing-case which he had opened out and which glistened silverly. He realised that he would have to leave that behind. If he took it – as he was taking the linen and the plate – then the blow to Mary would be too abrupt and cruel. It would be a great loss and Newton would be livid. Perversely, that gave him comfort.

Indeed the seed of thought that led to an expectation of Newton's malign outrage blossomed into a renewed sense of confidence – based on nothing at all – but now tingling through him, rushing to his nerve ends, fingertips, until he was in a state of intoxication and turned, tentatively, to Mary, to touch her shoulder, her thigh, to slide his hand around onto her breast, to kiss the hair and then carefully push it aside and kiss her neck and back until she turned to him and in the silvery silence, lit by the haloed dressing-case, they came together.

*

"I may say you are very unlike your brother. In appearance," Hardinge said.

"You are not the first to have noticed that."

"I could have sworn that in some company this morning there was mention of a piece which will appear in the *Morning Post* about the Member for Linlithgowshire marrying some local innkeeper's daughter."

"You are referring to my wife, sir." Hope's back stiffened and his eyes stared straight and challengingly into Hardinge's crimson, beetle-browed and jowly face. There was an apology needed.

"I beg your pardon, sir."

"I have not seen the report," said Hope, whose mind groaned as it worked out the inevitable consequences of such publicity. "No doubt . . . if it is as you say . . . it is an error which will be repeated. My seat is that of Dumfries."

"I am staying in the town for a few days. Perhaps you will dine with me this evening?"

"I may have left before then, but if I find myself here, I shall be delighted."

All this was delivered without warmth. Hardinge was not let off the hook.

"Good day to you, then, sir. And to you, sir."

After this last nod to Nicholson, he swung his bulk around and, glowering, made for Jenkins, as for a culprit. Hope noted that they went into an intense whispered exchange as soon as they left the room. Hope and Nicholson were left alone in the dining room of the Queen's Head.

Hope looked at Nicholson and smiled very sweetly.

"It is difficult to know the best way to deal with bores who insist on imposing their company on you," he said. "I often find that the best way is to take small and I am sure forgivable liberties with the strict truth. Otherwise one would spend a lifetime with fools. Don't you agree?"

Nicholson, splayed, nodded.

"Here you are, Colonel."

Nicholson almost jumped as Hope's rank was mentioned.

"Thank you. Now, Mr. Wood. I want you to do me another favour."

Wood nodded gratefully. There was no better demonstration of friendship.

"I am expecting a friend, a Mr. Newton. He is rather below average height, wiry, very slim faced, wears dark clothes –"

"I remember a Mr. Newton," Wood interrupted, helpfully. "He stayed overnight quite recently. A lawyer, I believe, from Chester, if I remember, and wore dark clothes as you say."

"That's the man. When he arrives, will you show him to your private parlour and tell him I will be no more than a few minutes."

"I will, sir, and here, sir." Wood had all the time had one hand behind his back: he now produced it, clutching a roll of paper. "'Romantic Marriage'," said Wood, beaming and a little bashful. "I heard that it had been sent off to the *Post* and got a fair copy made of it."

Hope read it rapidly, a haughty smile fixed on his face. He then handed it back to Wood, cutting out Nicholson.

"They write about anything these days," he said. "You will look out for Newton?"

"Like a hawk, Colonel."

Nicholson stood up and the two men walked into the street together.

"You'll be going down to Crosthwaite Church," Hope suggested and Nicholson nodded. "I'm off the other way. Good day to you, Nicholson: and good luck with Miss Skelton. Be bold, man: nothing lost."

He took the clergyman's thin hand, banged him jovially on the shoulder and went on his way. Nicholson stood quite still for a moment or two until a woman with two large wicker baskets strapped on either side of her as if she were a packmule bumped him back into movement and on his thoughtful way to the church.

Hope made rapidly for the nearby museum where he asked to see maps of the district and spent a pleasant half hour complimenting Peter Crosthwaite on the excellence of the penmanship and the aptness of the graphic illustrations.

On his no less rapid return to the Queen's Head he was hailed and congratulated by three or four of the more substantial townspeople. And did he spot Joanna? When he looked again there was her back only, walking quickly away. An illusion? He must be careful. He felt his inclination to speak aloud to himself grow stronger but "Calm," he said inside his mind, "calmly does it now."

Before he went into the Queen's Head he sought out the boy and instructed him to pull out the coach into the lane which led directly onto the main street. After scanning the street he went in and found Wood.

"Is Newton here?"

"No, sir." Wood was crestfallen: as if he were partly responsible. His subdued manner was not invigorated by the positive news he did have. "But there's two gentlemen for you in the parlour, sir."

"Who are they?"

"They made me promise not to say, sir." Wood hung his head as Hope's glance condemned him. "But," said Wood, talking to his boots, "if I was to say one was a man of the same rank as yourself, sir, and the other was a Welshman, I would not be breaking my promise head on."

Hardinge and Moore.

"Are you sure Newton is not here? It is not like him to be so late." Newton had virtually commanded him to be there by mid-morning.

"Positive certain, sir."

So he could not leave.

"I'll see these gentlemen, of course," he said. "But when Mr. Newton does come, don't hesitate to interrupt . . ."

"No, sir."

He entered without knocking and the men sprang apart.

"Am I intruding?"

"Not at all." Hardinge's self-possession was restored immediately. Moore, enraged at the very sight of Hope, had much more trouble in re-grouping.

"Will you take a seat?" Hardinge indicated a chair clearly placed by himself, near the centre of the room and away from the table, behind which Hardinge and Moore had set themselves.

"Thank you." Hope lifted the chair, took it to the end of the table, tilted it back in a rakish manner and took out a pipe.

"I've never seen such damned, barefaced insubordinate insolence!"

"Is Colonel Moore addressing himself to anyone in particular?"

"You have behaved abominably, atrociously, wickedly, sir."

Hope snapped the chair onto its four legs and took out his pipe.

"If I have been invited here to be insulted by a retired Irish soldier then I will go."

"Colonel Moore," Hardinge laid a hand on Moore's arm. "I think an apology . . .?"

"You will never get an apology from me, sir. I am sorry, Mr. Hardinge, but there will be no apology."

It was more politic for Hope to stay.

"What is it you want, Mr. Hardinge?"

"Colonel Moore swears that you have passed yourself off as Colonel Alexander Hope – when I know you not to be – and he further swears that the account of the marriage which has certainly by now appeared in the London *Morning Post* was written by one who lives locally and has access to all the facts of the case. He swears, in short, sir, that you are an impostor."

Hope lit his pipe but the nonchalance did not quite work: his hand, Hardinge noted, trembled a little with the flame.

"Do you have anything to say in your defence?"

"I was unaware that this parlour was a court."

"I am a senior justice of Brecon in Wales, sir, and where I am, there also, I tell you, is justice."

"But not a court."

"The man's a fraud from top to toe! Now that I know it I will never forgive myself for being blinded. I had my suspicions – his vulgarities – no wig – his fawning – no servant – his wild talk to the ladies – his self-abasing of himself before me –"

Hope laughed which caught the smoke in his throat and the laughter coughed itself out.

"To take on another man's name and character is a most serious offence, sir, and no cause for laughter or coughing or smoking, if I may say. You say that you are not the Honourable Alexander Augustus Hope, the Member for Linlithgowshire?"

"I do. And if I may explain to you the reasons for old Moore's anger and mistaken desire for vengeance . . . ? I paid attentions to his ward, Miss D'Arcy. Not to the extent described by the eminent local writer for the *Post* but I paid sufficient attentions to her for her to enjoy the expectation that I was pursuing a course which might well lead to marriage."

"Had I not been there you would have seduced her and taken her to Gretna!"

"As you see, Hardinge, your friend Moore is beside himself. He has every reason to be. It was due solely to his ill-intentioned interference that my suit failed – with some distress, I may say, to the lady. Nor, as I understand it, is this the first occasion on which Moore's ward has been denied marriage by his inexcusable rudeness and his devotion to the perpetual security of his own financial interest as guardian rather than any concern at all for poor Miss D'Arcy's happiness."

Moore howled out in fury and Hardinge had to grapple him around the chest and arms to force him back into his seat.

"You will pay for this! You will pay for this! You will be hounded until you drop and you will pay for this!"

Hope waited for Hardinge's next move, but as Hardinge finally sat down, he suddenly decided on a move of his own. He stood up.

"I think I have said all that I have to say, indeed," to Hardinge, "more than I would ever have intended. It was not my intention to provoke this man although he has provoked me greatly over the last few weeks and this absurd allegation comes as no surprise. Good day."

"One more witness."

"Witness?"

"Jenkins!"

The door was whipped open.

"Bring in Mr. Ismay. Will you give us a few more moments? I see you are puzzled by Mr. Ismay. Here he is. Do you recognise him?"

"No," said Hope, although a vague flicker – he could not catch it . . .

"Mr. Ismay holds the important office of postmaster in this town. In the execution of his duties in that office he has on several occasions from this hotel – while you, sir, were resident here – received letters to be sent free post by the authority of His Majesty's Parliament and franked by you both for yourself and for others 'A. A. HOPE, M.P. Free Post.' Now what do you say to that, sir?"

"Forging a frank," said Moore, to Hardinge's annoyance, "is a capital offence."

"Really, sir." Hope smiled at the three men and opened his arms. "It is all a very small error. For A. A. Hope read C. A. Hope, that is all."

"Speak, Mr. Ismay, speak!"

"We have received several letters addressed to Colonel the Honourable Alexander Augustus Hope, Member of Parliament, and that is you, sir, as I understand it – I have one here now with me, just arrived." He handed it over.

The writing was Newton's.

Hope steadied himself. What was Newton's game? Had he sprung this trap?

Mr. Ismay, who disliked all disturbance and was happiest with his spinster sister in the small cottage they had inherited behind the museum of which he was, for obscure but tenaciously held reasons, an obstinate critic, stood grey head bowed as if deserving punishment for this upright action.

Hope most deliberately forced himself to hand back the letter to the postmaster.

"It is addressed to my brother," he said, dry-throated.

"Thank you," said Mr. Ismay.

"Come, come, man, the game's up," said Hardinge, almost kindly.

"One Hope roving about the Lakes falling in love with innkeepers' daughters and affronting Colonel Moore and his ward is hard enough to believe: two of you circulating about the place puts too heavy a load on credulity: it breaks. You have been forging the name and signature and character of Colonel Hope and I am this moment – Jenkins! – applying to the magistrate, Sir Frederick Vane, Sheriff of this county – you are to take a letter to the Sheriff of Cumberland, Jenkins! – for a warrant for your arrest. You are not, sir, who you say you are: nor are you his brother."

"And who are you?"

Hardinge looked at the door, as if a stranger were about to enter.

"No. You. Judge Hardinge you call yourself. What is the proof of your identity?"

"Sirr . . . !"

Jenkins knew that crescendo and battened down against the Brecon gale.

"Out with it! How am I to know you are not hired by that man Moore who is mad to exonerate himself in front of Miss D'Arcy whose temper he fears as much as he loves her fortune? You come to me with these ridiculous charges and baseless allegations – sending for postmasters I have never set eyes on – have I seen you, Ismay? Have I ever seen you? Answer me!"

"No sir, I think not."

"Then your 'evidence' is of no account whatsoever. Go back to your office, Mr. Ismay, and think yourself very lucky I am not bringing actions against you which would ruin you for life."

"Stay here, Ismay," said Hardinge, directing his anger into this disputed territory.

"If you stay, Ismay, you will be a ruined and homeless man, I swear to that!"

"Take no notice, Ismay. I am the senior justice of Brecon in Wales."

"And it is Wales you will have to run to for peace, my man, unless you quit this room now."

"Ismay!" Hardinge's warning order was pistol sharp.

"Very well," said Hope. "Mr. Wood! I need an independent witness here. Mr. Wood!"

The landlord, who had been drawn to the parlour by the bruising and ungentlemanly sounds and crashes, came in on cue and, hiding his face behind Newton's letter, Mr. Ismay used Mr. Wood's entrance to make a decisive exit. What had Newton written?

"Wood!" said Hope – pointing to Hardinge – "How do you know this man is Hardinge?" He laughed as Hardinge crashed through yet another barrier of constraint and arrived at the very brink.

Wood, taking up Hope's cheerful tone, thought for a moment and replied, "He told me so. And I believe the gentleman to be Hardinge."

"Well spoken. And how do you know I am Hope?"

"The same reason," said Wood. "And all the other proofs anybody could ask for."

"Jenkins," said Hardinge, breathing with difficulty, braking his rage, "before you go to the Sheriff you will bring the constable. You will bring the constable now."

"Good,"said Hope. "It's about time Moore was put under guard. He's a menace to the young women of the parish – don't you agree? Ah, Nicholson. Welcome. Identify yourself immediately, sir."

The Lorton chaplain's disquiet had brought him back to the Queen's Head but confronted by Hope rampant his artfully composed enquiries were swatted aside.

"Of course he agrees but he is too courteous to say so. Well then, Moore, cornered at last?"

"If, sir," Moore began, drawn up to attention and under considerable duress . . .

"If I want satisfaction? There you are, Judge – if you are a judge – Hardinge – if there is such a name – of Brecon – if Brecon exists – more law-breaking. Does he not know that? But Moore, if you want satisfaction *now*, sir, *now*, well, we have the whole of that Paradise out there – what do you call it, the Eden of England, full of empty fields and lonely valleys where two men could give each other satisfaction all a long afternoon without a constable in sight."

"I will go now," said Moore to Hardinge. "I thank you for doing your duty."

"Fleeing the field, Moore? Just another Irish wild goose, eh?"

Moore left before he exploded.

"I will stay for the constable," said Hardinge.

"And I will take some air," said Hope, and moved out and down towards the main door.

Hardinge, Wood, Nicholson and several other quiveringly curious spectators followed him onto the street where they saw him beckon the brass-buttoned boy and whisper in his ear. As if a starting pistol had sounded, the boy dashed away.

"Glorious day for a steep walk," said Hope, looking at the uncompromisingly murky sky.

"You will stay for the constable," said Hardinge, "or I will lay hands on you myself."

"Surely that is what a bishop would say. Not a judge. What's your opinion, Nicholson? Is this fellow a bishop, a judge or a Welshman?"

Jenkins arrived with the constable, a young-looking thirty-year-old only lately sworn in, called Forrester. Monkey-boy had sought out Burkett, who now joined the growing crowd outside the Queen's Head.

"Constable! I am Mr. Judge Hardinge from the Welsh circuit." The crowd listened and grew even stronger. "I am sending to Sir Frederick Vane, Sheriff of this county, for a warrant for the arrest of this man who calls himself Hope. While we are waiting for this warrant it is your duty to ensure that this man does not leave this town or its most immediate environs, so that when the warrant reaches us it can be served swiftly. Are you clear on all those points, constable?"

"Yes, sir."

"Good. Jenkins! I shall write the letter."

Hardinge retreated, leaving an eager, inquisitive crowd, a constable flustered into unwanted limelight, and Hope – who waited for a moment or two and then turned to address them all but with especial reference to Mr. Wood and the Reverend Nicholson.

"Friends, let me try to explain this misunderstanding. You have heard, there, from a man who calls himself Judge Hardinge of Wales. I have no reason to doubt him, though what a Welsh judge is doing laying down the law in Keswick is a matter for speculation, look you." He managed the Welsh accent well and the unexpectedness of this talent drew a cohering lilt from the crowd. "Now what our Wizardy Welshman cannot worm into his suspicious Welsh mind is that I have a brother: not an uncommon condition, I would have thought, not even in Wales." He nodded at George Wood, who smiled back, 'carry on, my friend,' said the smile, 'everybody's on your side'. "I know it is difficult to understand the confusion which this brother has thrown on the Welshman but we must remember that in Wales they have only just abandoned human sacrifice!" George Wood laughed loudly at this, mostly because Hope's tone instructed him to. "There has been a mistake. And on today of all days, when I came to Keswick to settle a few small matters after my marriage to one of this county's greatest beauties – your Mary of Buttermere!" Applause and cheers greeted this confession and the still swelling crowd, which rather intimidated the Reverend Nicholson who preferred his congregation safely under a roof, ordered in pews. Already the mob was working towards a mood where it would have carried the speaker shoulder high up and down the street. "If I were guilty," he said, raising his voice, conducting them to silence with his hands, thickening his tone with emotion and reproach, "if I were guilty of any crime in the calendar, my friends – I may call you my friends?" "Yes!" shouted George Wood, and "Yes . . . Yes . . . Yes!" rattled around the street. "Then I would not need constables, I would not need warrants from my dear father's old comrade-in-arms Sir Frederick Vane, if I were guilty, I say," he paused, his voice dropped, "a hair would hold me." And ended.

The crowd applauded, individuals came up to shake his hand, and the constable, caught between Wood and Nicholson, tried to see what he could see over the rooftops opposite.

"Constable," said Hope, pleasantly. "You have your duty to do and I will not hinder you. There is no fault or blame in you. But, Constable, we wait for – how long before the warrant from the Sheriff?"

"About four hours, sir, I would guess, mebbe a bit more."

"Exactly. So. You do not expect me to stand here on this spot for four hours or 'mebbe' more?"

"Oh no, sir."

"Good. Well. I will tell you what I will do. I will give my friend the Reverend Nicholson of Lorton this guinea. Here you are. This guinea, Constable, is for a dinner – for the Reverend gentleman and myself – here in Mr. Wood's famous establishment at – let me see," he looked at his watch, "three o'clock – that is in two and a half hours. Furthermore, as my friend Mr. Wood will testify, there is a coach and four horses beside the Queen's Head – these I leave as surety. And all this, constable, is by way of convincing you that I am to be trusted to go down to the lake – come along by all means, if you wish – with Burkett over there and devote those two and a half hours before that excellent dinner to the catching of Keswick fish. Is that permitted, Constable?"

With a purpose now, that portion of the crowd which had nothing better to do proposed to give Hope an escort down to the lake. He halted them for a moment, went over to the boy, squatted before him and spoke rapidly, quietly, looking at him kindly.

"You did well to get Burkett. One last thing. Have you saddled up the fastest horse in the stables?" A nod. "Good boy. I want you to ride to Buttermere, to the Fish, to my wife and tell her – listen – Come immediately to Sprinkling Tarn. Bring the dressing-case. Your husband will wait for you there. Repeat that: quietly." The boy repeated it. "And again." He did so. "Good boy. This," he took out a guinea and pressed it into the small palm of the wide-eyed child, "is for you. Now then – go like the wind, boy!"

He stood up and watched the boy jack-rabbit around the corner.

"To the lake, then, friends," he announced. "To try our luck on the water."

There were only about half a dozen who lasted the course down to the lakeside where the boats and tackle were but they continued in the carnival spirit.

The sky was lowering; the lake mildly rippling, pewter heavy, hint of a wind in the snapping at the shingle of the wavelets.

"Well now, Burkett, is it fit to go out?"

"I've seen days like this turn out well."

"D'you think George Wood'll buy a few trout off me and cook them for my dinner, constable?"

The young man's head moved in a criss-cross way which indicated very clearly the helplessness he felt as the two older men calmly put the rods and the nets in the boat and then pushed it into Derwent Water.

The gaggle gave a cheer which reached thinly out onto the lake.

"Three o'clock, mind!" the constable shouted, sternly.

"To the minute!"

"I'll wait here for you."

"Good man. Good man."

Burkett rowed out steadily.

"I think we might go behind Pocklington's Island, Burkett," said Hope. "We've been lucky on that side before."

"And we'll be out of sight of the shore."

"More peaceful, yes."

Burkett took a wide arc around the island and calmly and naturally swung about until he disappeared from view. Hope, who had been rather ostentatiously examining the nets and busying himself with the bait and the lines, now hauled in all the gear and put it neatly on the bottom of the boat.

"I want you to row hard for the top of the lake, Burkett. For the Lodore Station. If the pull is too far for you, say. I'll set you down not here but on that next island over there" – much further from the mooring – "and finish the journey myself."

The man gave a sour knowing smile and rested on the oars.

"And after that?"

"I could use a guide I suppose. Just for a few hours. This comedy has come at an awkward time – all a stupid mistake."

Burkett still rested on the oars. The wind, which was beginning to move, slapped the water hard against the boards.

"It's a risky business," he said. "Very risky."

"You can say I ordered you."

"I can speak up for myself. That'll be right enough." He looked around and up at the sky. "I suppose a man might be wanting to get through the mountains and down to the coast. In weather like we're going to have, that could be very risky. You would need a guide – at least through the high passes. But am I your man, Colonel Hope?"

"Have I ever given you any reason to doubt my honesty?"

"Not with me. With my daughter maybe. But not with me."

The mention of his daughter appeared to dislodge an impediment to action. He pulled on the oars, taking the boat out of the shallows to which the wind had pushed it, and then paused again.

"I've always admired that watch of yours, Colonel Hope. Always admired that."

"I was thinking it would make a fine parting gift, Burkett."

"Better put a couple of rods out for another half hour or so. The lad has keen eyes."

Hope did as advised and Burkett licked his palms and stuck into the task. He was a strong man, used to the work, and the boat shifted rapidly despite the growing swell from the rising wind which veered and then settled dead against them.

As they rowed towards the Jaws of Borrowdale, the rain came in the wind and pelted Hope in the face.

At the Lodore Station they pulled the boat well up onto the shore and hid it deep under bramble bushes. Burkett's caution led him to bury the rods in the shingle.

They hurried into Borrowdale, single file, Burkett leading through the valley most notorious in the entire district for rock falls, rushes of stone, broken bridges. The last time Hope had passed through had been on his first ride over into Buttermere. They trudged soddenly into the sullen head-wind, soon wet to the skin.

"There's a pothouse a mile or so on," Burkett said, turning. "We'll call in there. We shall have to get something to warm us up. If it's bad down here it'll be terrible up there." Hope followed his eyeline up the volcanic hills: the tops were well hidden by galleons of dark cloud moving restlessly across the bare land.

It was the pothouse at which Hope had received such grudging hospitality but this time there was a fire going which drew steam from the greatcoat he held before it and some rum and water which took the chill off the bone. They ate hot black puddings with cold apple sauce and Hope bought bread, cheese and the bottle of rum.

Just before Seatoller, which led west to Honister Pass, entry to Buttermere, Burkett struck south along a valley bottom. The path was narrow and backed up beside a stream which was low after the long stretch of fine summer even though the rain now gushed down on them. Burkett waved Hope after him and they both stooped for protection under a rock.

"No sense in getting more soaked than we need," he said. "There's still a way to go. We haven't started to climb yet."

Hope nodded and saved his breath. In the grim slashing rain, the fells were all cloud which now appeared fulminous as the water haze from the force of the rain gathered to a smoking veil.

"It'll ease up soon," Burkett said. "It never lasts very long up here."

Within ten or fifteen minutes the rain, as good as Burkett's word, thinned, slackened and finally stopped. By this time the two men were on their way, picking out their footing carefully over the jutting stones made slape by the newly running mud.

"It could even be a good day yet," said Burkett, inscrutably pleased that the weather could be so twisted.

Across the neat hump of Stockley Bridge and up the first steep rise, the track often sending Hope slithering in his fashionable town boots. They skirted Aaron Crags and walked under Green Gable to Styhead Tarn, a small bleak pool like the last drop in the bottom of the gigantic bowl formed by the most fearsome fells in the entire area.

Burkett called a halt.

"From here," he said, "you can go straight over that road ahead –

smugglers' road we call it – down to Whitehaven – you can see the sea if we go up that bank a bit – or if you want to be more complicated, you can go into Langdale and then down by Coniston towards Ulverston – there's plenty boats there as well."

"Where's Sprinkling Tarn?"

"Langdale way." Burkett pointed. "Just up there. But after that it'll be more than your life's worth to go on without daylight. Bad enough when you *can* see: there's only a shepherd would tackle it even then."

"I'll have to take my chances."

Burkett nodded and looked about. The weather had cleared. The massed clouds had moved across the country leaving a sky pearl grey and a sun now fully in sight moving out towards the sea to the west.

"What time do you have?"

"Just past seven."

"If we strode out we could get some way to Whitehaven that way and the other," he pointed up towards Sprinkling Tarn, "at least I could pilot you over the pass while there's some light."

Hope shook his head, clipped the watch off its chain and handed it over.

"It's better if you don't know where I've gone. It'd be better still if you don't know I've come this far."

Burkett took the watch.

"I would still do it," he said and gave the lightest smack of a smile which said 'I'm enjoying it'.

"I'll be better on my own." Hope was conclusive. "Anyway, that young constable will still be there waiting for you to come back."

"He will!" Burkett grinned unguardedly now. "The same lad. He'll be a second cousin of my wife's."

With that, he nodded, turned and moved quickly down the high empty valley back the way they had come. Although Hope saw no sign of his looking back, he waited until Burkett was out of sight, to be quite sure, and then struck up for Sprinkling Tarn.

This was a larger but wilder stretch of water than Styehead. The high-massed and perilous crags of Great End were in prospect; and the name could have stood as the epitaph for the whole place. Hope could not recollect anywhere on earth he had been that was so barren, inhospitable, and full of potential terror. Even the sheep which scaled and gave some life to the most remote districts were absent from this spot which could truly be thought of, Hope considered, as

God-forsaken. Those who found a paradise in the Lakes should come here now and see what lay at the true heart of it. But then, as if directly sent to contradict and vanquish such thoughts, a rainbow grew into the sky coming up from where they had begun their upward climb and arcing perfectly across the front of the Gables to fall away towards Wast Water. Hope was entranced.

He was looking at it so fixedly that at first he did not see the small figure come up the twisting path, under the arch of the rainbow, a pack slung on the back, waving long hair loosened and struggling to be free in the milder evening wind. For a few moments he did not move. He had never known a feeling such as this: not that of her for himself – although he had some notion of the high passes she had been forced to climb and alone – a route more dangerous than that of Burkett and himself – but his love for her: that was what moved him. After all that had happened, he could still be capable of such ardent and uncomplicated love. He stood up and called "Mary!" and her name echoed around. He went to help her the last few dozen yards but when they turned at the top to look at the rainbow it was fading fast and they saw it die away.

He had found a flat seat of rock and Mary, who was warm and quiet when they had first embraced, soon, he noticed, relapsed into embarrassment and opened her pack to take out food.

"I have some," he said, pulling out the squashed and damp bread and cheese from one of his pockets. Mary laughed and Hope, amazed at his happiness, gratefully took the slice of pie she offered, and the milk touched with rum. He added more.

"Is the dressing-case safe?" He indicated her bulging pack.

"I didn't bring it."

Hope drank some of the rum and milk.

"Why not?"

"If I had brought that, I could not have carried the food or clothes – some of yours, some mine . . ."

"Is that the full reason?" He chewed at the pie less ravenously now but still he ate as he questioned her.

"No."

"You were afraid that I wanted the dressing-case more, perhaps, than I wanted you."

She was silent.

He looked directly at her now but she turned away. Sitting on the rock against the mountainous landscape, her profile and streaming hair gave her the appearance, he thought, of a princess in a fable, someone who had brought magic into the world, someone who was the object of spells and great trials of wit and strength, always and essentially apart from coarse fallible mortals such as he.

"There was something in the case I needed to have, that's all," he said. "I knew the boy would have difficulty enough in remembering the simplest message and I had neither the time nor the means to write out what I wanted. But had you brought it, Mary, I would have taken the few notes I wanted and the rest could have gone to the bottom of that miserable gathering of water."

"Why did you want me to come here?" She believed him, he knew that. She was so fine that the truth was always known to her and she responded to it like a flower to the sun.

"I am wanted by the law," he said, carefully. "There has been a mistake made about my identity, about who I am, my name, and everything to do with it – or I say there has been a mistake but the Judge –"

"Are you who you say you are?"

"I am the man you married. I am the man who talked and walked with you and bedded and wedded you, Mary. I am he who can't stop his arms from going around you and finds the best comfort in the world in dreams of a life with you alone."

"But are you – Alexander Hope?"

"I asked you to call me John. John I am."

Mary nodded and began to re-strap her pack. She would be more persistent later.

"Where are we going?"

"I have to tell you about myself before I can ask you to come with me."

"I want to know no more. You will be John." She looked about. "We had best make a move before we lose all the light."

"Mary, men will soon be pursuing me."

"You told me that." She stood up and for a moment her anger showed. "And some day you will tell me everything. Now, are we going along this path or back down there and over to Wast Water?"

"You choose."

"Langdale," she said, "is a much worse path but for that reason it will seem less likely."

She set off ahead of him and as with Burkett he walked behind.

As the path went up to Angle Tarn the mountains grew higher, the spikes and knots and boulders of rock more threatening and increasingly inclined to transform themselves into gargoyles and imps, or large shapes without recognisable form but menacing the two on foot who trudged between the heights in silence as if they dared not disturb either the other or the posse of the enemy crags.

Under Rossett Pike, Mary, who knew this area only slightly, saw a gully and below it the safe darkening plain of the Langdale valley, and decided to make down Rossett Gill. As the darkness gathered faster this direct route proved treacherous. A foot wrongly placed would skid and set off a rush of stones which could loosen rocks large enough to knock over both of them. There were unforeseen and sheer drops where Hope's strength was vital in lowering Mary down so that she could then make a stirrup of her hands to support the first leg of his following descent. Small trees grabbed for support gave none and the next dozen yards would be sledged on the back. There were moments when the balance between danger and stupidity struck sparks of disconnected hilarity, more a shuddering out of tension and fear than any real expression of cheerfulness, but uncontrollable, for a time, as they lurched, rushed, skied, fell, slid, rolled and most often edged hand holding hand down that cataract of loose, unreliable and potentially fatal rock.

At the bottom they were wringing wet with the effort, legs dithery, stomachs aching but embracing as tightly as they had ever done in their lives in almost delirious recognition of a deliverance.

By now it was black dark, no moon yet up and their way was signalled by the reactions of the beasts in the fields of the valley. They did not want to call in at a farmhouse and certainly not an inn but the sky was beginning to cloud over again: it would rain, they needed shelter.

Eventually, after two more hours, they saw a small chapel. It was open. They went in.

*

"We must talk now."

"I have to sleep," Mary said. "Please let me sleep first."

"No. Here: drink some of this."

"No thank you."

"It will help you to stay awake for a few minutes at least."

"I'll stay awake to listen."

"It's too dark to see you – can you come closer?"

"Can I stay here, John? I can lean against the side of the pew."

"Very well." He paused: and then he could not begin.

"I'm still awake."

A voice in the dark. Still no moon, only the faintest light in the small space. Rain scattering itself on the tiny windows, a low wind now audible, sounds now and then from the beasts in the fields.

"I want us to go to America together. To go to Liverpool or may be we will try to find a boat at a nearer port – and work our passage to America."

"What does that mean?" She was severe.

"I have very little money. But a man and a woman together, man and wife as we are, could always find some employment on a ship carrying passengers to America. We would work on the ship and that would pay for the passage – you see?"

"My parents are owed money."

"I know."

"You said you had –"

"I *know*. Now my circumstances have changed. Mary: I am a bad man. A very wicked man."

"Tell me."

"You would not believe it."

"You are my husband now. What you did before –"

"Mary. If I tell you, you will no longer love me."

"But how can I care for you if you will not tell me the truth?" Her anger once again threatened to break through and again she checked it back.

"You have to believe in me. Forget anything except the present and the future. In America we can start all over again – oh, imagine that! – nobody knowing who I am, what I've done, where I've been –"

"Tell me, John, and I will never speak of it again."

The voice out of the dark sounded to him like the song of the siren. To confess, to be absolved, to confess, to be embraced for it, to confess and be through with it: was that the promise?

"And I will stay with you for ever."

And suffer for ever? She might be able to endure it but how could he? How could he allow her to carry not only the knowledge of his evil but to force herself to live with and to love someone from whom every atom of her sensibility would strain to recoil, 'for ever', world without end. Amen. It was over.

"Good night, Mary."

"No . . . John . . ."

"Good night." His tone was as gentle as she could imagine and she took the comfort in that.

He waited until she was sound asleep and left. He wished he had some final eloquent gift to leave her but he had none. By dawn he was in Ulverston but abruptly he decided against escape by sea and made for the cross-Sands route.

22

'The Romantic Marriage II'

'The Romantic Marriage II' appeared in the *Morning Post* on 22nd October 1802. Coleridge's second account was dated 'Keswick October 15th'. When he wrote it he could not have been aware of the letter in the *Post* published on 14th October (in response to his first article) from the real Charles Hope correcting 'The Romantic Marriage I' and accusing the man who called himself Hope of being an impostor: nor of a further letter from Charles Hope on the 19th in which he stated that the real Colonel Hope had been in Germany for the past six months. The distance between London and Keswick, which was almost three hundred miles, would take several days to negotiate by horse and coach – Coleridge's pieces were published about a week after he had mailed them from Keswick. The Hardinge-constable 'arrest', for instance, happened on the 13th. Coleridge wrote on the 15th and his piece was printed on the 22nd: but on the 19th October the *Morning Chronicle* had scooped the *Post* with the Hardinge story.

Coleridge's first article had appealed to a wide constituency: the fashionable world was intrigued, sentimentalists claimed it as a modern fairy story, Lake lovers and those rising with the yeast of nature worship felt implicated and, through Mary, vindicated, the rich were amused and the poor given heart: Love, it seemed, could still conquer everything. Charles Hope's compulsion to write not one but two letters of rebuttal is some indication of the noise and interest the matter was raising both in town and abroad.

This second article, by turning all previous conclusions and expectations on their heads, set up a story with the makings of a notorious and cherishable lover-villain for its central character. Everything about it pointed to an enigmatic and powerfully Romantic plot which the public was invited to help unravel.

"The following," Coleridge begins, "are the particulars of the novel of real life, the scene of which has unfortunately been laid among our Mountains . . ." He chronicles in some detail the progress of "the pretended Alexander Hope" from his arrival in Keswick, claiming that "he had paid serious addresses to four women at the same time, one of rank and fortune, and three of humble life." Don Juan would have been present in Coleridge's mind. The implied comparison right there in paragraph one gave what was already a multi-stranded story yet another layer.

Coleridge then writes of the draft drawn on Crump by the "pretended *Honourable*" (his italics) and reveals "the draft was sent to Liverpool for acceptance: and it *was* accepted." Coleridge then moves on to the unexpected arrival of Mr. Judge Hardinge, the sending of his servant to Buttermere, the servant's "Here is some mistake – this is not Colonel Hope" and the reply "It is for my brother". He outlines the confrontation, the denial, the postmaster "respectable and intelligent", and the committal to "our constable while the examination was going forward". "He made light of it," Coleridge reports and "to amuse himself, he chose to make a little sailing expedition on the lake which the constable did not think himself authorised to prevent. Accordingly he went with his old friend, the fisherman; and all Keswick waiting for his return. Evening and darkness came on: he did not return." The phrasing points up a gaiety, a dashing quality in the man who is now someone of amusing and bold initiatives. "He probably escaped over the Stake," Coleridge writes, "a fearful Alpine pass." Not lacking in courage either.

There are some details and incidents which are not included.

George Wood for instance remained optimistic beyond all reasonable calculation. The constable finally left the lakeside at dusk. The Reverend Nicholson had to be down in Grasmere for the next morning and could not stay beyond six. Hardinge and Moore went into further conclave at the receipt of the Sheriff's warrant, drew up a plan of action and decided on what they would say to the local correspondent of the *Morning Post*. But Wood remained faithful, anxiously coming out onto the street even when the darkness had set in fast, refusing to let the horses be unharnessed – although he saw them well fed – in case his friend should need them the instant he returned. But he did not return.

Finally Wood led the horses into the rush-lit yard and gave orders for them to be stabled and brushed down. When he looked into the coach, he discovered the boxes of fine linen and the substantial mass of silver plate which, three months earlier, his servants had carried up to Hope's room, calling it his 'booty'.

The landlord went to the parlour to report.

"Then he came to Keswick ready to flit the coop," said Hardinge with considerable complacency. "I was right."

"And desert his poor wife."

"That would be of no account to the man we are dealing with," Hardinge said. "We are dealing with a type I have seen before. The type is a sensual type, utterly selfish, blind to the feelings of others, careless of the consequences of his actions and above all, Moore," he shoved over the port to give emphasis to his point, "self-indulgent, unable or unwilling – but it comes to the same – to distinguish between right and wrong, good and bad. We are dealing with a man who may have begun as a moral coward but has developed into what I have called, in one little article I wrote, a sincere liar, a self-deluder. You could see it in those thickety eyebrows, Moore . . . why would a man not pluck them or trim them? And the very pale eyes with the very heavy head of grey hair," the Judge scratched a scab on the cropped skull under his wig, "I have found that hair always gives me a clue. But it was the whole manner of the man –"

"That's it!" said Moore, "That damned swaggering braggadocio!"

"The common insolence –"

"The vulgar speech –"

"The lack of a sense of the dignity of the law –"

"Boasting of duels and India. Never set foot abroad. Never a soldier!"

"A performer," said the remorseless Judge, "happier playing a part than being the man he was – and despite the consequences, Colonel Moore, and," he added swiftly, to forestall any further interruptions, "despite consequences which could well be of the most severe – of the *most* severe –"

"I'd shoot him on sight."

"And yet," concluded the Judge, cheated and outsmarted but by no means disappointed by his day, "and yet – despite all the dangers – it is a performance that must go on. He cannot stop it, you see. The part has become the man."

Wood had listened in dismayed and affronted silence as his good friend was flayed across the port.

"There's no dressing-case," Wood said, without thought.

"Explain yourself, man."

"Colonel Hope . . ." Moore's animal sound stopped him, but

Hardinge nodded him on. "Mr. Hope had a very big, a very costly I would say, very costly, dressing-case. He showed it to me. Full of silver objects – and if he had intended to desert his wife – which I cannot believe from my knowledge of the man and I may say I have never seen him look better than he did this morning, I said to Mrs. Wood 'Marriage suits the Colonel, I have never seen him looking so well' – but why would he not take the case?"

"Are you sure he did not carry it down to the lake?"

"Fishing!" said Moore. "The constable is an ass."

"I am certain, sir. It is a big case – he could not have had it without my noticing."

"Did he speak to or contact anyone else apart from this Burkett?"

Wood graphically remembered his friend on his haunches before the child he had always called 'Monkey-boy' and the boy's immediate gallop off into Buttermere.

"No, sir."

"Keep the linen and plate in a safe place, Landlord. With the coach they are your responsibility."

"And your pledge," said Moore. "I believe the creature drew twenty pounds on you at breakfast."

"He did, sir."

"He is an accomplished villain, Mr. Wood. Do not be too cast down."

"Is that all, sirs?"

"Perhaps you could send in another bottle of your port."

"Thank you, sirs."

Despite the discussion, Wood held to his loyalty for several weeks longer and even a year later he was prepared to put forward a version of his own which matched most of the facts of the story and vindicated the behaviour of his friend 'Hope'. In 'The Romantic Marriage II' there is a reference to "the extravagant encomiums on the impostor's manner and address" in Keswick. The people, like Wood, loved him.

Coleridge finishes the second piece by returning to a concern for Mary which was guaranteed to move his readers and make her at least as beguiling as "the pretended *Honourable*". "I can truly say she would have been an ornament to any rank of life," he writes, "I cannot express the sincere concern which every inhabitant of the county takes in the misfortune of poor Mary of Buttermere . . . I am convinced that when the whole of the courtship is made known, she will rise in the opinion of the good and sensible instead of sinking."

It is a last flourish to a story which had now so many contrasting and mythic elements: sophistication and naïvety; the rootless and the rooted; ruthless and rueing; the ways of the world and worldliness and nature, simplicity, innocence; Don Giovanni and the virgin; the secret valley and the flamboyant intruder; high rank and low birth and all ignited by the still unfinished news of his escape – for he was now at large, somewhere among the readers of the *Morning Post*. They could play a part. Coleridge added a curious final snippet on Mary.

"It seems," he wrote, "that there are some circumstances attending her birth and true parentage which would account for her striking superiority in mind and manners, in a way extremely flattering to the prejudices of rank and birth." A hint that the child from the humble cradle might have been spirited there from a noble household, like the mythological and chosen heroes and heroines throughout history for whom circumstances or fiction seemed to reserve especial twists and treats of fortune. Was Mary really nobly born? Coleridge the journalist knew that it would titillate his readers to have that possibility also in their minds. He must have had some evidence beyond gossip. Or was it thrown in out of snobbery, his noted weakness for the aristocracy – such a lovely and intelligent woman could not possibly be of humble birth! There is no evidence since uncovered, and Mary's birth recorded in the Lorton Parish Register gives her parents as the Robinsons of the Fish Inn. It is a little odd, that having spent lavish sentences defending the honour and commending the sweetness of mind of Mary, Coleridge should deliver a public sentence guaranteed to upset greatly both her and her parents.

"Buttermere," he signs off – signposting and encouraging the tourists? – "is nine miles from Keswick by the horse-road; fourteen by the carriage-road."

Coleridge left his readers with the wronged heroine locked in her beautiful valley; the story spiralling up and down the English class system; the incident magnetised to attract clashing factions of current ideas; and the rogue at large, somewhere among them, on the run.

*

There were various spottings of 'Hope' in the next couple of weeks – one, for instance, recorded at Ravenglass and another at Whitehaven, where he was reported to be waiting on a ship to Liverpool. But there was no police notice yet out and few knew the slightest detail about him.

'Hope' was aware of the one man who knew everything about him, aware too that he was now that man's quarry. He was afraid of him and his whole strategy was now bent on eluding Newton.

He talked in Ulverston to a couple of midshipmen about the possibility of boats from Ravenglass (just down the coast) to Liverpool and let slip the Honourable and the Member of Parliament more than once. He then beat back a few miles north and called at an inn to take dinner and in the course of it quiz the landlord about boats from Whitehaven to Ireland. Then he cut across country to Cartmel where he made for the more remote, eastern edge of the cross-route and there he waited until he could make his way onto the Sands the moment the tide moved out. He was only beaten by the fishermen in their carts who plunged their horses into the receding sea. Hope had chosen his path shrewdly – no-one was near him.

By going onto the Sands immediately, he gave himself the maximum time to get across. It was a grave risk, without a guide, especially in the changeable October weather when the wind could cause the two river cuts to run so fast and deep that only a knowing hand could find the shallow fording point. He had hacked himself a long stick of ash and this he prodded in front of him whenever he saw the shining soft-featured surface which suggested quicksands. He took his time.

It took him almost the full tide to make the crossing – not only was he being careful, he was determined to avoid any cluster, even any single person. Once he waded chest high across a channel running so fast that only his great strength got him through. He had lain down on the Sands to recover and his fine clothes were badly disfigured by the mud.

When he finally arrived near Hest Bank it was eight in the evening, dark, and he was soaked, famished, exhausted and desolate after the lonely struggle across such an inhospitable landscape. He ought to have gone on towards Lancaster – not into the town itself but its suburbs – but he needed to rest. He found a sandbank where he was sheltered from the wind, the solid and comfortable sand wall at his back, the comparative warmth of the safe unharried spot, the slow shades of darkness in the clouds, the memory of Mary arriving on the high fell and then in the blank chapel, the abrasion of salt air . . .

Anne Tyson came across him at dawn. Roughened out of all description from the man who had gone through her life like an hallucination, she recognised him instantly and at first feared he was dead. The face was white, the mouth agape, the neck puppet-flopped on his left shoulder, legs spread-eagled out before him as if he had fallen unconscious to that spot.

She went the few hundred yards back to her hut and returned with a billy-can, a bowl and a twist from her secret store of tea. A small fire was quickly got going and she waited until the sun rose high enough to warm him back into life. The tide was once again on the turn way down the Bay and she was missing work but that was of no account.

When he woke up he saw her crouched beside the fire, almost a silhouette against the brightening morning light – white sun, clear. He remembered her. To his relief and her deep pleasure, he remembered her.

"Hallo, Anne Tyson," he said. 'Still listening out for cockles?"

"I have some tea," she said.

"Well now. Which wreck was that rescued from?"

"It was paid for at Lancaster Michaelmas Fair."

She poured some into the billy-can and stirred the boiling brew before adding a dash of rum which she poured from an unexpectedly elegant hip flask.

"*This* is what came from a wreck," she said, holding it up. "But I'll not tell you which one."

The tea was poured into a bowl, the bowl brought to the man who might have been in chains so little had he shifted since waking up.

"That's good, Anne Tyson. That's how a man should wake up."

"You'll burn your tongue out of your head."

"That's the object, Anne Tyson. That's the intention – to burn out the tongue and let the soul have a bit of peace."

"You can rest in my hut if you want to."

Hope looked closely at her: the woman who combed the margins of the Bay, the woman still in mourning for her lost child, the woman who chose to disguise herself as an old crone.

"Would anyone know I was resting there, Anne?"

"Only one or two of the likes of me. And if you kept out of their way I could say you were anybody."

"Anybody . . . Do you know who I am, Anne?"

"In the Bay, three months ago, you gave yourself a terrible long list of names and titles."

"Do you remember any of them?"

"Member of Parliament. Honourable. Colonel, wasn't it? And Augustus."

"You have a strong memory." He finished the tea. "And why should I want to rest in your hut?"

"You seem to need somewhere to rest."

Hope finished the tea slowly now and scarcely seemed to notice that she passed him a second cup. When he had finished that he took off his heavy gold watch chain.

"This is worth a considerable sum, Anne." He placed it on the sand and rubbed it in, picking it up only when it was thoroughly gritted. "I want you to take this to Lancaster. There's a jeweller called Harris just under the castle. Tell him you found this on the beach but a gentleman has told you its value and you will only sell if a fair price is offered. Take anything over twelve guineas but walk out if he offers less: it is worth at least twice that."

He handed it to her and stood up.

"Lead on then, Anne Tyson, let us to this hut."

First she kicked sand over the fire and then walked down through the dunes to a turf-covered hut. Hope looked at it and smiled.

"If you can borrow a broad spade, I'll go out and cut you some fresh turf sods for that roof, Anne: it may be a hard winter. And then you can teach me to catch the famous shrimps so that I can help you." He took off his coat. "First we need a fire for this –" he looked at his once proudly glossy Hessian boots, the tassels now ripped and bedraggled "– and these . . . let me chop you some wood – I mean to be no burden."

He would stay with her until the trail went completely cold.

For the first day or two she was ready for him to fly off. She could not believe he was not merely and temporarily down on his luck in a way unaccountable to her but just credible. He stayed for a week, though, and then a few more days after, helping her but taking care to be away from any others – spending long evening hours in his corner of the hut, smoking – she had bought him tobacco with some of the money from the gold chain, and two rough shirts, a plain coat, some sturdy boots (although she had mended and polished the Hessians almost back to their glossy glory and the dashing green greatcoat too was as cleaned and restored as was humanly possible). Occasionally he would go into long monologues about his travels or his family – talking of kings and lost records, of country seats, his rights and the nobility who had spurned his attempts to repair his broken inheritance. Once, at his most chilly and melancholy, he had said that he felt as alone and indifferent to the world as a pebble on the beach: that his wife had not followed him; his friend had betrayed him; and God offered him no answer to his prayers.

He did not attempt to molest Anne, not once, although he would kiss her on the cheek, now and then.

"It's the sound of the sea that keeps you here, isn't it?" he said. "Listen."

And Anne listened as if for the first time to the surge and suck of the ocean just beyond her door.

*

Miss D'Arcy and Mrs. Moore arrived at the Fish just before noon on Friday, 22nd October. Dan, the handyman from the Queen's Head, had driven them over in the trap which Mr. Wood had bought for himself and Mrs. Wood but never used and let out now and then to favoured clients. It was a mature October day, the leaves full of browns, yellows, still holding onto the branch and providing an extraordinary autumn tapestry which Amaryllis had been quick to point out to Mrs. Moore.

They had persuaded Colonel Moore not to come and it was with a feeling almost of light-headedness that they found themselves without him. Since Hope's flight he had monitored them like a warder. Nor did he approve of the visit they were making but Amaryllis was again and at last – after two weeks of shocked and subdued withdrawal – beginning to assert herself. Moore's declared reason for letting them go – under Dan's escort, of course – was that as the weather seemed settled and fair, the ride in the open would do his ward good. He did not want her health to suffer from this distressing and, as the Judge had reassured her, unimportant incident in what was certain to be a happy and fortunate life.

It was the Judge who had suggested the fresh air more than a week before on the day he left to strike south through Lancaster and by way of Chester into Brecon.

Miss D'Arcy had planned the visit. She had rehearsed her speeches many times.

The two women were shown into the parlour by Annie, who seemed wholly preoccupied with Damson who, she claimed, had scratched her ear. "But whenever I tell her that, she says to me, she says 'Noo-oo'. She won't own up and I can't be done with that."

There was no fire and the room was chilly and so Mary found the two women standing. When she saw Miss D'Arcy her self-possession, which had been remarkable for many days, all but failed her.

"Mary." Amaryllis held out both her hands and advanced behind an expression of terrible pity. "Mary – poor Mary. What can I say?"

She took Mary's hands – cold: she had been working outside, doing the old jobs.

"We must talk," Amaryllis said, "we two. But first I want to tell you that I know how you feel. Believe me. I know exactly how you feel. You and I are as one."

Mary was as plainly dressed – out of a kind of obstinacy she did not understand – as she had ever been. Amaryllis was wearing clothes the cost of which would have bought the inn, the cut and fashion of which would have been noted even in London. And whereas Amaryllis looked fresh from her drive, sufficiently healthy and cared for and determined (and unscathed) not only to slough off the affair but to discover a positive dynamic inside it, Mary felt that she looked heavy and worn, almost beaten. She allowed herself to be drawn down into a chair. Miss D'Arcy, still holding her hands, knelt disconcertingly at her feet. All the while, Mrs. Moore stood by the window and smiled: now and then she would peep over a shoulder to see if there was anything happening in the view.

"I am determined to be your friend," Miss D'Arcy said. "Until this whole business is resolved, I will be your true friend."

"Thank you," Mary was obliged to say and dared not express her real thoughts.

"It is only you and I who know him, you see." Amaryllis was eager and, Mary thought, genuinely sympathetic to her condition. "I am the only one in whom you can confide and I know," she continued, lowering her voice into which was introduced a slight vibrato, "that we two will have a great deal to confide in each other."

"But more than that, my dear, we want to help," said Mrs. Moore, making a surprise move and nudging her ward to the point.

"Yes." Amaryllis would have preferred to rest for some time on the mutuality of their experiences but she took her cue quite gracefully and stood up. "We want to take you back to Keswick with us," she said. "The curious will be bound to seek you out – now that the *Morning Post* . . ." the excitement of publicity tinctured her voice, Mary noted, "but with us you can be sure of the very sternest protection from my dear Colonel Moore, who will guard your position as firmly as he has guarded mine."

Mary looked up at the rather younger, elegant, totally unused figure and nodded, slightly but visibly. She paused and then:

"I thank you both," she said, "I know you mean to be kind." She stood up. "But I will stay here until my husband either returns to me or sends me word where I should meet him. Now," she continued, making the effort to be brisk which, together with her effort to seem calm, imposed a double strain she could well have done without, "I will find Annie and send you some tea. Excuse me."

They took tea and Mary came and went politely. She accepted a small yellow handkerchief marked around the border by Amaryllis in silk embroidery. "A first small gift," Amaryllis said, "first of many."

Eventually they left and Mary, for her own sake, stood prominently in view until they were well away.

Then she went to her room and, deeply, deeply tired, lay on her bed.

She ought to have followed him. She knew now, she could sense, that he had expected that. Yet, she forced herself to admit it, he was a wicked bad man. She could feel it and she was ashamed for him. But he was her husband and he had loved her and she him as she had never dreamt of. If only she could let loose her anger somewhere at someone!

To return and stay here was what he had intended her to do, clearly, and every day she waited for the mail; and after it had gone she began to wait again, tiringly self-questioning. Had she loved him at all? Had those couplings, those tenderly violent hours, been anything other than a gross exception in her life, an accident or intrusion, impossible to live with or absorb or build anything life-giving on?

Mary looked again at the dressing-case to which she had turned immediately on her return looking for the 'notes' he had spoken of: but she had found nothing more than a few business papers and some scribbles about his journey. Now she took everything out of the case, deciding that she would clean every object thoroughly and polish up the case itself until it glittered.

She found that the case had a double bottom ingeniously hidden and made visible to her only by a chance combination of pressures from her polishing.

In the drawer were letters which she began to read.

When she had finished those letters she howled aloud, uncaring, heard all over the tiny village, uncontrolled, a sound which came from a pain all but unendurable. People thought that an animal – a fox perhaps – had caught its leg in the steel jaws of one of the traps in Burtness Wood.

23

'The Keswick Impostor'

"Great was the emotion of Coleridge when he recalled to his remembrance of those letters," Thomas de Quincey wrote, about thirty years later, "and bitter – almost vindictive – was the indignation with which he spoke of Hatfield."

After Mary's discovery of the letters, Coleridge was to write: "Never surely did an equal number of letters disclose a thicker swarm of villanies perpetrated by one of the worst and miseries inflicted on some of the best of human beings."

"One set of letters," wrote de Quincey in *The Recollections of the Lakes and the Lake Poets*, "appeared to have been written under too certain a knowledge of his villainy to whom they were addressed: though still relying on some possible remains of humanity or perhaps (the poor writer might think) on some lingering relics of affection for herself. The other set was even more distressing: they were written under the first conflicts of suspicions, alternately repelling with warmth the gloomy doubts which were fast arising and then yielding to their afflicting evidence; raving in one page under the misery of alarm, in another courting the delusions of hope and luring back the perfidious deserter – here resigning herself to despair, and there again labouring to show that all might yet be well.

"Coleridge said often, in looking back on that frightful exposure of human guilt and misery – and I also echoed his feeling," de Quincey continues, "that the man who, when pursued by these heart-rending apostrophes and with this litany of anguish sounding in his ears from despairing women and from famishing children, could yet find it possible to enjoy the calm pleasures of a Lake Tourist, and deliberately hunt for the picturesque, must have been a fiend of that order which fortunately does not often emerge amongst men."

Yet, "it will hardly be believed," wrote Coleridge in the second of two articles entitled 'The Keswick Impostor' published in the *Morning Post* on 31st December 1802, "how obstinately almost all classes at Keswick were infatuated in his favour, and how indignantly they spoke of the Gentleman who had taken such prudent and prompt measures to bring the Impostor to detection. The truth is, the good people of the Lakes had as little heard, and possessed as little notion of the existence of this sort of wickedness as of the abominations of Tiberius at Caprae."

*

The morning after she discovered the letters, Mary went out to be alone. Her parents, cowed at the possible consequences of what they already knew and fearing even worse, heard her leave but made no move to discover where she was headed.

The weather was beginning to bite, the wet ground was cold. She had forgotten her old cloak and only the urgent strain of her steep ascent warmed her. But when she had climbed down to the pool and sat on its ledge, she quickly became cold and then so cold that it was very painful. That solid-seeming physical pain was a relief and she nursed it.

There were no questions easily formulated. Nothing so clear as – what shall I do? Should I make an end to it now? How can anything I feel or what anyone does be believed again? – and yet the circuit of those questionings moved about her retreating warm consciousness as the cold morning bleakly moved towards a chill, sharp noon. Nothing could be grasped except the body itself, hunched, hugging her knees on the rock. The longer she sat so still the wilder beat her fears, the deeper threatened the chasms of blackness in her mind. It had to be believed – what she had read – and yet she had no means of absorbing it and in her still passionate, though damaged, love for her husband, she longed to reject it.

It would be easiest for everybody, she thought, if she were just to slip into the bitterly cold pool and let it close over her life. She knew the thought was wrong.

Yet it recurred. It would release her, release him, end the shame. Let it happen. There was something in her wilful immobility which encouraged it. The cold had seized her and she was drifting towards a dizzy carelessness which could soon cause by apparent accident what she knew by design she ought to avoid.

There was no comfort in the valley which had given her so much before. It was no more than an arrangement of fields, a few paths, the lakes, hills, a handful of cottages – not even as defined as that now, in her severe stillness, but merely patterns; objects; becoming very strange and even, how could that be? unfamiliar as the cold penetrated deeper and her mind sought ease in emptiness.

After the sunless noon, a wind brought colder air from the north-east and Mary found herself drifting. She saw Hope riding towards her, she saw herself as a small girl with her father taking the flocks up the fells, Mr. Fenton by candlelight, Tom, fresh as an apple, the fire in the parlour of the Fish, the fire in her chest roaring like dry logs in a winter stove, the fire boring pains in her legs and arms, now enflaming and scorching her tongue until she spat it out.

"Swallow some more," said Kitty, "more now."

Mary looked at her friend as if she had crossed a barrier and was seeing someone in another world.

"I've always known this was your hidey hole," said Kitty in explanation. "Drink up now."

Mary put her mouth obediently to the top of the small flask of brandy but it was with no feeling of gratitude.

"I've saved this up," Kitty said. "I knew I would need it."

Mary felt ashamed of her ingratitude but the feeling of profound and tired indifference to her lifesaving friend and the alcohol now fairly stinging her into painful life was not dissolved.

"I'll have to help you up the rock," said Kitty. "You must get yourself moving. When I came here you were fast as a stone."

Mary uttered a moan as she levered herself to her feet: but even that did not come from her heart, from herself; it was merely a mechanical response, as many at that time thought the cries of animals to be.

"Can I come back with you?"

"No. You'd never be able to stand it. We'll get you home."

By the time the women reached the inn, the combined effects of the shock, the sleepless heart-rent night, the near-exposure and the forceful medicine had exhausted her. She managed to swallow a dish of tea and then fell deeply asleep before the fire in the parlour. Her mother covered her with blankets and let her stay there, feeding the fire right through until the morning. Occasionally Mary would seem about to break out of unconsciousness and with a series of indistinguishable syllables alert the older woman to some revelation but nothing was ever clear or coherent enough to give her a clue to the course the distress was taking.

When Mary woke up, well after dawn, she looked even more tired, her mother thought, than she had done when Kitty Dawson had brought her back the previous night.

Even the arrival of Colonel Moore – this time alone – failed to generate animation and Mrs. Robinson was quite upset to see how listlessly her daughter was prepared to greet such an important and splendidly spruce visitor. She was relieved to be occupied in fetching the Colonel some mulled ale – which had taken his fancy after a crisp canter over from Keswick.

"I see you are not well –" he had intended to be comforting but an unanticipated awareness that this woman had been preferred to his ward brought him to an abrupt stop and his observation hung there like an unfinished bridge. Mary did not help him by offering a response.

"Your – husband – is, as you know, wanted by Sir Frederick Vane over this unfortunate and disgraceful affair. It would help us all – and you too – if we had more information about him, more to help those Bow Street Runners – heard of them? Remarkable – ferrets to a man, better than a foxhound on a warm scent – Hardinge told me all about them – anything you have, or of course want to say – to me – it would be a great help."

Once again Mary gave him no help and the Colonel was grateful for the digression of the mulled ale which arrived with an oatmeal biscuit. He went across to the window, pretending to be absorbed in the view, but in truth seized by a feeling of all but intolerable agitation that his marvellous, beautiful, fashionable, wealthy ward should be tied, however loosely, to this great white-faced innkeeper's daughter, hair trailing down to the floor, staring out at him from under the grey blankets as if he had some hand in her downfall.

"We all feel very sorry for you," he said, easing his collar with his index finger. "Everywhere I go there is nothing but pity for you and understanding. Pity above all."

"Thank you, sir." The peculiarity of her tone made him turn around sharply.

She had stood up and stared at him "as if I were the ghost," he would say later, "although it was she who looked like one."

"What will happen if you catch him?" she asked.

"Oh, we *shall* capture him without doubt, without doubt."

"What will happen when you do?"

"He'll be brought back here and put up to stand trial."

"What will happen to him then?"

"That is in the hands of the jury."

"What do you think they will decide?"

"What he has done – if it is true, as it seems, that he is not the Honourable Augustus Hope, M.P. – what he has done in franking his letters 'Free: A. HOPE' is a capital offence."

"Does that mean he could be hanged for it? For not paying for his letters?"

"'Not paying for his letters . . .' That is not the point, young woman. That is not the point at all."

"But he could be hanged for it?"

"Yes."

"What might stop them doing that?"

"If he has no case – and he has *none*! – then he will be at the mercy of the court."

"What is the quality of that mercy?"

"I have answered your questions patiently even though I have found it uncomfortable to do so. I must ask you a question now. Do you have something which can be of help to the forces of law? – because if you do have information then it is your bounden duty to give it up. Should you be discovered to be shielding him *in any way* you become an accomplice. I have to warn you of that."

"What would make them merciful?"

"Why do you want them to be merciful?"

"I don't," she said. And at last her hurt revenge found its voice. "I have some letters."

*

One cluster of letters was from Michelli Nation, his second wife, to whom he was still married: there were two small children. The other, smaller bundle was from his first wife, the natural daughter of Lord Robert Manners, dead for some time, mother of three of his children, all abandoned by him. She herself had expired destitute.

*

Newton, on the same day – 27th October – on which Moore rode back to Keswick in a state of immense excitement, worked his way back to base and calculated that Hatfield must have slipped inland, possibly back to Lancaster.

He went to the traders who might have bought one of the few pieces of valuable jewellery which Newton knew well.

Soon enough he was on his way to that part of the beach where the coaches assembled which was where Mr. Harris believed that the old woman must have picked up the heavy gold chain. Anne Tyson refused to give him any information. She would yield neither to guile nor to bribes nor even to threats.

A little trawling, however, uncovered a pregnant young woman, Sally, employed as a labourer on a nearby farm. She had spied on the man and was very happy to help if Newton promised to take her with him. This he did, convincingly. She described his clothes, she remembered precisely when he had left, she had managed to track him into Lancaster and could even remember the details of the coach he had taken to Liverpool. Newton gave her half a guinea and told her to be ready for him outside the farm just after dawn the next day. He left for Liverpool immediately.

*

On 5th November, two pieces were printed which were to excite the public interest to an even higher pitch.

The first was an article by Coleridge published in the *Morning Post* and reprinted in the *Courier* the same day. Its dateline was Keswick October 30th. It was the shortest and most urgent of the articles – almost a newsflash.

The 'Impostor's' true name was discovered – John Hatfield . . . "Poor Mary of Buttermere, examining the box more narrowly, found that the box had a double bottom: and in the interspace were a number of letters addressed to him from his wife and children under the name of Headfield. This atrocious villain is therefore a bigamist, as well as guilty of felony for attaching the name of Member of Parliament to a letter for the purpose of fraud . . . It is greatly to be hoped that the wretch will be apprehended – a more detestable action was surely never perpetrated. Poor Mary is the object of universal concern."

Apart from the incorrect spelling of the name – which could suggest that Coleridge had *heard* about the cache of letters but not as yet read them, the mention of only one correspondent and the lack of detail suggest that Coleridge rushed off this story the moment he learnt of it and his later, mature, worked-on, 'vindictive' feelings over the letters (when describing them he would "*go white and weep*") came from a later, more careful reading. He saw the news value in what he had once called 'The Romantic Marriage' and now re-christened it 'The Fraudulent Marriage'. He saw that yet another dimension was given to this story which drew to itself so many contrasts: now we had a bigamist, a villain and a seducer – Hatfield would be referred to as 'the famous seducer'. The man seen to be attacking what the more pious and high-minded were combining to institute (against the liberties of the previous century) as the holy sepulchre of all true earthly morality: marriage and the family. Hypocrisy, scandal, prurience and public morality came on stage.

Hatfield read the *Post* on 10th November in his lodgings in the poorest part of Chester. He was there disguised as a Jew.

That act of faith in leaving the dressing-case with Mary was now revealed as it had always been in reality – an act of dangerous foolishness.

Sickened, he left his bare basement cupboard and went out to walk through the town he knew so very well. He had thought in some way that he could do a trade: abandon himself to good and good would be returned to him. God had not heard him and taken advantage of what was meant as an honourable loving gesture – the leaving of the dressing-case worth at least eighty pounds – to threaten him with destruction and to shock and distress Mary with those letters. And madden her. So much that she had given them over, he guessed, to Moore. Yet, involuntarily, he smiled at the recollection of how fine she looked when she threatened a temper.

As he walked around the ancient town in which so much of his childhood – as battling and attacked as the town itself – had been eased in just such ambling through the cosseting streets, he worked out his next move.

Mary would have to be persuaded to join him. Or be prepared to join him in a few months' time when he had settled. Or at least prevented from turning her face for ever against him. However much he had lost, the revelation at Hause Point and the falling in love with Mary still burned a light inside him where all else there was nothing but blackness.

He was the old fox slipped back to his lair in the middle of the hunt. He could move through Chester like a spirit.

About two hours of the place uncramped his mind – he was even quite cheerful observing people whom he had once known so well now totally ignoring this Jew or, occasionally, letting him see their contempt. The life of an actor, he thought – a dream inside the dream it seemed to Hatfield.

He saw his name on a page of the *Daily Advertiser* – again for 5th November – a London paper which someone must have brought up on the coach. The man who was reading it was ill-dressed; the copy was soiled; it seemed unlikely he himself had purchased it. Yet only by patiently waiting and humbly offering twopence was Hatfield able to secure it.

He folded it tightly and walked back to his lodgings, holding it in a fist like a cudgel.

Exercising even more self-restraint, he waited until his can boiled him the water for tea, took himself some bread and cheese, drew the curtain although the room was half below ground, wedged the chair against the door, lit the candle and lay on his bed.

It was a Police Notice.

Fifty Pounds Reward

NOTORIOUS IMPOSTOR, SWINDLER AND FELON

JOHN HATFIELD

Who lately married a young woman, commonly called
THE BEAUTY OF BUTTERMERE

under an assumed name.

Height about 5′10″, age about 44, full face, bright eyes, thick eyebrows, strong but light beard, good complexion with some colour, thick but not very prominent nose, smiling countenance, fine teeth, a scar on one of his cheeks near the chin, very long, thick, light hair, with a great deal of it grey, done up in a club, stout, square-shouldered, full breast and chest, rather corpulent and stout-limbed but very active, and has rather a spring in his gait, with apparently a little hitch in bringing up one leg; the two middle fingers of his left hand are stiff from an old wound and he frequently has the custom of pulling them straight with his right; has something of the Irish brogue in his speech, fluent and elegant in his language, great command of words, frequently puts his hand to his heart, very fond of compliments and generally addressing himself to persons most distinguished by rank or situation, attentive in the extreme to females, and likely to insinuate himself where there are young ladies; he was in America during the War, is fond of talking of his wounds and exploits there and on military subjects, as well as of Hatfield Hall, and his estates in Derbyshire and Chester, of the antiquity of his family, which he pretends to trace to the Plantagenets; all which are shameful falsehoods, thrown out to deceive. He makes a boast of having often been engaged in duels; he has been a great traveller also (by his own account) and talks of Egypt, Turkey, Italy, and in short has a general knowledge of subjects which, together with his engaging manner, is well calculated to impose on the credulous.

He was seven years confined in Scarborough gaol, from when he married, and removed into Devonshire, where he has basely deserted an amiable wife and a young family.

He had art enough to connect himself with some very respectable merchants in Devonshire as a partner in business, but having swindled them out of large sums of money he was made a separate bankrupt in June last, and has never surrendered to his commission, by which means he is guilty of a Felony.

He cloaks his deceptions under the mask of religion, appears fond of religious conversation, and makes a point of attending divine service and popular preachers.

To consummate his villainies, he has lately, under the very respectable name of the Honourable Colonel Hope, betrayed an innocent but unfortunate young woman near the Lake of Buttermere.

He was on the 25th October last, at Ravenglass, in Cumberland, wrapped in a sailor's greatcoat and disguised, and is supposed to be now secreted in Liverpool, or some adjacent port, with a view to leave the country.

Whoever will apprehend him, and give information to MR. TAUNTON, *no 4,* PUMP COURT, TEMPLE, *so that he may be safely lodged in one of his Majesty's gaols, shall receive Fifty pounds reward.*

November 5th, 1802

He read it quickly: then he stood up, stretched, took his tea, forced down his bread and cheese and read it very slowly.

It was Newton, of course. Apart from the amount of accurate information – how in hell's name had he traced him to Liverpool? – the piece was most markedly Newton's because it was so out of date. This was the man he had represented himself to be when first he had met Newton in prison. Then indeed he 'frequently put his hand on his heart': not so frequently now. Talk of Hatfield Hall and the

Plantagenets had been no more than thread to spin and swing him from one day to the next – always done merely for effect and never designed – post-prison, post-Newton – to take in anyone who was not a registered fool. Not many boasts about duels these days and not too fond of 'persons most distinguished by rank and situation'. But Scarborough Gaol, Devonshire, the bankruptcy and that far far too helpful physical description . . . Newton.

Was this a desperate throw or was he closing in?

Liverpool was the warning.

He wrapped up the bread and cheese.

Towards midnight, moving through the streets as cautiously as a rat, a Jew, unobserved, left the Border city of Chester.

24

Letters

November 15th

My darling Mary,

Though I give you the date of this letter, I cannot tell you where I am. Nor can I be sure when it will be posted – the risk is certainly too great at the moment. And so I am writing to you the most important letter of my life with no sure expectation that you will ever receive it. But read it you certainly shall. For we will be together again, my darling Mary, as soon as the hue and cry has died down; I will come back for you and we will be together always. If I did not believe that to be truly possible then I would walk out and surrender myself to the Bow Street Officers this morning.

It is only in you, the memory of you, the thought of you, the great wish that I have to redeem myself before you and to make you understand – for you are a pure soul – in you alone do I have faith. I have thought often enough that I have faith in Jesus Christ and Our Lord God but either He has cast me out entirely or I have lost that faith. I feel afraid to say that, afraid that His lightning might strike me, His plague set upon me, His curses hound me across the surface of the earth – but then I *am* plagued and hounded and struck by bolts of misfortune. I thought I had regained the shining armour of faith near your village one day some weeks ago when it seemed the heavens opened and the God of Hosts took me back into His fold. Since then – although the same sensation returned on other occasions – I have experienced nothing but that terrible blackness into which I have threatened to lurch since I was a boy. A blackness which has nothing to do with *anything*: neither what I am, nor was, nor will be. Only the love of you for me and my own true love for you gave any light.

If you were with me I could tell you better than I can write to you: but when I was with you I never talked, or but little, and that, sadly, often deceitfully of who and what I was.

> This letter and others I may write are in part to tell you who I am. I will do this without lies. You will by now have read the Police Notice: doubtless other slanders and libels will follow. You have to know my life from me: and then you can judge. And that is the main purpose of this letter – and any others – to let you judge me. Others are passing judgement all over the Kingdom. It is your judgement which matters most – matters solely, to me – and once you know what my life was and is, I am convinced that you will agree to be mine once more and come away with me to start life again outside this England which has done nothing but torment and taunt me since the day I was born.

He put down his pen and reflected for a few moments which stretched into minutes, into more than half an hour. He was lodged in a farmhouse in Aberystwyth – no longer a Jew but a Scottish traveller in linen making his way leisurely back to Dundee from Swansea after a successful trading trip abroad. He gave out that he had a prodigious amount of bookwork to complete and this excuse kept him in retreat in his room for as long as he chose. In the two days he had been there he had been helped by the rain which had scarcely stopped for more than an hour's clear space. When there was not rain there was low cloud, or mist, usually all three. This gave him every reason not to go scrambling after the views. He would move on in two more days: meanwhile he noted the speech pattern and manners of his host with care. At his next stop he would be a Welshman.

In Liverpool he had made detailed enquiries about ships to America and the East. He had asked specifically about any work which a respectable married couple (the wife young) used to keeping inns could do on board – work which would pay for their passage. Few of the responses had been encouraging: no-one saw any place for a woman except as a passenger, a whore or a prisoner. He had gathered information about fares and immediately gone over to a strict economy.

His first plan had been to sneak back to Buttermere, carry off Mary and, however meagre their resources, set sail for the furthest country they could afford. It was not Newton's Police Notice which had put an end to that. All the main ports would be watched, of course, but useful as that description of himself undoubtedly was to spies, informers and interferingly honest citizens he was confident of his disguises. But Mary would be so conspicuous as to leave them no chance at all. Her extraordinary beauty could never be disguised.

Now he intended to slip away – possibly only to Ireland or even Denmark – and from there arrange a meeting with Mary out of England. Two obstacles had to be overcome for that: the first was to keep out of the path of the law officers and, more especially, Newton until it was safe to look for a sea passage. For that reason he was tacking his way across the North of Wales with the very greatest caution. At Aberystwyth, for instance, he never enquired once about a boat, let alone a sea passage. He contrived to wear gloves on every outing, hiding the fingers; a staff helped conceal that hitch in his gait; the hair was concealed by a wig; the character was that of a reserved, even surly, man of his own business, non-conformist almost to a fault. He was all but certain that his scent was cold but nevertheless he would move on. The second obstacle was Mary. She had to be prepared to come when he called. Otherwise . . . speculation on those consequences only intensified his reverie.

He dozed.

The fire in his snug bedroom – almost crowded out by the great oak double bed – the heavy afternoon pot of stew, the bread pudding, ale, most of all perhaps the sense of release which those first few paragraphs of the letter brought him . . . he relaxed more deeply than he had dared to since the day of his marriage, perhaps even before then, even before he went into Cumberland . . . there was a sensation of floating and, half-awake, he imagined lines out and the fish biting, hauling them in – now the face of his mother on the body of the fish, now a friend, a lover, a child, a warder, a judge, a patron . . . he was reeling in his past and its weight drew him down into weariness, its variety confused him. If only he could say everything about himself just as the Catholics did in their confession – but even more than that. For he would want to hide nothing at all – to let free all the meanness, the pettiness, the vice, to let it leave him and be on the page instead of being stuck on his brain. He had a momentous impulse to show the world what one man was like for better, worse, rich, poor, bad, sick, healthy, in glory, in shame, feeling that in the end he would be much as other men were if they too were truthful, and though that was not a decisive factor, it would give him some comfort in the loneliness of this battle against those who were out to capture him.

After an hour or so he found himself in a state which fluctuated between excited discovery and exhaustion: it was as if he had arrived unexpectedly and suddenly at a cliff edge after a wearing journey: and some imperative inner voice told him 'Jump! Leap! Fly!'

He went out into the brutal winter afternoon – grey cloud, grey sea, landscape lowering and unpeopled, and took what he had been told was the most common walk. The cold settled on his face, infiltrated to the tips of his toes, found small gaps in his over-hasty dress and nipped him into a fit of shivering which soon had him hurrying back for the hibernated burrow of the overheated bedroom.

He would write no more that night, he decided. What he had written so far would serve as a general prologue. He would take a night's sleep before attempting the next letter.

*

November 16th

My darling Mary,

I was born about the middle of the last century in Mortram in Langdale, Cheshire. I have an idea that we do not look hard enough into childhood to find what has made us. In my case there are conflicting impulses: I want to look in order to see – and above all to show you – what I am, but to look is painful, distorted by a sense of injustice and scarred by wrongs. But I want you to know everything about me so that you can be armed against the multitudes of denigrators and, as I have said, have before you the evidence on which to judge me.

My parents were as humble as yours. My father worked in the woods belonging to Lord I——. My mother was the youngest of fourteen children of a schoolteacher. We were eight: my mother lost three girls and one boy all before they had reached one year. I was the youngest of those four who remained. My oldest brother was so far ahead of me – about eleven years, I guess – that he had left the house before I could know him. Much the same with my oldest sister, who went out to service when she was ten. My next sister – only three years older than myself – was sickly and kept at home where she could be of some help to my mother.

As my father was away in the woods for great spans of time – charcoal burning, felling, cutting the coppice for baskets, living the life of an Indian while he was working – I was brought up by a mother who doted on me and a sister whom I revered. For illness, as sometimes happens with children, gave my sister a great serenity and sweetness which was saintly. She looked very like my mother who herself, at that time – I was about seven – was wasting away. I can see their eyes now – large, brown eyes so kind and fond of me that I would never again know such care.

The village was extremely modest – though larger than Buttermere – and we were well liked. The local clergyman found a special sympathy for my mother and he would call in to see us, often enough bringing some treat his wife had sent for one of the children. I was quick and bold and he loved to question me on the bible, set me tests and see me succeed: he would often give me a few coppers but, precious as they were, they were little compared with the glory I felt in making my mother – as I could see – so proud of her small son.

That time with the three or four of us – for when my father came back, there was little disturbance: he was utterly devoted to my mother and my sister – seems to have gone on for ever. It cannot have been much more than two – at the most three – years of my life and yet even now I can slip back to that small room with the peat fire, my mother reading to us, my sister sewing and smiling her angelic smile, myself listening intently to the story, perhaps even on my mother's knee, unaware of the pain even my childish weight could cause her. And then all of us to bed together, the most innocent and untroubled nights of my life.

One day my father came home with the news that Lord I—— had fallen on bad times, needed fewer men and had set him off. After almost twenty years' continuous drudgery, ill paid, loyally rendered. At first my father was cheerful: there would be other work and the change might do him good. We had all been prudent and there was no immediate anxiety. The anxiety soon grew, over the next few weeks, when my father found that Lord I——'s case was a common one. He searched all over the county but there was no work.

At this time, something happened to me which should have been a small event but had the most dire results. I fell painfully in love – and if this seems impossible for a boy of seven, I can assure you that it did happen. The object of my total adoration was a young daughter of Lord I——. She was a few years older than I and I saw her on her pony, with her groom and a lady who may have been her aunt or her governess. The instant I saw her I was enslaved. I talked of nothing else to my at first amused but soon bewildered and then alarmed dear mother and sister. I begged them not to tell my father, fearing – rightly, I'm sure – that he would force me to stop what he would see as idle and even dangerous play. I spent every minute either scheming how to see her or putting myself in her way. Just the sight of that erect back and the beautiful hard face which never gave me a single glance. Perhaps it was that which drove me mad – for was I not mad?

I became bolder – crept into the grounds and up to the stables to see the divine creature walk as well as ride. I would race through the woods to cut across her route three or even four times in a morning. I dreamt of her and saw her face before mine plain as a church window.

That the gap between us, between my dream and her life, was wider than the Atlantic Ocean never entered my head at that time. All I knew was that I was compelled to seek her out: that life without her was without life. I had no choice.

I arrived home one day from the chase to find my mother and my sister outside our small cottage, barricaded about by such furniture as we had. News of my attentions had reached Lord I—— whose response was to drive us out of the district. This he did. My father could find no accommodation at Mortram or anywhere about – no-one wanted to antagonise the great Lord – and after two days spent in the leaking barn end of the one neighbour less fearful than the others (though even he regretted his charity after a few hours and was constantly urging us to go) we set off for Chester.

My father had said little about the reason for our abrupt eviction. But as we were leaving the village with such chattels as we could stack on a hand-pulled cart, my mother perched on top of them, a most reluctant Majesty, my sister setting us all an example in finding something to bless even in this, the small, irresistible, erect, unlooking object of my fascination rode by – forcing us off the path. I could not resist running after her, leaving my father alone between the shafts, racing down the autumn lane for one more glance. The groom by now had received his orders: he brought his crop down across my face so viciously that I fell immediately, half-stunned and bleeding. The horse party rode on without a word.

This blow released my gentle father's sense of grievance and stoked his anger. My mother was made ill by the sight of my bloodied, bruised face and we stopped at the nearest pothouse where she insisted on spending the night although the expense worried my father greatly. I raved to be allowed to stay. I could not bear it, I said, if I were to be sent away from the ground over which my divine creature rode, from the air she breathed, from the trees and streams she saw. I would surely die of such a loss.

My fever lasted more than two days but as I revived my mother failed. The vehemence and strangeness of my condition added to the terror she felt and the violent uprooting was too much for her. My father was forced to keep us all in a room at the pothouse and the prospect of continued expense began to work on him. Moreover I would not give up my crusade. I would attempt to run back the few miles to our village so that I could catch one more glimpse: weakened as I was my father had no trouble in catching me but the absurdity of his child's behaviour added to his growing distraction. He tied me up like a dog to a stake in the yard whenever he went off to see if he could chop some wood or do some labour for a few pence. When I broke away even from that, he had to pursue me to Mortram after a day's frustrated attempts to get money for the medicines my mother now needed and the bread we all wanted. He beat me. This was the first time he had done so: he was remarkable among his neighbours for never beating his children and although I was hurt, it was my mother who was the more badly injured.

Now she began to fade fast and my father, desperate for means, turned thief. He broke into the grounds he knew so well, made his way in black night with ease to that stretch of the wood most fortunate in game and took from the gamekeeper's snares not only enough to feed ourselves but enough as he thought to make it worth our landlord's while to give us free lodging. Alas, he misjudged his man. The landlord saw more to be gained from turning evidence than taking game and he delivered my father to the law.

While he was in Chester gaol, my mother died. I was apprenticed to a linen draper in that town. My father was sent off for five years' hard labour. My sister attempted to follow him to be near him but within a month she too was dead. I never saw or heard of him again.

Within a few months we had been ravaged and all, I could not avoid it, on account of my uncontrollable passion for a girl who never once glanced at me.

Hatfield put down his pen and a spring of images, memories, smells, sights flooded into him too fast to capture on the page, too incoherent to summarise; he was invaded by those few months of almost forty years before. He sat and watched his candle dwindle to its base and then gutter out completely: only the ember in the fire gave any light. But that was enough for him to add one sentence:

"What you are to make of this," he wrote, "I do not know for still today I have no idea of what I myself conclude." And then a final word. "Except that I dreamt and dream still that I killed them: all."

*

November 18th

My darling Mary,

Yesterday I changed my lodging and am now housed in the poorest district of a populous city. I have been anxious all the time of moving to race on with my life, both for your sake and mine. But I cannot be too careful. The enemy who stalks me is the most tenacious and cunning man in the Kingdom and it is the greatest test of my wits to keep him off. Yesterday I felt I crossed his path. He was going away from me but I scented the man and shivered to think of the consequences for me, and for you, dare I say it, Mary? were he to have me captured. He stalks me with his hook and I must be always on my guard . . .

My first year in Chester was the worst year of my life. I was apprenticed to an evil man. There were four of us boys, none of whom had a life better than that of a nigger on a plantation. We worked sixteen hours a day, sometimes – you must believe me – even longer and two of the boys – older than I, with some spirit left – were chained to their benches and slept in chains. We were given half an hour for food at midday and a quarter hour in the evening – vile food, bread and gruel, hardly enough for a rabbit let alone a growing boy. On Sunday mornings we were scrubbed by the callous-handed mistress of the house and marched to church as a sort of dwarf escort to the great man and his wife and their three fat daughters. There were four servant girls also, but they were considered so very mean that they were not even allowed to church. Every sign of independence or humour or sympathy was checked and beaten out of us. If we had not been beaten in the week then he would still beat us on Saturday night just to make sure, he said. He was free with the small servant girls, the youngest of whom would be no more than ten: he would occasionally unshackle one of us and haul us off to a cockfighting ring where we would be made to set to with other apprentices – all naked, bare fists and feet flying – while the sporting gentry tossed us coppers and laid side bets and rewarded us with ripped chunks of burnt game flesh so rich and strange we were sick on them. I was taken once and fainted at the end of it.

He cheated his customers wherever possible and equally fawned on them wherever possible. We would hear him above us ingratiating himself in the most silken manner to some local gentleman or lady and then through the trapdoor he would come like the devil in a melodrama and scorn those he had flattered, slander them and tell us how he was going to hoodwink them and so subtly they would never know it. When anyone from the parish or – as happened twice in that year – a clergyman came to see us, we were terrified to do anything but swear to his overwhelming benevolence, which they seemed to accept at face value although, God knows, any close look at the faces and starving bodies of the four grey-faced runts must have given the lie to our protestations of health and happiness.

He was caught in some doubtful transaction, further crimes were uncovered, he was sentenced to imprisonment, I think for ten years, and we were taken over by a new owner, Mr. Seyward.

I can hear you say that I am playing on your sympathy for this boy I was. And so I am. Whatever your poverty you had loving and constant parents. Whatever your straits you had freedom.

Whatever your lacks you had sufficient fresh water, nourishing food, fresh air, use of your limbs, friendly neighbours. I have no need to be told of the rude distresses existing in the country, often worse than those in the cities. But those of us buried alive in the catacombs of those cities know a life which needs to be told to be understood. Further, I believe that what happens to us in those tender years of childhood sets up a reel that unspools through the rest of our lives. I know we are urged to 'put away childish things' and I see all around me children being treated as playthings or slaves or merely small adults. But I believe there is a world of childhood which is a world different to that of our own and what is sown there though buried and forgotten for years on end must one day be reaped. And I have thought back on that evil man many times since and wondered what he destroyed in me and what he planted. He was my first experience of a Tyrant.

My new master was kind enough. We worked almost the same number of hours but the terror was gone. The food was a little better. He did not abuse us except boisterously, when he was drunk – then, to take one instance, he would shave our heads bald, paint the bare skulls with paste and stick chicken feathers all over us. But he meant no harm; and Mrs. Seyward was an extremely pious woman who gave us all bible classes, responding most favourably to myself who was well trained in that discipline. It was through her favour that I began to prosper and soon Mr. Seyward was taking me around the towns with him as a 'rider', selling his linen. It was there I learned to lie.

At first I entered into it innocently enough – Mr. Seyward was very encouraging, he told me that all the 'riders' had to exaggerate (his word for it) but that this was no more than a common form of speculation. You would say, for instance, that you could offer such and such a cloth for sixpence less than your keenest competitor, even though you could not. Come the day of delivery you had then the task to sell something else he had not ordered, at a higher price, so as to make up your money, or chisel the sixpence down to a tolerable twopence by tales of misfortune, or *discover any way* to wheedle through it. And he observed that I was greatly attracted to women and they – although I blush now to write it as then, a virgin, I blushed, though pleased, to understand it – were to me. Mr. Seyward saw this as my *principal asset.* From then on I was to play on the womenfolk – those who were not kept as serfs (for it seemed to the boy I then was there were only three kinds of women: slaves, monsters and mistresses who governed all before them) – and conduct business as far as possible through them. This I did. And with lies and flattery to the female kind I prospered.

There is one further small fact I want to tell you. It was just after I began with Mr. Seyward that I began to experience a very strange sensation from which I have never since been wholly free. It happens to me usually when I am alone and may be associated with fear of solitude or with that greatest fear of all. (Indeed, once one truly begins to fear Death, I believe that everything else in the mind lives in that shadow.) It is hard to describe without sounding ridiculous but, begging your indulgence, and because I think it is important, I will say, briefly, only this: it is as if a distinct part of me – is it my soul? It is certainly an intelligence – leaves my body entirely and completely, totally and unmistakably – hovers above it looking back on this vacated thing of flesh, bone, blood, breath, water, matter. Once freed, this 'intelligence' is suspended as if in waiting – for what I do not know. The body which has been abandoned dares hardly breathe for fear – of what I do not know, but it is a vice-powerful tyranny of fear which allows no slightest rebellion against its law. At times it can happen when I wake up from a drowse and then there is a sensation of nothing: my body seems nowhere with no limits and no form; beyond it are the spirits which make it what it is and then I pause as if about to topple off a cliff edge, balanced finely, as I sway forward, between falling and staying upright, the whole existence in the balance . . .

I have written enough – although it has come to fascinate me and I would like to discover more scientifically what it is that I suffer from or, perhaps, more theologically, what it is I enjoy – but I wanted to tell you this. Because I am convinced that this split in myself was responsible for much of the evil I am said to have done and much of the misfortune I have endured. For just as the 'spirit' will go out of me and be outside the control of whatever mass it is which is left behind, so too, at times, I have seen and known a 'spirit' inside me *and yet independent of me*, always a malign force, a dæmon resolved to wrench me its way however terrible the effects might be. And just as I have been numb before that which has left me, so I have been powerless before that which has appeared inside me. It is to be pitied, Mary, but more than that, it is to be driven out: I tell you of it because I sensed in you someone who had the power and the innocence to exorcise the devil just as you have the beauty to make me whole to myself.

I have digressed further than I intended and I am aware that I have not yet got to the two subjects most harrowing for you – my wives. It is true that I hesitate through fear of what you will think and how you will judge. But I wanted you to know a little of the boy who became the man: of my lovely and pious mother; my affecting, uncomplaining sister; a father driven to what the world of property calls crime; an evil master and a kinder couple who drew me out – the woman in religion and pleasing, the man in trading and in lying. And the strange nature which grew out of all this. I will next tell you what I made of that inheritance.

*

It was five days before Hatfield wrote another letter. On the morning of 19th November, he was seized by panic and for no reason that made sense to himself he went back into Liverpool where he lay by the docks for two days and left after having laid a multitude of false trails. He headed across to Manchester, made to go north but then slipped over into Derbyshire, staying at the Rutland Arms in Bakewell for one night as a Mr. Whitehead, druggist. By this time his beard was full and black.

In Liverpool he had pawned whatever would fetch cash but even so he was becoming anxious about his finances and once again he turned west for Wales where he could live most cheaply. This time he struck south.

On his way he bought a copy of the *Morning Post* for 25th November. In it, dateline 'Keswick 11th November 1802. Thursday', he saw 'The Keswick Impostor: I. A Narrative of what is at present known at Keswick of the Keswick Impostor.'

This had been commissioned by Stuart, the Editor, from Coleridge following the increasing, even fervid, interest in the story. Plays were under way; portraits were being issued; hacks were flying north; the Bow Street Officers were out across the land; ports watched; hotels checked; informers called in; pawnbrokers visited; the Police Notice issued and re-issued. This long article by Coleridge was promised to be, as the title declared, the first part of a larger piece: Stuart was to hold back on the second, philosophical half. The length and prominence were a testament to the widespread interest. Hatfield read it alone, sitting behind a hedge on a blustery day – the paper shaking in the wind – somewhere in mid-Wales.

There was little new in it and that was a relief. Much of his physical description, he saw, had been plucked all but unchanged from the Police Notice and, he guessed, much else which posed as locally gathered and tested information had been extrapolated from that same source – "full of compliments, skilful and discriminating . . . frequently put his hand to his heart . . ." He was pleased to be credited with "an astonishing flow of words" – the man might have spoken to dear old Wood – and moved to see the commendation of the People faithfully recorded – "It was common in persons who spoke of him to exclaim 'What an *entertaining* man he is! What prodigious *information* he possesses!' Expressions of admiration which were usually followed by the phrase – 'and then he is *so* good!' "

At this point, Hatfield lifted up his head to the big-bellied clouds sailing low over the fields and hills of Wales and prayed aloud that Mary might read that passage.

He was accused of making "a promise of marriage to Burkett's daughter" and also "if I am not grossly misinformed," continued Coleridge, the anonymous author, "something very like a promise of marriage to one of the maidservants at the Queen's Head." Hatfield was saddened by such lack of loyalty. He supposed they had been bribed.

He was interested in what the writer had to say of his religion. His fondness for religion or, as the writer typically put it, his "pretensions to religion and to religious exercises" was noted but so also was the fact that "he never attended a church at Keswick but once." Was this Wood? Or Nicholson? Surely Nicholson would not yield up information on him until his side of the story had been properly aired. What was amusing was that once again he was excused by "the people of Keswick who . . . candidly attributed this neglect (in churchgoing) to his being of a Scottish family and education."

His real name was not mentioned this time. Perhaps when it was, the writer would this time take the trouble to spell it correctly.

But the hunt was up.

*

November 25th

My darling Mary,

Let me tell you about my first marriage which was the cause of all my future problems.

By the age of fifteen, I was Mr. Seyward's best 'rider'. I could sell more than any other man he had, more than my Master himself. I had all the confidence in the world and although I still thought of my parents and my sister, time had largely erased them from my mind while that year of torment with the man whose name I will not dignify in writing was also a phantom in a lost past.

About a dozen miles from Chester was a farmer who sold us some of our best wool. Mr. Seyward had kept him for his own as he did with all the better and richer clients and customers. An illness on his part – his regular drunkenness made him very susceptible to minor but disabling ailments – gave me the responsibility and it was there I first saw Emma.

She was sixteen. I, as I said, fifteen, but the sight of her encouraged me to promote myself four years. Luckily I was big for my age, all but fully grown and with that sense of decorum necessary for my business which can easily be mistaken for maturity. I was not as madly enraptured as I had been at seven but then – until I saw you – I never recognised that feeling again. Yet I liked her very much: there was something fine and also rather fragile about her – a curt mouth, dependent eyes, a firm nose, nothing of a chin. A tendency to flirtatiousness, easily cowed. I fancy – and so she said – that she took to me as I to her, at first sight: indeed I believe in no other kind of love.

I went back several times and we always contrived to pass looks, be alone together for a moment in the kitchen or the stable, in short, inform each other of our mutual regard – no, Mary, you will excuse it in a boy – passion! The passion, though, *of* a boy: blind, urgent, ignorant, content with mere conquest and show. But it was, for all that, a true feeling, and a powerful one.

Mr. Powell – the successful and most friendly farmer – noticed all this without much comment until it came to the stage where he had to intervene. Taking me aside one day – out of the stable yard and into the orchard – he asked me how serious were my intentions. I replied that their seriousness was 'beyond question and beyond reproach'. I remember that phrase to this day: I was very pleased with it. He then enquired of my prospects and here I claimed more than my due but I was convinced I could somehow get Seyward to back me up.

Mr. Powell then informed me that Emma was not his own child but the natural daughter of Lord Robert Manners (this was still unknown to her) who intended to give her one thousand pounds on her marriage provided he approved the bridegroom. Mr. Powell then conducted me to my horse, helped me mount – I must have been in a daze – slapped the flanks of my old cob and asked or rather ordered me to think it over and bring him an answer. If it should be 'yes' then he would inform both Emma and Lord Robert of the truth of their respective situations. He would, though, of course, want Mr. Seyward to confirm the brightness of my prospects in the wholesale linen business.

I cannot say I rode back to Chester. The old cob just piloted me there.

Let me confess that it was like being in a fairy story. The daughter of a *Lord*! 'Natural' or natural, she was still part of that Mighty and All-Powerful Connection which could crush my people like so many beetles under the heels of their boots. *Lord!* The estates, the court, the titles, the banquets, the jewellery, the manners, the seasons, the gardens and acres and all the magnificence I had peeped at time and again through back doors, side windows, framed in carriages, gasped at from a crowd, applauded entering a ball, made way for, been exhilarated by the slightest notice of: they were our rulers, our living history, our wealth and our greatness, our Past – Norman, Plantagenet, Tudor, Stuart – and through Emma my children would be part of them. I almost choked to think of that.

And one thousand pounds! To me, then – indeed, Mary, to me, now – but to me, then, one thousand pounds would buy the grandest house, the finest carriage, the most gorgeous clothes and society in England – in Europe! It was wealth incalculable for a boy who – let me illustrate. Kind as Mr. Seyward was, he was nevertheless a tradesman by default: he came of gentlefolk and had descended to business through penury. He had the coarse habits and the haughty affectations of the true country gentleman. One day, after I had been in service with him for well over a year – perhaps nearer two – he saw me on one half-holiday in the middle of Chester looking through the stalls. Are you looking for something to buy? says he. That I am, I replied, cocky with liberty. And what will you use for money? says he. This, I incautiously replied, opening a hand to reveal a guinea which was all I had saved and taken in tips and scavenged over the two years. Give that to me, says he: people of your kind should not have that sort of money to spend. And he took the guinea from me.

But one thousand pounds. Who could take that from me?

My dream was wilder than the Arabian Nights. Surely you can understand that. Admit it now – just something, just a mite of that same fifteen-year-old exhilaration entered your ten years older and much purer, much more sober mind when I first proposed to you? I hope it did because it would not be human had it not: and shy and innocent as you are – the rarest woman I have met – and though you repulsed me with all your strength and took me finally only out of love, yet that little pedigree and those larger prospects must have affected you. Imagine, then, how it agitated the brains of that boy I was!

I thought that Seyward would be a problem and so I told him the truth. To my surprise he was delighted but his delight was mostly to do with putting one over on the good and upright Mr. Powell whose ceaseless probity and sobriety were a little taxing to merry Master Seyward. He also thought Powell beneath him in those infinite gradations of classification practised in England for so long and polished to the perfection and, I now say, futility of those mediaeval schoolmen's debates about the number of angels who could dance on the point of a needle. It served my purpose very well. On the road there I made certain he had a few stops for refreshment just to be on the safe side, but my Master got me through it with as convincing a performance as ever I have witnessed.

We were married within the month, left her guardian loaded

down with gifts and received a banker's draft of no less than one thousand five hundred pounds from Lord Robert who declared himself delighted with the pair of us.

We went to London thinking that nothing on earth could injure a couple so young, so full of life, so bold and so rich. We rented a small but fashionable home in Mayfair; I hired a phaeton, visited the coffee houses in Covent Garden, went to the theatre, talked about politics, soon found friends for my wife to entertain in a style which was a galloping melange of invention and imitation and, still not sixteen, late a cowering drudge of an apprentice, played the part of a young blood flawlessly.

It was not difficult. Nor had I much need to gild the lily but I did and boasted of my wife's connections to the Rutland family – on which Lord Robert Manners had very kindly offered me some information during our short but pleasant interview. I admit also I boasted of a certain Hatfield Hall in Derbyshire which would be difficult to discover on a map and this hall I dressed in a certain style – explaining that I had come to London while two hundred men laid out water gardens to my new wife's taste. I spoke of my prowess as a huntsman and boasted of the foxes ripped to death by my fast and fearless hounds. I did, dear Mary, tell such and other untruths.

But they were the barkings of an overexcited pup, no more. No harm in them for anyone save myself. And it made good company even better – as did wine.

In a few months, to our astonishment we found that we were out of capital and appeared to owe money over half of London. Emma sped off to her 'natural' father who was, at this time, more amused than displeased – the money which seemed mountains to us, to him was a cowpat – he paid our debts and gave us a final sum on condition we left Town. This I was glad to do – too ashamed to stay, for even though I had met sharpers and gamblers, boasters worse than myself and dubious characters unimaginable to a country boy, I had also met some good fellows and I wanted them to remember me not down on my luck but as Young Jack Hatfield roaring with the best of them.

Nor did I want to go back down to Chester.

We went to Bristol and embarked for America.

Up until that time, Mary, although I did much that was foolish

> and some things that would not sit well on the shoulders of a Reverend Nicholson – I do not mock him, Mary: he is a good man and I rest easier as I write this now knowing that you can turn to him should you have need – but I did nothing *evil* or *wrong*. I was high-spirited and, if you wish to go further, irresponsible. I will not claim any sympathy from the fact that my wife not only helped me but urged me on, mad as I was to grab all the life the capital offered as fast as possible. But we learnt our lesson and arrived in America chastened, determined to succeed and, just after my sixteenth birthday, parents of a daughter.

*

Hatfield felt very depressed after this stint. Perhaps it was the letter or perhaps the memory of those retrospectively innocent and cavalier times of gregarious fun in London contrasted too strongly with the growing loneliness and desperation of his present fugitive life. And he had loved his wife for a time: and their three daughters. He had not seen the daughters for more than twenty years and Emma had long since died.

He went out into Brecon for his daily constitutional. Here he was known – though to very few – as Mr. Ludor Henry, a Welsh gentleman down from London to pursue amateur scholarship – a short History of Wales before Henry Tudor became King of England – and searching for a small property for his retirement. So far, though, he had made no contact with agents and on being told by his landlord that a Mr. Dafyd Pryce-Jones was the local expert on all things ancient and Welsh he had almost gruffly declined a meeting.

The solitude and the interminable recourse to writing – the letters or, more copiously at that time, his Journals – were bringing on a pattern alternately lethargic and jumpy. The laudanum did not help. There were hours on end when he would merely slump in his chair in front of a strip of blank white paper in a kind of stupor which, far from refreshing him, left him groggy and indecisive. His sleep was never untroubled and sometimes so violently uneven that he woke up terrified that he had given everything away in his unconscious babble. And those walks, far from clearing his mind, as once they had done, were now leaden affairs, weary in anticipation and even more exhausting in practice. He returned from them uninvigorated, in a sulky fatigue of body as well as mind. He had stopped exercising.

Brecon had been chosen because it was the home base of Judge Hardinge. Hatfield's calculation was that Newton would never guess that he would seek out the home base of the man who had exposed him (after that damned journalist in the *Post*), the man moreover being a judge and, as Hatfield had learned, uncommonly tenacious. Newton himself, Hatfield believed, would be very wary of visiting a place holding such a mastiff of the Law. Hatfield, with his Welsh accent perfected though not too strong and his manner flawless – surly, but not over-remarkably so, reserved to a fault perhaps – his face clean-shaven, the hair dyed, the gait corrected, once more the gloves, the unimpeachable excuse for being alone . . . ought to have felt as snug as a badger. But on this walk he felt uneasy. No-one followed him; he checked that; there was no-one conspicuously out of place; there was nothing at all to alert him except that sixth sense which had as often failed as served him but sometimes was as quick as paint.

He returned to his room tired but not ready for sleep. He poured a little of his now meagre store of laudanum into the last glass in the bottle.

The letters so far had been easy: ingratiating even, reflecting very well on him.

Would he have the courage to tell her the harder truths?

He took out his Journals and in a shorthand he had perfected for himself he began to write out, in headline and greatly abbreviated form, the subjects which a true confessor would have to reveal to redeem a true lover from such wounds and deceits as he had visited on Mary. Only the truest confession could cut clean through all this, he felt, believing confession to be an Excalibur, a weapon of unopposable righteousness. Perfect truth would cancel out wickedness: exposure of evil would render it harmless. If he were to recover Mary then he must confess all the worst. Nothing less would work.

She seemed so far away now. How many days and nights had they had together? How did he know it was not just another sincere lust? Was that belief that there was something extraordinary, something unique in Mary and in the two of them anything more than merely wished for?

She had given up the other letters, why should she not give up these? Safer to put what he had to say in his Journals – expand on them later when he might somehow be surer of Mary – there was bound to be some sign sooner or later – or show them to her when they met – the letters so far written must surely be enough to persuade her that she ought to listen to him and give him a chance to prove himself.

He scratched around trying to start what was to be a list but he had no heart for it. The landlord himself brought up the summoned pint of mulled ale – an unusual mark of respect – and Hatfield nursed it thriftily until he decided to attempt to sleep.

*

November 27th

My darling Mary,

I am writing in my Journals but this is a continuation of my letters. I know now that I will never be able to send them to you. You will have to read them when I have delivered them by my own hand. There is none other I would trust. I am very lonely as I write this, Mary, and cold as if I were ill and yet I have no great symptoms. My mind flies to alarm at the slightest provocation and as this ancient Welsh inn creaks like a ship in a storm I am constantly agitated. I have not been out for my walk for the last two days: perhaps that was a mistake but a compelling foreboding kept me from crossing the threshold of my own room. I take all my meals here now and would not be surprised had I the reputation of a hermit. I must move on but for the life of me I cannot think of anywhere more safe than this.

Oh I am weary, Mary. To lie in bed with you – a simple cottage bed – to look at candle shadows playing on the wall, to hear together those outside sounds which can be an aid to the deepest comfort just as they can be a prompt to the greatest fears, but to be at rest with the woman I love more than I have ever loved, saying nothing . . . will I be given that again?

And now, for reasons which defeat my poor Reason, I must tell you that:

In America I quickly found that I was of the Revolutionary party and much informed by Tom Paine who became my hero. I have written all this elsewhere in my Journals – especially and in detail the course of my struggle on the side of the Republican

Americans against the tyrannical British Monarchists. What is germane to this account, however, is that my wife disapproving of my principles (though that only provided me with a helpful excuse), I eventually abandoned her and betrayed her although by that time she had three small daughters and no visible means of supporting either herself or them. I have since heard she died in great distress. Our daughters are unknown to me.

On my return to London I found my radical principles unwelcome and unpopular. I presented myself as an Englishman of gentle birth from Northumberland waiting for an inheritance after an over-extended tour through Europe. By this means I kept afloat for three months, when I was arrested for a debt of one hundred and sixty pounds and committed to the King's Bench Prison. There I met several of those who had known me across the tables and in the coffee houses and taverns but none seemed to object when I called up the good Lord Robert Manners and began to boast of my estates in Rutland, etc. As usual I found women who would supply me with essentials often for the smallest return. And if a larger return were demanded I would fulfil that obligation as a justifiable quid pro quo.

I sought out the visiting clergyman and told him of Manners and Rutland and lied to him about my young wife and three daughters now distraught, I said, in Dorset awaiting the return of a husband and father whose carelessness had been misconstrued as criminality. I begged him to call on the Duke of Rutland and describe my condition. Easily and grossly flattered by proximity to the aristocracy as all Anglican clergymen have ever been he instantly put my plan into operation. After a slight hitch (I believe the clergyman – the Duke being rather a forgetful character and for that afternoon out of sorts with Lord Robert – was at first slung out by the tradesmen's door), two hundred pounds came my way and out into the world I came, born again.

This Duke, I thought, was worth my while. He was appointed Lord Lieutenant of Ireland in 1784 or thereabouts and I followed him to Dublin, engaged a set of rooms at an hotel in College Green and boasted of my relationship with the new Viceroy. Once again it did the trick – and how satisfying, how wonderfully deeply satisfying it was to the revolutionary I had become that I should be able to bamboozle the gentry at whim. I was the central feature, the bouquet of the famous Lucas' coffee house, and if a sixty-pound bill had not interfered with my progress I would have stayed on to become Viceroy myself.

This time I was lodged in the Dublin Marshalsea, but here I was in luck for the gaoler's wife, who came to see all new prisoners in fine clothes, was soon convinced that I was a close relative of the Viceroy, locked up in error. That day I was taken to the best apartment in the Marshalsea which, like the food I ate in the company of the said gaoler's wife and her amiable spouse, was far superior to the hotel in College Green.

As I anticipated, my notes to the Duke embarrassed him into action. I was released and, most thoughtfully, conducted under a personal escort to a packet that sailed on the next tide to Holyhead.

By this time I knew that the only life for me in this rotted country where the loyal patriotic gentlemen crush their fellow countrymen without a Christian care or any smallest notion of justice was to use this great gift I had for all it was worth. Lies were my passport, disguise my visiting card. Revenge was pleasure, pleasure revenge. For months on end I plagued the spas of the south – proposing here, drawing credit there, now as an Englishman, now Irish (most favoured), occasionally Scots – always full of news of the wide world and always a hop, skip and a jump ahead of the law until, that is, Scarborough. Here I made the mistake of entering politics.

That is to say of threatening to enter politics. Because I was bored and wanted to attempt something new I announced that by the interest of the Duke of Rutland (he has been mighty useful) I was soon to be one of the representatives in Parliament for the town of Scarborough. Naturally this was accepted. I believe your own premier Lord, Lord Lowther, controls about ten seats in the Commons – that is, in our great democratic assembly of freely elected representatives. At all events, the burghers of Scarborough took me in, feasted me, introduced me to their salty daughters, tried to seduce me into business ventures which might lead them onto the ducal highway and only fell out with me when it was again discovered I could not pay my hotel bill. Imagine the life I might have led had one or two landlords been a little less pressing! Nothing for it, though: I hopped up to London. Unfortunately, I had become rather fat and the Scarborough men were nimble. They hopped up to London faster than I did, met me on arrival, brought me back and threw me into prison.

I was in that prison for eight years. Of those years there can be nothing more truthful written than that they changed my life utterly and broke my spirit.

It was here I met Newton and, sensing his power, still full of myself, I charmed him with stories, some true, some false, stories of wars, duels, visits to exotic lands, women, escapades in coffee houses and boudoirs. I spent an age entertaining him in order to strike off the deadly clamp of boredom on my own brain and to win the good favour of one I knew could help me if he would. Alas I succeeded too well and that is a story for another part of these Journals.

In Scarborough prison, too, I saw my second wife, Miss Michelli Nation, of Devonshire. She had taken holiday rooms for the sea air just opposite the prison and caught sight of me and I of her as I looked out of my small square of light on one summer's day almost mad for air and then maddened when I had got it. Something in my plight, my appearance, moved her. We looked at each other as if we were already lovers, she, I dare say, because of what she wanted to be – already and at once – me because I sensed that here was another possible key to liberty. Every day we looked at each other, every day at the same hour for six and a half years. This I swear. The only time she was absent was when she went up to London to try to plead my cause or down to Devonshire for more funds to pay for what had become a permanent suite of rooms.

Eventually, she paid my debts, had me released from prison and on that very day, by special licence, married me. The first words I said to her were "My thanks". The second "I do". But I was free and now I was determined to make money by legitimate means. I was also determined to armour myself against what I feared would be the demanding influence of Newton.

In Tiverton in Devonshire I had a fine scheme which was guaranteed to make a number of the local tradesmen rich. And so, in the first eighteen months, it proved. The town – the wealthy in the town, that is – regarded me as something between a wizard and a benefactor. In truth, my scheme was a copy of a scheme which Newton had outlined to me and which in his case had all but worked out perfectly. After eighteen months of exemplary behaviour, a solid citizen now with one child born and my wife – whom I could not now endure but stayed loyal to for what she had done for me – well gone with another, I set off for London to exercise gaiety. Here I fell once again into the company of Newton and, at his suggestion, to secure an invincible refuge against my growing debts, turned to politics and canvassed the rotten borough of Queensborough. My bills were enormous as I tried to match the bribery and corruption of my opponents – but I declare, Mary, once in Parliament, where my debts could not have been called in, I would have done radical things for my fellow men. All was not vainglorious shows and vaunts! But I failed to be elected and, to cut the story short, I was set upon by creditors and bankrupted.

Newton offered me a way out and in my maddened, bemused and Godless state I accepted it, abandoning my wife, whose letters have followed me like an ancient curse in a Greek Tragedy.

I was broken. I would propose to almost every woman I met and I admit openly, Mary, I would seek out women for pleasure with no other aim but animal satisfaction, whose need for satiation sometimes made me lunatic with lust. That other batch of letters is from a young woman I met, proposed to and seduced in London just a few weeks before Newton and I fled the place with the dressing-case you have in your room now. But I was broken not by debts or crime: not even by the way I had behaved to women and children, nor even by the impossible weight of privilege as Hope which made a mockery of my principles. I was broken because I had lost God and with Him, lost myself. I knew neither Him nor myself.

You redeemed me, Mary. You and then a great and true revelation I had at Hause Point. That is why you must now be the recipient of my confession. For only you can absolve me.

*

The relief gave him his first good sleep for many weeks. In the morning he woke humming, ordered the hot water for his shave and told the maid to have his bill ready: he would move on. He was so eager to do this that he packed immediately – he was travelling very lightly – and took his Journals and letters with him down to the parlour for breakfast.

The Bow Street Officers were waiting there. Newton, at the door, smiled, nodded to the Officers and then skipped away.

25

The Maid of Buttermere

It was Mr. Fenton who hurried across to Buttermere with news of Hatfield's arrest. He had been in Keswick to seek out a meeting with Peter Crosthwaite to discuss the stone circles when the *Post* arrived and the news blazed across the town. Keswick opinion seemed undivided. A good man had been brought low by misguided and perhaps malevolent forces.

Fenton's diffidence, and a distant sense of guilty implication in this whole business, had kept him away from Buttermere even though he had felt he ought to go ever since that first report in the *Post*. He knew that Mary would need support. Nevertheless he found excuses for himself as he drew the coverlet of bachelor habit ever more snugly over his cosily favoured existence.

But this was a spur and he rode over to Buttermere – taking the shorter Newlands road – arriving there in the afternoon. Snow transfigured the valley. Yet again he wondered how he could have left it. He rode on a little towards Hause Point, stretch of Crummock Water before him, steep white hills to left, to right and straight ahead the great Vale of Lorton, draped with a bridal train. Just to ride back over the hillock and down to the village, the lake of Buttermere itself now wholly visible and glittering white from the white sun and the deep-powdered steep mountain sides – just to *be*, and *there*, was for the timid, over-secured and perhaps even cowardly soul of Fenton, an undeniable joy.

Mary, he was told by her father, was inside with Miss D'Arcy and Mrs. Moore. He saw the coach and enquired when they had arrived: too soon to catch the *Post*. He was reluctant to break up the meeting of the three women and re-mounted to walk his horse over towards Burtness Wood where he could further relish the day – the sun now striking the snow hot-white – and feel the cleansing cold on his face, further draw out the anticipation of tea and warmth before the parlour fire: prepare himself for the meeting with Mary.

Mary would have wished him to come in, though not for reasons which would have flattered him. She was feeling ill, increasingly upset, and there was an unaccustomed lethargy which could not be solely accounted for by the increased measures of laudanum and wine she had been taking. Above all, she wanted to be rid of her solicitous guests.

"Can we not persuade you?" Miss D'Arcy repeated for – was it the eighth time? Mary had kept count but now that she needed it to fill the gap after the question, she had foggily forgotten.

"You are very kind, but no," she replied in a voice which sounded very thick-tongued.

Mrs. Moore sat rather as if posing for a portrait, upright and unblinking in a hard chair. Miss D'Arcy flitted about the small parlour like a newly captured humming bird in a cage too small. Mary felt an invalid by comparison, lumpenly settled in the largest and most deeply comfortable chair which both women had positively commanded her to occupy.

"The change," said Mrs. Moore, for the fourth time, "would do you good."

"It is very kind of you," Mary began, but she failed to finish the sentence, struck as she was by the subversive thought – *was* it very kind of them? Through her fatigue – as a glimpse of sun is suddenly visible through a gap in clouds – came the piercing and hotly illuminating notion that they might want her as a curiosity. Certainly Miss D'Arcy's constant visits and gifts – clothes, books, knick-knacks – went far beyond anything Mary had heard of before. It seemed as if she were driven to come and talk to Mary in order to be able to discuss the subject which she could not forget – Hatfield: a subject which Mary herself wanted to forget as finally as possible. Well-intentioned and unimpeachable as Miss D'Arcy's visits were, they had precisely the opposite effect to that intended. What would Miss D'Arcy do with herself when she no longer had Mary to talk to? With whom else could she as richly, as ironically, as sensually even, discuss the man they still called Hope?

"London," said Mrs. Moore, for only the second time, "will be a tonic. There are sights to see, visits, playhouses –" she waved her hand, unable to summon the energy for an alluring list but hoping to indicate London's possibilities by this gesture.

He would be there, Mary thought: sure to be. She could not bear to be anywhere he might be. She was safe only in Buttermere. He would never dare return. Nor, perhaps, she had confided to herself in the honesty of more than one sleepless night, would he want to after her betrayal over the letters. But such letters. Just to refer to them and so fleetingly as the lightest thoughts drifted through her mind was the sharp turn of a knife. They had shocked her, heart and soul.

"I couldn't leave my parents," said Mary, very firmly.

"Surely," Miss D'Arcy had prepared for this objection, "they have little to do in these winter months. No Lake Tourists. And, I am told, the animals indoors – no shepherding again until spring."

"They need me for their comfort," said Mary.

"Really, Amaryllis," Mrs. Moore was anxious to be on her way before it grew too dark: only a fortnight before a woman and her two children – vagrants – had been discovered frozen to death on the top of Whinlatter Pass, just a mile or so from where they were sitting, "I do think we have tempted dear Mary quite enough. Determined as you are to have her as your companion, she is more determined to stay at home. And," Mrs. Moore added with no disguising the relief, "I can sympathise with her decision. To look after aged parents is always the right thing to do. It is time we were on our way, my dear. The snow was only light but it may become frosty and I would not like to be stranded in Buttermere." That surprising thought took Mrs. Moore aback.

"I would love it!" Amaryllis replied. "To be hidden away in this valley with Mary to talk to day after day and no-one able to disturb us – surrounded by snow and ice and unpassable mountains!"

Mrs. Moore moved towards the door in a state of some agitation.

"Amaryllis, I really must command you to leave now." Her husband's vocabulary came to her aid and Miss D'Arcy complied.

"We will be back, dear Mary, once more before we go. We shall come and tempt you a final time."

"If the road is safe," said Mrs. Moore, now standing by the open door almost rudely impatient to be off.

"Goodbye, dear Mary, and do take that honey mixture."

"Goodbye, Mary – you are a sensible young woman."

"Goodbye. Goodbye."

It seemed expected that she would not get up to show them off the premises and Mary took advantage of that expectation. It was her mother who saw them to the door, her father who saw them to the carriage, the old couple who stood as if compelled to do so until the carriage had pulled out of sight.

Damson came in and Mary, who had grown greatly attached to the cat over the past weeks, took her on her lap and stroked her . . . the peat fire burned. White light came through the two small windows. Snow muffled sounds. It would be a hard winter, they said, pointing to the behaviour of badgers, moles, squirrels . . . she took a few drops of laudanum and dozed.

When Mr. Fenton was shown into the room by her mother he found her asleep. Her mother moved to wake her but the former schoolteacher put up his hand and she let her daughter alone. Following his whispered instructions, she brought him in some tea and he sat beside the fire prepared to wait until Mary woke up. He had already arranged to stay over and his horse was warmly stabled.

He looked at Mary in dismay. She was heavy, pale, even pasty-faced, her hair was loosely tucked about and dirty, her whole expression lacked sweetness and the entirely singular beauty which had made her so remarkable was, surely wilfully, obscured. The hem of her dress hung unstitched in one noticeable length. Instead of feeling immediate pity – that was to follow – Mr. Fenton experienced something akin to relief that she was not, as she just might have been, his responsibility. Ashamed of that he composed his mind to charity and drank the tea before the fire with his contentment largely unimpaired.

When she woke, the unfocused look ought to have alerted him to what was becoming a new habit, but he was too entrenched in his past certainty of her innocence and health.

"Mr. Fenton?"

"Yes, Mary."

She smiled, a rather lopsided, over-open-mouthed smile which thoroughly disconcerted him.

"Ah, Mr. Fenton," she repeated, clipping the syllables rather cuttingly, he thought, and felt a little uncomfortable.

"How are you, Mary?"

"How *am* I?"

She looked at him searchingly – no smile now – a long gaze which triggered a rush of guilt. His throat went dry.

"Do you have to ask how I am? Can you not imagine how I *am*, Mr. Fenton?"

"Of course."

"Good!" Briskly she reached down and took the wine glass which was already charged with laudanum and enjoyed a few sips. Thinking the wine was no more than a useful restorative, Fenton saw nothing to comment on.

"It must have been very trying for you."

"It has been trying, Mr. Fenton."

"I thought to visit before now."

"I hoped you would. Your health." She raised the glass.

"I calculated you would prefer to be alone."

"Well. At least you thought of it."

There was a harshness, even a brashness?, quite new, quite out of character with the gentle, head-bowed pupil who had for so long adored him. Mr. Fenton did not like it, but, realising that she was much more distressed than he could have imagined, he tried not to let it jostle his equanimity.

"You know what has been happening to me, Mr. Fenton. Leave that. Tell me what has been happening to you."

As best he could, he took up what seemed very like a challenge and in his careful, amused, dry way outlined the life he had plotted so comfortably for himself. He saw that Mary was crying – soft sentimental tears which came with no sobs, tears alone unforced. He stopped.

"Please go on," she whispered. "Please go on. It sounds so lovely – don't you see? It sounds so warm, so civilised and safe. I can imagine everything as you talk. Your room, your books, the desk you bought at Wigton, the cloth you bought at Rosley Fair, the wooden candlesticks carved by Mr. – Metcalfe was it? in Caldbeck – you, there, reading or making your notes. Oh Mr. Fenton, if only I were in that picture too, bringing you your tea, seeing to your comfort – I would be the happiest woman in the world instead of what you see – the most miserable on earth."

He ought to have moved to comfort her. Perhaps after such an open effort of devotion he might even have thought and began to think of eventually – let time and fame pass – marrying her. Or at least say something – he could have done that. But he neither moved nor planned nor spoke, sat silent and on his guard in case old obligations and new pity might catch him unawares. After the silence had spoken for his reaction to her call for help, he produced the newspaper from inside his jacket.

"They have arrested him," he said, reading, "he has been brought up to London by a Bow Street Officer, from 'Breaknock in Wales', it says."

"Arrested?"

"Yes. He will be charged 'on a warrant from Sir Frederick Vane Bart., a magistrate for the County of Cumberland'."

"So they have got him." The sentence was spoken as heavily as a judgement.

"Yes."

Fenton leaned out to hand the paper over to her but either she did not want it or she did not see it.

"Shall I read it all to you?"

It seemed that Mary did not hear him. After a slight pause, he repeated his question. She turned to pick up the glass and drain it.

"Yes," she said. "But first, I shall take a little more wine."

She got up heavily and slowly, almost dreamily, Fenton thought, went out of the room leaving him in silence but for the irregular hiss of the peat fire which sounded a little eerie to his jangled nerves.

She did not return.

*

The newspapers reported that public opinion everywhere supported Mary. Coleridge became her champion. In 'The Keswick Impostor I' – his third piece – he writes: "In my second communication ('Romantic Marriage II') I ventured to affirm that when the particulars of her late unhappy connection were made known, her former character for modesty, virtue and good sense would only receive confirmation and poor Mary would rise, not sink, in the opinion of all wise and good men. The circumstances which I am now to detail will fully verify my assertion . . ." Towards the end of the same article he goes into detail to underline his point and mentions "Mary Robinson's first refusal to go off with him (Hatfield) to Scotland" and commends her further for being "determined at all events to do nothing which she could not do openly."

In 'The Keswick Impostor II', which was not published until 31st December, Coleridge again defended Mary against any charges which might be brought or even thought against her. "Is there on earth that prude or that bigot who can blame poor Mary?" he writes. "She had given her lover the best reasons to esteem her, and earned a rational love by innocence and wise conduct. Nor can it be doubted that the man had really and deeply engaged her affections. He seemed to have fascinated everyone in all ranks of society; and if Mary had remained an exception, it would have detracted more from her sensibility than it would have added to her prudence."

Coleridge's logic in the cause of his gallantry flattens all possible opposition.

Apart from Coleridge's naturally quick sympathy and indisputably altruistic desire to see that an innocent woman was not harmed by an error, there is perhaps something deeper. It was vital to Coleridge and to Wordsworth – to their choice of how and where to live, to their radical reappraisal of poetry's subject matter and to their philosophical re-grouping after what they saw as the failure of the revolution and the ideal of Reason in France – that a new and uncorrupted touchstone for life and for thought be found. Nature was the solution. Mary was a 'natural' person of humble birth born and bred in Nature, tutored it seemed by a wholly benevolent Nature and living in uncorrupted rusticity. To be outside Society was as important as being part of Nature.

Thomas de Quincey's interest in the story had been aroused before he met Wordsworth and Coleridge. At the back of his 1803 diary, there is an entry 'Mary of Butter' and a sum 10s. 6d. – the sum paid for 'Augustus and Mary, or the Maid of Buttermere: a Domestic Tale' by William Mudford.

Thirty years later, writing about the poets who had become his friends and commenting on Coleridge's absorption in the affair, a distanced and in some ways soured de Quincey never wavered from the line: "It could be no blame to a shepherd girl, bred in the sternest solitude which England has to shew, that she should fall into a snare which hardly any of her betters had escaped."

In this passage, de Quincey most firmly followed the faith of his primary and tutelary hero, Wordsworth. After describing the events and dwelling particularly on Coleridge's fascination with Hatfield's behaviour, he turns his attention to Mary.

> She, meantime, under the name of the Beauty of Buttermere, became an object of interest to all England: dramas and melodramas were produced in the London theatres upon her story: and for many a year afterwards, shoals of tourists crowded to the secluded lake, and the little homely cabaret, which had been the scene of her brief romance. [He goes on:] It was fortunate for a person in her distressing situation that her home was not in a town: the few, and

> simple, neighbours who had witnessed her imaginary elevation, having little knowledge of worldly feelings, never for an instant connected with her disappointment any sense of the ludicrous, or spoke of it as a calamity to which her vanity might have cooperated. They treated it as an unmixed injury, reflecting shame upon nobody but the wicked perpetrator.

How can de Quincey or Coleridge be so sure? Although her neighbours were certainly few, were they necessarily simple? The dialect stories and ballads of that time are almost exclusively concerned with acts of cunning, often including lies, bluff, double-dealing, a range of worldly accomplishments. Oppressed often enough, yes; sometimes in these years of war, enclosure and bad harvests, near starvation; subdued through fear, yes again; under or uneducated and living in the bleakest comfort, yes. But simple? Unable to snigger, to take satisfaction in another's misfortune? Feeling nothing but thoughts of supportive tenderness? Perhaps. But statements such as "they never for an instant connected with her disappointment any sense of the ludicrous, or spoke of it as a calamity to which her vanity might have cooperated" do provoke the question – how did de Quincey know? Did he talk to those few and simple neighbours? If so, he does not mention it. And if he did and they told him what he reports, could he be sure they were telling the truth? Or had Mary become unreal? Did she allow Wordsworth to see her 'real' self?

Wordsworth felt himself intimately connected with Mary and her story from the start. He took her over.

> For we were nursed, as almost might be said,
> On the same mountains; children at one time
> Must haply on the self-same day
> Have from our several dwellings gone abroad
> To gather daffodils on Coker's Stream.

Almost 'twin souls'.

It was about this time that Wordsworth began once more to think over his autobiographical poem *The Prelude*, charting the 'growth of the poet's mind'. The first version had been completed in 1798: the second would be finished by 1805: the third by 1850: none would be published until after his death. De Quincey and Coleridge were two of the very few to read it in his lifetime. It is in the 1805 version that Mary figures and quite prominently.

She appears as part of the promiscuous spectacle of London:

> Spectacles within doors – birds and beasts
> Of every nature . . .

And then he writes of the theatre, the "Half-rural Sadlers Wells", with its "giants and dwarfs/Clowns, conjurers, posture-makers, harlequins" and as well, representations of:

> . . . recent things yet warm with life; a sea fight,
> Shipwreck, or some domestic incident
> Divulged by Truth and magnified by Fame;
> Such as the daring brotherhood of late
> Set forth, too serious a theme for that light place –
> I mean, O distant Friend! a story drawn
> From our own ground – the Maid of Buttermere.

He points out that he and Coleridge (the distant Friend) had known and admired Mary "Ere the broad world rang with the maiden's name". He mentions her "patience and humility of mind", her "discretion" and "delicate reserve" although she could clearly express "her just opinions". He praises her as one "unspoiled by commendation and the excess/Of public notice –"

It is no more than a coincidence that Wordsworth married his wife, Mary, within a couple of days of Mary Robinson marrying Hatfield. What is important is that he praised in his wife – and came increasingly to depend on and glorify – the very virtues which he found both traduced and upheld in the public drama and private integrity of Mary of Buttermere: loyalty to a region of great natural riches; the probably consequent exemplification of 'natural' virtues and domesticated habits, thoroughly supportive, dependent and feminine, yet strong enough to resist the seduction of 'The Spoiler', as Wordsworth called him, 'a bold bad man'. He pledged his life, as he had committed his work, to an ideal he found in part realised in both Marys.

It may also be without much significance that there is another country girl in *The Prelude* who is the radicalising catalyst for Wordsworth's political ideas. When he was in France and became friends with the extraordinary revolutionary, M. Beaupuy, they were out walking when they encountered a poor, sickly, desperately deprived "hunger-bitten girl", hopelessly leading a single cow down a lane. "'Tis against *that*," Beaupuy said, pointing to the girl, "which we are fighting." And it is this incident more than any other which is given us by the poet as explanation of his conversion to revolution. Mary is joined to her just as she is allied with his wife. For it is the near-poverty and perilous social hold of Mary Robinson which makes her position so vulnerable and her innocence and sense of morality all the more remarkable, especially when compared with the corruption of indulgence and critical sophistication. In the Maid of Buttermere, then, he saw not only the absolutes of good living, not only the highest form of simple, pure manners, but a cause worth defending in the name of post-revolutionary ideals. Indeed, she was a seed of the new and truer revolution.

Perhaps Mary herself got a little lost in all this. Wordsworth was Cambridge educated, a poet, a man who lived, however frugally, without having to 'work' in any accepted sense, just beginning, at this precise time, to move up the gentry scale, eventually to become a little lordling himself; devoted to domesticity, not necessarily best placed to understand the private 'intimate' possibly wild reaction – as distinct from the show put on for visitors – of a very modestly brought up, careful, even shrewd country girl. How well *did* he know her?

When de Quincey – his acolyte and devoted friend – married a farmer's daughter some years later, the Wordsworths thought he had married beneath him and refused to receive her.

*

In her bedroom, Mary lit a candle, gathered the blankets about her and as she had done on many such nights, took out the large block of writing paper.

"Mr. Fenton came," she wrote, making an effort to keep the script both neat and elegant. "I wish he had come much earlier. I have thought about him several times and wanted him to come but he was so long about it that when he did arrive it was too late. I was too tired. Miss D'Arcy and Mrs. Moore tried to persuade me to go to London with them but I think I have finally dissuaded them. I wonder if Miss D'Arcy has any idea how cruel her kindness can seem.

"Or if anybody does. I thank God it is the middle of winter and we are about to be barred into the valley. Pity is so hard to bear. I do not know why."

She folded this sheet of paper and, rather clumsily, leaned across the narrow room and pushed it beneath a stone which served as a paperweight and held down a few score of such sheets. She drank from the re-filled glass, looked for a long while at the frosting lacework on the moonwashed window and then once more began to write.

Dear —

Yet again I do not know how to address you. Husband? Colonel Hope? Both false. And John Hatfield – him I never knew. I only write 'Dear —' for the sake of good manners. Good manners could break my spirit: the good manners of everybody in the valley pretending that you are all to blame and I altogether the innocent. That makes me witless. I would rather they came out with their crowing and 'told-you-so's and get it done with. But my own good manners will not let me challenge them. Everybody pretends that I must be treated as if nothing had happened when my world has turned on its head and fled on its heels.

But I will not have them break my spirit. I am being unfair. They do not want to break me – they are truly kind - but you have broken my heart, wherever you are, you wicked, bad man, you LIAR and CHEAT of my life, you have taken me from the LIGHT and driven me into DARKNESS where I am so alone, SO ALONE, it is horrible and you knew, you knew all the TIME that you were DECEIVING me, even in those moments when we were ONE, even then you KNEW and how can I BEAR it – you are worse than a MURDERER – you leave a body with no LIFE but without the peace of a corpse, I hate you and want you to be HANGED, I am GLAD they have caught you, I am . . .

Sobbing, choking the sound back into herself, she took the letter and, as she always did, burnt it on the candle flame, watching it curl, seeing it was all destroyed.

26

The Examinations at Bow Street

The *Morning Post*, like other papers, reported the case intensively from the day of Hatfield's arrival in London from "Breaknock in Wales". These reports were rushed to Coleridge whose second extended piece appeared at the end of the month with the promise of a third to follow. An earlier print of Mary by Gillray was pulled out and re-sold on the streets: seats in the courtroom were fought over. 'The Famous Seducer' and the 'Maid of Buttermere' became the leading characters in a whirlwind production of gossip, scandal, legal niceties and fashion which swept everything aside in a society transparently inflamed with threatened upheavals, stresses and rumours of wars, but pausing, at that moment, after a great conflict.

Perhaps it was the first clash of two centuries: the licentious, bawdy, rational eighteenth century and the nineteenth; romantic, sentimental, increasingly strapped in a rigid public morality with its consequent hypocrisy. For though the charge was forgery, the pull was seduction. Perhaps this was one of those moments when a nation in some major though indefinable way decides on a different course, determines to look for a different self – and the force of attention on Hatfield and Mary's case could have been because it was a harbinger and a symbol. Or maybe the crowds lined up to look at a Great Seducer who had been caught: a Great Seducer, moreover, who had not only beguiled women for sex, but men of the world for cash and aristocrats for titles. While Mary, back in that famous paradise of the North, could be seen as any image of innocence, purity or trust the conversation demanded. Or perhaps the masses came to view because this was another stage in the story they had followed for two months – and a story they could all join in. These factors and others took the London crowds to Bow Street in Covent Garden where Hatfield had twice spent weeks as the tyro of the coffee houses. As one examination succeeded another – there were to be four – the numbers along the street grew into one of those London spectacles described with such superficial cheerfulness and fundamental disapproval by Wordsworth. Urchins, Earls, flower-sellers, ladies of fashion, singers, young bloods, scribblers,

Negro ladies in white muslin gowns, Turks, Moors, Lascars, Chinese and very likely Charles Lamb, all came to gawp and talk.

The report in the *Morning Post* on 7th December – which began with his crimes in Tiverton some months before he went to the Lake District – was simply headed

JOHN HATFIELD

Already he needed no other explanation or sub-title.

> Sunday evening, this famous character was brought to town from Brecknock in Wales by Pearks, one of the Bow Street officers, under authority of a warrant, signed by SIR RICHARD FORD, before whom, MR. GRAHAM, MR. ROBINSON, MR. KINNAIRD and other magistrates, he was examined yesterday at Bow Street.
>
> The solicitor for the Prisoner's Bankruptcy attended and identified his person and stated that the commission was issued against Hatfield in June last: that he attended the last meeting of the commissioners, but the prisoner did not appear although due notice of the bankruptcy had been given in the *Gazette* and he himself had given a personal notice to the prisoner's wife at Washfield near Tiverton, Devon. MR. PARKIN, the Solicitor to the Post Office, produced a warrant from Sir Frederick Vane, Bart., a magistrate for the County of Cumberland, against the prisoner by the name of the Hon. Alex. Augustus Hope, charging him with felony by pretending to be a Member of Parliament of the United Kingdom, and franking several letters by the name of A. Hope to several persons and which were put into the post-office at Keswick in Cumberland in order to evade the duties of postage. There are other charges against him for forgery and bigamy, which were explained to him, but not entered into and he was committed to Tothill Fields, Bridewell, for further examination on Tuesday next. Hatfield conducted himself with the greatest propriety during his journey to town, and on his examination; but said nothing more than answering a few questions put to him by SIR RICHARD FORD and the solicitors. He was dressed in a black coat and waistcoat, fustian breeches and boots, and wore his hair tied behind, without powder; his appearance was respectable though quite in dishabille.
>
> His Royal Highness the Duke of Cumberland, Earl of Aylesbury, Sir Charles Bunbury, Sir Edward Pellew, Hon. Mr. Ashley, Mr.

Andrews, M.P., Hon. Mr. Macdonald, Colonel Fuller, Colonel McMarne, Colonel Stevens and a number of other gentlemen were present at the examination.

*

8th December, 1802

My darling Mary,

You may have read that yesterday I was taken into Bow Street to be examined. I was told that the reporters were there – indeed the world and its mother turned out and my progress was more like that of the Prince of Wales along the front at Brighton than that of a man charged with forgery, felony and every other 'y' in the statute book.

I feel sound in mind and very steady and I do not quite know what I must attribute this to. I am being well served here in the prison. The apartment is one of the best. The irons are taken off before I am securely locked in so I can move about without pain or hindrance. There is paper, ink, pens, a bible and books – including *The Letters of Lord Chesterfield*, one of my favourites and a text I used to live by. Little I ask for – except liberty! – is denied by a gaoler who is nice in every particular including his regular jest that he will not introduce me to his wife for fear . . . etc. So you see how buoyant material comforts can make you. I have no notion who might be the provider of these feasts but I lift my glass – I have wine – to whomever it is and wish him Good Health and Long Life.

Yet I believe my steadiness, even my ease of mind is not wholly to be accounted for by the wine and the outward show I am afforded. I feel a stirring in my deepest self which affirms life. Does this mean I have renewed my Faith? I hope so but I fear not. No, I believe it must be construed as a certainty I have that my Love for you is my faith – not the greedy, lustful, convenient, even politic thing it has been so often – but something that is as strong and as obscure as Faith and just as unmistakable when it arrives. That is why I wanted to write you this letter – a letter of thanks from a prison cell, a letter of joy from a man whose days and perhaps many of whose remaining years will be spent in irons, a letter of hope that you will believe in me: if you can do that, I will fear no evil, not even my own.

John Hatfield

This letter he posted.

On 14th December, the *Morning Post* headed one of its columns:

PUBLIC OFFICE, BOW STREET

Hatfield was yesterday brought up for a second examination before SIR R. FORD and T. ROBINSON ESQ.: the office was crowded long before he entered and some hundreds besieged the door in vain. Hatfield wrote a note to SIR R. FORD requesting he might be permitted to have his irons taken off while under examination which was humanely complied with; and Mr. Fenwick, the governor, brought him into the office himself.

Nothing could be fully entered into at the examination, the necessary witnesses not being present. Mr. Taunton, the solicitor for the Bankruptcy, produced the *Gazette* where it was recorded on the 15th of June last, and also the Lord Chancellor's order for enlarging the time of appearing to the 18th of Sept. But he did not appear to such an order.

Mr. Taunton also produced a bill of exchange for the sum of 30L. drawn in the name of Hope which, he had reason to believe, had been written and negotiated by the prisoner. The gentleman to whom the said bill had been passed, not being in town, this affair must stand over.

A copy of the register of the prisoner's marriage: in the name of Alexander Augustus Hope with Mary Robinson (the Beauty of Buttermere) at Laughton on the 2nd of October 1802 by the Rev. John Nicholson was produced; and SIR R. FORD said he should certainly write to this unfortunate young woman immediately to inform her that he is in custody and that she may come and prefer the charge against him.

The Prisoner, as before, made hardly any reply, except in answer to some few questions respecting the said marriage. Mr. Taunton said he would undertake to allow him a guinea and a half per week for the present. The prisoner was then remanded back to Tothill-fields, Bridewell.

Some gentlemen have proposed to set on foot a subscription, for the purpose of defraying the expense of the Beauty of Buttermere to town, in order to appear against Hatfield. Mr. Graham, Mr. Kinnaird and several other gentlemen in the commission were present; and the Duke of Roxburgh, Lord Grenville, Earl of Aylesbury, Earl of Ormond, Sir J. Molyneux, Sir E. Pellew, Sir E. Nagle and a number of gentlemen attended out of curiosity.

London wanted both of the leading players and was willing to pay for them. Mary wrote to Sir Richard Ford, confirming that "the man whom I had the misfortune to marry . . . always told me he was the Hon. Colonel Hope, the next brother to the Earl of Hopetoun" but she refused to come up to London. It was partly for this, for what he saw as her deep understanding of the place and strength of her roots, as well as for her refusal to be drawn into a 'spectacle' that Wordsworth admired her.

There was another reason. She discovered she was pregnant. A few days later, on December 18th, the *Morning Post* announced it in the following terms: "It is with much sorrow and sympathy we mention that poor Mary of Buttermere is with child."

*

This only intensified the public's interest and it was in the second half of December that the ballad by Robert Bomford was taken up first on the streets "by shameless women and children" and then "all over the town in whatever society you found yourself". It was called 'False Hope and the Beauty'.

> One day there rode to Buttermere
> A bold and wicked man.
> He said "Here's where I'll find some cheer
> And mischief if I can!"
> False Hope! False Hope! Dear Mary take alarm!
> False Hope! False Hope! He'll do the Beauty Harm.

He rode up hill and down the dale
He wore the devil's mask.
He saw a lovely maiden pale
To win her was his task.
  False Hope! False Hope! etc.

She did not know, the beauteous maid
That on villainy he fed.
He took her in his arms and said
Oh! Thou and I must wed!
  False Hope! False Hope! etc.

There are seven more such verses which manage to include the bigamy and the felony as well as giving Mary a dying father and a bewilderingly happy ending. Children used it as the basis for a street game.

As well as the reports of the examinations in Bow Street, the *Post* was also interested in anything which plumped out Hatfield gossip.

These 'fillers', like everything else in the *Post*, appeared anonymously. Those articles written by Coleridge have been attributed: these fillers may – it is thought but not proved – have been written by Charles Lamb.

The Lambs were certainly interested in Mary's case and in a position to know the location and the details of the story at first hand. They had spent some of that August in the Lakes with Coleridge and it is inconceivable that they would not have read his articles in the *Post* and discussed with others in their circle the implications and particularly for the Lambs as for the Wordsworths, the implications for Mary. There is a letter later – in July 1803 – from Mary Lamb to Dorothy Wordsworth in which she describes a visit by Southey, John Rickman and his sister and her brother Charles and herself to Sadlers Wells, "the lowest and most London-like of all our London amusements".

". . . the entertainments were Goody Two Shoes, Jack the Giant-killer and *Mary of Buttermere*! Poor Mary was very happily married at the end of the piece to a sailor, her former sweetheart – we had a prodigious fine view of her father's house in the vale of Buttermere – mountains very like large haycocks and a lake like nothing at all . . ."

Whether or not Lamb himself wrote the 'fillers' it has been pointed out that they clearly reflect his moral indignation directed both against

Hatfield and against the London gentry whose values he could not respect. So on 21st December, an entry reads "A great crowd of *Men of Fashion* went to see Hatfield examined at Bow Street yesterday desirous, no doubt, of receiving a lesson from the *accomplished seducer*." The contempt for the idle and the immoral is unmistakable. On 29th December, the sarcasm bites further into Hatfield: "*Hatfield* complains bitterly of the calumnies of the public prints. Indeed, they use him cruelly, considering that Sir Richard Ford has evidence of his having been an invariable swindler for *no more* than thirty years." The author is as scathing about Hatfield's supporters as about the man himself: "HATFIELD'S panegyrists allege in his defence that he seems addicted to no one kind of vice in particular." And, on 1st January 1803, "the *Bond Street* loungers already dress *à la Hatfield* with large black eyebrows, rolling eyes, a ruddy complexion and even a hitch in the walk."

Even from this brief selection of 'fillers' we have a sackful of impressions: of Hatfield's case being taken up and defended by a vociferous and fashionable section of London – the bustle, the crush, the cheers and jeers; of the story being debated at levels of intensity and stridency which indicates not only support for him but a desire to champion him.

It is extraordinary, for instance, that a man indicted for so many crimes should have had such an impact on fashion. The Bond Street Loungers were serious men in such matters. Their adoption of Hatfield's style was, perhaps, not just subversive fun: it could have been the applause of those who wanted liberty at all costs even if it came in the form of licence. It was a time of boiling frustration: the war with France had outlawed the great swell towards revolution and forced it into the drilled lines of patriotism which was encouraged by oppression. Draconian laws had terrorised radicals and Treason Trials had sent sensible reformers flying for cover; and yet, even at the peak of national danger, revolution, mutiny and rebellion broke out. It was the time when London ought to have been in the van – Burke had praised the American Revolutionaries partly on the grounds that their belief in Liberty was a noble creed acceptable because they were, fundamentally, British and so *had* to love freedom. English men and women – including Wordsworth – had passionately welcomed the French Revolution and wanted the dictatorships, privileges and corruption in their own country overthrown. Everywhere among good-hearted people there was a wish for change. But the war had put a block on it. Indeed, the British became, by that one act, the great force for conservatism. Yet the feelings of the time, the romantic-revolutionary feeling which was still the most powerful moving force of the day despite the war, had to get out somehow and perhaps – in its own way – the unrestrained behaviour of Hatfield called up a response from that deep current.

For it was not only the Bond Street Loungers who adopted him. Much to Coleridge's annoyance, in the 'Keswick Impostor II' (31st December, 1802), everyone seemed to support him. "It will hardly be believed, how obstinately almost all classes in Keswick were infatuated in his favour" . . . While Mary was "universally the cause of concern". So we have the intriguing situation in which the people of sensibility and the law are judging harshly over right and wrong, legal and unlawful, and the generality – 'high' and 'low' – seem inclined to support and delight in *both* parties. Innocence and Wickedness equally were the talk and toast of the town.

*

At his third – and even more crowded – examination at Bow Street on 21st December, another warrant was issued against Hatfield for "having forged and uttered a bill of exchange".

Hatfield was now cheered through the streets and there would still be part of the crowd tagging along all the way back to Bridewell.

On this day, Newton was waiting for him in his cell-apartment.

Hatfield was silent while his irons were taken off and waited until the gaoler – abstractedly accepting some gold from Newton – had left them together.

"Did you not guess all this was me?"

Newton looked around the well-appointed cell as a man pleased with what he had wrought.

"There are others."

Hatfield pointed to a table crowded with knick-knacks – some of them silver, a few obviously expensive.

"You always did have the trick of being popular, John."

Hatfield was so nervous he had begun to tremble. He kept as far away from Newton as was possible within that space. He had to resist.

"You wonder why I am here and why I have taken such care of you after what I did?" Hatfield, head lowered like a bull pondering the next move, said nothing. Newton advanced towards him a step or so and the bigger man shuffled back, finding that he was now against the wall.

"You betrayed *me*, John. Twice. Once by that ridiculous marriage – which I doubt is legitimate as you were married already – and then by your unfriendly attempt to conceal it from me. In return I betrayed you twice. Once in Keswick when I put Hardinge onto you, and a second time in Brecon. Now we are even."

"Save that you are free and I am in prison."

"When I heard of your marriage to that village belle, I too felt that I had been sentenced."

"My sentence is likely to be the noose."

"It is a capital offence. But it is unlikely they will make it a hanging matter."

"I would be glad of your certainty."

"I'll make you a gift of it, John, if we can be friends again."

Another step forward: Hatfield pressed against the wall but found no comfort in the cold stone.

"I can do a great deal for you, John. You know that. You know how well we have done together."

"I could . . ." Hatfield's voice was hoarse.

"You would not tell them about me, John, would you?" Another step forward. "And if you did – what could they prove? *I* was not bankrupted: *I* did not fail to appear in court: *I* am not a felon: it was not *I* who franked the letters, obtained credit falsely, married bigamously . . ."

"You have done much worse. Much worse than I." The words came pantingly: the strong, impressive man was now all but cowering against the wall away from the white-faced figure in black, his hair, even his eyes consistent with the uniform blackness of his clothes.

"Only you know that, John." He paused. "And who would believe you?"

The last sentence was all but whispered in Hatfield's ear. The blackness of Newton seemed now like a sudden fever which set off a violent ebb and flow of darkness in his mind. He thought of Mary as he remembered her that night the young couple had arrived at the inn in disguise: he thought of Hause Point: he thought back to his mother and her face swirled clear of the enclosing throb of darkness now threatening to flood him back into Newton's power.

"Please leave me now." The voice was a whisper. "Please leave me now."

If only Newton would not touch him. If only he could escape untouched then by the next day he would have made his preparations.

"Please." He swivelled, stood upright, pressed himself against the wall, arms outstretched and pleaded to the glittering white face only a few feet from him. "Tomorrow," he added.

Newton smiled and nodded very gently. He was about to put out a hand to take Hatfield's shoulder, but withheld it, seeing the terror on the man's face.

"I am sorry if my sudden arrival shocked you, John. But there was no warning I could safely give you."

He wandered over towards the door and called out for the gaoler.

"Is there anything you lack?"

"No." Hatfield still held to the wall.

"Then I will see you tomorrow."

Newton was gone as magically as he had arrived.

Hatfield was clammy with sweat. He called out for the gaoler, who was delayed, presumably seeing Newton ceremoniously off the premises. When he came, brisk with even more respect for his famous and profitable captive, Hatfield ordered a bottle of claret and some venison pie for his meal. While the man went off, he pulled out his Journals and began to write as if he had only a few hours of life left.

On the 22nd and 23rd December, Hatfield was in a fever. He vaguely saw Newton – who appeared, disappeared and reappeared with a physician who bled him and prescribed drugs immediately purchased by Newton. The fever, though, was as brief as it was savage and on Christmas Eve Hatfield woke up clear-headed, rather weak but not, when he got to his feet, in any serious way enfeebled, even able to carry out a half-course of the exercises he had re-instituted on a daily basis since his confinement.

There occurred – on Christmas Eve – an event which impressed and astonished everyone, from Hatfield himself to the press, to the general public and even, perhaps, to the Bond Street Loungers.

*

"Your wife," said the gaoler, "is here and wishes to know if you will receive her."

The gaoler made no attempt to hide his glee. The arrival of Hatfield had made his Christmas with *cadeaux* arriving from the ladies (and, consequently, tips for himself) every day and a gentleman like Mr. Newton free with his guineas. And now the drama of the great reunion. His own wife, whom he had sworn to introduce to Hatfield on Christmas Day when her two sisters from Twickenham would be joining them, would be wild to be the *first to know* of this latest astonishing twist in the tale.

"One minute. Just – stay there, don't let her in yet – one minute."

The man watched in wonder as Hatfield raced to the mirror, slapped the blood into his cheeks, brushed his hair and swiftly re-tied it, fluffed up his collar, heaved on his bottle-green coat, shook a large measure of the contents of a small scent bottle over his handkerchief which he then dabbed across his jaws and cheeks and finally stopped, stood, poised and posed.

"Show her in."

In Hatfield's heart there were hosannas in those moments alone in his cell. She had come! She had read and understood his letter and she had come. His love was now proved to be something which could outreach lust, ignore misfortune, forgive sin – it was there that the proof of his new life would be seen. He forced himself to remain absolutely still – quite suddenly and luxuriously reminded of Kemble in a scene – what was the scene? What was it . . . ?

"John?"

The tentative enquiry was a natural reaction because it was as if he had not seen her. He stood, hands apparently locked – perhaps they were, she thought – behind his back, his eyes fixed on her but apparently not seeing her.

"John?"

She moved forward as gently and tentatively as her voice.

"Michelli," he said, as if testing her name on his tongue.

"Yes." She stopped, some feet away from him, knowing how strange he could be about being touched.

"They said my wife . . ."

"I am still proud to call myself your wife, John. I never want another or a better title."

He nodded and that small action brought her into focus. He saw a woman in her late thirties who could just have been described as handsome though very careworn. Her dress was of silk but well out of fashion and although well-kept, well-worn. Her auburn hair, rather severely dressed, was greying and her face was pale. Two or three of her teeth were bad but otherwise it was a sweet if rather sorrowful face. Her figure was still good, not stout but no sign of wasting. She would have made another man, Hatfield thought, a devoted, creditable and loving wife. It took him considerable force of will to summon the courtesy of an embrace which both knew, as his listless arms ungripped her, was hollow even as a courtesy.

But she would not be daunted. With that dread persistence which had wasted her best years staring silent across a space in Scarborough at the face of an unknown criminal she was determined to marry, she began to unpack her things and make it quietly clear that she was now sharing his cell.

"Michelli." The impetus to do right which spun off his elevated thoughts on Mary now pushed him to try to clarify and be honest about his feelings. If he did not do it immediately, he knew that the complicity of the passage of time shared would make it impossible to speak other than with venom. "Michelli, you have nothing to gain by being with me. The examination is going badly. I shall certainly be sent for trial either in Tiverton or in Cumberland: in either case it will be humiliating for you. You have endured more than anyone could be expected to endure. I have failed you: I have been faithless: I have abandoned you . . . Michelli, your forgiveness would crush me. Please . . ."

She turned to him with a considered sweet-tolerant-unhappiness which all but made him cry out for mercy.

"I know you find it hard to like me, John," she said and stumbled in her pause: the admission, however deeply accepted, was still very hard to make, "but I am your legal wife."

"My conduct has taken away any rights I have and any duties you might have had."

"I want to be with you."

"Michelli, I am poor company."

"You cannot be alone at Christmas."

"I fear I shall be alone a great deal now. One Christmas . . ."

"Do you want me to go?"

"For your sake, Michelli: for such future as you might have."

"I want no future without you."

"You must not say that! You *must not*!"

"Why do you so very much dislike me to tell you how much I care for you?"

"I am not worth it! I have ruined your life! I am the Black Death to you! You ought to flee from me, paint a cross on the door, leave me to do you no more harm, Michelli."

"I have brought the children."

"Oh God!"

"They are with the gaoler. They want to see their father." She paused. "I will go and fetch them and then if you still want us to go – then we will go."

"Michelli . . . I am sorry."

"Never mind." She smiled, inasfar as he could judge, a smile of simple love, unladen, untainted by any contagion of inducing guilt. "Ever since the moment I saw you, ever since that first moment," she said, "I have been wholly and eternally in love with you. Perhaps that is hard to bear."

*

On the 27th December, Hatfield underwent his fourth and final examination at Bow Street: on 3rd January, 1803, the *Morning Post* announced that it had been decided Hatfield was to be tried in Carlisle – at a date to be arranged – for forging franks.

On the 28th December, Hatfield was peremptorily and unexpectedly moved from Bridewell to Newgate Prison. Less than a week later he was shovelled over into the Marshalsea. A few days after that – on the 9th January – he was taken off to Bristol.

Perhaps reports of his comparatively comfortable living had disturbed the law: perhaps his popularity with the young bloods and the old London mob had worried the authorities: no explanation was given for these moves.

The gaoler at Bridewell was cast down by the matter and, in the lengthy discussion with his wife – who tended, he thought, and quite unjustifiably, to hold him personally responsible for losing their most famous prisoner – he came back time and again to that incident on Christmas Eve. The answer, he said, lay there.

As promised, the gaoler had taken his wife, her sisters – all a little too primed with port – and one of the husbands (the other was a religious man and would have nothing to do with "such capers") to see Hatfield. They had come across a most affecting sight. Mr. and

Mrs. Hatfield together and their two young children happily singing a round together. Hatfield had been even more charming than the gaoler could have imagined – he was to say later that he had never in his life seen a man change so much from one instant to the next: he could scarcely recognise the solitary rather self-absorbed captive he had known hitherto. The ladies were entranced, enchanted and, he would say, would readily have become enchained by the seducer, who offered them claret, praised their gowns, gave them tittle-tattle about what the Duke of Cumberland had remarked at the examination and how the Earl of Aylesbury had made special mention of this particular in the evidence. Mrs. Hatfield, not a bit perturbed, it seemed, had stood modestly to one side, and answered in the most ladylike way all the questions put to her. It was, his wife answered him – with firm promises of certain pleasures to come – the best Christmas she had ever had.

Soon after he had taken them back to his quarters, he had been summoned to the gate where a coach had drawn up. In it was the man Newton, in a sea of packages for which he asked the gaoler to find assistance to take into Hatfield's cell so that, as he said, "the poor prisoner could enjoy some Christmas cheer". This was done.

The gaoler was not invited to stay with the party but he took care to hover nearby. His prescience was canny. In a very short time, after what seemed a period of near silence in Hatfield's cell, Newton came out and demanded to be taken to the main gate.

"I looked on his face once," said the gaoler, "and dared not look at it again. Would not have done for ten guineas. It is that man who now harries John Hatfield. I thank God he is not pursuing me."

27

Waiting

When Mary finally received his letter she knew that she was pregnant. The words of the man she had loved so fiercely were like omega to the alpha of the unborn child, the balance, the completion, and that love unfroze from its past tense into the present. The pregnancy had in some indescribable way purged her feelings. She wrote back almost immediately.

20th December

Dear husband,

I wish to tell you that I am with child. I know you will be pleased to hear it because we did talk of it and you said how much you wanted a child by me. I received your letter which I think I understand. There is such a great deal to say between us that it is fruitless for me to try to put it into a short letter. Nor do I have your fluency. I am a little sick at the moment but that is nothing out of the ordinary run. When I am feeling fully myself and if you wish it I shall come and see you.

Mary

She hesitated for a few days but Christmas Eve decided her – in that moment when she went into the tiny toy church perched on the rock outcrop like Noah's Ark landed up on some height. There she heard the old Christmas story and recited the psalms, the litany, the creed, was absolved, redeemed, blessed and came out thinking that she could follow both her faith and her deepest feeling. She would send off the letter to Bridewell.

It was cold, ice on the lake, a moon hung above Haystacks like a large friendly faced yellow lantern. She had stopped taking the laudanum, revived her interest in her health and her appearance, settled back with remarkable ease into the routine she had known for more than twenty years. As she walked down the steep slope, Alice and Tom came each side of her and took hold of her arms so that she would not slip and damage the child.

*

Journals, 17th January, Bristol.

They are trying to kill me before they bring me to trial! This is the fourth prison I have been in since Christmas and it is the worst. There is freezing water almost half an inch deep on the floor. I am covered with almost every article of clothing I possess but the cold still finds chinks despite all my wrappings round. They say my wife has not been to the main gate. Either they are lying or they have shifted me about so confusingly that the puzzle and expense of it has thrown her off the trail. It is *torment* to sit or lie still: even as I write this my fingers – twice gloved – tingle and cramp with the bitterest *cold* I have ever known. I get up and stamp about like a dervish and that does some good but only for a few minutes and then the *cold* assaults me once again. The gaoler is my only visitor: he says I am locked in the deepest part of the prison and that the cells on either side are empty because flooded (and now frozen, I'll be bound) and unfit even for the vermin they take us to be. He gives me hot gruel and in large quantities – he knows I have silver and gold – but he will not be drawn on *any*thing and when I asked him amiably enough about his wife he looked as startled as a rabbit caught by a flare. There is no news of when my trial shall be except I know it will be at Carlisle which bodes ill as the jurymen will be publicly bound to condemn me for my marrying Mary bigamously. But why this *torment*? I have money. My legal wife is willing to follow me and do me service. Poor, terrible, awful place though this is, it is at least a better home for my two dear children than an icy ditch – why is it that they keep me in such ignorance and throw me from place to place and outlaw me in this dark and cold and unknown spot?

*

When she saw the letter on the table, Mary thought for a moment that it might be from her husband. The leap inside her body as if the child – though that would have been impossible – had reached up for pleasure, emphasised how much she wanted to join up with him again.

It was from Miss D'Arcy and she decided that it would keep until after the departure of the Reverend Nicholson whom she had discovered in the parlour, after her slow return from Kitty's.

Sometimes she thought that the young clergyman had suffered too much from all this. He was constantly visiting the Fish to see Mary and reassure himself that she was well as if her health were his direct responsibility. He felt that he ought to have been far more wary of the stranger who had so easily seduced him with his open manner, his lightly carried title, his unexpressed but quick understanding of the clergyman's desperation over Miss Skelton. Mary ought to have been his chief concern: she was his parishioner, one of his flock, and as a shepherd he had let a wolf come among that flock and steal one of its most precious lambs. And there had been a sign. When he had discovered her with 'Hope' in a state of over-affectionate embrace outside his church door – he had shut his eyes to it! God had plainly sent him there at that time to be warned and he had been so blinded by the man's title and good humour and amiable plausibility that he had ignored the sign. Mary's fall, then, the deceit practised on her and the punishment that would now be visible and accompany her for the rest of her life were his fault.

Equally, he was upset and unappeasable on the matter of the marriage itself. Although he had not known that 'Hope' was already married – had he transgressed beyond redemption in marrying in His holy church one already married? He wanted to debate this with other clergymen but whenever he saw the opportunity, his nerve failed him and that crippling diffidence held him back. The issue troubled him a great deal.

Though unaware of his theological confusion, Mary had soon understood his anxiety over her and knew that he came to be reassured. But no matter how skilfully she did reassure him, he would return for more.

She brought him some tea and, protesting that he could not stay, he had to get down the valley before dark and these were short days, the Reverend Nicholson thankfully sat and sipped.

"I saw Miss Skelton yesterday," Mary said, having found from her recent intimacy with the young clergyman that she could afford to be bold. "Isn't it unusual for her to stay in the valley through the winter?"

"Is it? She likes the valley." His lame reply warned her off immediately. But he had only paused. "It must be difficult for her – a beautiful young lady of considerable expectations, a prize for every man in the country I should think, and shut up here by her father who seems to plan to buy up all the free land he can find and will not leave the place for a week in case he misses a bargain. It is very hard on her."

"It must be," Mary agreed in a tone of firm neutrality. She did not like Miss Skelton much – liked her at all, in fact, only through her relationship with Nicholson whom she thought the young heiress treated very badly.

"But then, marriage . . ." said the clergyman gloomily and then, realising that he appeared to have made a tactless opening, he blushed.

"Yes," said Mary, quite cheerfully, considering, and after some practice, "it can be a misfortune."

"My dear Mary," he rushed on, his wound bare as new, "I should have been more circumspect."

"No-one could know."

"I rushed in like a fool."

"Everyone believed him."

"I was ordained to counsel against such unbelievers."

"Even the landlord at the Queen's Head was taken in."

The unexpected invocation of the wrestling figure of George Wood silenced the young man. Wood still swore by the greatness of his 'old friend', doggedly believing that somehow or other 'his' man would 'come right in the end'. His own losses in the affair he thought of as nothing more than the normal run. 'Hope' had been a 'true gentleman' and a favourite and the *Morning Post* was heavily criticised in the parlour of the establishment of George Wood Esq.

"And I was taken in," she added softly. "So what were you to do?"

"So you do not blame me?"

"How could I blame *you*?"

"But you *do* not?"

In his pleading, she thought, he looked beatific: how could Miss Skelton play her callow game with him?

"I do not," she replied solemnly. "And I never shall."

"Thank you, Mary."

He jumped up and only her swift hand preserved the integrity of the dislodged teapot. Apologies effusive, hurried, jolted, several farewells, whenever of service, see her on Sunday, call again soon . . .

Mary cleared away, came back, built up the fire and settled down to read Miss D'Arcy's letter. The benefit of winter was the leisure to do such things as this. Peace and isolation returned to the valley; thoughts could be collected in tranquillity.

January 10th

My dearest Mary,

London is so wonderful! Next to the Lakes it is my favourite place on earth and everywhere I look I think – 'If only Mary were here to see that! or that!' or 'I know dear Mary would love this! And this!' We have seen so many people and spectacles and so much of this Great City that I burst to tell you about it but it must wait for another letter. Here I want to say that we arrived safely, we are well lodged in one of the best addresses in London, and if only my Mary were here, life would be perfect.

But I must tell you about Hope – Hatfield!

The town has been full of him. I have never heard so much talk on one man unless it was Mr. Pitt or Bonaparte. And I, of course, because of my special position in all this, have been much sought out for my opinion. Indeed some of the best families in London have cared to engage me in conversation which has been made all the easier since the article in 'The Post' on 31st December. Did you read it? It was called 'The Keswick Impostor II' and in it, the writer (whom Colonel Moore knows: he is the poet Mr. Coleridge and he lives in Greta Hall) apologises, very handsomely, for having falsely said that I had *fixed a day for marriage* with the Impostor. "The day was not fixed," he writes and goes on to commend me on my safe escape and gives me credit for my "good sense and virtue". I could not have manufactured a better advertisement had I tried.

I wanted to go to Bow Street whither, it seemed to me, half the town would resort to see Hatfield at his examinations. Colonel Moore forbade it very sternly. But I outwitted him on one day, the 27th December. On that day, Mrs. Moore and myself, having discovered the route taken by the post-chaise (!) in which Hatfield sallied to and from his prison, stationed ourselves along it in the afternoon and where we could get a good long look at him. Oh, Mary!

How either of us (you see: I include myself) could have thought him anything but the blackest villain I do not know! He sat with his hair blowing free in the cold air, raising his hand to the huzzahs of the mob as if he were the Prince of Wales himself. But such a study in baseness! As he came nearer our carriage I confess I shuddered that he might see me and hid my face: as his carriage went past ours, I shivered with terror that such a beast of evil should be passing so close by me. I shook so frenziedly that my poor Mrs. Moore thought that I was suffering from an attack but it was only the effect of his unfathomable wickedness on my soul, causing it such faintness that when we reached our lodging I had to go to my room to lie down for at least an hour in order to compose myself.

And I thought of you, my dear, dear Mary. Of what you must have suffered and must still suffer. Yet there is no end to the monster's ingenuity. You will have read that his wife, formerly a Miss Nation, took his children to his cell on Christmas Eve and was received by him with open arms and stayed with him throughout the rest of the examinations and, as far as I know, stays with him still. Well, they say that Hatfield engineered all of that himself in order to be in a position – when the trial should be held – to point out not only his true penitence but the perilous state in which the poor woman and her small children will be thrown should he be given the capital sentence which his crimes clearly deserve. Colonel Moore met a friend of his, Judge Hawkins, and . . .

Mary read no further. Had she written too late? Or had he forgotten her so completely?

Her mother came in, but, seeing her daughter wrapped in herself so privately in front of the fire, she left and cautioned all the others against disturbing her.

The room darkened: Mary lit no candle though she put more peat on the fire and two small logs to give quicker heat.

The flames came slowly and danced in front of her bleak staring eyes as if trying to distract her, console her, help.

Later, she put the pages of the letter on the flames and watched the edges catch and wrinkle, the sepia burn spread to the final patch of white, the large flakes of ash blue grey on the back of the peat. Outside the black valley was gripped by cold and silence.

*

Journals, February 26th, Oxford.

Another dank cell! Another dismal and brutal place. They have brought me to Oxford Gaol. The gaoler said it was because I had so much learning, having written, as he had heard, several memorable works which was more than could be said for the inhabitants of the University. I would have enjoyed his wit but, like all the others, he keeps away from me. It is as if I have the *Plague*. They rush in with my food and rush out again. I have money to pay for a few luxuries – and some monies still come freshly to me, sometimes from an admirer, mostly from I know not where – and they will bring me pen and paper, fresh candles, wine now and then, clean linen – *but they will not stay to talk.* Who has put this edict on them? When I ask them they are uncomfortable with the question and run away from it. When I ask them about their wives – to test them – they turn green and tumble backwards in terror.

So I am isolated. Michelli will have little chance of finding me. They have moved me too often, trailing me under the belly of England as if I were being keel-hauled. I know what is happening: but I will not be broken.

I have decided to outline my philosophy as well as my adventures. I will propose a system of political order (with a Bill of Rights and all men enfranchised) and a system of domestic economy (with the poor given land and a minimum wage and the rich dispossessed of vast tracts of their generally illegally gotten gains). I will examine religion and education and make recommendations in each area based not on extensive knowledge – for mine is very random matter spread wide but thinly – but founded on what I myself have found and experienced in a lifetime which has had several vivid chapters. And I shall lay down rules of behaviour both for adults and children. I do not talk of family life because I do not at this moment know whether family life will survive my closer scrutiny.

I will begin, as all men in solitude must, with love.

Love, it now seems to me, is sacrifice: the greater the sacrifice the greater the love. I now see Michelli's affection for what it is: the willingness to give all of her character, her life, her virtue, her means, to me. That is sacrifice and there is nothing else which more distinguishes love. The rest is lust, whim, fashion, imagination, greed or custom. The sacrificial nature of human love finds its example and its great justification in the noblest act performed on earth – the sacrifice of Jesus Christ for all mankind that we should be born again and be with Him in His Father's kingdom. The life of Christ is the perfect life and its acts and meanings are all founded on sacrifice. Where He goes, we follow.

Once the sacrifice of love has been offered, it cannot be reclaimed: nor can it be offered a second time. Therefore we have one love just as Christ had one sacrifice. The problem arises when, as most frequently happens, we misuse that one opportunity. This misuse partly comes from ignorance – which is excusable and questions the justice of the Almighty – but mostly through intemperance. If we are fortunate enough to offer the sacrifice to the right person at the right time then that love will be true and lasting and neither Beelzebub nor all his fiends can break it. If, though, we offer it to the wrong person at the wrong time or even the right person – as I believe my Mary was – at the wrong time – then like the house built on sand it shall surely fall.

In this, the finding of the object for sacrifice is like finding the key which will unlock your fear . . .

*

The frost bit in until a late Easter. Mary was glad of it for some weeks because it confined her and cut off the valley, bringing her the simple peace and quiet she had been used to and sadly needed to repair the damage that had been done. And she wanted to be careful for the child. Alice and her mother rather scolded her for the precautions she took to make sure that she was eating well, sleeping well, breathing fresh air even through the night, but Mary took no notice. And they did not tease her over-much. It was clear to both of them that the child was overwhelmingly important to Mary. She would stop, as she walked, listen to her body's feel of it and only then, reassured, walk on, smiling that sweet internal smile. She read in her books of medicine and talked at length to Mrs. Smallwood, who acted as the midwife in the valley, so that she would be able to land the child safely on her own should she not arrive in time. She used the herbs dried in the autumn to season her food and went to the apple store every day for fruit. She would have liked John to share this, she would think: and then her hurt would deny any such wish.

In early April, though the frost was still set, the sun drew her irresistibly out for a walk and she went down the east of Buttermere up towards Moss Force. It was a walk she had taken with John and she passed the spot where he had first proposed to her. As she did so, she was engulfed by an unexpected rush of joy. She *had* been in love and been loved. It was not hopeless, or worthless – something remained: she touched her swollen stomach and longed for him.

In that late August when she and John were circling about each other, Coleridge had come through Buttermere. He had rarely been as full of passion or of a sense of power in his own genius. At that time he described the waterfall called Moss Force in a way which represented the mood of Mary's present reflections as she, in this rare respite, remembered the marvel that part of that summer had been for her.

> It is a great torrent from the Top of the Mountain to the Bottom . . . the mad water rushes through its *sinuous* Bed, or rather prison of Rock, with such rapid Curves, as if it turned the corners not from mechanic force but with fore-knowledge, like a fierce and skilful driver: great Masses of Water, one after the other, that in twilight one might have feelingly compared them to a vast crowd of huge white Bears, rushing, one over the other, against the wind . . . what a sight it is to look down on such a Cataract! The wheels, that circumvolve in it, the leaping up and plunging forward of that infinity of Pearls and Glass Bulbs, the continual *change* of the *Matter*, the perpetual *Sameness* of the *Form* – it is an awful Image and Shadow of God and the World!

She held onto the mood represented by that passage, held it as long as she could, wanting to remember this memory so that she could return to it for nurture, starved as she had been of the comforts of any pleasant thought of him. But finally it slipped away and she was left looking at the water as it was now, in winter, trickling down a middle channel narrowed by ice, the ice at the furthest edges forming into twisted vines of thick icicles, distorted shapes of water frozen into limbs, bellies and udders of ice too thick to be broken off by hand.

Mary felt the chill catch her throat. She wrapped the cloak even more firmly about her and walked back to the village as quickly as her caution would allow. Perhaps the child would bring him back.

*

14th April, 1803

My dear husband,

I have landed up in Oxford but they told me that you were taken away from here more than six weeks ago. It is not that I am weary going from place to place – although the little ones now call themselves 'the gypsies!' – but the expense is proving too much. Some of our friends in Tiverton kindly made up a subscription but it is not large and I must guard it. What I need is to be settled somewhere so that I can earn some small sums to provide me with daily necessities. I thought of starting a small Dame School which would also serve to educate our own. Do you approve? I am not a learned woman but I was well enough taught and I have always read books whenever they were available to me.

My decision is this. I will go to Carlisle so that I shall be there whenever you arrive for your trial. No-one can tell me when the Assizes are fixed but it is better to be early than late and I shall go directly. I hope to get there well enough before you to have found lodgings and perhaps even some employment. I know your temper in these matters and I shall not embarrass you. I will come alone to see you and if you are morose or deeply engaged with your lawyers, I shall understand. To make it easier for us all I shall call myself Mrs. Benson (Ann Benson was a friend of mine at school) and have myself announced to you in that name. It will also protect the children from the chaffing and injury which comes to anyone associated with notoriety.

To save expense, I intend to walk a good deal of the way. The spring is a beautiful one. (How cruel that must seem to you, locked away in your dungeon – please believe that I intended no wounding in this.) I merely wish to reassure you that I will not be over-tiring the children, who are used to walking long distances, in such gentle weather.

Oh, my dear husband, how often and how tenderly my thoughts turn to you! It is strange, but I believe the most contented hours we have ever spent together were over Christmas and into the New Year. Unlikely surroundings for such a resurgence of affection on, I dare hope, both our sides. Yet when you consider how we met, perhaps the setting for such happiness is not so strange. You must know that in Scarborough when I waited for you to appear at your window and spent all other hours of the day and night scheming to have you released from that cage, my greatest dream was to be with you in that cell, to have the world locked out and you for myself alone.

I know you do not like me to be sentimental. I know that I make you angry in many little ways but you must know that you have brought me the greatest happiness. I wish life had been different in some ways but not in this: to have known and married you and borne your children has been a fulfilment richer than I could ever have imagined and for that, dear John, I will always, always be grateful and ever

Your loving wife,
Michelli

Michelli and her children set out north the next day. There is no record of their having reached Carlisle. There is no record of what happened to them. At the end of April, freak snowstorms struck the north–west and many vagrants were discovered dead from exposure.

*

Journals, 23rd June, Chester.

They have landed me back in Chester which is very cunning. And I am suddenly ripped out of the abandoned solitude with which I have been tested for several months and put in the large open pen where crones and overnight drunks, harlots, madmen, thieving children and some of the most vicious of both sexes are deposited with less ceremony than hogs in a sty. They mean to shock and break my spirit but I have determined that they have done me a favour. I will use this assembly as a laboratory for my ideas. I will have a Parliament. I will institute laws of common nourishment. I will set up schools and institute religious study (the clergy will be bound to help me here). I will have cleanliness an obligation and all this will be done in the most democratic way.

Journals, 6th July, Chester.

After less than three days my system failed. I have to consider whether it failed because of the CIRCUMSTANCES (a Prison) and the MATERIALS (common criminals for the most part) or because of the SYSTEM ITSELF. This is the crux of all political theory.

It began very well and with the warmest enthusiasm. Within two days we had new fresh straw for the floors (some silver I had was of assistance there) and we had regular and communal eating times – preceded by prayers – at which everyone got at least one bowl of soup or gruel. The prison clergyman – the Reverend Scott, a handsome young man, too handsome and too *clever*, I thought, for a cleric – set up his schools and the gaoler's wife – a most buxom, fleshy, jelly-breasted but, it has to be confessed from the depths of my enforced and lengthy chastity, covetable woman – set to for cleanliness so that on the second day the place was cleaner than many an inn.

The difficulties began with the elections. We were proceeding in a constitutional manner, they having adopted my suggestion that one in seven should be in the Parliament, when a harlot (who swore she had 'known' me as a boy although I had no recollection) called 'Red' (because of her hair: now much faded) Jennie took from her mouth the pipe that rarely left it and demanded that women too should be admitted to this Parliament. As there were almost as many women as men in the place, this was received with loud cheers on the one side but groans on the other. I thought it a good revolutionary suggestion and pointed out that if we followed it we would be going beyond both the American and the French Revolution and putting these islands once more in the forefront of change as it had been in 1688. This was greeted with ringing cheers by the women but only by some of the men.

Unhappily there was a resolute faction among the male prisoners which would have nothing to do with this suggestion and resented it mightily. This faction was led by two brothers – the Thomases – whose acts of violence after drunkenness had finally passed the usual tolerance of market-day behaviour and landed them in gaol for several months. As they were small hill farmers whose beasts and crops were every day wasting away without their attention, they were for ever irritable and seeking trouble. They were also very strong men and no-one dared contradict them. Nevertheless in the interests of my principles, I argued with them that woman, though not the equal of man, was nevertheless equal in the eyes of God and therefore in a good society – such as we were trying to create – they should have a vote. They should not, I agreed, be allowed into the Parliament itself – but they should be allowed to vote for those who were.

Here Red Jennie demurred (in her characteristically fierce fashion) and said that if she could not get in the Parliament then she wanted no vote and if she had no vote she would take no notice of the Parliament. She said she had enough trouble with parliaments outside of Chester prison without having the same thing inside where the least you could expect was some peace and quiet and the chance to gather your wits without being ordered about by parliaments. The women now were hotly on her side and only the gaoler's calling the good-night and ordering the candles to be quenched averted what began to look like a troublesome affray.

In the night Red Jennie came to me and said that for a guinea she would climb down from her opinions and that for another guinea I could pleasure myself in her for as long as I pleased as she remembered me as a boy and she too was a little aroused. As she spoke she stroked me with the most skilful provocation but I refused both her requests. The first because of my principles – which would not allow her to desert *her* principles – the second because I was certain she had the pox.

On the following day – the third day – the first having been a great *Rebirth*; the second a storm of activity followed by a *Great Disputation* – matters came to a climax and one of the fomenting elements was my old master, Mr. Seyward, who was suddenly thrown in among us ragged, half-drunk and the other half-crazy. But he recognised me – from the Police Notice – and immediately embraced me which almost made my gorge rise up. Perhaps he sensed my less than friendly feeling (though in truth I was pleased enough to see the old bully and sorry he had fallen low) and when the debate began again he most forcefully opposed the whole idea of an elected parliament and said that Parliament should be constituted only of the worthiest and the most eminent men in society. Plainly he thought of himself as their leader. To my horror and astonishment, he gathered some sort of party about him – largely from local people who anticipated favours, for he still had connections – but also from that irresponsible rabble which will do anything to spite what is good and helpful. Red Jennie, meanwhile, furious no doubt at my lack of sympathy in the night, took off her fighting womenfolk and their children into a corner of the large cell-room and marked it off as their own territory not to be entered by any MAN elected or unelected in the room. It was with some difficulty that I prevented the Thomas brothers from moving in with fists flying.

And so we held our elections without the women although they gave us not a moment's peace and Seyward's faction baited and heckled us at the tops of their voices urged on by that demented old scoundrel himself.

To my annoyance, one of the Thomas brothers was voted Prime Minister and it was then, I think – and here I must blame not the SYSTEM, which had weathered the most turbulent crosswinds, but the MATERIAL, which proved unequal to the task – that the experiment lost its purpose. This Thomas decided to punish the women by withholding food from them. He also made an alliance with Seyward and his party to banish education from the State. Naturally I protested and with my few brave and gallant supporters (the most educated but also, alas, the most timid in the room) made what I thought were bold and moving speeches on the founding principles of the republic we had attempted to establish. To my surprise – but also to my disadvantage – Red Jennie was so moved by my fine talk that she brought her camp over to mine and rashly challenged the Thomas brothers to do their worst.

Which they proceeded to do. The riot that followed saw several badly injured, many with minor contusions, the cell wrecked and finally a number of soldiers rushed in to enforce order.

I was moved back to a solitary cell but with my lessons learned and the bruises and cuts well paid for in such a direct lesson in politics.

*

Journals, 28th July, Lancaster.

I am in Lancaster Castle, the dungeons, and once more alone. This must be my last place before Carlisle. The world goes round in circles. I have regained my Faith.

Since my experiences at Chester I have thought of two things. The first is how futile sensual pleasures prove as aids to future contentment. In my life I have enjoyed many and powerful, often excessive, sometimes quite miraculous pleasures of the senses. With women, of course, particularly, but also with wine, with food, in luxury and privilege. Yet now that in my emptiness I seek renewal and restoration, these bring nothing to me. It is as if they are like fireworks: lit up and spent at once with nothing remaining save a husk. I would have thought that the laying up of sensual pleasure would have been like the laying up of learning or of wines but it appears not to be so: those peaks of the past are impossible to re-scale and they leave behind nothing much more than a sense of strangeness that once I was the man who did such things.

My second thought is of God. There are men I have known and respected who have been atheists but I cannot see the proofs of it. To me God is the central mystery and that mystery is everywhere. Even to a sinner such as myself He brings some comfort. Not in what He does – because He does nothing for me that I can say is 'mine'. And I know that for a long time I was dejected and felt spurned after what I thought had been the great gift of revelation which was followed by silence and indifference. But now His indifference seems the greatest wisdom, His silence the voice of purity and truth. I worship His name.

The cell, though a dungeon, is better than most others I have been in. The gaoler is friendly. I have fresh shrimps and cockles every day which the gaoler says are brought from the Bay by someone who will not give her name.

*

The boy was born at the end of June. The birth was safe but the child was always weak. Mary would not sleep for worrying over it and she got into such a state of anxiety that her milk dried and Alice suckled the child. For some reason this saving act made Mary half-mad with jealousy and poor Alice was frightened to go down to the Fish. Tom persuaded her that she had to.

Despite the summer date on the calendar, it was cold in the valley and the child grew bronchial and then caught pneumonia. Mary was quite frantic with nursing, coddling, desperately looking up and preparing all sorts of herbal medicines, sending to Cockermouth for the doctor, driving herself into illness as she strained to save the child; but in vain. He died three weeks after his birth and few could bear Mary's violent tears and despair.

Wordsworth wrote the following lines on the final state of Mary and her child's death:

> . . . She lives in peace
> Upon the spot where she was born and reared;
> Without contamination doth she live
> In quietness, without anxiety:
> Beside the mountain-chapel, sleeps in earth
> Her new-born infant, fearless as a lamb
> That, thither driven from some unsheltered place,
> Rests underneath the little rock-like pile
> When storms are raging. Happy are they both –
> Mother and child!

His own son, John, also born in June, was thriving.

28

Carlisle Assizes: August 1803

Carlisle, Hatfield thought, made a creditable setting. He was brought there in the first week in August with nine days in which to prepare himself for the trial. His gaoler, Mr. Campbell, as round faced, obliging and merry as a naughty monk, welcomed him for all the world as if he were a counterpart of George Wood and Carlisle Gaol the equivalent of the Queen's Head. "So pleased," he said. "Trust everything to your satisfaction" – the very treatment which brought out the best in him, who gave the man a guinea with such a mixture of hauteur and bonhomie that Mr. Campbell was immediately signed up as pro-Hatfield.

His first visitor was the Reverend Mark who would share the duties of ministering to him with the Reverend Patterson. It was from Mark that Hatfield learned something of the history of Carlisle – its Roman importance, its claims to be the capital of King Arthur, the Norman establishment, the great wars with Scotland when the Castle changed hands like a fortune in a card game, when a King of Scotland was crowned in the Castle and one of the greatest warrior kings of England was buried nearby at Burgh-by-Sands. And after the national armies had grappled over the Border and seen their armies swept over by the sea in the nearby Solway, the local families then feuded on for three centuries with Carlisle as often the only sign and security of any law for a hundred miles north or south until James united two of the fiercest kingdoms in history. Finally the postscript, when Bonnie Prince Charlie was led into the town by a hundred pipers only sixty-seven years ago – people still living in the town had seen the sight as children.

Hatfield, who had taken little notice of Carlisle on his two passages through it with Mary, felt complimented. This was a worthy stage.

He planned to use the nine days. There was his appearance to work on, his relationship with visitors – especially the clergy – his defence, his demeanour, his strategy. He was confident that Michelli would arrive before the trial and allow him to employ herself and the two small children as part of his case. He had no illusions over what would be the publicly expressed views of the jurymen on the issue of Bigamy – their wives would see to that; and although he was not charged with that offence, it ran under this whole operation like a river under a mill. He was being charged with a capital offence but there was the discretion of the judge and always – as was not infrequent – the possibility of a reprieve from London. He had a fighting chance.

But from now on there must be no blemish, not even a hairline crack: the character had to be wholly and finely finished.

He asked for a few small items to make him more comfortable – ordered more paper and ink, a new pen and claret. The tyrannical destitution of the last eight months had given him little opportunity to spend the money he had taken with him from Brecon – and he also had that which London admirers, and Newton, had added to his store. He was sufficiently in funds to be careless and confident enough to speculate on the arrival of more funds as soon as news of his arrival was generally known.

Mr. Campbell was rather anxious to show him around the gaol and even though Hatfield had to be put into irons for this little tour he agreed benevolently enough. It was certainly a well-used and well-kept place. Mr. Campbell pointed out improvements and features at every stop and if he had closed his eyes, Hatfield could have forgotten entirely that he was in a place of incarceration and dreamt himself in some thriving lodging-house.

"Here we have the come-and-go cell – when the lock-up is full as is often the case on Saturdays," said the gaoler, pleasantly, looking through the bars at four glum ruffians slumped each in his corner, the straw between them scuffed and heaped up as if it had recently been kicked to bits. "Public disorder generally," he said, smiling, and Hatfield could have sworn his tone was proud. "We see the same families and faces almost every week." He pointed to the smallest of the men, a cherubic figure with tranquil blue eyes. "That is Henderson," he said. "Probably a sheep-stealer, certainly a cattle-thief although never committed, and a Scot with a radical notion of politics that would give heart to Mr. Paine and all his friends in Paris. That small man causes much trouble. Over there," he pointed to a large, black-curly-haired individual wound up in a foetal position, "is Graham. One of the scores of Grahams about here. He's a great one for breaking pots when drunk, which he always is in Carlisle. That man," a lean, fine-faced man who disdained all the gaoler's coercive benevolence, "is Hetherington. Hetheringtons drink until they drop. Boys of eleven are sent out on missions of revenge. He'll swing one day." Mr. Campbell seemed especially pleased about that. "And he," he pointed to a body asleep, breathing as regularly as the tick of a clock, "is the Pearson we've been trying to catch for years. And now we have him, how long can we hold him? No more than a week." He nodded, admiringly. "All he does is sleep."

Hatfield wondered if he ought to propose a vote of thanks. Mr. Campbell was so pleased to show off his cage of rare birds. But he understood. Mr. Campbell was a born host and he wanted nothing to be lacking in making Hatfield feel at home. None of the men had said a word.

"You see, the families up here will keep on fighting; they've done it for centuries," said Campbell, happy, it seemed, to be part of such a long history even in this rather tangential way.

"Perhaps I could . . ."

"Of course . . ."

The gaoler led him back to his cell, returned a few minutes later to introduce his wife who curtsied and presented Hatfield with an apple pie and only after some time, his few items delivered, could Hatfield settle down quietly to steep himself in the part.

But Mr. Campbell had been very reassuring. For all its wars and ancient glories, he knew now that he was in a provincial city very remote from the capital and his larger Fame was a considerable factor. The gaoler, like a landscape painter, had drawn from the setting the features to look for and these provided Hatfield with a perspective.

*

The Reverend Nicholson was not surprised to see Mary when he came out of Lorton Church although second thoughts should have made him so. She had no reason to be there on a Tuesday evening. It was only three weeks since he had buried her infant son, Lorton was a stiff walk for someone as distraught and physically feeble as she had been and, she had told him, she would never again set foot in Lorton Church. His unsurprise was due to his constant thinking about her. To see her was merely the embodiment of his thoughts. He went over to her immediately and they turned towards Buttermere with the evening sun moving out of their eyeline over to the west.

They did not speak for some time, until they were well clear of the village.

"Well then," she began, always bolder than him, "he has landed in Carlisle."

"The trial will be next week. It will soon be over."

"I hear so many different voices," Mary said, plunging into what had beset her since learning of Hatfield's arrival. "I want to see him – I can say that to you –" she gave Nicholson a quick glance of gratitude which he slightly regretted: perhaps he would have preferred it had she not been so sisterly a parishioner to him? "– and yet the thought of seeing him after all . . . I wrote to him but he never replied – possibly the letter did not reach him – and then I heard about . . ." she hesitated a moment and he wanted to take her arm as if to help her over a rough stretch of ground but his diffidence forbade it, ". . . his other wife joining him in prison and that made me hate him more than I had ever hated him before, even more than when I discovered the letters. I want to leave the valley while he is in Carlisle but where would I go? He is reported on everywhere and I would be picked out even worse than I am here, although here . . ." The young clergyman knew that she was thinking of the party of Lake Visitors who had attended, respectfully but still obtrusively, the funeral of her child as if it were a legitimate stop on their Tour. ". . . Here the world comes to gawp and stare at me as if I were a freak show and yet – where could I hide?"

Nicholson had no helpful reply and he did not attempt to be merely soothing. It was important for Mary to talk: what he said would be no more than marginal. As she walked on, though, the sun, about to slide behind the fell, caught her hair in a haloed radiance, which crystallised an insight for the clergyman. Mary had never been able to 'hide'. Her Beauty had marked her out; her fame from early youth had further emphasised her difference. The work she did in her father's inn meant that she could never rest from the awareness that she was being examined; and now her marriage had increased that attention to an intolerably cruel degree. Even when she had been fully pregnant, the Tourists would still stalk the village for a glimpse of her. And the whole valley knew of the increase in traffic from Keswick along the Newlands road since the good weather had come in. Now that Hatfield was about to go on trial the crowds would grow even greater.

The insight gave him yet more respect for the tall, graceful and, he thought, fairer than ever young woman walking by his side. If only he had the courage to reach out and let her know of his own warm feelings for her. But a screen of public obligations shut him off from her and he would never have the audacity to break through it.

"Can you not visit a relative for a time?"

She ignored his pallid suggestion.

"It has been worst of all for my father," she said, again following thoughts of her own which had been honed to the sharp edge of pain. "The man, Hope, Hatfield, had not paid bills and there was more drunk at the wedding than my father could afford which he said he would make good and then there was a bill for ten pounds he drew on my father which he told me about only recently – all in all nearly twenty-eight pounds which is a ruinous amount – but it is not even that amount which has cast him down. It is the matter itself. He cannot understand how the man could do such a thing, and to me, his daughter. He sits and stares ahead of himself for an hour or even more and I know he is trying to understand it but he cannot and because he cannot he is drawing in on himself rapidly."

"Do you yourself understand, Mary?"

At last a contribution which she heard and addressed.

"Sometimes I think I do. When I have thought hard about every single thing I remember him saying, every action he took, every look, I think that I know him. And then something will come along and shatter my picture of him like a stone thrown on a sheet of water. But when I think I know him I begin to feel a great pity for him and I must resist that pity because what he did was wrong. To me, to the others, to so many people, what he did was wrong. It was bad. It was *wicked*." She breathed the last word almost as a whisper, as if she herself stood in danger of being accused of wickedness for accusing someone else of it.

The certainty of her morality touched the young clergyman profoundly. Her '*wicked*' breathed a loving God and a Devil who had to be grappled with and overthrown every day. Her '*wicked*' was the loving force of Christ which turned its face against the ways of the world. Her '*wicked*' called up the pity of hell fire, the bodies in torment and souls damned everlastingly.

"Mary," he said, "wicked though he was we must pray for his soul. And wrong as he was, I must remember how flattered and pleased I was to be in his good company. And we must recognise that even *in* the wicked there can be goodness. Just as the good man can stoop to evil, so the evil man can have moments of blessedness and truth." He took some letters out of his pocket. "He loved you very much and that love was good in him. Perhaps that is what will save him on the final day. When you were at Longtown he wrote me two letters – and in both he spoke lovingly of you." Nicholson read out, "He talks about his 'dear Mary' and the discourse you had with Mr. Graham and says 'All this hurried my dear Mary a little but nothing can be more pleasing than the *manner* she at all times possesses' and later on in the same letter he asks me to give your parents 'the most lively assurance of our mutual happiness'."

He passed the letter to Mary who read it several times until finally she returned it to him.

"I did not know he had written," she said. "And you wrote back?"

"As he asked me to."

She nodded and walked on in silence. At Hause Point she insisted on taking him no further out of his way. When he had finally given over watching her walk towards Buttermere, she turned aside into the copse on the brow before the village and thought through the letter again. At first it had puzzled her: he had written of going to a church service, hearing 'one of the finest lectures ever I have heard' by Mr. Graham, 'brother of Sir James', of footmen lighting them back to the hotel and other lies. Only at the very end and only then after she had read it several times did she realise what it was about. 'This will be a short letter,' he had written, 'let us have a long one from you as soon as possible addressed to Colonel Hope M.P., Post Office, Longtown, Cumberland, and you will greatly oblige, very dear and Reverend Sir, yours most truly, A. Hope.'

Even then, when, of all times, she had thought their love was for those few days set apart from the contamination of the rest of his life, he had been deceitful, using poor Nicholson to verify his imposture and inventing whatever he fancied to see him through.

She had gone to Lorton half-persuaded that the good deed to do was to go to Carlisle and at least show the world of Assizes and courts that she was not a poor broken creature but a woman who would survive and did not need or call on their vengeance to help her do so.

Now, she would stay here, bound in the valley.

Wearily she walked down the hill. When she saw the three coaches outside the inn she closed her eyes and swayed with dizziness. But she could not indulge in illness now. As she came nearer the door she stopped, breathed as deeply as she could, and walked in quickly.

*

Within a week Hatfield's impact on Carlisle society was astonishing.

It began in the gaol. The *Carlisle Journal* reported: "His readiness on all occasions to befriend his fellow prisoners procured him their most marked regard and esteem. He was often employed by them in writing letters and petitions, in many of which he evinces a benevolence of disposition highly honourable to him. The sufferings of the unfortunate excited in him the most lively sympathy, as will appear by the following letter addressed to a medical gentleman in the city."

The *Journal* quotes the letter:

Dear Sir,

I have for some time purposed addressing you, but the sensibility of your heart towards me, when we have met *lately*, has deprived me of an opportunity.

Thomas Hetherington, a prisoner for debt, applied *too late* to the Society for the relief of such persons *to sue for his sixpences* and he is left to the cheerless prospect of a *long cold winter*; without any hope of relief. He is eighty-three years of age; his son, who was confined with him for the same debt, died by his side soon after my arrival here. The debt was only £23. The costs are £24 10s.!!!

The Society never gives more than ten pounds to any one case; for that sum I have already recommended him, as it is the last recommendation of a man whose pleadings they have kindly and invariably attended to for many years, we will hope *that will* be complied with . . .

The debt was contracted for beer, with a brewery at Alstone Moor: the old man has been their customer eighteen years! *as a publican.* The Principal Proprietor is said to be Mr. Christopher Blackett residing at Newcastle. Pray do be so good as to solicit the very excellent Chancellor, now in residence here, to use his benevolent influence with Mr. Blackett, that he will condescend to accept all we can offer for this poor man's liberty . . .

May HE who comforts me beyond expression ever bless you and yours.

Dear Sir, I am yours
With affection and gratitude
JOHN HATFIELD

This is one of a considerable number of letters.

Hatfield, with the benign connivance of Mr. Campbell, who kept reminding Hatfield that as a boy he had sung in the Cathedral and *knew his scriptures well*, first influenced and then, rapidly, ran the gaol on Christian principles. He gave an outstanding example of faith and charity: he took on the grievances of everyone who sought him out and those reluctant to approach him were delicately made aware of his availability should they need help. The Reverends Mark and Patterson reported the salvation and transformation of the gaol throughout the city. On that indisputable foundation, Hatfield built.

He received Carlisle society as if he were a minor princeling. Somehow, in the space of a few days, he forced a radical alteration on the city's perception. He was no longer a curiosity, much less a freak, not even a notorious seducer, forger, felon, impostor – but a man of unique distinction from whose presence one came away enhanced. A feeling of reverence mushroomed for Hatfield and, later, it saturated the speeches at his trial as much as it moved the leading citizens of the Border capital.

Just as the gaol was his open laboratory, daily proof of his good works, so his relationship with the clergy – not just Mark and Patterson but clergy all over the county with whom he entered into copious correspondence – was the visible evidence of an overpowering inner faith. Indeed there is the impression at times that the clergy rather wilt or seem winded at the vehemence and frontal certainty of Hatfield's religiosity. They were convinced, though, of that there can be little question – judging from all the evidence – and their stories of his muscular piety were told around the county with all the acclamation of the story of the Prodigal Son: yet again Hatfield – now Don Juan, now Spartacus, now Zeus in his many shapes, now the Man of the People – had winkled out a role of immense cultural resonance – the rescue and return of Man from the Fall. Carlisle welcomed the Prodigal.

"His demeanour during his imprisonment here," reported the *Carlisle Journal,* "was such as to excite admiration mingled with sorrow in those that visited him: admiration of his natural and acquired accomplishments; sorrow that abilities which, if usefully employed, would have done honour to himself, and promoted the welfare of society were, by deviation from the path of rectitude, fatally obscured and lost . . . The Clergymen who attended him found him a man of good understanding, conversant with the scriptures."

*

Journals, 14th August 1803, Carlisle.

Tomorrow I shall be taken to the ancient Town Hall of this historic and admirable city (it has no Court House: I have heard that the Judges and the newspapers have frequently complained of this) and tried.

I am prepared. I shall conduct my own defence although Messrs. Topping and Holroyd – well read gentlemen who make extensive notes – have been deputed as my counsel. I am surprised that Michelli, my dear wife, has not arrived: as I have had no reply to my letters to London and Tiverton, I presume she has turned away. To my dear Mary I have sent a letter asking forgiveness. I wronged her cruelly and HE has punished us both by taking back to HIMSELF the child. Poor Mary: and yet I know her well enough to believe she will survive this with HIS help.

HE is now my constant aid. As a sign HE has taken away from me that species of madness I endured for so long, since I was a child, whereby 'I' seemed to leave my own body and see it as an object no more than a stone on a path. With that has gone my nightmares, my crying aloud, all my fears, and although I know that Newton is somewhere in this city, I am no longer in dread and mortal terror of him. I am myself. I act as I want to be and that brings me favour wherever I turn. If only I had been myself throughout my life then HE would not need to intercede for a sinner.

*

"Never perhaps in this city," reported the *Carlisle Journal*, "did there a cause come before a court of justice which claimed such a general interest." The town was overflowing: no room could be had in any hotel. Coaches had come from all over the county.

The trial was widely reported but the reports in the *Carlisle Journal* are the longest and the most detailed. It is the *Journal* which is most quoted here.

At ten thirty, on the morning of Monday, 15th August, 1803, John Hatfield was taken from Carlisle Gaol to the Town Hall for the Assizes. He was accompanied by the gaoler Mr. Campbell and by an escort taken from the yeomanry. The crowds were so great that he was given a post-chaise. He was applauded down the streets of the city and had some difficulty entering the Town Hall because of the size and pressure of the crowd.

29

The Trial

The trial began at eleven a.m. on Monday, 15th August, 1803, "at the Assizes for this county, before the Hon. Alexander Thomson, Knight."

The mediaeval Town Hall was so overcrowded that some newspapers complained it hindered their reporters. The county was there, the city was there, and the general public seemed solidly for Hatfield and besieged the Town Hall throughout the day as resolutely as many an English and Scottish army had besieged that city in the past seven hundred years.

"The Prisoner," said the *Journal*, "is a handsome and genteel person and his behaviour in court was proper and dignified and he supported his situation from first to last with unshaken fortitude."

Hatfield saw one or two old friends around the court: and one enemy. Of his solicitors, Holroyd was already scribbling notes before the proceedings had got under way and it was Topping who brought Hatfield to his seat. Sir Alexander Thomson arrived to meet turmoil and threatened that the court would be cleared if the uproar did not cease. The silence indoors accentuated the market sounds and crowd roars of those locked outside.

Hatfield had dressed carefully and well. A new but sober jacket and waistcoat; new stout black shoes from George Johnston, 'Bootmaker to the Aristocracy of the County'; his thick hair tied back unpowdered. He looked around the faces as he had once looked around the great Bay of Morecambe when rehearsing his lines. As on that previous occasion, he reached back to the example of the glorious actor Kemble as he was asked to rise to his feet and hear the indictment brought against him. He managed that 'rise' with such modesty but also with such panache that he felt the whole of the packed room rise with him and let out a corporate exhalation of satisfaction that this was to be a rare piece of theatre indeed and they were to be a part of it.

The Clerk read out the following:

John Hatfield, you stand charged upon three indictments:

1) With having assumed the name and title of the Honourable Alexander Augustus Hope and pretending to be a Member of Parliament of the United Kingdom of Great Britain and Ireland and with having, about the month of October last, under such false and fictitious name and character, drawn a draft or bill of exchange in the name of Alexander Hope upon John Crump, Esquire, for the sum of thirty pounds payable to George Wood, of Keswick, Cumberland, innkeeper, or order, at the end of fourteen days from the date of the said draft or bill of exchange.

2) With making, uttering and publishing as true a certain false, forged and counterfeit bill of exchange, with the name of Alexander Augustus Hope thereunto falsely set and subscribed, drawn upon John Crump, Esquire, dated the 1st of October 1802 and payable to Nathaniel Montgomery Moore, or order, ten days after the date, for twenty pounds sterling.

3) With having assumed the name of Alexander Hope and pretending to be a Member of Parliament of the United Kingdom of Great Britain and Ireland, the brother of the Right Honourable Lord Hopetoun, and a Colonel in the Army and under such false and fictitious name and character, at various times in the month of October 1802, having forged and counterfeited the handwriting of the said Alexander Hope, in the superscription of certain letters or packets, in order to avoid the payment of the duty on postage.

Oh no, Hatfield murmured to himself: in order to convince the world that I was indeed A. Hope.

"How do you plead?"

"Not guilty to all three," said Hatfield, allowing no pause.

The public sank back on their seats in contentment: the prologue had been well played. As Hatfield sat down, the court buzzed with the accumulated whispers of scores of private observations and Sir Alexander Thomson once again threatened them with banishment. He did not like this case. Carlisle was usually a merry stop on his circuit with cattle-thieves, sheep-stealers, a murder from some local feud, good Border stuff not this fashionable nonsense about forgery and impostors. He had dined at Netherby Hall the previous evening, with Sir James Graham – as he usually did in the August Assize, for the fishing – and the talk had been of nothing but Hatfield, Hatfield, Hatfield! The ladies had cajoled him into getting seats for them in the court and there they were, the flower of the land – (Sir Alexander was noted for his gallantry to the ladies and considered himself no mean charmer) – squashed in a sweltering and stinking old room about to listen to the sordid history of a miserable bigamist who had fooled certain susceptible folk – Lord knows how, looking at that disgustingly thick hair and the clearly faked-up scar on his cheek which dimpled when he smiled (though what he had to smile about . . . ! He would wipe the smile off his face soon enough). Who had been convinced that he was a gentleman? The port at Netherby Hall had been too plentiful and he was more liverish than he liked to be at the start of what would be a long case. He called for a jug of cold lemonade.

Mr. Scarlet rose up to open the case for the prosecution and began by stating "at great length the enormity of the crimes for which the prisoner stood indicted". As Mr. Scarlet laid out his groundwork – in all the methodical detail of one constructing great engines and ditches for a long and sustained attack – as he pointed out with gravity and example the ruination that mass forgery would bring on the realm and the debauchery which would be let loose should imposture go unpunished by the severest penalties – Hatfield took up a pen and began to make his own notes. Topping occasionally whispered a word behind Hatfield's back to Holroyd – still deep in his note-taking; was he compiling a vast book? – and, provoked, Holroyd would assent or dissent – usually monosyllabically – but as the conversation appeared to have little direct bearing on his case and concerned itself with observations on style or points of presentation, Hatfield realised that he would be best served by serving himself.

The Judge was not on his side and would never be. In Sir Alexander Thomson, Hatfield saw a lifelong adversary: a man who had hated the French Revolution, pressed for the Treason Trials, supported William Pitt in his censorship of the press, despised the liberal Fox, considered Wilberforce, Clarkson and the entire Anti-Slave-Trade lobby to be fools, admired Napoleon, deplored the Prince of Wales and his set, feared all members of the British public below his own class except for 'honest' (by which he largely meant deferential) tradesmen and thought the solution to the discontents of the poor lay in mass starvation and increased hangings. They caught each other's eye and immediate and mutual detestation was registered.

Mr. Scarlet developed an interesting digression on the relationship between the validity of a nation's coin and the viability of its commerce and health. He had several impressive instances from Roman history and as he was rather addicted to Latin, all of this would be drummed up for service by one means or another.

Hatfield's only chance was the jury, twelve 'good men and true' who sat assuming an impossible Sunday-school air of reverence as they nodded to the Latin of the learned prosecutor. This jury – in their best clothes – were shiny faced as if an extra polish had been given their faces whereas it was only the first glistening of sweat as the day broiled up to noon. These men would all have known of his tornado of virtue during the past nine days. Some of their wives might have visited him and although they would certainly disapprove they would most likely draw the line at the death penalty which, in any event, was sometimes mitigated for these offences and transmuted into 'life'. Life was all he wanted and with a ferocity he dared not admit even to himself in case it wrenched his equilibrium. The jury was his target.

Hatfield made some notes but then his attention was caught by Mr. Scarlet who, clearly quite affected by the impact of Hatfield and his good works, was now taking leave of the Roman plain of generalisations to make a reluctant advance on the particular. "I must point out to the jury," he said, "that the prisoner came qualified to act a conspicuous part in society by the gentility of his manners and by the extent of his information. I am sorry to observe that a man so qualified could become, alas, such a dangerous member of society. It is well known that the crimes singly with which the prisoner has been charged meet with the punishment of *death*: but here was an accumulation of guilt which, I trust, I shall be able to prove by a chain of evidence which will challenge the strictest investigation."

Here Topping cast an agitated word to Holroyd but Holroyd wrote on and did not reply.

Mr. Scarlet wiped his face with his handkerchief and looked enviously at Sir Alexander's cold stone jug of lemonade.

"I have to say," said Mr. Scarlet, "that I am extremely sorry that the painful duty should be mine to point out more particularly the surety of his offences" – and here he paused to glance at Hatfield as if to beg his pardon: Hatfield recognised the moment, sensed the jury following the prosecutor's example and brought up an expression of greatly wounded but deeply tolerant dignity: as if waved on, Mr. Scarlet continued and addressed the jury firmly. "But however painful my sensations are, I trust that neither my own feelings nor those of yourselves, gentlemen of the jury, shall induce you for a moment to forget the momentous duty which your country has imposed upon you." As if sharply aware of the rigid presence of the Judge, he added, "You must waive all considerations as to feelings of Humanity and consider this question as it materially affects the happiness and welfare of society."

Hatfield saw the jury brace themselves to this call to duty. To counteract this, he fixed their foreman with a stern and admonishing look as if to convince him that there were matters more important than 'the happiness and welfare of society' which he would understand if he put his mind to it.

"Mr. Scarlet, then, with a great deal of moderation, sketched an outline of the character of the prisoner from the time he became known to the world in the assumed character of *Colonel Hope*."

The outline was quite detailed and included excerpts from the letters to the Reverend Nicholson, a reference to Mary – "in these letters he speaks with great affection of his 'Beloved Mary'. Indeed it was allowed on all hands that the prisoner conducted himself with singular propriety . . ." The arrival of Hardinge was described and on up to the flight across the lake.

Mr. Scarlet then concluded his strangely double-jointed prosecution: "Painful as the task assigned to me is, I feel an inward satisfaction while I discharge a duty which I owe to my country, and to its liberties and laws. I shall now call evidence in support of what I have advanced and I rest my claims of justice on your unbiased verdict."

There was a nod from the Judge: the jury slumped out of its tension, the court murmured but did not applaud.

As Mr. Scarlet's opening had taken longer than anticipated, the Judge ordered a break for refreshments and retired to a side room for cold beer, ham and pickled onions. Topping and Holroyd sent out for their beer: Hatfield would take only lemonade. As no-one in the court wanted to risk losing his seat by quitting it even for a few moments, shouts, bribes and orders winged through windows and ricocheted across the sweating courtroom. Outside small boys made fast pence rushing to and from the Crown and Mitre with tankards and plates.

Once again it took Sir Alexander some time to tame the court: once again he was not pleased: and the pickled onions threatened to repeat.

Mr. Quick was called. Had Mr. Quick known the prisoner previously? He had. By what name? John Hatfield. In which place? At Tiverton in Devonshire where the prisoner entered into partnership in 1801 with Dennis & Co. in consequence of which the firm was changed to Dennis, Hatfield & Co. The prisoner had left Tiverton in April 1802 on pretence of transacting some of the company's concerns in London.

The word 'pretence' shuttlecocked between busy Topping and scribbling Holroyd but neither seemed inclined to consult Hatfield himself about it.

Mr. Quick was then shown some papers and swore positively on his oath that it was the handwriting of the prisoner both in the letters and in the Bills of Exchange.

Hatfield was thereby established.

Next to be called was the Reverend Nicholson who had finally been too confused and overcome to tell Mary that he had been called on to play this role. As he took his oath he remembered most vividly the last time he saw her on her way into Buttermere and as he took his hand from the bible he knew that she would never wholly trust him again.

Hatfield smiled at him in such genuine friendship that Nicholson was startled and choked on his first few words. Water was brought and Sir Alexander's opinion about the reliability of the lower clergy was reinforced.

The Reverend Nicholson stated that he was introduced to the prisoner – by Mr. Skelton – and he understood him to be the Honourable Colonel Hope, brother to Lord Hopetoun. Later in his evidence, Nicholson said that he had accompanied the prisoner to Whitehaven "to procure a licence for his marriage" to Mary of Buttermere "whom, if I may say so, the prisoner spoke of as a *lovely girl*." A buzz and appreciative murmur went around the court as Mary's association with Hatfield was so tenderly – and in terms of the reference to the 'lovely girl' – unexpectedly referred to.

The Reverend Nicholson then went through the meeting with

Hardinge in Keswick in great detail, differing only from previous versions in saying that when it was clear that he could not use his carriage, he had said "that he had to get to Buttermere and the quickest way without a carriage was to go across the water and over the mountains into Buttermere". This difference to the account which has him give Nicholson a guinea for dinner and go 'fishing' with Burkett is not one which changes the case but it is intriguing. Was Nicholson ashamed of accepting the guinea and being left at the hotel? Or did he wish to cover up for the constable who might have been in some trouble had Hatfield's flight been seen to follow his utter stupidity in letting him 'go fishing'? Burkett is not mentioned at all and yet it seems certain he led Hatfield into the high passes.

It all suggests some innocent and face-saving doctoring of the evidence on the part of the kind-hearted clergyman whose permanent characteristic was embarrassment, whose liability was diffidence and to whom the undertaking of giving public evidence was the most distressing experience in his life. Nevertheless, the Reverend Nicholson produced damning evidence, for "yes," he replied to a leading question from Mr. Scarlet, "I do clearly remember the transaction taking place for which the prisoner stands charged. I saw him take a stamp out of his pocket and draw a bill for twenty pounds on John Crump for which he received cash from Mr. G. Wood, innkeeper at Keswick."

Nicholson then swore to being the person who married the prisoner to "Mary Robinson, commonly called Mary of Buttermere, on 2nd October, 1802."

Mr. Joseph Skelton was then called and he confirmed that the prisoner had informed him that "his name was Hope, that he was brother to Lord Hopetoun and a Colonel in a regiment of Dragoons. I also frequently heard the prisoner speak of his estates in Herefordshire . . ."

Mr. Scarlet then called Mr. Crump, whose crisp manner was a relief after the tentative low-pitched rambling of Nicholson and the tendency to garrulity on the part of Skelton. The case was already taking much longer than Sir Alexander had planned and he was beginning to be disconcerted by the composure of the prisoner and his intelligent, collected air in circumstances which ought to have crushed him.

Mr. John Gregory Crump confirmed that he met the prisoner at

Grasmere and that he had no knowledge of him before that time. He understood his name to be Alexander Augustus Hope. He had frequent conversations with the prisoner during which the prisoner "spoke of his fortune and said he had an estate near Stockport and others." Mr. Crump confirmed that he "left Grasmere and returned to Liverpool where he cashed a bill for the prisoner for thirty pounds." "No," he agreed, "he had no connection with him before about business." Mr. Crump stood down.

The saddest sight of the day was the doleful figure of George Wood, strapped in his best rig-out – a purchase designed for winter – and sweltering in the heat which was now immense despite all the doors and the windows being open and the ladies rapidly quivering their fans. He had arrived on the previous evening for fear of being late on the day itself although he would have given a tidy sum to have avoided the occasion altogether. His journey had not been improved by the company of Monkey-boy who felt impelled to remember his previous journey along the route – with Hatfield and Mary – and seemed to Wood to hold him responsible for what was a mandated appearance. All his friends in Keswick were in a similar frame of mind. They spoke as if he were volunteering to set off for the Assizes delighted at the prospect of putting an end to Hatfield's existence. Mr. Wood felt very badly done by.

"No-one will ever know what Colonel Hope and myself went through together," he would say, allowing images of war and conflict to arise if they would, but prepared, under challenge, to tell the more mundane truth of their few drinking sessions. "I have never known an Honourable more honourable and if they say he is not in title then I say he is by nature." All this stirring loyalty had made him the keeper of the grail in Keswick. And then he received this summons to appear as a witness for the prosecution. After the implications were unravelled and news got about, Wood had little peace.

"I have to go, otherwise it will be my neck they'll want next," he said, "that's what none of them understand."

But Monkey-boy was not one for giving in easily: Wood found no comfort there.

Hesitantly and ponderously, Wood was sworn in. Sir Alexander liked the look of him.

It became very drawn out as Wood sniffed and lumbered around every question – now and then catching Hatfield's eye and always in his glance craving an apology – happily given by Hatfield who found himself touched that his old drinking partner should be so protective. Skelton had stretched out his time; Nicholson had meandered and wandered through twice or even thrice as long as necessary. Mr. Scarlet's long prologue had been succeeded by long questions and longer summaries: but Wood set the record – and the courtroom all but jellified in the mid-August heat.

Reluctantly he admitted to having seen the prisoner. He had been at the Queen's Head frequently and would be welcome – please to stick to the answers to the questions asked, Mr. Wood – Sorry, Your Honour – Yes, he had his own carriage and a very handsome affair too, horses particularly well looked after and – And how was he known? That seemed to give George Wood a problem. Indeed it seemed to cause an acute attack of migraine from the spasm of pain which seized his face. How was he *known*? Yes – how was the prisoner *known*? What *name* did he use? What name? He could never recollect the gentleman, the prisoner, using his name, not what might be his full name. Did he answer, then, shall we say, to the name Colonel Hope? After a scowling silence, Mr. Wood was forced to agree that this, occasionally, was the case but in making this admission he kept his head down low. How were parcels addressed to him? Which particular parcel was His Honour after? Any parcels. There were all arts and parts of parcels. Well then, letters. The Colonel, that is, the prisoner, tended to stroll down to the post office for his own letters – said he liked walking through the streets of Keswick because all the people were so friendly as indeed they still were and if ever he needs a place – Mr. Wood! Did ever any parcels or letters arrive at your hotel sometimes known as the Queen's Head and sometimes simply Wood's Hotel, did any missives arrive addressed to 'The Honourable A. A. Hope, M.P'? You are on oath, Mr. Wood, and the court is waiting. They did. Thank you, Mr. Wood.

It was when Mr. Scarlet attempted to lead Wood through the meeting with Hardinge and Hatfield's escape that the labyrinth was fully revealed. It became necessary for Mr. Wood to explain which room he had been in at particular times, which rooms he had just left, which rooms he was just about to enter, the precise displacement of accommodation on the ground floor of the hotel, the distance between the front door and the side alley next to which the honourable prisoner had made a speech which he had not in all particulars caught in its entirety . . .

All Sir Alexander's prejudices returned but Wood went back to his seat feeling in some obscure way a better man than he had been when he vacated it.

Mr. Scarlet's final witness was Colonel Parke. Yes, he was well acquainted with Colonel Hope: yes, Colonel Hope was brother to the Earl of Hopetoun, a General in the Army and Colonel in the 17th Regiment of Dragoons. Yes, he had been in Ireland with him for about three years. No, the prisoner at the bar was not Colonel Hope.

Mr. Scarlet drew some sonorous and, Sir Alexander thought – especially after the excellent example of Colonel Parke – unnecessary conclusions.

It was going on for six o'clock and the Judge broke for refreshment. Topping and Holroyd took Hatfield to a side room and sent out for beer and lemonade.

Topping went through the witnesses he intended to call – the only one of any substance being an attorney from Stockport in Cheshire who had been employed by Hatfield in 1801 for the recovery of some property in Kent.

"But all that he will show is that you are in fact John Hatfield although that you were a man of some wealth might weigh in your favour."

It was at this point that Holroyd broke silence. This he did not do lightly nor without a warning salvo of preliminary cluckings and hawkings. But once the passage was clear, the message came succinctly.

"Scarlet has all the evidence and that's the truth of it. He has proved his case."

"I have to agree," said Topping. "I wish I could dissent but I find I agree."

"And so do I," said Hatfield. "What sort of speech do you advise?"

"An honest one," said Topping.

"Gentlemen," Hatfield replied, "I am on trial for my life and my case has been entrusted to you both. So far you have been no help. I cannot blame you for that, seeing I had so little to help you *with*, but I can ask you to be helpful now. What sort of speech do you advise?"

"Fairly short," said Holroyd, thoughtfully, drawing out his words, "unless you change your plea you cannot admit anything but somehow you must make it plain you admit everything and then you must make them feel you deserve to be treated leniently."

"It is a great shame that your wife and children are not here," said Topping. "You could have pointed to them. The children might have looked distraught. It can be very affecting."

"It's been a long day," said Holroyd, for whom Hatfield now felt respect. "Be as simple as you possibly can be." He looked at his notes rather sadly. "None of these will be of any help to you, I'm afraid. And it is not so much the argument they are waiting for as *what you seem to be*."

"Then it is in God's hands," said Hatfield.

"Amen."

"Leave me alone here for a few moments, please."

The counsels went out of the door and stood with the yeomen who were guarding it. In the room, Hatfield got onto his knees.

"I know, O Lord, that I am Thy unworthy servant and I am composed for death. But O Lord, I want to live. I know now how to live and what to live for – to be an example, however poor, of the truth of Thy Glory on earth, to help my fellows, as I can, O Lord, Thou hast seen that. I have good feelings in me and there is much in this world needs to be done. I could be of service. I beg You, in the name of Jesus Christ, to give me the opportunity to do it."

He heard only distantly the knocking on the door and when his counsels came into the room for him they found him, as Topping was to say, "locked in prayer so deeply we had to wake him out of it".

To give Hatfield some time to collect himself, Topping called the attorney who said he knew the prisoner as Hatfield, had acted for him over a property in Kent and knew that the prisoner kept a carriage.

Topping then called Hatfield, who stood and turned into the sun which made him flinch and swing the other way. The court was more attentive than it had been all the day. To Hatfield it seemed an eternity before he began. The very condition he had thought had left him for ever now returned to debilitate him utterly. The spirit had gone out of him, he had felt himself drained away as he was praying, when he had asked for help in his time of greatest need, then he had been weakened. Whose was this voice? What were these words? The thing he was stood in the middle of the floor, swaying to escape the sun which, now low in the sky, streamed through the windows incandescently. He saw himself there and, without power, had to begin: perhaps the Lord would be merciful.

"Gentlemen." He paused and the women in the court thought he had never looked so affecting, so romantic, and so perfectly tragic as he did in that dramatic pose, a hand on his heart, his head turned to look at the jury although his body stood four-square to the Judge, his hair catching golden lights from the sun. "Gentlemen of the jury, I will say to you with all the honesty I have that I am glad to be here and in your unbiased and unprejudiced hands. For in one way or in another my sufferings will soon be terminated. Over the past eight months, I have been dragged from prison to prison, from place to place, and seen myself referred to in the most injurious and vicious terms. Yes, gentlemen," his voice, instead of something apart from himself now eased back into his body; the dry horror of his mind filled with a suffusion of relief; he raised his voice a little and turned more directly now to the twelve men who would decide on his life. "I am even happy to be here with men such as you for I know that you will see things for what they are and not for what they seem – as our Lord sees us for what we are – not for the outward show, not for the appearance, the cut of cloth, the pile of gold, but for that which is eternal and fine in us, that which gives the truest proof of all – proof of His reign on earth. And that is what you can judge as *you too will be judged* and at that time this day will weigh heavily in the scales. 'Judge not,' said our Lord Saviour, 'lest ye be judged.' But of course you must do your duty as Mr. Scarlet has said so eloquently and as he did not need to say because of *course* you will.

"But, gentlemen of the jury, wherein lies that duty? That is the question. And, what are you judging? Are you judging a man who drew a few pounds on those he thought of as friends at a time when he needed them and distances made explanations impossible? Surely not. For by the sale of my carriage and horses – which I authorised many months ago and am sad but not surprised to see that my enemies have not acted on and indeed deny all knowledge of – by that simple sale, all can be repaid to the generous Mr. Crump and my good old friend George Wood. I authorise that the sale be done now: as I can get no action from a letter let me beg your indulgence to clear these few debts in this courtroom today. And so there is no matter of debt, no matter of fraud, no matter of any theft at all involved, a hastiness for which I beg forgiveness, a carelessness for which I crave pardon, a presumption on friendship which I now realise, in the case of Mr. Crump, merchant of Liverpool, was too great. For this I ask forgiveness and clear all debts.

"So it is not for that you will judge me in your severest testing of the *real* evidence. As for the other matter, as to who I am, who I was, what I seemed, what I did with the name of a noble and ancient family, gentlemen, as God is my witness I tell you this. I solemnly swear – see, I take up this great bible once again – on this eternal book from which all blessings flow and before my Maker whom I am prepared to meet even face to face, on this Thy word, I look up to Heaven and I SOLEMNLY SWEAR that in all my transactions – all, ALL – in all my transactions I never intended to defraud or injure the persons whose names have appeared in this prosecution. GOD HEARS ME AND HE ALONE WILL JUDGE and if I swear falsely then I invite and embrace damnation and the worst of Hell. I meant no harm, gentlemen of the jury, no harm; this I will maintain until the last moment of my earthly life!"

Unable any longer to hold back the tears, he sat down and, after a gasp of emotion from the court, the room rippled into applause and softly weeping bravos. Holroyd leaned across and tapped his arm in congratulation.

Sir Alexander called for silence three times and finally achieved it. He would take five minutes, he said, sat where he was, to prepare his summary: any disturbance in that time would result in immediate expulsion from the court. He charged the constables to see to it.

The jury, he could see, had been quite as moved by that extraordinarily irregular defence as the general public. It was his duty to direct them back to the evidence – which he could have done as soon as Hatfield sat down – he kept good notes and was widely appreciated for his speedy and concise summaries. But the court needed to change its mood, he thought, shake off the dangerous enthusiasm aroused by that all but inadmissible speech.

The gavel was banged – he fixed the jury directly in his sightlines and summed up the evidence "with a great deal of perspicacity and force". He went back to the three indictments, read them out rapidly, commended Mr. Scarlet on the high-mindedness of his opening remarks and seconded his calling the jury to a proper sense of their great duty in a matter of such national significance. He praised the evidence of the Reverend Nicholson and pointed out how it accorded with the evidence of Mr. Skelton and George Wood. He drew attention to Mr. Quick's knowledge of Hatfield, and in very dubious circumstances, in Tiverton in Devonshire, and to Colonel Parke's clinching assertion that the man before them was not the man he had claimed to be in October last. He drew particular attention to the precise evidence of Mr. Crump. Topping's attorney was dismissed in a line and Hatfield's speech was referred to as 'the rhetoric of a clever but desperate man'.

"It is my view," he said, "nothing could be more clearly proved, than that the prisoner did make the bill or bills in question under the assumed name of Alexander Augustus Hope with an intention to defraud. That the prisoner used the additional name of Augustus is of no consequence in this question. The evidence proves *clearly* that the prisoner meant to represent himself to be another character and that under that assumed character, he drew the bills in question. If anything should appear in mitigation of the offences with which the prisoner stands charged, you must give them a full consideration; and though his character has long been shaded with obloquy, yet you must not let this in the least influence the verdict you were sworn to give."

This time Holroyd's pressure on Hatfield's arm was sympathetic. The jury looked chastened. The court murmured almost mutinously.

The jury retired and for the last time, Hatfield went into the small side room with his two counsels.

"'Character long been shaded with obloquy'," said Topping, "that was a blow, Holroyd."

"He wants a conviction and he wants it quickly, Topping," Holroyd replied. "No doubt he is late already for his dinner."

"I must say," Topping turned to Hatfield almost bashfully, "*your* speech . . ."

"Would have turned them," said Holroyd.

"With anybody but Thomson," Topping concluded. "He had an eleven-year-old boy hanged at the last Assizes for poaching on the Lonsdale estates. Afterwards we found out that the principal witness – one of the gamekeepers – had a grudge against the boy's mother and may well have sworn falsely."

"Even if he did not," said Hatfield, quickened out of his reverie by the thought of the boy, "to hang a child for a few fish . . ."

"All *your* offences are capital," said the blunt Holroyd, "but what have you done? You have given back the money you took on false pretences. You have abused the name of a man who will surely not suffer any direct inconvenience . . ."

"He may be rather amused by it," said Topping, who had been hardly done by in having to put his own private appreciation of Hatfield's escapades under the discipline of his gravitas as a counsel.

"He will certainly not be *harmed.* All the harm done is in Scarlet's windy philosophy about the foundations of the state. Unprovable. And yet . . ."

"There could be a reprieve," Topping said.

"The bigamy goes against us," Holroyd ground on. "And I fear that the bigamy is playing its part in the jury room at this very minute. That is where Sir Alexander was so sly, you see, with that 'character shaded with obloquy' – they will refer to that since he directed them so forcefully to the phrase and then Mary of Buttermere will become a consideration and all of them will want to spring to her defence."

The jury returned after only ten minutes.

The verdict was 'Guilty of Forgery'.

"After the verdict of the jury was given, Hatfield discovered no relaxation of his accustomed demeanour, but after the court adjourned he retired from the bar, and was ordered to attend the next morning to receive the sentence of the law. The crowd was immense and he was allowed to have a post-chaise from the Town Hall to the gaol."

That night the city was in a mood somewhere between carnival and near riot. The yeomanry were alerted. The Commander-in-Chief at the Castle was told to be prepared to bring out the troops. The hotels and inns surged and rocked with crowds wanting to drink, eat, but above all talk about the trial and gamble not so much on the sentence as on the chance of a reprieve.

The jury was widely condemned. The story put out by their rather nervous apologists was that they had been unwilling to bring in a verdict which might see him hanged for having forged a frank but his heartless conduct to "their fellow countrywoman" had reconciled them to their harshness. Messrs. Topping and Holroyd visited Hatfield after their late dinner – the trial had not finished until after seven o'clock – and Holroyd once again pointed to 'obloquy' as the turning point.

"They did not need reminding of Mary," Hatfield objected, quietly. "Even in London the crowds were chanting her name, the children sang songs about her, there are pictures of her and books about her.

She is a woman who remains marvellously modest and insists on doing what she would do if she were as plain as a bucket but yet you just have to see her to know that she has been plucked out for grace and favour by Him on high. They would need no word from Sir Alexander Thomson to bring Mary of Buttermere into their minds. She has been hovering above this trial like the Archangel over the shepherds. It is not for lying or forging but for letting loose a passion that I am to be sentenced. Surely you see, gentlemen? That is why the city is full. That is why, as Mr. Campbell tells me, claques are running in from the English gate shouting her name and clashing with those coming in from the Scottish gate who call out 'A. Hope! A. Hope!'"

"If the verdict is the worst," said Holroyd, "then this will not influence those in London who can grant a reprieve. I have confidence there."

"Perhaps not."

"Let us not pre-empt the sentence. Sir Alexander is dining with the High Sheriff and Lord Inglewood's party in the Crown and Mitre tonight. Possibly that will mellow him . . ." Topping's optimism was scarcely strong enough to carry him to the end of the sentence.

After a few more exchanges they left Hatfield who was glad to be alone. Since his return he had been beset by visitors and however strongly he urged Mr. Campbell to let him be in peace, the gaoler – who had never in his life made as much money in as short a time – would find an imperative reason for the next arrival. When Topping and Holroyd had left, Hatfield ordered Mr. Campbell to let in no more visitors: he held up the bible as if to ward off the evil they might bring.

"I want to read this book, Mr. Campbell."

"I understand, sir. When I sang in the Cathedral as a boy I developed a taste for the Scriptures myself."

"I have everything I need – candles, wine, I have eaten well; I need peace to prepare myself for tomorrow."

"Take my word for it, sir," Campbell's solemn round face became firmly sincere, "you will be undisturbed. Never fear."

He banged the door as he left to emphasise his determination.

Hatfield turned to the Second Epistle to the Corinthians and read quietly for half an hour or so and then began to write more of his Journals. This writing compulsion had been noted in many of the reports: letters, of course, and often of daunting length, but also what he described as 'personal writings' which he was to parcel up and send to an attorney in London.

As he wrote with the noise from the town booming outside with an occasional closer splash of sound when one of the claques came to serenade or denigrate him outside the gaol, he concentrated on Mary. He was describing how he had met her and what that had led to. He could see her with total clarity – standing outside the door of the inn, as tall as the door height so that she stooped, a little, when she went in, her face wrapt, it seemed to Hatfield, in an inexpressible love which responded exactly to his own immediate feeling about her. He saw now the valley, the 'secret chamber of the Lakes' as he had heard it called, and his old prejudices against Nature faded at the memory: the place was a haven. It had bred Mary and kept intact her virtues against the predatory world of Fame and Reports. He could believe now, even though he was as ignorant of detail as ever, that to let yourself be supported by Nature and learn from its steady flux was to be strengthened. "And yet," he added, "this does not apply to those who have not the means to be beneficiaries. For them, Nature is no more than the indifferent backdrop in a hostile world."

Mary, though: how little time they had had. The pleasure of Mary would have been the long pleasure of a long life, unwinding daily the amity and richness she spun so effortlessly, seeing a fit of passion weave into a tapestry of loyalty, devotion and as life went on, deep companionship. He had known none of that nor ever would now, but he had seen the possibility in Mary. He had enjoyed the strength of her gratification in a pleasure so long postponed. But that was no comfort. "The great misfortune in life," he wrote, "is to meet the true person at a false time. I have never loved anyone as I loved Mary Robinson, but by the time I found her I was not only married but weakened by a life of promiscuity, long periods of enforced chastity and sexual luxury. Yet I know that in the better world – the world in which we have what we desire! – she would be mine. It is always a mistake to try to imprint the world we desire on the world as it is."

The town quietened down. The candles were long flamed, only halfway burnt, soft streams of wax slowly slipping down into the holders. The burning heat of the day had gone but the stones retained the sun's warmth, the cell was as comfortable as he could have wished and the bottle of wine was only half-drunk. "It is very strange that at a time when my life is literally in the balance, I am able to enjoy comforts in a more acute, and, I may say, a more leisured, appreciative way than before."

The rattle of the cell door startled him and he botched a line.

"Mr. Campbell!"

"I am sorry, sir, I beg you, really I am very sorry!"

The gaoler stood at the door in a contortion of apology.

"I requested you –"

"I know, sir. Please don't be angry, sir. But he will not go away. He came just after I left your cell, sir, and he will not go away." The gaoler was bewildered by this fact. "I tell him that you will see no-one, no-one at all, but he insists and he stands his ground – and he will not go away."

Hatfield put down his pen, picked up his bible and spoke kindly.

"How much has he given you, Mr. Campbell?"

"Three guineas, sir."

"Ask for another two. He is rather a slight man, is he not? Dressed in black, distinctively white-faced – a delicate face with eyes which seem as black as jet?"

"You know him then, sir?"

"I expected him."

Campbell went out pell-mell and Hatfield went over to the window. When Newton came in, he saw the broad back of his former accomplice, the hair loosed from its ribbon hanging down to the shoulders, a bible held in the right hand, seemingly intent on the small barred window which framed the night sky. Campbell closed but did not lock the door and went a few paces away to count over, yet again, the mint he had accumulated over the ten days.

"I am only surprised you took so long," said Hatfield.

"You moved about so much and so confusingly."

"You know all about that. I smelt you in every rat that walked across me in the dark."

"Your speech today was very powerful, John. Everyone in the city is praising it tonight."

"And tomorrow night they will have forgotten it. What do you want?"

"I can be of some service to you."

"I doubt it. Why should you be after tormenting me for so long?"

"I was settling accounts, John. You know that is part of my bargain with everyone I deal with. Remember when I was in your debt in Lancaster only a little more than a year ago and how obedient I was, how I let you run as you wished and rule me as you wanted."

"Because I was doing what *you* wanted. I have thought of that time a great deal. You only appeared to be my accessory and in my command because I was doing what you wanted. Though why you wanted that . . . were you in earnest or were you testing me?"

"I saw in you one of the rarest spirits I have met," said Newton, his words soft as the yellow candle flames. "I saw in you more possibilities, more unused energies and forces than I have *ever* found."

"You wanted me to become your creature. You wanted to make me what you desired but could not achieve. And first you wanted to let me run 'free' – a freedom you controlled so that even at the limit of what I wanted I would sense and you would *know* that I was in your power."

"I can help you now."

"I want no help from you. Your help is never given: it is traded. And I have nothing I want to trade."

"Freedom."

"That is in the hands of God and the Law."

"Escape."

"To be hounded again – and by you? I would escape only back to Mary who would turn me away and then I would be trapped and dragged about worse than a slave."

"A reprieve."

"A reprieve? Even if you could accomplish it that would merely put me back in your debt which, if I did not repay, you would collect in more torment. I'll get my own reprieve."

Hatfield turned, quite unexpectedly at his ease. He saw the man he had feared so much and smiled broadly at him.

"I am no longer afraid of you," he said. "Look at me. I am no longer afraid – God be praised." He raised up the bible and held it aloft while he went on: "In the name of the Father, the Son and the Holy Ghost, I forgive you for all you have done to me and I implore and beg you in the body of Christ to confess all your sins and be received at His holy altar."

Newton turned away.

*

"At eight o'clock the next morning (Tuesday 16th) the court met again, when John Hatfield, the prisoner, appeared at the bar to receive his sentence." Once again the *Carlisle Journal* – in line with all the other papers – felt it necessary to point out the popularity of the case and the attraction of the man.

> Great numbers of people gathered together to witness this painful duty of the law passed upon one whose appearance, manners and actions have excited a most uncommon degree of interest. After proceeding in the usual form, the Judge addressed the prisoner in the following impressive terms:
>
> JOHN HATFIELD – After the long and serious investigation of the charges which have been preferred against you, you have been found guilty by a jury of your country. You have been distinguished for crimes of such magnitude as have seldom, if ever, received any mitigation of capital punishment, and in your case it is impossible it can be limited –
>
> Assuming the person, name and character of a worthy and respectable officer, of a noble family in this country, you have perpetrated and committed the most enormous crimes. The long imprisonment you have undergone has afforded time for your serious reflection, and an opportunity of you being deeply impressed with a sense of the enormity of your crimes, and the justice of that sentence which must be inflicted upon you, and I wish you to be seriously impressed with the awefulness of your situation. I conjure you to reflect with anxious care and with deep concern on your approaching end, concerning which much remains to be done. Lay aside now your delusions and imposture and employ properly that short space you have to live. I beseech you to employ the remaining part of your time in preparing for eternity, so that you might find mercy at the hour of death and in the day of judgement.
>
> Hear now the sentence of the law: THAT YOU BE CARRIED FROM HENCE TO THE PLACE FROM WHENCE YOU CAME, AND FROM THENCE TO THE PLACE OF EXECUTION, AND THERE TO BE HANGED BY THE NECK UNTIL YOU ARE DEAD. AND MAY THE LORD HAVE MERCY ON YOUR SOUL.

*

George Wood took the Reverend Nicholson back to Keswick. Wood was first with the news in Keswick. He loaned Nicholson a horse and the clergyman took the news over into Buttermere, where he spent some hours walking beside the lake with Mary.

30

The Sands Between the Bridges

A few hours after Hatfield's condemnation, he was visited in Carlisle gaol by Samuel Taylor Coleridge.

This is recorded in Dorothy Wordsworth's Journals. Dorothy, her brother William – whose wife, Mary, had, in June, been delivered of their first child, John – and Coleridge had set out in a most uncomfortable Irish jaunting car on a Tour of Scotland. Coleridge left behind his three children. This latest of his many long absences from his family – coupled with increased addiction – was to be the precursor of his final move away from them. Wordsworth, by a contrast which Coleridge envied greatly, was settling into what would be a lifetime's feast of domesticity. Adored by his wife and sister and by several other women close to him, Wordsworth in his fidelity also contrasted with Coleridge, whose violent quarrels with his wife and eagerness to fall in love with a pretty face helped spoil his chance of a settled married life.

They set off from Keswick on the 15th, spent the night at "Mr. Younghusband's public house, Hesket, New Market" and came on to Carlisle the next day. "This day Hatfield was condemned," Dorothy wrote. "I stood at the door of the gaoler's house where he was; William entered the house, and Coleridge saw him." Wordsworth, it seems, did not. The focus of his interest was Mary. Even so, it seems a rather remarkable act of restraint.

But there was no doubting the attitude of the Wordsworths and Coleridge: it was that of Sir Alexander Thomson. Of Hatfield, Wordsworth wrote in *The Prelude*:

> Unfaithful to a virtuous wife,
> Deserted and deceived, the spoiler came . . .
> And wooed the artless daughter of the hills
> And wedded her in cruel mockery.

Dorothy confirmed this. The same Journal entry that brought them to Carlisle took them on to Longtown where they stayed at "The

Graham's Arms, a large inn". She wrote, "Here, as everywhere else, the people seem utterly insensible of the enormity of Hatfield's offences: the ostler told William that he was quite a gentleman, paid everyone genteelly, etc., etc."

But it is the meeting between Hatfield and Coleridge which is intriguing, not the least fascination being Hatfield's willingness to 'receive' a few hours after he had been sentenced to death. September 3rd had been fixed for the execution: barring a reprieve.

It is impossible to discover whether or not Hatfield knew that Coleridge was the author of that first *Morning Post* article which so effectively (and so soon) set off the hunt. Hatfield, from his time in Keswick and the general credit given to his "wide information", would surely have known that Coleridge was a poet, though whether he had read *The Ancient Mariner* is doubtful. It is not too absurd to speculate that the originality and capaciousness of Coleridge's mind, and his devotion – growing stronger at this time – to Christianity would have delighted Hatfield. It might be offered as one of several symmetrical speculations that Hatfield's many and varied essays in sensual fulfilment and the accumulated variety of his personal adventures might have excited a corresponding attraction or even envy from Coleridge, who longed for such pleasures. Perhaps Hatfield represented the darker side of Coleridge, a man who had done all he himself had – in his worst moments – wanted to do: the lasting hatred would then have the added dynamic of self-hatred. Hatfield was writing, as he stated to several visitors, in order that his life's story might be understood: those writings have been lost. Coleridge was already the author of works still read, every scrap of his writing is preserved and cherished. One a man loved by 'the people': the other a man who loved 'the people' only in an abstract mass. One a creator of fictions, the other a man who made himself into fictions. Both men whose looks and manner immediately impressed their contemporaries. But Coleridge, from portraits at that time, an unhealthy-looking young man: Hatfield in the bloom of strong middle age. One bound for great and lasting fame, the other for temporary though clamant notoriety.

We have no record of what passed between them.

"Vain," was Coleridge's verdict after that meeting in the gaoler's house, "a hypocrite." And then he added the most puzzling and memorable remark anyone wrote on Hatfield. "It is not by mere Thought, I can understand this man." One wonders what mystery and profundity he imagined or sensed there. This sentence by Coleridge confirms the potency of Hatfield as a man and for what he represented – not just as an important marker on the new drawn human map of Romanticism, but as a figure who could lead to the very darkest and most obscure areas of the human psyche.

It is, then, not altogether surprising that Coleridge some years later writes of Hatfield when he is considering the character of Iago; that he may well have brought Hatfield into his reflections on Richard III; that in an indictment of Universities of the time he links Hatfield together with William Pitt and Napoleon – his two most hated public figures; that in 1810, Hatfield yet again crops up: "An excellent remark, that the Devil can serve his turn even of the virtues which we have – at least, of those amiable and useful qualities, which have a natural tendency to unite themselves with virtue and are its appropriate companions – Hatfield." And, of course, there are de Quincey's recollections of Coleridge's obsession: "Great was the emotion of Coleridge when he recurred to his remembrance of those letters, and bitter – almost vindictive – was the indignation with which he spoke of Hatfield . . ."

And yet on that day in Carlisle, as in Keswick, as they were to find in Longtown and elsewhere, Dorothy reported: "the people seemed utterly insensible of the enormity of Hatfield's offences."

*

Right up to the day appointed for his execution, Hatfield occupied himself intensively with three matters: (i) helping his fellow prisoners – there are many letters which he wrote on their behalf pleading their cause, arguing at great length and with ingenuity; (ii) his own writings on which he set great expectations; and (iii) private religious preparations for his death.

Those were thorough and involved him in substantial correspondence with several clergymen as well as claiming a good deal of the energies of the Reverends Mark and Patterson. He was keen to be buried at Burgh-by-Sands – where King Edward the Hammer of the Scots had his grave – and the Reverend Mark agreed to try to negotiate what would be a most unusual concession. He was keen to have a very plain oak coffin and sent out for Mr. Joseph Bushby to take his measurements: Mr. Bushby was more agitated than Hatfield who chatted pleasantly with the coffin-maker and his assistant, a young apprentice called Ike Wilkinson who was trying desperately to remember every detail of his visit so that he could turn it over to his parents in Ireby when next he went home. And Mr. Campbell seemed to spend his entire life as Hatfield's factor.

The character of his religious feeling and his admitted state of mind can be seen in these extracts from a long letter he wrote to the Reverend Mr. Ellerton of Colton near Ulverston. It was authenticated by the Editor of the *Lancaster Gazette* on September 10th, 1803.

Carlisle, 29th August 1803, Monday.

Dear and Rev. Sir,

I take the earliest opportunity to say how very much I am obliged by your excellent letter; it reached my hands whilst Mr. Mark was doing duty in the chapel, after having bestowed the comfortable sacrament of our blessed Lord upon me. The state of my mind is very pleasing to Mr. Mark and Mr. Patterson whose attendance on me is very valuable – but solitude suits me best; alone with GOD and his word I find a peace which passeth all understanding; and it produces a desire to go hence not in spleen or disgust: oh no! very far, very far from it . . . Nine months of previous confinement and an accurate knowledge of the dispositions of those who were set against me were circumstances of great value – they led me to seek help . . . I am indeed sensible of the goodness of GOD in granting me the abundant preparation I have had . . . I have sought, and I hope I shall to the last continue to seek all, through a blessed REDEEMER – in him only do I trust – through HIS suffering and HIS MEDIATION ALONE can I hope to see my GOD in Peace . . . For your prayers on Saturday next I shall be truly thankful for here – instigated doubtless by humane motives, they do not execute me until after the post comes in and that is sometime near three o'clock . . .

It is a fine irony that, charged for defrauding the post office, it is until after the second and last postal delivery of the week that the time of his execution will be delayed. A reprieve was widely and devoutly wished for.

In a breezy postscript to that letter, Hatfield gives an indication of his day:

> P.S. I could with much pleasure to myself extend this Epistle very much, but many affectionate claims are made on the time I allot for writing, and four of yesterday remain unanswered. May every blessing be yours.

This was the public face and it is reported as being consistent and, clearly, to the reporters and to the wide range of those who visited and corresponded with him, it was convincing.

"The calmness, composure and recollection of his mind while in prison did not desert him in the hour of trial," the *Journal* reported. "This, we think, is no weak proof of supernatural aid . . . He had found, by evangelical repentance, mercy with God which, consistently with order, could not be granted him by the laws of his country."

It was also reported on the 29th August – the day on which he wrote the letter to the Reverend Ellerton – "His hair, which was remarkably thick and long and of a beautiful flaxen colour, he had cut off and sent it along with the whole of his papers etc. to a friend in London."

*

On the night before the execution, Friday, 2nd September, the gallows were erected on the Sands, "an island formed by the River Eden, on the north side of the town, between the two bridges".

Soon after ten o'clock the next morning, Hatfield had his irons struck off and Mr. Campbell was sent out to buy the *Carlisle Journal.* Hatfield read this for a while and then received the two clergymen who had attended on him – Mr. Patterson of Carlisle and Mr. Mark of Burgh-by-Sands. They prayed with him for about two hours. After they had drunk coffee with him they left: Hatfield explained that he did not want to cause them the distress of seeing him prepared for the journey to the Sands.

He wrote letters, one of them to Michelli in which he enclosed his pen-knife for his son. To a young and rather slow-witted prisoner – who had become infatuated with Hatfield, who had allowed him to carry out some rather menial tasks for him – he gave the new Bible which he had sent out for the previous day.

Just before three o'clock, a desolate Mr. Campbell came in to tell him that the post had arrived but no reprieve. He asked the gaoler to leave him alone for a few minutes.

In two hours, then, and for certain, he would be dead. He looked at the bare walls in puzzlement, trying to imagine what it would be like not being: not being there, not being anywhere else, knowing only through the intercession of Christ that there was another life. The truth was that for these moments, faith deserted him. He did not want to die – and for such a thing! To die – never to see that sky, breathe air, touch flesh, eat food, drink: never again to try and fail, to travel, to adventure, be part of the time you were born into. He longed to go out of this place and just walk, say 'hello' to somebody, eat an orange, stride across a street. A rush, an avalanche of memory came into his mind, of faces, moments, events, bodies, himself alone, the song of his life: now it would be silenced.

How could he bear it? He was as well prepared for death as any man had any right to be, but Oh God, he did not want to die: he did not want that end. Like a sob grown into a growl grown into a bay of trumpeted pain, a sound came out of him which wrenched the hearts of those who heard it. But then, with his blemished hand, he stopped his mouth: pressed his glistering brow to the cool wall: let the shudder, like a tremor, quaking through his body, his mind and his spirit, pass.

He called for the gaoler to bring him some hot water and a razor and to fetch some cold game pie, a bottle of claret and two glasses – he would be obliged if Mr. Campbell would dine with him.

Back to the self he had chosen to lead him out of this life, he shaved with full concentration and made not the slightest nick.

He instructed Mr. Campbell on what to do with the few trifles he had not already disposed of and gave him five guineas to distribute among the poorest prisoners whose names he had written down on a list. While the gaoler went out to bring in the coffee, he read a chapter from the Second Epistle to the Corinthians which he had already marked.

He was informed that the Sheriff and his forces were at the door but he asked if he could see the executioner privately for a moment. The man had been brought down from Dumfries at a fee of ten guineas. Hatfield forgave him for what he was about to do and gave him some silver in a paper, urging him to make certain the knot was well tied.

A few minutes before four o'clock, he stepped out of the gaol, out into the light of a fine clear late summer, a golden afternoon, out to streets lined and crowded with coaches, carts, horsemen, street sellers, gypsies, parties at windows and youths on rooftops. Waiting for him were the Sheriff, bailiffs, his post-chaise, the full Carlisle yeomanry and a hearse. He went out and a subdued but deep-sounding roar, as of applause, came from the crowd, a roar which gathered outside the gaol and then rippled like a gathering wave down the streets of Carlisle to break at the gibbet on the Sands.

"He is here!"

Hatfield looked up, looked around him, nodded slowly at the world he saw and turned to face the multitudes.

*

Half the cavalry went in front, the other half made up the rear. Hatfield sat in the chaise, pinioned, between Mr. Campbell and the executioner. The crowd was so numerous that their progress to the Sands was very slow. Sometimes they were forced to stop by the pressure of the crowd which the yeomen did not wish to charge down and merely asked to disperse quietly.

Hatfield heard his name called out a score, two, three score times but kept as steady as he could, glancing aside only rarely and never sharply except for once when it was not his name but a distinctive "Sir! Sir!" he heard.

He turned and saw struggling to stay alongside the chaise . . . Anne Tyson! He smiled. "Good luck, Anne Tyson!" And she dropped back, out of his sight.

Faces he had seen once, twice, voices he had known – "God bless you, John Hatfield!" – the crowd at the Town Hall surged against the light post-chaise and rocked it on its wheels but eventually the cavalry cleared the way and the condemned procession moved on.

George Wood had been too overcome to make the journey, but Monkey-boy had come and he would swear for the rest of his life that Hatfield had caught his eye and nodded to him. The Reverend Nicholson had decided to stay in the valley and be on hand to comfort Mary, but when he got to the inn at midday, he was informed by her father that she had been up before dawn, taken some provisions and gone into the fells, telling them not to expect her back until well after dark. Topping and Holroyd, with the Reverends Mark and Patterson, had secured themselves positions near the gibbet.

By the time the procession reached the fatal tree, it was only a few minutes from five o'clock, the time appointed for the execution.

Hatfield closed his eyes for one moment, prayed for those he loved, and took a sudden breath and steadied himself. "He stepped out of the carriage and ascended the platform with unshaken firmness."

The executioner followed him. Hatfield looked at the rope and asked the executioner to make an adjustment to the noose which he did. He then turned and faced the crowd.

What numbers! Faces across the Sands and up to the Scotch gate. Noises still from within the city walls! The River Eden moving slowly after a dry summer but no doubt there would be boys a mile or so away, fishing, as he had done. And wives to love as he had, and all the inexplicable, unknowable, astounding business of life from the smallest to the greatest things, all there to be done: but not by him. The faces turned up to him – hundreds of open eyes, mouths that breathed, ears that heard. The executioner asked if he wished for any support and Hatfield realised that he must have shivered a little. But "No," he said, "though my body may appear weak, my mind is perfectly firm." And now he longed for that affliction which had plagued and frightened him many times. At this moment he prayed that 'he' might leave his body as he had so often done before. For that had been an intimation: now he knew: that had been his gift.

He untied his neckerchief and placed it as a bandage over his eyes. The executioner put on the noose. Hatfield tried to make his last thought of Christ and urged on his spirit to leave his body and soar, for the last time to eternity. Many of the crowd, especially the women, sank to their knees.

He hung about an hour and then they cut him down.

Though he had ordered a plain coffin, it was reported that the coffin which took him away was highly ornamental, adorned with plates and extremely handsome in every way.

The Reverend Mark had not been able to get permission for Hatfield to be buried at Burgh-by-Sands – royal burial place – and he was taken to St. Mary's graveyard, close by the Northern Gate, the usual cemetery for criminals. The coffin was lowered in without prayers: no clergyman attended.

Anne Tyson stood apart and alone, occasionally squinting her eyes into the bright sunset now turning from copper to crimson over the sea to the west.

Epilogue

Four years later, Mary Robinson married Richard Harrison of Caldbeck, by whom she had four children. Caldbeck, in the Northern Fells, was then a town of over a thousand people, about the size of Keswick. Mary lived in a handsome farmhouse, Todcrofts, behind which is a perilous and virtually unknown waterfall called the Howk. She was still famous enough for her death to be reported in the London Annual Register for 1837 under the date 22nd February, 1837.

"Lately – At Caldbeck, Cumberland, Mary, wife of Mr. Richard Harrison of that Place. This amiable individual was formerly the far-famed and much talked of 'Mary of Buttermere' or as she was more commonly termed 'The Buttermere Beauty'."

Her descendants live on in these valleys yet and her grave is a few miles over the common from where this novel was written.

Melvyn Bragg
High Ireby
1983–1986

"Not only William Wordsworth, but Dorothy Wordsworth, Samuel Taylor Coleridge, the Lambs and Thomas de Quincey, all left records of their interest and involvement in the story of the Beauty of Buttermere. When analysis of these documents is combined with a brief glance at the attitudes of the British Public generally, it will be easier for us to understand why [the story] of Mary Robinson in 1802 caused a public reaction comparable to the kidnapping in 1932 of the infant son of Charles A. Lindbergh . . . or to the assassination in 1980 of John Lennon."

Donald H. Reiman,

The Beauty of Buttermere as Fact and Romantic Symbol

The following is a list of those characters based on real people and of historical figures who also appear in the novel:

Alice
Monsieur Beaupuy
Broussais
Captain Budworth
Burkett and his daughter
Mr. Joseph Bushby
Earl of Carlisle
Christine, the maid at the Queen's Head
Peter Crosthwaite
Mr. and Mrs. John Crump
Duke of Cumberland and others attending the London examinations
Miss Amaryllis D'Arcy
Thomas de Quincey
Earl of Derby
Dr. Edmonson
Reverend Ellerton
Mr. Fenton
Mary Fisher
The Flemings
Sir Richard Ford
Constable Forrester
Dr. John Gillies
Lady William Gordon
The Grahams at Netherby
George Hardinge
Richard Harrison
John Hatfield
Thomas Hetherington
Jonah Hogarth
Mr. Holroyd
Earl of Hopetoun, MP for Linlithgowshire
Mary Hutchinson
Sara Hutchinson
Kemble
Mr. Kinnaird
Charles and Mary Lamb
The Lonsdales
Emma 'Manners'
Lord Robert Manners
Reverend Mark
Colonel and Mrs. Moore
Michelli Nation
Reverend John Nicholson
Mr. Otley
Colonel Parke
Reverend Patterson
Colonel Peachey
The Penningtons
Mr. Pocklington
Mr. Powell
Mr. and Mrs. Joseph Robinson
Mary Robinson
T. Robinson
Mr. Scarlet
Miss Skelton and Mr. Joseph Skelton
Mr. Slack
Captain Spence
The Stricklands
John Summers
Mr. Taunton
Earl of Thanet
Honourable Alexander Thomson
Tom
Mr. Topping
Sir Frederick Treese Morshead
Annette Vallon
Sir Frederick Vane
George Wood
Dorothy Wordsworth
William Wordsworth
Wright of Derby

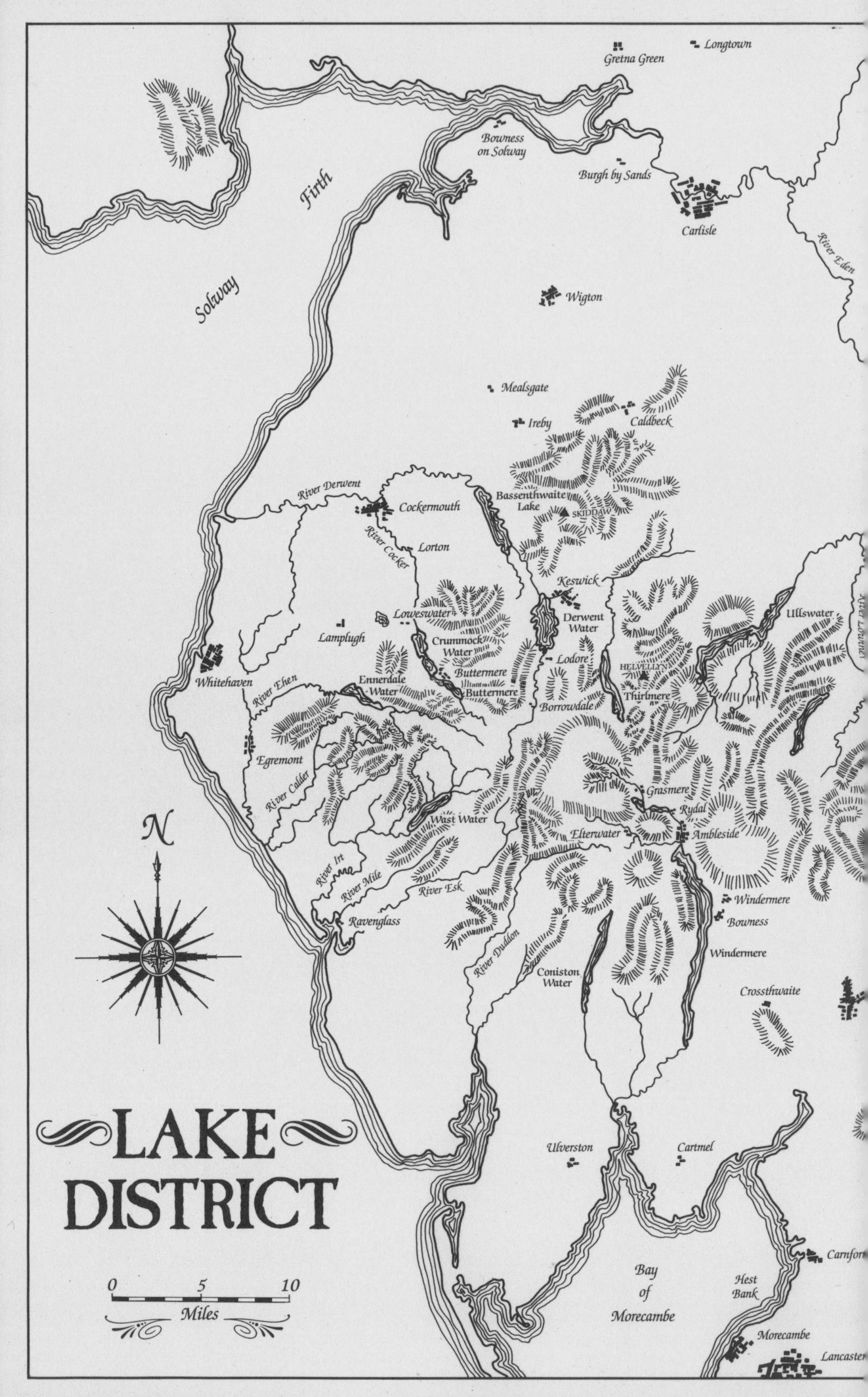
LAKE
DISTRICT
Gretna Green
Longtown
Bowness
on Solway
Burgh by Sands
Carlisle
River Eden
Solway
Firth
Wigton
Mealsgate
Ireby
Caldbeck
River Derwent
Cockermouth
Bassenthwaite
Lake
SKIDDAW
River Cocker
Lorton
Keswick
Derwent
Water
Loweswater
Lamplugh
Crummock
Water
Buttermere
Buttermere
Lodore
Whitehaven
River Ehen
Ennerdale
Water
Borrowdale
HELVELLYN
Thirlmere
Ullswater
Egremont
River Calder
Grasmere
Rydal
Ambleside
Elterwater
Wast Water
N
River Irt
River Mile
River Esk
Ravenglass
Windermere
Bowness
Windermere
River Duddon
Coniston
Water
Crossthwaite
Ulverston
Cartmel
Bay
of
Morecambe
Hest
Bank
Morecambe
Lancaster
0
5
10
Miles